THE WORLD OF
DARKNESS

BLOOD WAR

Masquerade of the Red Death Part 1

Based on **Vampire: The Masquerade**™

ROBERT WEINBERG

WHITE WOLF
PUBLISHING

Cover illustration by BROM.
Design by Michael Scott Cohen.
Printed in Canada.

White Wolf Publishing
735 Park North Blvd.
Suite 128
Clarkston, GA 30021

Blood was its Avatar and its seal—
the redness and horror of blood.
            "The Masque of the Red Death"
            Edgar Allan Poe

<u>Book One - BLOOD WAR</u>

Dedication

To Edgar Allan Poe, for obvious reasons.
And
To Bram Stoker, who started it all.

Author's Note
While the locations and history of this trilogy may seem familiar, it is not our reality. The setting of *Vampire: The Masquerade of the Red Death* is a harsher, crueler version of our world. It is a stark, desolate landscape where nothing is what it seems. It is truly a World of Darkness.

PROLOGUE

Rome—June 15, 1992

They met at twelve noon, on a bright Sunday in June, in a small outdoor restaurant a few blocks from the Coliseum. The phone call the night before to an unlisted number in the heart of the Vatican had been sharp and to the point. The unknown speaker stated the place and the time, the person to attend, warned of "no tricks," and mentioned an incredible sum of money. But it had been the final sentence of the conversation that had assured the rendezvous would take place. "We will talk," declared the mysterious voice in somber, cold tones, "of *The Kindred*."

Father Naples arrived first. He was always early for meetings. Especially ones of importance. A big, powerfully built man in his late fifties, with thick, curly gray hair, matching beard, and piercing dark eyes, even in street clothes he looked like a priest. He carried himself with the quiet air of authority, of someone used to giving orders and having them obeyed instantly. A man of unshakable beliefs and determination, Father Naples walked with the absolute conviction of many hundreds of years of Church history.

As specified by the late-night message, he came to the meeting unarmed. Not that he was worried. His faith served as his shield. Along with the five other agents of the Society of Leopold in the restaurant, including two women disguised as streetwalkers. All combined, they carried enough firepower on them to start a minor war. And, though he had retired years before as a field operative, Father Naples still maintained his training in the martial arts. An expert at both kendo and karate, he could kill an attacker a dozen different ways.

Following the specified instructions, the priest requested a table for two at the rear of the patio, away from the hustle and bustle of the kitchen. A hundred yards away, in a rented hotel room, a directional microphone was focused on this exact location. Every word spoken at this meeting would be picked up and recorded for playback and analysis later. The priest smiled faintly as he instructed the waiter to bring a bottle of the house red. God provided, but the miracles of modern science and technology helped.

He was just finishing his first glass of wine when the other man arrived. The stranger, perhaps twenty-five, tall and slender, with wavy blond hair and bright blue eyes, wore a white suit with an open-necked white shirt. He moved so silently that Father Naples wasn't aware of his approach until his shadow fell across the table.

"Father Naples, I believe?" said the stranger. His voice, low and vibrant, was definitely not the same as the speaker on the phone the night before. The priest nodded, as much to himself as to the other. There were at least two involved in this mystery. He wondered how many more? Hopefully, he would soon know the answer.

"That is my name," he replied, rising to his feet. He offered his hand and the young man took it. His grip was surprisingly strong. Dark, harsh eyes met and held bright blue ones. Few men could endure Father Naples' unyielding glare for more than an instant. The stranger never blinked. He matched the priest stare for stare, with an inner serenity undaunted by the priest's fierce scowl. Grunting in annoyance and surprise, the older man finally broke the contact. A brief pain flared in the priest's chest but he ignored it. Another glass of wine would help him relax. He had a sudden feeling that he would need a great deal of *vino* before the afternoon was over.

"You are . . . ?" he asked, resuming his seat. The other sat down directly across from him. Carefully, the young man rested a shiny new black leather attaché case against the base of the table.

"Call me . . . Reuben," said the blond stranger. He grinned. "Like the sandwich."

"There was a Reuben in *The Bible*," said Father Naples. "It is a good name."

"The firstborn of Jacob," replied the young man smoothly. "His father's strength. One of the founders of the twelve tribes of Israel."

"You know *The Old Testament*," said Father Naples. "Not many young men do anymore."

"I have an exceptional memory," replied Reuben, with a grin. "And I'm not as young as I look."

"A glass of wine?" asked Father Naples, pouring himself a second helping.

"No thank you," said Reuben. "I do not drink wine."

He paused for an instant, almost as if awaiting a reply from the priest. When none came, he beckoned to the waiter. "A Coca-Cola, please. And a menu."

"We did not come here to eat," protested Father Naples.

"Agreed," said Reuben. "But conversation flows easiest over good food. Besides which, I'm hungry. I spent most of the night traveling. Airline food might satisfy some, but not me. I need substance." He chuckled. "After all, you'll be doing most of the talking."

The priest nodded, his thoughts whirling. Things were progressing well. The Kindred neither ate nor drank. Nor could they tolerate exposure to bright sunshine. The stranger was definitely human. And not very clever.

Reuben's chance remark about flying played right into the Church's hands. Father Naples felt confident that his crew manning the microphone were already on the phone with the airport. Checking the flights that had arrived last night would not take long, especially with the authority of the Vatican behind the request. Before this lunch concluded, the Society of Leopold would have Reuben's real name and point of origin. It was all quite simple if you had the right connections. And knew what strings to pull.

"You have the money?"

"Right here in this attaché case," replied Reuben. He reached down and hoisted the black leather bag onto the table. Inserting a thin key, he snapped open the lock. Carefully, he raised the lid of the case a few inches.

Involuntarily, Father Naples gasped. The box was filled with neat stacks of $100 bills.

"Twenty million dollars in US funds," said Reuben softly. He closed and locked the case and replaced it beneath the table. "With more, much more to come, if you answer a few questions to my satisfaction."

"Your satisfaction," said Father Naples, hoping to learn yet more. "Or your employer's?"

Reuben merely smiled and said nothing. With a wave of a hand, the young man summoned their waiter and ordered a plate of linguine with meat sauce. Father Naples politely declined. He rarely ate lunch. Afternoon meals made him feel sluggish. The red wine was all he needed. It helped with the nagging pain in his chest. He poured himself another drink.

"What questions?" he asked, once the waiter had left the table. "Ask me what you will."

"The Kindred," said Reuben, his bright blue eyes twinkling in the sunshine. "The children of Caine. Your Order has hunted them since the Middle Ages. The Society of Leopold knows more about them than anyone else in the world. Tell me the history of the Kindred."

The priest scowled. He had expected no less. But that didn't mean he liked it better. "There are some secrets that I cannot reveal. Not without permission from Monsignor Ameliano."

"Understood," said Reuben. He nodded as the waiter deposited a salad in front of him and a Coke, then departed. "Speak. I will decide afterwards if I need to know more."

"Exactly where do you want me to begin?" asked Father Naples. "The Kindred have existed since the creation of mankind. They are the spawn of Satan himself. Though they claim to be descended from Adam and Eve, we of the Society know differently. They are tools of the devil. They are as old as humanity, and their history is as complex."

Reuben chuckled. "Start at the very beginning. With Caine. But please feel free to summarize."

"Summarize?" replied Father Naples, sarcastically. He

poured himself another glass of wine, emptying the bottle. With a wave of a hand, he signaled their waiter for another. "How does one summarize ten thousand years of absolute evil? An impossible task, but let me try."

The priest lowered his voice. Though it remained sunny and bright, the day no longer seemed so warm. Or pleasant.

"Thirteen vampire clans secretly rule the world and have done so since before the beginning of recorded history. Few in number, immortal though not indestructible, they call themselves The Kindred. For they all trace their origin back to a single common ancestor. You said his name. He is Caine, the Third Human. The first child of Adam and Eve, he was tempted by Lucifer, the Fallen One. In his weakness, he yielded to Satan's words and became the first killer— and the first vampire."

Father Naples gathered in a deep breath. Reuben sat patiently, his bright blue eyes undisturbed by the revelations being stated. As if it was nothing new. For the thousandth time since last night, Father Naples wondered who Reuben was. Or, more importantly, who he represented.

"For slaying his brother, Caine was cursed by God with the mark of the beast. It was not a physical sign but a mental one. Caine had brought murder into the world, and by murder he was forced to survive. As long as Caine killed and drank the blood of his victims, he remained alive. Immortal, he became an undying symbol of the monster that lurks within every man. Satan was very pleased.

"Moreover, the blood gave Caine powers unmatched by ordinary mortals. He needed these supernatural abilities to survive the hatred and loathing he encountered wherever he went. Lucifer taunted him, making Caine bitter against God. The Third Mortal suffered mightily under the weight of his curse. Alone, haunted by demons, he yearned for others to share in his grief."

Father Naples paused dramatically and sipped his wine. The story, though he had told it a hundred times to new recruits of the Order, still fascinated him. It was a tale of evil personified. And it was all terribly true.

"It was then, in his darkest despair, that Caine learned from Satan a monstrous secret. Not only was he damned, but he could pass along his suffering to others. The *Embrace* Lucifer called this unholy ritual, in mockery of human love. A drop of the Third Human's blood, given to one of his victims at the moment of their death, transformed that mortal into an undead, immortal vampire. These childer, as these dread offspring became known, were not as powerful as their sire, but commanded potent forces nonetheless.

"Encouraged by Satan, Caine created three such monsters. Together, this trio of undead monsters lived with their creator in the first city, Enoch, where they were worshiped by the human inhabitants as Gods. Immortal vampires, Caine and his brood. And Satan laughed at his triumph."

"The Second generation," interrupted Reuben. "Caine was the first. The three that followed were the Second."

"Exactly," said Father Naples. "And, in time, urged by Lucifer, they, too, bestowed the gift of eternal life on a select group of their victims. For the Second generation learned from the Evil One that any vampire could pass along the curse to one of their prey by the same method as Caine used. A drop of Kindred blood given to a dying victim resulted in a new childe. Again, the vampire created had powers diminished from that of its sire, for it was yet another generation removed from the very first."

"In ten thousand years, there have been how many such generations?" asked Reuben, then smiled as their waiter delivered his plate of pasta.

Father Naples waited until they were alone before answering. "Twelve, perhaps thirteen. Caine's curse has grown so weak that those of the later generations barely possess any supernatural powers. They are minor annoyances. Abominations in the eyes of God, they deserve to be destroyed. But the Order of Leopold rarely wastes time hunting them. We are concerned with those of the earliest generations. The elders of the Kindred are our quarry. They are the spawn of the devil, and thus, the true enemies of the faithful."

"Delicious," murmured Reuben as he sampled the linguine. He seemed as intent upon his food as upon Father Naples' lecture. "Please continue. You were telling me about the third generation."

"They were thirteen in number," said the priest, scratching his thick hair in confusion. He prayed that his compatriots could make some sense out of this bizarre escapade. He definitely could not. "Childer of the Second generation, they were the true founders of the Kindred race. For these thirteen Antediluvian vampires were ambitious. Caine's guilt meant nothing to them. They knew not the Lord God, only Lucifer, the Dark Angel. Thus, they felt no shame, no remorse for Caine's actions. So, prompted by Satan, they duplicated the Third Human's crime. They rose up against their sires and destroyed them. In that great battle, Enoch was destroyed. Caine vanished, never to be seen again. And the third generation reigned supreme.

"They built a Second City, populated with human slaves, and ruled it with the aid of their new progeny, vampires of the fourth generation. For two thousand years the Antedeluvians kept humanity in bondage. Until, one morning, mankind finally rose against them in revolt. For the vampires were immortal but not indestructible. Bright sunlight or fire killed them." The priest chuckled, not a pleasant sound. "*Or beheading.* Like Enoch before it, the Second City was destroyed. And what remained of the Kindred were scattered throughout the world.

"The third generation, incredibly ancient by this time, disappeared. Many of their own kind thought them destroyed. Other, wiser ones, suspected that the Antediluvian vampires had gone into hiding. After many thousands of years of existence, they needed rest.

"Kindred legends say that the third generation lie in a death-like sleep known as torpor in hidden tombs throughout the world. Someday, these tales predict, they shall arise, and the world of the Undead shall tremble." The priest spat on the ground. "Spawn of the devil, their return has been foretold in *The Revelations of St. John.*"

"What happened to the fourth generation?" asked Reuben. He had finished his linguine and now sat patiently sipping his Coke. "Did many of them survive the fall of the Second City?"

"A small number," replied Father Naples. "No records say how many. These Methuselahs, for they too were thousands of years old, became secretive. They realized that their continued existence depended on mankind thinking the Kindred destroyed. Thus, they instituted what became known as The Masquerade. It demanded that all vampires keep their existence hidden from mankind. The penalty for violation of the Masquerade by a member of the Kindred was death. Centuries passed and, in time, humanity forgot that vampires ever actually lived. They became creatures of myth, of legend. Just as the Kindred elders had planned.

"Then, and only then, did the fourth generation create new progeny. After the fifth generation came the sixth, then a seventh, and so on through the ages. Thirteen clans arose, each possessing certain traits and characteristics of the third-generation Antediluvian who was its original founder. Working in secret, guided by Lucifer and his minions, these vampire clans schemed, fought, bargained, and conspired for control of the Earth. Using their supernatural powers, they became the hidden masters of the world. They were the Kindred and mankind, their unsuspecting victims, the kine."

"But since each vampire can create innumerable others, the Earth should be overrun by monsters," declared Reuben, his eyes sparkling with amusement. "Doesn't that prove this entire history just myth?"

Father Naples shook his head. He felt a little groggy. Too much sun and too much wine this early in the day. "The Kindred are no fools. The Masquerade is just one of their laws. They have Six Traditions governing the major aspects of their lives. One of the most important edicts controls the creation of new vampires. The elders of the thirteen clans have carefully kept the number of Kindred in existence small, so as not to exhaust the available blood pool. Always remember, my young friend, that we are their food. One of the undead for tens of thousands of humans is the rule. Which nonetheless means there are well over a hundred thousand of the Kindred scattered throughout the world."

"A sizable but extremely influential minority," chuckled Reuben. "Yet, for all of their great powers, the Kindred cannot function during the daylight hours. Sunlight destroys them. I find it hard to understand how they maintain this stranglehold on mankind when they are so vulnerable. How do you explain that inconsistency?"

"Traitors," spat out Father Naples. "Devil worshipers. Humans willing to betray their kind for eternal life. Damned like their unholy masters, they are known as Ghouls."

The priest paused, trying to regain his composure. "A drop of a vampire's blood given to its dying victim transforms that person into a member of the Undead. Killer and prey become sire and childe. That same vitæ, given at regular intervals to a ordinary human, halts the aging process. It also bestows on the drinker superhuman strength and minor supernatural powers. However, the price the Kindred demand for their blood is eternal service. Able to function normally in the daylight, these Ghouls perform those tasks impossible for their undead Masters. It is immortality in exchange for freedom."

"A deal with the devil is hard to refuse," said Reuben somberly. He signaled the waiter for another Coke. "A few more questions and I think my curiosity will be satisfied. Tell me about the Camarilla. And the Sabbat?"

The priest snorted in derision. There was a bare trace of wine left in the second bottle and he drank it thirstily. All of this talk made his throat dry.

"They are the two major sects of the Kindred," he declared. "The Camarilla believe that the Antediluvians met the Final Death when the Second City was destroyed. They feel that the basic threat to the Kindred comes from the possibility that mankind someday might learn that vampires are real. The Masquerade governs their actions. They are the traditionalists among Caine's descendants.

"Seven major clans make up the bulk of the cult. The

Ventrue are power mongers, the unofficial leaders of the sect. The Toreador are involved in the arts. The Tremere are a line of vampire wizards who rose to prominence in the Middle Ages. The Nosferatu are monstrously ugly because their leader was cursed by Caine. A few of their fourth-generation progeny are rumored to be grotesque monsters, known as the Nictuku. The Malkavians are tricksters, seemingly mad, but probably more cunning than most imagine. The Brujah are rebellious in nature, while the Gangrel, master shapechangers, maintain close ties with the gypsies and werewolves."

Reuben sipped his Coke and said nothing. He had come to listen, not to comment.

"The Sabbat are the rebels of the Kindred. My Order considers them the more dangerous of the two sects. Two major clans, the Lasombra and the Tzimisce rule the order. Most other clans are represented by small groups of rebels known as *Antitribu.*

"Leaders of the Sabbat firmly maintain that the third generation lives and that they are secretly manipulating their descendants for reasons of their own." The priest's voice sank very low. "They fear an approaching Armageddon that they call Gehenna. A time when the Antediluvians will rise to take control of the Kindred. The Sabbat suspect that the third generation plans to devour their descendants."

"The longer a vampire survives," said Reuben, his expression never changing, "the more potent the blood it needs to exist. *Human vitæ no longer satisfies third- or fourth-generation Kindred.* They need a more powerful stimulant. Only the blood of their descendants, of other vampires, slakes their unholy thirst. *They have become cannibals.*"

"Correct," said Father Naples, undaunted by this unexpected revelation from his companion. "No one knows for sure if the Antediluvians still exist or if they turned to dust millennia ago. But, if they are merely sleeping, when they awaken after ages without food, their hunger will be all consuming."

"You named only nine cults," said Reuben, switching

subjects. "What are the others?"

"There are the Ravnos, a society of outcasts and drifters," intoned Father Naples, using his fingers to count the remaining few. "Then the Assamites, an Order of Assassins, much feared even among their own kind, The Followers of Set worship a long-dormant third-generation Egyptian horror, the embodiment of that land's ancient evil. And last, we must not forget the Giovanni, another fairly new clan, who are preoccupied with two subjects—death and money."

"Good," said Reuben, putting down his empty glass. "Now I know all the clans. But I am unsure about their interactions."

The young man's bright blue eyes burned with an intense inner fire. "What is the Jyhad?" he asked.

Father Naples was feeling very strange. Yet he felt that he had to answer. It was extremely important to himself and the Society of Leopold that he answer Reuben's every question. Extremely important.

"A legend among the vampires," said the priest. "It is the title given to a war that supposedly has endured for millennia. Most say it rages between the few remaining members of the fourth generation, the Methuselahs, using their unsuspecting childer as pawns. Beings of incredible supernatural power, they each seek to gain absolute control of the Earth for reasons of their own. Others claim that the Jyhad is really a game played by the third generation, expertly manipulating the Methuselahs from behind the scenes. The world of the Kindred is filled with treachery and deceit. Remember, Lucifer, their patron, is the Father of Lies. Wheels spin within wheels within wheels. None other than the Antediluvians, if they actually survive, know the truth."

"On that subject," said Reuben, "you might be mistaken."

The young man signaled for the check. "Is there anything else, anything of importance about the Kindred, that you think I should know? Perhaps about the Inconnu? Or the recent disturbances in Russia and Peru?"

Father Naples shook his head. "Inconnu? Russia? Peru?

11

No, I don't think so. Why do you ask?"

"Just confirming a few of my own suspicions," said Reuben. He pulled some cash from his wallet and paid the waiter. "It's time for me to leave. You've told me everything I wanted to know."

The young man rose to his feet. "No need to get up. I can see myself to the door. Thank you for your time, Father Naples. I appreciate the information you've given me, though I think your views concerning the devil tint your narration slightly. That's always been a problem with the Inquisition. You worry too much about demons and too little about evil. I'm sorry, but you can't be permitted to describe our conversation to anyone. Especially to your superiors in the Society of Leopold. May God grant you peace."

None of the five Society of Leopold agents stationed in the restaurant noticed Reuben leave. Nor could they remember afterwards anything at all about his appearance. When rewound, the audiotape from the directional microphone was found to be completely blank. And none of the technicians working the post could recall a word of the conversation they had supposedly recorded.

Father Naples remained unmoving at the table until fifteen minutes passed and a curious waiter came over to see if anything was wrong. To his horror, he discovered that the priest was dead.

According to a secret report prepared by a team of investigators, Father Naples had died from a massive heart attack. One suffered by the priest a few minutes after sitting down at noon. No one could explain, nor even attempt to answer, how a dead man managed to drink two bottles of wine. The black attaché case found beneath the table was empty.

PART
1

There are some secrets which do not permit themselves to be told. Men die nightly in their beds, wringing the hands of ghostly confessors, and looking them piteously in the eyes—die with despair of heart and convulsion of throat, on account of the hideousness of mysteries which will not suffer themselves to be revealed.

"The Man in the Crowd"
Edgar Allan Poe

CHAPTER 1

St. Louis—March 10, 1994

Someone was following him. A sixth sense, the result of years of detective work, warned McCann that he was being watched. And tracked.

Softly, the detective cursed. He leaned against a nearby building and casually scratched his right ankle. At the same time, McCann swept the street around and behind him with relaxed gaze. It was late, nearly midnight, but in St. Louis' "adult" entertainment strip, things were just starting to happen.

Dozens of people crowded the sidewalk. Men and women, black and white, they were all part of the usual weeknight crowd. Cheap whores in black leather outfits that exhibited all of their charms mixed with high-class hookers dressed in silks. In a tough economy, both were anxious for business. Teenagers and college students hunted for drugs, bargaining with street dealers for the best price. Red-faced drunks begged for quarters. Young kids, dressed in rags and violating the curfew, danced on street corners, looking to grow up fast.

Young and old, they shared one trait in common. None of them expressed the least bit of interest in the motionless figure of Dire McCann.

With a sigh of annoyance, the big detective shook his head. Friends didn't track you. Just enemies. Mentally, he reviewed anyone he might have insulted or annoyed lately. The list wasn't very long. He hadn't been actively involved with the St. Louis underworld recently. Instead, he had been traveling around the USA for much of the past six months tying up loose ends of his personal life. What little he had accomplished while in the city had been in the employ of Alexander Vargoss, a rich and powerful industrialist. And those jobs hadn't crossed paths with any gang chieftains or

Mafia Dons who directed the majority of St. Louis' thriving criminal community.

McCann couldn't believe that his missions for Vargoss had anything to do with his tail tonight. Nobody with any intelligence, even major crooks, hassled the secretive industrialist or interfered with his plans. Besides being incredibly wealthy, with connections in both the police department and the mayor's office, Vargoss was the most powerful vampire in St. Louis. In the argot of the Kindred, he was the Prince of the city. And, like the medieval princes of old, from whom the term had been taken, Vargoss ruled with an iron hand. Any Kindred or kine foolish enough to cross him ended up dead. The permanent end of the Final Death.

Mysteries annoyed McCann. Especially when they revolved around him. Though he possessed extraordinary patience, the detective never delayed the inevitable. As he repeatedly told acquaintances, he liked to face the devil straight up. Oftentimes, that policy led to bloodshed. But McCann, though he deemed himself the quiet type, was no stranger to violence. When necessary, he was quite deadly.

Straightening his jacket, McCann started walking again. Clutched tightly in one hand was a small box and a stack of letters he had just retrieved from the all-night delivery center where his mail was sent. Maintaining odd hours and being out of the city for long stretches of time, McCann preferred not using a post office box. The clerks had a bad habit of stealing anything that looked the least bit valuable. The shipping depot charged more money for their services, but they guaranteed the safety of anything sent there.

Back in the city tonight after weeks on the road, McCann checked in first at his office. There were only a few messages on his answering machine, nothing of importance. With a cool breeze blowing off the river making the weather tolerable if not comfortable this June evening, the detective decided to walk the five blocks to the mail drop. He needed to work the soreness out of tired, old muscles. The certainty of being watched had not started until after he had retrieved his mail. That perplexed McCann. A stakeout meant a long-term commitment of time and resources. He wondered who was after him? And why? The detective meant to find out.

The black hole of an alleyway loomed up to his left. Smoothly, without breaking stride, McCann swiveled into the narrow corridor. An unbroken wall of brick twenty feet high lined both sides of the passage. Just as he had remembered. It was the perfect location for a trap.

A big, broad-shouldered man, standing four inches over six feet and weighing near two-fifty, the investigator moved with astonishing swiftness. McCann raced along the walkway, eyes quickly adjusting to the gloom. Thirty feet from the street, the alley made a right turn into near absolute darkness. The only illumination came from a bare hint of moonlight peeking out from between the rooftops. Rats burrowing in stacks of days-old garbage scurried out of the detective's path.

McCann stifled a snort of disgust. So much for keeping the neighborhoods clean. The main streets looked fine, but out of sight, just beyond the bend, urban decay ruled. Decades of graft and corruption had taken their toll on basic city services. St. Louis was no different than every big city. The rich and famous received all the benefits of modern life, while the poor and middle class suffered with the crumbs. Things never really changed, McCann decided, his gaze searching the walls. At least not in his lifetime.

Finally, the detective spotted the boarded-up doorway recessed behind a thigh-high pile of trash. He nodded in satisfaction and headed toward it. A dozen steps further, the alley ended in a twelve-foot high steel privacy fence. Soundlessly, McCann slipped into the alcove. It effectively made him invisible from anyone trailing behind. Then, he waited.

From underneath his topcoat, the detective pulled out his gun. Few humans knew of the Kindred. A mere handful of those, like McCann, dealt with the vampires on a regular basis. The big detective was quite aware of the unnatural strength possessed by his undead clients. Vampires were stronger and quicker than mortals. While they were not invulnerable, killing them was almost impossible. However, though they regenerated damaged or lost body parts, it took them time to heal. They could be rendered helpless by enough force.

Thus, instead of a .45 automatic or a .375 Magnum, McCann carried an Ingram Mac-10 submachine gun pistol. Just eleven inches long, it held thirty .45 caliber rounds that could be fired in one continuous burst. The impact of those bullets could rip any normal man to shreds and smash a vampire flat. In the harsh netherworld of crime in which the detective operated, the gun had proven to be an extremely effective tool.

Nearly a minute passed before McCann's shadow made the turn and came into sight. Hugging the shadows, the newcomer was a short, stocky man in his mid-thirties, with swarthy, cruel features. Dressed in a dark pullover and faded jeans, he appeared unarmed. Appearances, McCann knew full well, gripping his gun tighter, could be deceiving.

Spotting the steel fence in the dim moonlight, the stranger muttered a curse. Angrily, he moved forward, head moving from side to side as he looked for a break in the barrier. Intent on the bars blocking his way, the man walked right past McCann.

"Lose something, brother?" asked the detective, stepping out of the alcove. The stranger stopped moving, then slowly turned. Less than six feet separated the stalker from his quarry. The man's eyes widened in sudden shock as he spotted the submachine gun pistol in the investigator's left hand. Its muzzle, gaping wider than the entrance to hell, was pointed in a direct line with his stomach.

"McCann, right?" the swarthy man asked, his voice low and guttural. Slowly, very slowly, he spread his hands apart, as if demonstrating he was unarmed.

"That's me," admitted the detective. "Which hardly matters. What's more important, is who . . . "

The detective never completed the sentence. The

stranger's right hand twisted unexpectedly. As if by magic, a thin cord flashed out from beneath the man's arm and wrapped whip-like around the Ingram. McCann was caught completely by surprise. Before he could squeeze down on the trigger, the gun went flying from the detective's hands. Pistol and strangler's rope disappeared into the trash, leaving the detective unarmed. And in a fight for his life.

Free of the threat of the submachine gun, the swarthy man attacked with a ferocity that had McCann reeling. A series of savage karate kicks to his chest sent the detective stumbling backwards. Steel-tipped boots felt like hammers striking McCann's body. Growling deep in his throat, the assassin leapt into the air, aiming a sideways thrust for the detective's head. Enough force propelled the blow to crush McCann's skull like an eggshell. But it never connected.

Moving with blinding speed, the detective dropped beneath the kick, thrusting both of his arms upward as he did so. Catching the outstretched assassin's leg between his hands, McCann twisted hard. The attacker screamed as cartilage and muscle in his knee exploded. Howling in pain, he collapsed to the pavement.

Cautious of another surprise, McCann circled the injured man until he stood behind his head. A swift, brutal blow from a wooden box knocked the assassin unconscious. Shaking off the pain of bruised ribs, the detective searched the alleyway for his pistol. In minutes, he had retrieved both his weapon and the strangler's cord. A long thin strand of black fiberglass, it was knotted in three places to crush a man's windpipe on impact. The weapon successfully melded modern technology with ancient sacrificial ritual.

It also served as an effective rope to tie the assassin's hands tightly together behind his back. By the time the swarthy man regained his senses, brought back to reality by a series of sharp slaps, he was securely trussed up in a sitting position, his back resting against one wall of the alley. He whimpered in pain as McCann, squatting nearby, tapped his damaged kneecap with the barrel of the Ingram.

"Time for us to have a little chat," said the detective

pleasantly. "I dislike being followed. More so, I really hate it when somebody tries to murder me. I want to know why, and I want to know why . . . quick."

"I won't talk," declared the swarthy man angrily. "I demand you turn me over to the police. I want a lawyer."

McCann smiled. "Funny thing about this part of town. Cops don't come around here very often. They figure anyone crazy enough to wander about deserves what they get." McCann rapped the muzzle of the gun against his prisoner's undamaged knee. "You're on your own, my friend. Back here, we're isolated from view. Nobody can see or hear a thing. There's no cops, no lawyers. Just you and me. And my gun."

Small beads of sweat dribbled down the assassin's face as his gaze flickered to McCann's eyes, then to the submachine gun, then back to McCann's eyes. Mentally, the detective shrugged in disgust. He was wasting his time threatening this clown. It took a lot more than a veiled threat to worry a true professional. The swarthy man was cheap talent, hired merely as a diversion.

A *decoy!* The thought slammed through McCann as the sensation of being observed suddenly flared. Instantly, the big detective flung himself flat to the ground in the darkness. Twenty feet distant, at the corner in the alley, a heavy caliber automatic bellowed. A dozen shells exploded in the swarthy man's chest, jerking his body about in a grisly dance of death. They were bullets meant for McCann, baited by the hapless assassin's life.

Squeezing the trigger of the Ingram, McCann fired a useless burst in reply. He felt sure that his unseen opponent had already fled the scene. Strike quickly, then move. That was the operational procedure of a true professional. Never waste time on meaningless chatter or second tries. Mistakes like that were for amateurs like the dead man sprawled up against the wall. The real assassin was gone.

A short, muffled gasp and a flash of white leather indicated that McCann had jumped to the wrong conclusion. The detective shook his head in disbelief. The night held more surprises than he liked.

Three figures stepped into the moonlight. Their leader was a tall, aristocratic man with a face that appeared to be carved from weathered stone. He wore a black tuxedo with a ruffled white shirt, a red bow tie, and a matching red cummerbund. To McCann, it was a costume right out of wedding. Or a funeral. The detective, though, knew better than to speak his thoughts. No one dared insult Alexander Vargoss, Ventrue Clan elder. And the vampire Prince of St. Louis.

A step behind him stood two nearly identical platinum blondes. White leather jumpsuits clung to their voluptuous figures like second skins. High cheekbones, pitch-black eyes, and wide sensuous lips gave them a predatory look. McCann had encountered them before. They were Fawn and Flavia, Vargoss's twin bodyguards. Silent and deadly, they never spoke. Or acted without direct command of their Ventrue employer. Assamite assassins, the twins enjoyed their notorious nicknames as the Dark Angels of the Kindred.

Held effortlessly in one Fawn's arms was the lifeless body of a man. The pale white light glistened off the horrified expression frozen on his face. A hint of blood coated the blonde's upper lip. With a flick of her long tongue, she wiped it clean. Then, mischievously, the vampire smiled seductively at McCann.

The detective shuddered. Though she looked to be in her early twenties, McCann knew the girl and her twin were actually hundreds of years old. Oftentimes, the pair mocked him with suggestive gestures. They enjoyed pretending that passion still stirred within their perfect forms. But McCann wasn't fooled.

Along with food and drink, vampires no longer craved sex. For them, hot blood was the ultimate high. Carnal pleasures meant little to them. However, McCann had heard tales of Kindred who had taken human lovers in a desperate attempt to regain some of their lost humanity. The notion made his flesh crawl.

"We were on our way to your office when we spotted you entering the alley," said Vargoss dryly. "Two lowlife scum followed. We stayed in the shadows, assuming that you preferred us not to interfere. However, when your adversary chose to flee instead of fight, I demanded he stop." Vargoss shook his head in mock despair. "The fool chose instead to point his weapon at me. Fawn, of course, reacted."

"Of course," repeated McCann, bending over to search the first assassin's pockets. As expected, they contained nothing.

After Fawn dumped the second man to the ground, McCann checked him out as well. The dead man yielded a wallet holding five hundred-dollar bills and nothing else. McCann pocketed the money and slipped the billfold into his back pocket to examine later.

"You could have warned me before he started shooting," said the detective as he gathered together his mail from the alcove.

He pushed the corpses together against the wall. Sooner or later the police would discover the pair of lifeless bodies. They would be listed as two more vagrants murdered for no reason in the wrong part of town. With fifty unexplained deaths or more in St. Louis every month, the death of a pair of bums wouldn't rate a line of newspaper space.

"Nonsense," said the Prince, smiling. "I had absolute confidence in your ability to deal with the situation. Circumstances proved that my trust was not misplaced."

"And if you were wrong?"

"There are other humans, McCann," said the Prince. "Never forget that. I find you vastly entertaining. And quite useful despite your mortal limitations. I would mourn your passing. But you are not indispensable. There will always be others to take your place. In five hundred years, you will be no more than a pleasant memory. I will still remain."

"What a cheerful sentiment," said the detective. He picked his words very carefully. Vargoss appreciated his honesty and his sarcasm—within limits. No vampire in St. Louis mocked the Prince of the city. Much less a human, no matter how entertaining. McCann tiptoed on a tightrope where undead horrors feared to tread.

"I cannot afford the luxury of emotions," declared Vargoss, almost wistfully. "Nor friends. We Kindred are an ambitious race. It is part of our heritage. More than a few of my loyal subjects believe that they should rule this city, not I. Too many of my nights are spent squelching their ill-conceived plots."

"Uneasy lies the head that wears the crown," said McCann.

"Shakespeare understood the politics of power," said Vargoss, with a smile. "He should have been one of us."

The vampire turned to leave. "Enough chitchat. Come to the club tonight around midnight, McCann. I am entertaining a visitor from overseas. I want your opinion on what he has to report. Strange events are taking place in the former Soviet Union. *Extremely disturbing* events."

"I'll be there," said the detective. "At midnight."

Then Vargoss and his Dark Angels were gone. Leaving McCann standing alone in the alley with two lifeless bodies. Holding in his hands a small box and stack of letters, several with foreign postmarks. And an enigmatic smile on his face.

CHAPTER 2

St. Louis—March 10, 1994

McCann's office was located on the third floor of the Dempster building in the heart of the tenderloin district. The small suite consisted of a tiny reception area and an inner office beyond. Big, bold, black letters on the glass door proclaimed, *D. McCann, Investigations.* Beneath his name, in much smaller print, was the disclaimer *Consultation by Appointment Only.*

Twisting his key in the lock, the detective pushed open the door to the outer office and turned on the light. He was greeted by a low coffee table stacked with several old issues of *Sports Illustrated* and three worn red leather chairs. McCann shrugged. It wasn't much, but he didn't require any better. Recently, his only clients had been the Kindred, and none of them worried about his taste in furniture. At least, he noted with a small measure of satisfaction, the cleaning woman had kept the place tidy during his long absence. She almost made the outrageous rent he paid worth the price.

Walking through the reception area, McCann entered his inner sanctum. The office was dominated by a massive oak desk. On it sat an elaborate telephone answering machine. To one side was a low table with a dedicated fax machine, personal computer, and inkjet printer. Several metal cabinets hugged an inner wall, while behind McCann's armchair a row of windows looked out on the street. The glow of a nearby streetlight gave the room an eerie, ghost-like interior. Two more red leather chairs, matching those in the outer chamber, completed the furniture. No cheaply framed photos with hearty endorsements or tacky paint-by-numbers artwork hung on the walls. McCann believed in a strictly functional workplace. Besides which, it made a better impression on potential clients.

Tossing his coat on one of the red chairs, he dropped

into the seat behind his desk. Removing the submachine gun pistol from his shoulder holster, he reloaded it from a box of ammo stored in the desk. Considering what had happened already tonight, it seemed like good policy to stay ready for trouble.

Once that task was finished, McCann checked his answering machine. There had been three calls since he had gone for his walk. He reviewed the messages quickly.

Two came from people needing an investigator to handle divorce work. Pulling out a pad of paper and a pen, he jotted down names and phone numbers. Such work didn't interest him, but another detective in the building specialized in marital problems. The man appreciated the leads and paid McCann back in favors. It was an arrangement that benefited them both.

The other message was from an insurance agent anxious to sell him a health care policy. McCann grinned. Considering his present circumstances, he wasn't sure he could afford the premiums.

Answering machine reset, he opened his mail. The junk flyers he tossed into the garbage can; the bills he pushed to the side for later. That left him with five letters and the box. Three of the missives came from Italy, the fourth from Australia, and the fifth from Peru. The box was from Switzerland.

McCann read the correspondence from Venice first. Dated approximately a week apart, the letters contained detailed records for financial deals made during the previous seven days. The facts and figures covered hundreds of major business transactions throughout Europe and the United States. The detective scanned the documents carefully. There were no unusual expenditures or unexplained expenses. Not that he expected to find any. The masterminds of the Giovanni Clan were the greatest financial wizards in the world. They kept a tight watch on their investments. McCann merely wanted to make sure no one other than him was skimming the profits. The longer he lived, the more cautious he became. And, though he appeared to be in his mid-thirties, Dire McCann had lived a very long time.

He opened the envelope from Australia next. The only thing it held was a month-old newspaper clipping from Darwin, Northern Territory. The piece discussed how a recent influx of nomadic Aborigines from the Tanami Desert had created a shanty town at the edge of the city. Local officials were trying to get the troublemakers to return to their reservation, but with no success.

No one could offer an explanation for the natives' unexpected migration. Nor were the unwelcome Aborigines willing to discuss why they had abandoned their primitive shelters and made the long trek to the coast. Their only reply was to point in the general direction of the Macdonnell Ranges and utter the word "Nuckalavee, Nuckalavee," over and over again. Unfortunately, no one other than the natives understood what the term meant. The story ended with the mayor promising city residents that the shanty town would be gone shortly.

McCann grimaced. He understood why the Aborigines had fled. But he doubted that the government officials in Darwin would believe his answer. Or care. Mentally, McCann noted that he should request that his clipping service search for any follow-up stories. Or reports of unusual disappearances in the Northern Territory.

Shaking his head in frustration, the detective ripped open the letter from Peru. A color photograph and a short, handwritten note tumbled onto his desk. McCann swallowed hard when he saw the picture. Tonight's mail was filled with bad news. In major doses.

Scribbled in black ink around the margin of the photo were the words, "Found at entrance to huge cavern, Gran Vilaya ruins, Peru." The picture showed a massive stone statue of a crouching demonic figure with a misshapen, bloated female body and the face of a snarling jaguar. Circling her feet in a ring were a dozen stone heads. Judging from the size of the skulls, the demon stood at least 15 feet tall.

The accompanying letter was short and to the point. It was written by a member of the Explorer's Club. He described uncovering the statue at Gran Vilaya, located in the fog-shrouded region of Peru known as the "jungle's eyebrow." It fronted a huge network of previously unknown caves that honeycombed the Andes for miles. No one knew for certain the purpose of the underground warren. Several members of the expedition thought it might have served as a ritual burying ground for the mysterious Chachapoya civilization due to the numerous skeletons found scattered all through the tunnels. Which would therefore identify the demonic figure as the guardian of the dead. The writer ended his note with the hope that McCann felt his research money was being well spent.

The detective had contributed nearly five hundred thousand dollars to help finance the Gran Vilaya expedition. The money had come from a secret Giovanni slush fund whose existence, if they ever discovered it, would surprise a number of clan elders. The results definitely justified the cost. Though McCann would have been happier if the archaeologists had not found a thing.

The statue was not a representation of the spirit guardian of the dead Chachapoyas. It showed their murderer. A creature who abhorred all life, she was named Gorgo, the One Who Screams in Darkness. And the empty caverns in Gran Vilaya indicated that once more she walked the Earth.

Sighing, McCann ripped open the small box from Switzerland. He recognized an old friend's handwriting. Inside were photocopies of more than three hundred pages of hand-written memos and high level classified documents. They were a mixed selection from a half-dozen different European security agencies. All were marked TOP SECRET. Roughly arranged in chronological order, the earliest was dated approximately four years ago, while the most recent was less than a month old.

Written on the first page of the stack was a short note. *I thought you might find these reports interesting.* There was no signature. None was needed.

Glancing at his watch, McCann saw it was eleven-thirty. Time for him to leave if he was going to be at the Club Diabolique by midnight. Alexander Vargoss did not like to be kept waiting.

Gathering all the letters and papers together, the detective shoved them into the second drawer of his desk. It didn't have a lock, but he wasn't worried. No one besides him would understand the meaning of the material.

He was donning his overcoat when the telephone rang. McCann checked the caller ID feature on his phone system. He didn't recognize the number. Curious who could be calling this late, the detective picked up the receiver. "Dire McCann," he announced, as his tape recorder automatically started recording the conversation.

A man whose voice McCann didn't recognize spoke in clear, crisp tones. "Lameth," said the stranger, "beware of the Red Death."

Without another sound, the man hung up, leaving a stunned McCann holding the receiver. Lameth, the speaker had called him. It was a name from the dawn of history, one that McCann believed long forgotten. A master schemer, the detective did not like unexpected shocks. Especially ones of this magnitude.

Anxiously, the detective rewound the audio tape. He wanted to hear that voice again. Pressing the play button, he waited for the speaker to begin talking. And waited.

After a minute and several more tries, McCann was forced to accept the fact that his recorder had not picked up the conversation. Angrily, he checked the caller ID screen. It was blank. The digits displayed a few seconds earlier were gone. The detective rubbed his eyes in amazement. Some unknown power was working hard to make sure he didn't trace that call.

Hurriedly, he jotted down the telephone number from memory. Machinery could be tampered with, but not his mind. A quick push of a button connected him with the local police station.

"Harry? Dire McCann. Yeah, I'm back in town. You enjoy

the whiskey I sent for your birthday? Good. How about returning the favor? Can you check a phone number in your reverse directory? I need to know the location of the caller. Fast." McCann rattled off the code. "I'll hold."

It didn't take very long for Harry to reply. "The booth in the front lobby of my building," repeated McCann wearily. "I should have guessed. Thanks, buddy. I owe you another bottle."

Hanging up, McCann pulled his coat closed and walked to the door of his office. The phone booth on the first floor had been out of service for months. Frowning with concentration, he shut off the light, then locked the door.

First there had been the assassination attempt in the alley. Next came the ominous reports from across the globe. Monstrous beings were stirring. Finally, a mysterious caller used a name out of the distant past. A name McCann preferred forgotten. Not a believer in coincidence, the detective knew the three events had to be linked together. But how?

The voice on the phone had warned him to "beware of the Red Death." McCann had absolutely no idea who or what the Red Death might be. He had a terrible suspicion that he would soon find out.

CHAPTER 3

St. Louis—March 10, 1994

The Club Diabolique was located a few miles from McCann's office, in the middle of one of St. Louis' older industrial parks. Driving there in his late-model Chrysler, the detective went through three red lights and violated a half-dozen rules of the road. However, he reached his destination with five minutes to spare.

Leaving the car parked on a back street several blocks away, McCann walked to the nightspot. Originally an abandoned warehouse, the building had been converted into a disco by several ambitious young capitalists ten years earlier. When that craze had died, so had the club. It passed through several hands and incarnations before being bought by the present owner, Oliver Pearson. After several months of extensive interior redesigning, the nightspot had reopened with a new name, The Club Diabolique, and a new attitude. Converted into a Gothic-Punk haven, with live music, a huge dance floor, and an exclusive, "Members Only" upper level, the bar had quickly developed into the hottest place to be seen in town.

Virtually none of the mortal patrons realized that the club also served as a gathering place for St. Louis' small community of Kindred. Even the undead needed a place to socialize and relax among their own kind. They found it at The Club Diabolique. It was here, too, behind locked doors, that the Prince of the city, Alexander Vargoss, held court, dispensed justice when necessary, and greeted vampires new to his territory. Which was the situation tonight.

McCann arrived at the front door exactly as the hands of the big clock over the entrance pointed to twelve. As usual, a crowd of anxious patrons waited impatiently on the sidewalk outside.

There were rich, middle-aged businessmen wearing expensive suits, accompanied by much younger women dressed to kill in skin-tight designer dresses and five-inch spiked heels. Club Diabolique catered to mistresses and expensive ladies of the evening, not wives. Morals and inhibitions were checked at the door.

Crowding them for space were the Goths. They were Punks with an attitude. Generation X-ers without much money and without much hope, they felt cheated by a world spoiled by their elders. Their quest for identity had led them down strange paths. Searching for meaning in a meaningless world, they turned to the 19th-century Gothic traditions for inspiration. Their look was a mix of black leather and Victorian finery. Many of them, not realizing the bitter truth behind the legends, fantasized about becoming vampires. Sometimes it happened, turning their dreams into nightmares.

Goths dressed the part. Their hair was black—short and spiky, long and flowing—or white, bleached colorless and cut close. They wore chalky white facial makeup and heavy dark eyeliner, giving their faces a hollow, unearthly look. Clothes were usually loose-fitting and black, though white lace was also popular. Skirts and dresses tended to be mid-thigh high and velvet, worn with net stockings. Ruffled jackets with vivid purple linings were the latest rage. What little jewelry they wore, ankhs and earrings, was invariably silver.

McCann sympathized with the Goths. Most of them were bright, sensitive young men and women trying desperately to cope with a world of diminishing returns. Lonely and bored, they had created a whole new subculture based on a romanticized view of decadence and death. Their view of the undead came from erotic novels and movies, not the Kindred. As he strolled past them, he uttered a silent prayer that they remain forever ignorant of the truth.

A giant of a man, seven feet tall and weighing close to 400 pounds, guarded the entrance to The Club Diabolique. Dressed in undertaker's garb, he exuded an air of restrained menace. This was Brutus, nicknamed the Arbitrator of Souls. In more mundane terms, the ex-wrestler worked as the doorman.

Brutus controlled admission to the club. His word was law. Bribes meant nothing to him. Nor did social status, or lack of it. No one was sure how he selected who was granted access to the nightspot and who was not. Brutus never explained his choices, and no one dared ask.

McCann nodded to the doorman. Brutus nodded back. "He's been expecting you," said the giant, his voice rumbling like distant thunder. There was no need to identify to whom the doorman referred. Along with being the gatekeeper and occasional bouncer, Brutus was also one of Vargoss's ghouls.

McCann stepped through the door into the club, then paused, letting his eyes adjust to the gloom. The dim lighting and a thick cloud of tobacco smoke made it difficult to see. The ever-present pounding of rock music played at the threshold of pain made conversation impossible. Nobody cared. The Goths, the straights, and those in between came to The Club Diabolique to be seen. To dance. To drink. And to forget their ordinary identities in a night of sin and debauchery.

The huge promenade was crowded with hundreds of patrons moving frantically in time to the eardrum-shattering sound of tonight's band. With a wry smile, McCann noted that the four entertainers called themselves Children of the Apocalypse. After the news from Peru and Australia, the words seemed quite appropriate.

Accompanied by a backbeat that refused to quit, McCann climbed the narrow stairway leading to the second floor. Another figure stood guard outside the ornately carved door marked *Members Only* at the top of the landing. Tall and slender, with greased-down black hair and skin so white as to be almost translucent, he was "Fast Eddie" Sanchez. Though Eddie looked no older than eighteen, he was closer to a hundred. Eddie was one of the Kindred, Embraced as a young man on the frontier at the turn of the century. He was gifted with extraordinary reflexes, amplified by his vampiric powers. Sanchez was the fastest person with a knife McCann had ever seen—living or dead.

"Evening, Eddie," said McCann. "What's the good word?"

"Nothing good tonight, McCann," said Eddie. "The boss is waiting inside for you. Got some big shot Tremere sorcerer with him. Word out on the street is that bad times are coming."

"Sounds like a good reason to keep your blades sharpened," said McCann, as Eddie opened the door.

"*I always keep my knives ready, McCann,*" *said Eddie, seriously, as the detective walked past him into the next room.*

There were a dozen round cocktail tables scattered about the private chamber, with perhaps fifteen Kindred and twice that number of ghouls present. A small bar served whiskey for the ghouls and blood, both human and animal, for the Undead. Neonates, recently Embraced vampires, worked as the waiters.

To the rear of the room, on a small raised stage, an undead trio of jazz legends were playing some of their greatest hits for a small but appreciative crowd gathered nearby. Alexander Vargoss hated rock music and refused to allow it in his domain. The walls and floor of the private club were soundproofed. They kept the noise outside, and, sometimes, held the screams inside. Humans other than McCann had entered the private chamber. But he was the only one who had ever left alive.

A stunning redhead was singing with the band tonight. Wearing a green sequined dress that sharply delineated a near-perfect figure, she possessed a deep, syrupy voice that blended in perfect harmony with the three musicians. Though the detective was positive he had never seen the woman before, her face looked vaguely familiar. Snagging a passing waiter, McCann asked, "Who is she?"

"One of Iverson's ghouls," replied the fledgling, recognizing McCann immediately. All of the Kindred in Vargoss's domain knew the rogue human who served as their Prince's advisor. The waiter gestured at a flashily outfitted Kindred male sitting alone in a corner, eyes fixed on intently on the singer. Iverson belonged to the Toreador Clan, known among the Kindred for their obsession with the arts. He had been visiting St. Louis for the past month on business. "He watches her real, real careful. Doesn't like anyone else taking an interest in the lady. Can't say I blame him. She's good."

"She's terrific," said McCann. "I'm surprised he's left her mortal. Having her as his childe would really boost his prestige in the clan."

"I think he's worried she might lose her sultriness if Embraced," replied the waiter. "Makes sense to me."

The neonate pulled free of the detective's grip. "I wouldn't gawk too long, McCann. The Prince looks like he's getting impatient. Plus, that Tremere he's with is a real obnoxious bastard."

"Yeah," said McCann, giving the singer a long last stare, unsuccessfully trying to place her features. Shrugging his shoulders in defeat, the detective strolled over to Vargoss's usual table at the far wall.

"Sorry I'm late," said McCann, nodding to the Prince. As usual, Vargoss sat with his back to the bricks. Like Wild Bill Hickok, he was obsessed with the thought of being attacked from behind. Considering the ambitions of his subjects, McCann didn't blame him a bit. Flanking the Prince on either side were Fawn and Flavia, clad as always, in white leather. The fourth Kindred at the table, dressed entirely in black, was a short, rat-faced man with wispy gray beard and beady little eyes. A Tremere magician, according to Fast Eddie. He stared at McCann contemptuously.

"You delayed our conversation until this kine arrived?" the wizard snarled at Vargoss, making it quite clear he considered McCann one step below a monkey. *The Tremere Clan were not noted for their social graces.*

"Good evening, McCann. You find our new singer interesting?" the Prince asked the detective politely, his voice icy cold.

Like most Ventrue elders, Vargoss considered bad manners a deadly insult. That a closely trusted Tremere counselor had sought to betray him a few months earlier in a plot uncovered by McCann further aggravated the situation. Suddenly aware that he had offended his host, the rat-faced Tremere magician nervously folded his hands together on the table and said nothing more.

"She's quite talented," answered McCann blandly, as the woman finished her song. He was anxious to learn what brought the sorcerer to St. Louis. But he knew better than to try to play peacemaker between two Kindred of rival clans. "I've heard few better."

"An exceptional performer," said the Prince. He gestured to one of the Kindred at a nearby table. "She is Melville's ghoul. Her name is Rachel Young."

As if hearing her name, the redheaded singer raised her eyes and looked across the room. For an instant, her gaze met McCann's. Rachel had the bluest eyes the detective had ever seen. The briefest hint of a smile flickered across her lips. McCann smiled back.

Vargoss turned and focused his gaze on the Tremere. The Prince's eyes blazed and his voice had the bite of a knife. "I refuse to tolerate rude behavior in my domain, Mr. Benedict. Especially to one of my guests, kine or Kindred. You have been warned. I do not believe in second chances."

Vargoss gestured for the detective to sit. "Not that McCann needs me to defend his honor. He is no ordinary mortal."

The Prince showing off his pet human, thought McCann sarcastically. But he knew better than to disappoint his mentor. Leaning forward, he traced a certain proscribed cabalistic phrase on the table. For an instant, the letters glowed red before disappearing. Benedict's eyes widened in shock.

"You are a mage?" he whispered. "Of what tradition?"

"Euthanatos," replied McCann, naming the infamous Death cult. Several of their number cooperated with the Kindred, lending credence to the detective's lie.

"My apologies," said the rat-faced vampire. Like most Kindred, he was extremely wary of mages. Those beings foolish enough to cross magicians usually ended up perishing in peculiar fashion. Including the Undead. "I am Tyrus Benedict. I meant no disrespect. To you or your order."

McCann nodded, struggling not to break out laughing.

Deceiving Vargoss with a few parlor tricks had been extraordinarily simple. As was the case now with Benedict. The Kindred were masters of deceit and deception. Yet they much too easily accepted the unbelievable when confronted by the obvious. They saw complications where none existed. It was a basic character flaw that Dire McCann understood and exploited quite effectively. And had done so, in various guises, over the millennia.

Vargoss raised a hand and a waiter immediately appeared. "A drink, and then we shall talk," he declared. "The best blood we have for myself and my guest. McCann, would you care for something?"

"I'll pass," said the detective. "Your whiskey is too smooth for the likes of me, Prince. I prefer my rotgut cheap and with a punch."

"As you will." Vargoss snapped his fingers. "Serve us."

McCann watched in silence as the two Kindred drained their blood cocktails. As usual, Fawn and Flavia abstained. They preferred their vitæ straight from the vein.

Vargoss, his cheeks flushed crimson, placed his glass on the table. "All right, Benedict. I understand the Camarilla elders sent you here to bring me up to date on the recent troubles in Russia. Speak. I am listening."

"A little over three years ago," began the vampire wizard, *"at the height of Boris Yeltsin's unexpected rise to supreme authority in Moscow, all communication with the Kindred inside the former Soviet Union abruptly ceased. In the period of a few days, an Iron Curtain of silence descended across Russia. It was as if the earth itself had swallowed up our brethren. No one was sure what had taken place, but all agreed it warranted serious action. Several fact-finding missions made up of powerful members of the European Ventrue and Toreador Clans entered the country searching for answers. None of them returned."*

Vargoss shrugged. "Obviously it was a Sabbat takeover. The Brujah elders in Moscow underestimated the discontent among their kine. Their puppet rulers spent too much money on weapons and not enough on food. Without a strong leader like Stalin to keep the commoners in line, discontent and anarchy flourished. The fall of the government, and the Brujah with it, was inevitable. No mystery there. We saw it take place on television."

The Prince paused. "The Sabbat are demon-worshiping lunatics. But they are also experts at staging revolutions. They caught the Brujahs unaware and slaughtered them before a counterattack could be organized. "

"So we thought as well," said Benedict, his gaze darting to the Prince, then to McCann, then to the Prince again. "Until our spies high in the ranks of the Sabbat learned that they too were unable to contact their agents within the country. A half-dozen Paladins and Bishops vanished in the purge."

"Liars," said Vargoss. "The Sabbat thrives on deception. Even among themselves."

"Not so," said Benedict. "The Lasombra elders desperately wanted to know what had happened. They sacrificed dozens of packs in suicide missions to break the barrier of silence."

"Did they?" asked McCann.

"No," said Benedict. "They failed. Something stronger than both the Camarilla and the Sabbat ruled Russia. And it wanted no interference from the outside world."

"Something stronger?" repeated Vargoss, turning the statement into a question. "What organization exists that is mightier than the Camarilla?"

"The Army of Night," said Tyrus Benedict, his voice rising in intensity. "An unholy band of demonic Kindred belonging to no clan, they are allied with the forces of hell. The fiends belong to the brood of the most feared sorceress of all time—the Hag, Baba Yaga. She awoke from torpor several years ago and has now reclaimed Russia as her own. Armageddon approaches. The Nictuku are rising!"

"Nonsense," said the Prince angrily. "The Nictuku do not exist. They are myths, invented by the Nosferatu elders to frighten their rebellious childer."

"Baba Yaga is no fable," said Benedict. He reached into an inner pocket of his jacket and pulled out a handful of photographs. "A dozen Tremere wizards met the Final Death obtaining these pictures. Look at them and then tell me if I am lying."

Vargoss's eyes narrowed as he stared at the photos. Raising up one particular picture, he showed it to Fawn and Flavia. "She has teeth of iron and six-inch claws," he stated in hushed tones. "Just as the legends claim."

McCann, anxious to see the evidence but knowing his place, waited patiently as Vargoss closely examined each photo. In the meantime, he glanced over at the Tremere wizard. Benedict had not said a word since revealing the pictures. That seemed odd.

The rat-faced vampire sat perfectly still, as if frozen in place. There was an odd look on his face. His eyes were focused on the jazz trio across the room. The musicians had suddenly gone silent. McCann wondered why.

"Benedict?" said McCann, mystified. "What's wrong?"

The detective never received an answer. Instead a scream of absolute, utter terror rocketed him to his feet. He turned as he rose, so that he faced the rear of the chamber where the noise had originated. In one hand, he gripped his machine gun pistol, ready for action. At his side were the Dark Angels. Each of them held a pair of short swords they were capable of wielding with deadly efficiency. Right behind them stood Alexander Vargoss. The Prince of St. Louis was no coward.

"Who in hell's name is that?" whispered McCann. *Now he understood the shocked expression on Benedict's face. The surprises were coming fast and furious tonight. He felt sure they were all linked together. The trick was discovering the common thread. "What in hell's name is that?"*

Tall and gaunt, a lone figure dominated the center of the chamber, a few feet in front of the stage. It had not been there a minute ago. Somehow, it had materialized out of thin air. That was what the Tremere wizard had seen. It was a magical feat that challenged even the most powerful of the Kindred.

The newcomer wore a single garment consisting of a

ripped and tattered shroud held tightly in place about his body with moldering white bandages. His chalk-white face was that of a long dead corpse. Ancient, decaying skin stretched tightly across a hairless skull. Paper-thin lips, a beak-like nose, and hollow, gaunt cheeks combined in a look of utter malevolence. Huge unblinking eyes, like the black pits of hell, took in all those in the chamber.

A creature of blacks and whites, streaks of brilliant crimson marked his face, his chest, and his arms. Hands and fingers glowed ghastly red. The bright scarlet of fresh blood. There was no question in McCann's mind that here stood the Red Death.

Behind the spectral creature, at the rear of the stage, crouched Rachel Young. She had been the one whose screams had first alerted the crowd. Now, though, her lips were pressed together in an expression of helpless despair. She was terrified of the Red Death. Yet she made no move to flee the horror. Looking down, McCann understood why.

The floor surrounding the walking corpse sizzled. The vinyl bubbled like lava beneath the creature's feet. Waves of superheated air rose around the figure, giving it an eerie, unearthly vagueness. The Red Death blazed, but did not burn.

"In three hundred years I have never seen its like," muttered Benedict, still seated. "How can such a monster exist?"

McCann wondered the same thing. And he based his observation on a much greater span of time.

"Who are you?" The Prince's voice rang like a bell through the silent chamber. "And how dare you violate the traditions and enter my domain without permission?"

The figure raised its head until its eyes glared directly at Vargoss. "I am the Red Death," *the monster declared in slow, deliberate tones.* "I go where I want. Your petty territorial claims mean nothing to me. My will is the only law."

"That ain't the way I sees it," said Fast Eddie Sanchez, emerging from the crowd of Kindred closest to the Red Death. Squinting from the heat, he took a step closer to the monster. Then another. In one hand, he clutched a needle-thin stiletto. "Entry to this club is by invitation only. And it don't sound like you got one."

Fast Eddie wasn't terribly smart, but he was extremely loyal to his Prince. Before anyone realized what he planned, the guard lunged forward and buried his knife up to the hilt in the Red Death's chest. Or, at least, he attempted to do so.

The metal blade flared incandescent. It vanished in a flurry of steel tears. Leaving Eddie unarmed and very near the Red Death. Reaching out with its claw-like fingers, the spectral figure snared the guard by the throat. Effortlessly it raised him into the air. Eddie shrieked in sudden, overwhelming pain. Then, arms and legs flailing about wildly, he ignited.

Gouts of blue flame burst from Eddie's nose, eyes, ears, and mouth. Tongues of fire erupted from his chest. His fingers blasted into bits like firecrackers. Legs and arms exploded like dry wood thrown into a blazing fireplace. His skin blackened and crinkled like burning paper. A blast of incredible heat roared through the chamber. And Fast Eddie Sanchez was gone.

Laughing insanely, the Red Death opened his hand and let a trickle of ashes fall to the floor. "He was the first. But not the last. A fitting end to all those who defy the Sabbat. Or challenge the might of the Red Death!"

The crowd went berserk. Screeching like wild animals, Kindred and ghouls bolted for the exit. Fire destroyed vampires, and though most had existed for hundreds of years, they clung to their unnatural existence with all of the hunger of their mortal counterparts. More, for they knew beyond any doubt that they were the damned.

Panic-stricken, they fought and clawed for the door. Only to discover that it refused to open!

Kindred who had been sharing a table minutes before ripped and tore at each other in a blind fury to escape the monster in their midst. They bolted from place to place, pushing chairs out of their path. For, walking slowly and deliberately through the chamber, burning a ghastly trail of blackened footprints in the floor, stalked the Red Death.

Methodically, it grabbed hold of any Kindred foolish enough to venture close. Clasped the vampire to its chest and turned it to ashes.

"It's searching for me," whispered Tyrus Benedict, huddled fearfully in his chair. "It wants the pictures from Russia. They are what drew it to this place. We are doomed!"

McCann shook his head. "Nonsense," he snapped at the wizard. But wondered if perhaps the Tremere sorcerer wasn't correct.

"Attend me," snapped Alexander Vargoss to his Dark Angels. "He must be stopped."

Features grim but determined, the Prince stepped forward directly into the path of the Red Death. Vargoss' body pulsated with raw energy. A fifth-generation vampire, he was over 2,000 years old and controlled incredible powers. Raising his hands high over his head, clenching his fingers into fists, Vargoss extended his mighty will. "Halt," he commanded in a voice that never before had been denied. "HALT!"

The Red Death laughed in defiance. It continued to advance.

"Halt," repeated Vargoss, his voice uncertain. The first traces of doubt showed on his face. The Red Death was very close. It was too late, much too late, for the Prince to turn and run.

Desperately, McCann squeezed the trigger of his submachine gun. Thirty bullets slammed into the monster from nearly point-blank range. And slowed it not at all.

Slowly, with great deliberation, the Red Death reached out for the Prince. To the detective, always suspicious of being manipulated, the monster seemed to hesitate for an instant, almost as if waiting for an interruption.

Two blurs in white leather hurtled forward. Moving with inhuman speed, Flavia and Fawn grabbed the Prince by the shoulders, spun him around, and sent him flying. Crimson fingers clutched empty air.

Saving Vargoss from the Red Death had been the Dark Angel's primary purpose. However, that accomplished, they could not resist the challenge the monster presented. Assamite assassins, they thrived on death and destruction. Two sets of matched blades, the finest weapons in the world, slashed in wide arcs. The blows were not aimed at the Red Death's face or chest, but at its wrists. The twins sought victory not with brute strength, but speed.

Moving faster than the eye could see, the blades connected. Then passed through! McCann cursed aloud, astonished. In his entire existence he had never before seen the like. The specter appeared composed entirely of frozen flame. Which meant that nothing physical could harm it. The Red Death was invulnerable to normal weapons.

Tentatively, McCann reached out telepathically with his mind. He hated revealing any hint of his true essence. But there was no other choice. He had to know the truth. What type of being was the Red Death? For a bare instant, thoughts crossed, as mind touched mind. Then McCann recoiled in shock.

The Red Death was one of the Kindred. That much the detective read easily from the monster's surface thoughts. It used a discipline McCann had never before encountered—Body of Fire. Transforming into this form took the combined efforts of several vampires, which meant the Red Death did not work alone. McCann caught a fleeting memory of a group calling themselves The Children of Dreadful Night. Then the thought was gone, swallowed up in the creature's obsession with destruction. In its present state, the Red Death was more elemental fire than vampire. It hungered to destroy life. It existed to kill.

More frightening was the fact that the Red Death immediately detected McCann's mind probe. It closed off its thoughts—then returned the favor with a mental stream of hellfire that would have burned the detective's brain to cinders if he had remained in contact. McCann had no idea who the Red Death really was. But there was no question that the monster recognized him!

Undaunted by their initial failure, the twins danced away, preparing a second attack. "No," cried the detective, but his warning was ignored. The Dark Angels leapt forward, their blades now aimed at the Red Death's eyes. This time, the monster was ready.

Though not as fast as its two enemies, the spectral creature still moved with incredible swiftness. Long arms lashed out in sweeping motions in both directions. Flavia dropped to the floor, diving beneath the creature's swing. Fawn, caught leaping forward, was not so fortunate. Crimson fingers raked across her face.

The Dark Angel screamed, the first time McCann ever heard her make a sound. Then, an instant later, she exploded in a fireball of white flame. Involuntarily, McCann's eyes snapped shut.

Behind him, he heard a gurgle of sound. Unable to see, the detective swung his arms about, making brief contact with someone hurrying past. Then, as the pain faded, his vision returned. And he found himself staring at the headless body of Tyrus Benedict!

In the chaos of the past few seconds, an unknown killer had crept behind the frightened Tremere sorcerer and decapitated him. Already, dissolution had begun. Benedict's body collapsed inward upon itself, a rotted husk consumed by decay. The grave, cheated for three hundred years, was not denied. In seconds, all that remained were the wizard's clothes in a crumpled heap on his chair.

Benedict was gone, and with his death, so too was the Red Death. The fiery specter had vanished as suddenly and mysteriously as it had appeared.

The crowd in the chamber were just beginning to realize they were safe. At the door stood Alexander Vargoss, his features a mixture of despair and relief. Exerting his overwhelming force of majesty, he was bringing order to his restless brood.

Whatever power had barred the exit disappeared with the Red Death. However, until calm was restored, the Prince refused to let any of his progeny depart. What had taken place inside this chamber was not the concern of the patrons of Club Diabolique. The Masquerade must be maintained.

Alone, on her knees in the center of the room, Flavia cried tears of black blood. Dark Angel and Red Death. McCann felt certain their duel was far from over.

The photos on the table were gone. As were the contents of Tyrus Benedict's clothes. The Tremere wizard's mysterious executioner had taken everything.

Or so McCann thought, until his gaze unexpectedly fixed on a gleaming bauble on the floor. Bending over, the detective picked up a shimmery green sequin. He remembered blindly hitting someone. Here was solid evidence of that contact.

Hurriedly, he scanned the crowd. Though no one had been permitted to depart, there was no sign of Rachel Young. The singer had disappeared. McCann was not surprised.

CHAPTER 4

Washington, DC—March 11, 1994

Makish glanced impatiently at his watch. It was one minute before 2 A.M. The letter had stated *two o'clock tonight, at the front entrance to Union Station.* The hour approached. But there was no sign of his mysterious employer.

A small, slender male, with mahogany skin, slicked-down black hair, and too-wide smile, Makish attracted little attention other than that of an occasional bum asking for a handout. Or a hooker hoping to make some spare change. The few policemen, anxious to make it through the shift without any trouble, treated him as if he was invisible. Whenever one of them walked by, Makish grinned widely and sang out in a high-pitched, nasal voice, "Good evening, officer. I am waiting for my ride home, officer. Good to see you, sir."

The cops nodded and continued their patrol. Lots of loonies and weirdos hung out at Union Station. It was well lit and comparatively safe. Not more than one or two killings took place there in a week. Which made it one of the most secure buildings on Washington's southeast side.

The nation's capital was infested with drug lords, crime bosses, and crooked politicians. Each controlled packs of thugs who engaged in a violent, ruthless war for territory. The small, outmanned, and outgunned District of Columbia police force had long conceded the street to the outlaws. North and West, where the major government buildings stood, was comparatively safe. The National Guard helped keep the peace. South and East, near Capitol Hill and the train station, justice came from the muzzle of a gun.

Makish couldn't understand the senseless violence. The cheap hoods who killed for gang honor and loose change disgusted him. They acted like wild animals, with no appreciation for art. Murder needed to be done with style, with panache. Makish was a connoisseur of extermination. Most Kindred thrived on blood. Makish drew his sustenance from murder. He was the supreme assassin in the world of the undead.

"I believe you are waiting for me?" asked a voice slightly behind and to the right of Makish. It was exactly two hours past midnight.

Startled, the assassin turned. Cautious by nature, he had positioned himself close to the front wall of the station. No one had passed in his direction in minutes. Yet, where no one had been seconds before, now stood a stranger.

A tall, lean figure wearing a dark raincoat, with a slouch hat that hid most of his features, the sardonic smile indicated he found Makish's bewilderment amusing. Stepping out of the shadows, he beckoned with one hand. "Come, walk with me. We need to talk business, and the street offers unmatched privacy. Besides," the newcomer added, "there is work to be done."

They headed east, into Washington's worst slums. At this time of night, in the midst of a cold snap, the dark streets were empty of life. The glare of a single streetlight sent long shadows scurrying ahead of them into the blackness.

"You hired the two kine as instructed?" questioned the stranger.

"I followed your instructions as written," said Makish. The assassin possessed a talent for sensing the bloodline of any vampire he encountered. There was no question in his mind that the figure at his side was a member of the Kindred. But, inexplicably, Makish could not place the other speaker's clan. It was quite frustrating. And very disconcerting.

"I dispatched them to St. Louis the other day," continued the assassin. "The first, of course, had no knowledge of the second. They received half their money in advance, the other half to be paid on completion of their assignment. I have not heard from either human since."

"Nor will you," said the stranger. "I was informed a short time ago that both killers died in the unsuccessful ambush.

As I expected. They served their purpose admirably."

"The other arrangements you requested proceed on schedule," said Makish. "The work will be finished tomorrow."

"Excellent," said the stranger. "Though I expect no less. You come highly recommended. And cost too much for the services you provide."

"I charge what I am worth," replied Makish. "Success cannot be measured in mere dollars."

"A wonderful sentiment for these times," said the other dryly. "You have an artist's temperament. In a few minutes, we shall discover if your skills match your arrogance."

Reaching up, the stranger removed his hat. Makish's eyes widened when he saw his employer's features. The speaker's chalk-white face was that of a long-dead corpse, with decayed skin stretched across his hairless skull. Streaks of crimson stained his cheeks and forehead. With a smile, the horror turned to the assassin. "I am known as The Red Death. Touching my flesh would be a terrible mistake."

Makish nodded, watching the stranger remove his raincoat. Beneath the garment, the Red Death wore a tattered shroud held in place by moldering bandages. Though he stood several feet away from the grim figure, Makish could feel the heat emanating from the Red Death's body. It felt as if the mysterious vampire was on fire, without the flames.

"You are a renegade, no longer obeying the commands of your clan?" said the Red Death. It was more statement than question.

"The Society of Leopold killed my sire," declared Makish defensively. There was little respect among the Kindred for those vampires without a clan. "I demanded revenge, but the Assamite elders worried that such action against our human enemies would jeopardize the Masquerade. I thought differently."

"So you disobeyed their orders," said the Red Death, "and murdered the kine involved."

"They died, along with those who issued the directive," said Makish. "As did their families. I thought it only proper to make a personal statement of my grief. My sire deserved a fitting memorial."

The Red Death smiled. "In total, how many did you kill?"

"One hundred and fourteen," answered the assassin. "Shortly afterward I received word that my presence was required in Alamut to explain my actions. I politely but firmly declined the invitation. That was when I began working as an independent contractor."

"Six Kindred disappeared delivering that request," said the Red Death, chuckling.

"They refused to accept my decision as final," replied Makish. He spread his arms apart, as if appealing to a jury. "I had no choice but to convince them that I meant what I said. Five further failed attempts finally persuaded Hasan's minions to leave me alone."

The assassin paused. "You are quite well-informed about me," he said politely.

"My plans involve both the Camarilla and the Sabbat," said the Red Death. "While the Camarilla claim this city, there are traces of the Sabbat here as well. I require an assistant loyal to neither sect. You are the best available choice."

"I am flattered," said Makish, with a slight bow of his head. "I will do my best to justify your confidence in me."

Walking east as they spoke, the two Kindred had traveled nearly three blocks since the start of their conversation. They were deep in the heart of gang territory. With the ruins of rusted cars, weed-infested lots, and seedy tenements, the street resembled photos of war-torn Sarajevo more than the capital of the United States.

The Red Death halted in front of a gutted brick structure. It appeared deserted. The spectral figure raised a bony arm and pointed. "I sense several Kindred inside. The Camarilla rules the capital, but they cannot be everywhere. A Sabbat pack controls the drug traffic in this part of the city. It is time for them to learn the meaning of fear."

He stepped to the doorway. "I will deal with the vampires. Kill all of their associates but one. I desire a survivor to spread the tale."

"News travels best when conveyed with passion," said Makish. "I will strive to make a strong impression."

"Follow me," said the Red Death and entered the hallway. Behind him, like a dark shadow, came Makish. The slender assassin flowed from place to place. It had been several hundred years since he had last worked in tandem with another. But adapting to any situation was another of his many skills. Makish followed orders. As long as his fee was paid.

The spectral figure moved confidently to the center of the building. Despite his strange appearance and outlandish garb, he walked swiftly and without a sound. A ramshackle wooden door when opened, revealed a brightly-lit steel stairway leading down into the basement. Two video cameras were mounted on the ceiling at the far end of the corridor.

"Childish toys," said the Red Death. "I assume you can neutralize them."

Makish nodded and pointed a finger at the devices. After a few seconds, he smiled. "I froze the picture on their screen," he declared. "Anyone monitoring the hall will see nothing unusual. I disabled the traps in the floor and walls at the same time."

"Fools," said the Red Death. "Depending on machinery for protection is the mark of incompetents. They deserve to perish."

Together they descended to the lower level. The door opened into a small foyer containing the twin video screens monitoring the corridor. A heavyset ghoul, with shaved head and thick handlebar mustache, guarded the chamber. He was armed with an Uzi machine gun and sour expression. His first glimpse of Makish was his last. He died silently, his head twisted about a full 360 degrees. Though not very big, the Assamite assassin had incredibly strong wrists.

"Impressive," murmured the Red Death and pushed open

the door leading to the Sabbat headquarters. For a second, he stood there, unmoving, with Makish at his side.

"Greetings from the Camarilla," he announced in a harsh voice. "I am the Red Death."

There were two Kindred and eight ghouls in the room. The vampires were greedily sucking the last drops of blood from an attractive young black woman, her shocked eyes wide in death. Their servitors sat clustered around a large-screen television set, watching "Beavis and Butthead." Typical young punks, dressed in black leather with cutoff shirts and multiple tattoos, they were armed with an impressive assortment of knives, chains and automatic weapons. Makish didn't care. His only concern was that the ghouls might accidentally kill each other while trying to hurt him, leaving none alive as requested.

Ghouls were tough, stronger and quicker than normal human beings. The taste of vampire blood heightened their awareness and their physical abilities. But they were helpless as children against the assassin.

Makish moved so fast that his actions blurred. He raced from punk to punk in an intricate pattern resembling a complex dance. His fingers, hard as steel, ripped and tore at the bodies of his foes. Blood gushed across the room in bright crimson geysers. It splashed on the floor and walls like red paint, as the chamber transformed from drug den to slaughterhouse.

Unlike most vampires, Makish held the beast within his soul under tight control. So much warm blood would have sent other Kindred into a mad frenzy. Not Makish. He drank blood when necessary, for the physical nourishment it provided his body. Killing gave him *life*.

To the assassin, art meant style and substance. Makish served as his own worst critic. A satisfactory murder required a minimum of effort with the maximum result. He strove to waste not a motion. Death was a broad canvas on which he painted masterpieces of destruction. Whenever possible, he worked with Thermit. The explosive powder provided flash and color to an otherwise drab business. Though the

Assamite's expression as he worked remained fixed, mentally he strove to attain the blessed state of the perfect kill.

The first ghoul died with its throat torn out, nearly decapitated. The second collapsed to the floor in a steaming pool of its own insides, ripped from it with a disemboweling stroke from needle-sharp claws. The third screamed once, then choked to death on his own blood as Makish slammed his nose into his brain. Thirty seconds, three corpses.

Victim four, Makish hurtled headfirst into the hallway, slapping it across the shoulders with a glancing blow. Normally a killing smash, Makish pulled his punch, so that the punk suffered a few bruised bones but no serious injury. Dazed and confused, the young ghoul crouched helplessly in the outer foyer as he watched his comrades systematically destroyed.

Using a variety of simple but effective maneuvers, Makish finished off the rest of the ghoul pack in less than a minute. The triumph of his art rushed through him like a powerful drug. He found the exercise an invigorating, if short, encounter. Simple, uncomplicated deaths, they required little effort. The truly satisfying kills, those done with explosives, would come later. His own task complete, Makish focused his attention on the Red Death.

The specter held a Kindred in each hand. The two vampires struggled weakly, tugging ineffectively at the skeletal fingers clasping them by the throat. Their features were contorted in pain, while faint, mewling sounds issued from their mouths.

A dreadful smell permeated the room. It came from the Sabbat duo. Makish's nose wrinkled in distaste. He recognized the stench of burning flesh. Tiny wisps of smoke rose from the pale, white skin of the drug lords. The Red Death was slowly cooking his undead prey.

The monstrous figure laughed. A wave of incredible heat poured out of his body, sending the temperature of the chamber soaring. With a faint popping sound, a trace of fire appeared around the Red Death's fingers, like a crimson set of brass knuckles. The imprisoned Kindred shrieked in unbelievable agony as the tiny flames touched their cheeks, setting them ablaze.

They burned like dry, rotted wood. Flesh melted, eyeballs exploded, bones crackled and burst like rotted sticks. Makish, no stranger to violence, shook his head in amazement. In a thousand years of murder he had never witnessed anything like this before. The Red Death was appropriately named. He was flame incarnate.

Behind them, a scrambling on the stairs indicated that the remaining ghoul had made his escape. The Red Death spread wide its fingers, letting the pair of shriveled husks drop to the floor. Stepping forward, he ground the remains into ashes.

"I expect news of our escapade will circulate through the city and suburbs swiftly," declared the specter. "The Sabbat anarchs will demand immediate revenge against the Camarilla. Prince Vitel and his council of advisors will retaliate swiftly to any such action. They know the Sabbat hungers to control the capital. A push or two more in the right direction should finish the job. A single incident will escalate quickly into a major battle between the rival cults.

"The Camarilla has controlled Washington for nearly two centuries. However, it is one of the few major cities in North America they still dominate. Their grip has been slipping here for decades. We have merely hastened the inevitable. A Sabbat attack is assured. Leaving me free to pursue my objectives without interruptions."

The Red Death smiled. "It is almost too easy."

"You plan to start a major blood war merely to further your own desires?" questioned Makish. "Hundreds, perhaps thousands, of Kindred will perish."

"The existence of the entire Cainite race depends on the success of my mission," said the Red Death, all humor gone from its voice. "If I fail, entire generations of vampires will die in a slaughter unmatched in history. I must succeed, no matter what the cost."

Makish, who had been employed by fanatics many times in the past, knew better than to respond.

CHAPTER 5

St. Louis—March 11, 1994

It was close to 3:00 A.M. before McCann returned to his office. With a sigh of relief, he sank into his armchair and put his feet up on the desk. It had been a long, brutal evening. One filled with more surprises than he imagined possible. Both during the reign of the Red Death . . . and after.

The room cleared of his brood, Vargoss had spent more than an hour raging to McCann about his progeny's cowardice. The detective and the Dark Angels had been the only ones who had attempted to save the Prince from the Final Death. Vargoss made it quite clear that in nights to come, the regulars of the Club would pay for their weakness.

Although the Prince didn't address the issue, there was no question that the Red Death's attack had frightened him badly. Vargoss had exerted the full power of his will against the monster, without success. The vampire knew he had escaped the Final Death by luck alone. And there was no certainty that the Red Death would not return.

Finally, his temper spent, the Prince bade McCann goodnight. After instructing the detective to return to the club the next evening, Vargoss retreated by a hidden passage to his inner sanctum in the subbasement of the building. McCann suspected the vampire planned phoning the other Ventrue elders throughout the United States to warn them of the attack. His exit left McCann alone with Flavia.

The rest of the Kindred and their accompanying ghouls had departed the minute Vargoss had allowed them to exit. Tonight, none of them evidenced any desire to wear the Prince's crown. The Red Death served as a grim reminder of the perils of leadership.

The remaining Dark Angel, however, had not exited with the others. She remained sitting on the floor, silent and unmoving, throughout Vargoss' tiresome outburst. In her hands she still held the scorched remains of Fawn's white leather jumpsuit. She seemed frozen in place, her face a mask of despair. Though anxious to return to his own office, McCann felt compelled to say something.

"She died fighting," he declared softly, stepping within a few feet of Flavia. Sympathy was fine, but not stupidity. If the Dark Angel took offense at his words, the detective wanted enough room to defend himself. "It was an honorable death."

Flavia turned her face and stared at him. Her cheeks were stained with crimson. Vampires cried tears of blood. "Your concern for my feelings is appreciated, McCann" she said, in a mellow, low voice, with a surprising trace of a British accent. It was the first time the detective had ever heard the Dark Angel speak. She cast a quick glance in the direction of the secret stairs leading to Vargoss's hideaway. "Sympathy is often in short supply among the Kindred."

"The Prince always lavishly praised the services provided by you and your sister," said the detective, nervously. The last thing he wanted to do was stir up trouble between Vargoss and the remaining Dark Angel. "He treated you with respect."

In a smooth, catlike motion, Flavia rose to her feet. She was, without question, one of the most beautiful women McCann had ever seen. She had platinum blonde hair, high cheekbones, and wide, sensuous lips. Her white leather jumpsuit accented her full breasts, narrow waist, and long, long legs. Sex might no longer hold any pleasure for the Dark Angel, but her body defined seduction.

Flavia laughed bitterly. "Respect? Vargoss never truly cared about us. We were his servants. He enjoyed bragging about our skills because it reflected onto himself."

She smiled sardonically at the detective. "You understand, don't you, McCann. He does the same with you."

Without thinking, McCann nodded in agreement. The Prince liked showing off. And he treated his associates as prized possessions to be displayed whenever possible.

"My sister and I originally lived in England in the early 19th century," said Flavia. "Our given names were Sarah and Eleanor James. We were touring the continent for our fifteenth birthdays when we were kidnapped from our party. Our blonde good looks, lightning-fast reflexes, and notorious taste for cruel delights caught the attention of a traveling Assamite assassin. He arranged our abduction and had us brought to Alamut."

"A taste for cruel delights?" repeated McCann.

"Fawn and I dallied in what now has become commonly known as bondage and S&M," said Flavia, chuckling. Her long tongue circled her wide lips. "As sisters, we often shared our lovers. Even after we were Embraced. Despite what you think, McCann, vampires can still enjoy sex. Especially if the stimulation is mental as well as physical."

The detective took a step back. He definitely did not like the Dark Angel's tone of voice. Or the hint of an implied invitation.

"We trained in the mountain fortress for ten years," said Flavia. "The Assamite elders marveled at our skills. We fought well separately. However, as a team, we were unmatched. It was there that we earned the title The Dark Angels. When we turned twenty-five, our years of preparation complete, we were Embraced and became neonates of the Order."

Flavia glanced at the charred leather in her hands. With a shrug of her shoulders, she let it slip from her fingers. "Together, Fawn and I served the clan for over a hundred years. We traveled the world, working for many masters, never fighting alone, always staying together. Thirty years ago, we performed several minor executions for Vargoss. Impressed, I suspect, more by our appearance than our skills, he agreed to a long-term contract with the Assamite elders. In three decades, we never failed in our duties to our lord. Until tonight."

"I doubt stopping the Red Death constitutes a failure on your part," replied McCann. "I don't think a Kindred in existence could have dealt with that monster."

Flavia nodded. "Perhaps. Someday, I hope to meet the Red Death for a second encounter." She paused, her expression turning grim. "Fawn's death will be avenged. I swear it."

"What discipline did the Red Death use?" asked McCann, warily. He did not want to appear too curious. "I've never heard of a Kindred who controlled fire."

"Nor I," said Flavia. "I suspect he travels on the Path of Evil Revelation."

McCann grimaced. The Path of Evil Revelation was a secret discipline practiced by many members of the Sabbat. It taught that evil was good and that vampires were the agents of corruption. Followers of the path routinely dealt with demonic forces. "I once heard talk of a forbidden rite called the Body of Fire," said the detective, hoping for a response.

"I am not familiar with that discipline," said Flavia. "I know only of Fires of Inferno. It is one of the Paths of Dark Thaumaturgy practiced by the Corrupters. I know little about it. But I intend to find out more."

She stepped closer to McCann. "You are an unusual human," she declared. "Even for a mage, you are aware of too many of the darkest secrets of the Children of Caine."

Without warning, Flavia's right hand lashed out at McCann, second and third fingers stiff and aimed directly at his eyes. The Dark Angel's limb moved with incredible speed. Equally fast, the detective reacted, grabbing her wrist with his left hand, holding her hand immobile inches from his face.

Flavia laughed, a wild, untamed sound. "No ordinary man could move that swiftly, McCann. Nor stop me from making contact."

"I'm not an ordinary man," said the detective. Mentally, he cursed himself for letting the Assamite get so close. Flavia was much more cunning than he realized. He pushed her arm to the side. "As you stated, I am a mage."

Flavia shook her head, grinning. "No kine could have

halted that lunge. Nor any mage. Don't worry. I won't betray you to Vargoss. He pays for my fighting skills, not my thoughts."

"What are you babbling about?" asked McCann, fearing the worst.

"There are rumors," said Flavia, "of certain fourth-generation Kindred with incredible powers of domination. They are called Masqueraders. Their minds are so strong that while they lie in torpor, they can reach out and overwhelm a mortal's personality. They literally possess their victim, body and soul. In this manner, these Methuselahs again experience true life. Puppet masters, they masquerade in mortal form—eating, drinking, sleeping, making love. For safety, they endow their marionette with some of their powers. Enough perhaps for the person to claim to be a ghoul—or a mage."

McCann laughed, trying to appear amused. "What utter nonsense."

Flavia smiled. "Protest all you wish, Dire McCann," she said. "If you didn't, I might be worried."

Slowly, provocatively, she leaned forward and pressed cold lips to his. Her tongue, a sliver of ice, darted for an instant into his mouth. "I would be very grateful for the patronage of a Methuselah." Her lush body pressed against him, her taut nipples hard against his chest. "Extremely grateful."

McCann forced himself to remain quiet. He had said too much already.

The Dark Angel seemed undisturbed by his silence. "I must go and attend to the Prince. Sooner or later he will wonder where I am. Do not expect me to address you aloud unless we are alone." She chuckled. "Vargoss prefers his bodyguards never speak. He enjoys the air of mystery it creates."

McCann, sitting behind the desk in his office an hour later, sighed heavily. The detective folded his arms across his chest. For all her grief, the Dark Angel had not stayed in mourning very long. He trusted Flavia not to reveal her suspicions to the Prince for as long as it suited her purposes, and not a second more. If not handled properly, the Dark Angel could prove to be as dangerous to him as the Red Death.

The thought of that bizarre specter stirred the detective to action. McCann reached for the telephone. He needed to make a number of calls. A careful man reacted immediately to any threat. And McCann liked to think of himself as very wise.

Nearly an hour later he put down the receiver. Arrangements had been made and instructions given. Money was diverted from a dozen secret bank accounts into the proper channels. Already, a team of researchers was investigating everything available on the Path of Evil Revelations. And another group was studying whether any of the Kindred legends about the Nictuku described a horror similar to the Red Death.

Satisfied that he had done everything possible, McCann reached for the desk drawer containing his overseas mail. He felt sure that the coming of the Red Death and the reappearance of the Nictuku had to be related. The detective did not believe in coincidence. Especially when it involved the Kindred.

The drawer was empty. The documents were gone. McCann cursed, steadily, in seven languages, including two that had not been spoken on Earth for over three thousand years, until he was out of breath. Angrily, he slammed a fist into the side of the desk. Wood splintered, delivering a small amount of satisfaction along with a strong recognition that he was acting foolishly.

While he had been at The Club Diabolique, a thief had entered his office and stolen the papers. He had obviously underestimated the intelligence and ability of his unknown adversary. Or adversaries, since McCann did not know if he faced one enemy or many. It was not a mistake he would make again.

It was then that he noticed, resting on the edge of his desk, almost like a calling card, a bright green sequin.

CHAPTER 6

Paris—March 12, 1994

The official smile of Paris is the sneer. The rich sneer at the middle class. The middle class sneer at the poor. And they all sneer at the hordes of tourists who flood their city each year.

Their mockery, according to the guidebooks, is part of the charm of Paris. The city, with its great restaurants, fabulous museums, superb monuments, and long history, breeds contempt for the lesser achievements surrounding it. The average Parisian citizen considers himself far superior to anyone from outside the city. That attitude explains, at least in theory, the joy the natives get from telling tales of the Phantom of the Paris Opera.

The story, first immortalized in the novel by Gaston Leroux, then brought to vivid life first by films, then by stage productions, told of a demented genius living beneath the venerable Opera House. A master musician with a hideously scarred face, he ruled an underground kingdom of labyrinthine catacombs and secret waterways. Parisians loved to elaborate on the fantasy for gullible tourists, saying how, though he had reportedly been destroyed, the body of Eric, the Phantom, had never been found. And that every year, a few unwary tourists to the Opera House disappeared without a trace.

It was typical malicious Parisian humor. Often, the story was accompanied with a breathless attempt to sell bootleg souvenirs such as an authentic map of the catacombs or a page from the score of the Phantom's infamous lost opera.

Not all such stories, however, provoked the gales of laughter generated by the Opera Ghost. Late at night, the poor shopkeepers of Paris met behind locked and barred doors and exchanged tales not told to tourists. They spoke in whispers of the unexplained disappearances that had plagued the Île de la Cité, the oldest section of Paris. They repeated the same stories they had heard from their parents, who had been told similar tales by their parents, stretching back into the dim recesses of history. Common to every narrative was the same name. A title that when said aloud could cause the most elegant Parisian to blanch in terror. *Phantomas*.

Officially, the French Sûreté dismiss such rumors as the insane ramblings of demented poets living on the West Bank. No mention is made of a file, five inches thick, hidden deep in the files of police headquarters. Contained in it are hundreds of reports, dating back a hundred and fifty years to the time of Chief Inspector Vidocq, detailing the circumstances surrounding hundreds of disappearances in the vicinity of the famous cathedral of Notre Dame.

Of special interest is a heavily underlined, six-page document prepared in 1963 by a special historical commission appointed to study the 800-year history of the church. The article, never made public, summarizes hundreds of myths and legends about Notre Dame. A mysterious thread binding them together is the presence of a ghostly figure haunting the cathedral grounds at night. Though he is called by a dozen different names in the tales, he is always described as being incredibly ugly. And a drinker of human blood.

In turn-of-the-century France, the vampire's name had gained such notoriety that a series of mystery thrillers featuring an arch-fiend called Fantomas became best-sellers. None of the stories explained the origin of the mastermind. Or why he preyed on the citizens of Paris. They were works of fiction, not fact.

The subject of these various novels, reports, and studies found them all vastly amusing. He had enjoyed the Fantomas novels immensely and had even sent the author several anonymous letters suggesting future ideas for plots. To his intense disappointment, none of his ideas had ever been used. Once or twice he had mentally debated visiting the novelist to plead his case. But Phantomas suspected his physical appearance might do his cause more harm than good.

The vampire readily acknowledged his ugliness. Standing exactly five feet tall, with skin wrinkled as a prune, eyes like raisins, and a nose the size and shape of a sweet potato, he had caused more than one drunken Parisian to swear off red wine forever. A gaping mouthful of yellow teeth and bulging red eyes propelled his face out of the realm of bizarre into the domain of the grotesque.

The second police charge, that of murdering hundreds of innocents over the course of centuries, he regarded as cheap slander. While he occasionally satisfied his thirst on some poor unfortunate, Phantomas rarely killed innocents if it could be avoided. A quiet, gentle soul, all he wanted was to be left alone in his underground lair, pursuing his research.

Over the years a host of villains had used his presence on the Île de la Cité as an alibi for their murders. Their victims ended, not in his hideaway, but dumped in the Seine. Most had escaped the guillotine. However, Phantomas was less forgiving. And his justice was as sharp and final as any blade.

Tonight, Phantomas was in excellent spirits. François Villon, the Prince of Paris, was throwing a party. Villon, a Toreador Clan elder and patron of the arts, held court once a month in the Louvre. Dozens of Kindred, along with several hundred of the Prince's favorite ghouls and kine, attended the festivities. This evening the Prince entertained an important Tremere wizard visiting from Vienna. Phantomas loved such events. Though never invited, he never missed one.

The Prince was under the mistaken impression that he was the oldest, most powerful vampire in the City of Lights. He was neither. Phantomas had come to the Île de la Cité with the invading legions of Julius Caesar in 53 B.C.

Known as Lutetia, the small island served as a natural crossing point across the Seine. A small village of Celtic tribesmen, the Paris, lived there. They were no match for the soldiers of Rome. Dwelling among the tribes, amusing himself by playing a forest God, though, was a fifth-generation Nosferatu vampire, Urgahalt. Fascinated by the invaders, the Kindred secretly embraced Varro Dominus, a young noble traveling with Caesar to carefully record his triumphs. Urgahalt intended to use Varro as his introduction into Roman society.

Unfortunately, the Methuselah had not counted on the discipline or fury of a Roman soldier whose entire career had been unexpectedly destroyed by a chance meeting with one of the Kindred. Urgahalt underestimated his new childe and the mistake cost him dearly. Varro knew more about vampires—lemures as they were called in Rome—than the Nosferatu realized. A wooden stake through his heart and a huge bonfire that burned him to ashes showed him the error of his ways.

Left to his own devices, Varro decided to remain on the island when the legions departed. Nosferatu Kindred were cursed with incredible ugliness. Like most of his kind, the young vampire preferred solitude to company. Two thousand years and several name changes later, he lived in much the same location as before. He was as much a part of the city as the Eiffel Tower.

More than two hundred Kindred inhabited Paris and its suburbs. The Toreador Clan held control of the central city, but several other bloodlines roamed the streets, including rebel bands of Brujah, Gangrel, and Malkavians. Rumors spoke of a Sabbat pack anxious to spread dissension and revolt, with headquarters in the slums. At least a half-dozen Nosferatu lived in lairs beneath major museums and churches Yet even among the Kindred Phantomas was a legend, an unseen presence with no firm basis in reality. He was a phantom to the living and the undead.

Phantomas maintained his invisibility two ways. He lived alone in a huge underground lair situated hundreds of feet beneath Notre Dame. Its entrance to the surface world was located in the ruins of the Paris settlement in the Crypte Archeologique in the main square of the cathedral. However, the vampire rarely used the secret doorway, preferring instead to travel the vast network of tunnels he had established over the centuries throughout the metropolis. After hundreds of years beneath the ground, Phantomas felt uncomfortable without a protective layer of earth over his head.

Equally important to Phantomas' invisibility was his incredible mastery of the vampiric power known as Obfuscate. It enabled him to walk among other Kindred without being noticed. Wearing the Mask of the Thousand Faces, Phantomas cloaked himself with anonymity. Those who saw the Nosferatu dismissed him as a minor, unimportant vampire. Numerous Kindred had actually encountered Phantomas. They just didn't realize it.

Shortly after midnight, he strolled past the two Assamites guarding the glass pyramid that served as entrance to the Louvre. They nodded without interest as he displayed an imaginary invitation and walked into the main hall. Phantomas muttered a word of thanks to his Roman gods that Villon considered electronic monitoring devices provincial. His psychic camouflage worked flawlessly with humans and vampires. It was useless against cameras or television monitors.

In Phantomas' opinion, the Prince was a pompous dandy who wouldn't recognize true art if it hit him in the face. Master of the Louvre, the finest art collection in the world, Villon ignored the treasures of the past for the ephemeral pleasures of the moment. His mercurial tastes dominated the Parisian fashion scene. He surrounded himself with the most beautiful models in Paris, blood dolls who sipped on blood and dreamed of immortality. Like too many of the Kindred, Villon had never come to terms with his undeath.

The party was being held in the glass-roofed Cour Marley, but Phantomas was in no hurry to go there. Though he had visited the Louvre many times, he never skipped the opportunity to visit the galleries housing the Greek, Roman, and Egyptian antiquities. The museum housed perhaps the finest such collection in the world and, though Phantomas had the face and body of a monster, he possessed the soul of a poet.

Ten minutes he spent staring at the "Venus de Milo." Then, it was on to "Winged Victory of Samothrace." The huge "Winged Bull" from Assyria drew his admiring glances, then it was on to the veiled statue of Queen Nefertiti in the Egyptian section. As always, he stopped to stare at the crypt of Osiris with its depiction of many of the gods of the New Kingdom. It had been old when he had served with Caesar.

The bust of Agrippa drew him to the Roman section. The famous general, the hero of Actium, had served Octavius, the grandnephew of his mentor, Julius Caesar. Staring at the statue made Phantomas feel old. Two thousand years separated him from his heritage. If not for a chance encounter in Gaul, his children might have fought against Mark Anthony. Or served in the Senate with Cicero.

Tour completed, he crossed into the Richelieu wing, where the Cour Marly was located. As he drew closer to the courtyard, he frowned. There was no music. Villon's parties always featured a loud rock band playing the latest hits. Tonight, the corridors were strangely silent.

A tall, young man slender, with blond hair and bright blue eyes, stood in front of the door leading to the Cour Marley. Dressed in a white suit with an open-necked white shirt, he nodded in greeting as Phantomas approached. It was almost as if he had been waiting for there for him.

"Do not enter," said the young man, catching the vampire by surprise. No one spoke to him directly when he employed the Mask of a Thousand Faces. Especially not a human.

"The Final Death waits inside," continued the stranger, evidently not troubled by Phantomas' concerns. "If you enter, you may never leave."

"I am no coward," stated the vampire simply. "After twenty centuries, I fear very little."

The young man smiled. "I suspected you would say that." He stepped to the side. "Beware the Red Death, Phantomas."

"Who are you?" asked Phantomas, startled. "How do you

know my name?"

But the stranger had vanished. It was as if he had never been there.

Trembling for the first time in centuries, Phantomas pulled open the door to the courtyard.

The smell of charred and blackened human flesh assaulted his nostrils. A horrified glance around the courtyard revealed a dozen bodies of Villon's favorites, their beautiful features burned beyond recognition. The fashion runways of Paris would be missing a number of familiar faces tomorrow. Mixed among the dead were the remains of twice as many ghouls. Nowhere was there life.

Villon was gone. As were all other Kindred. However, dark shadows on the ground indicated to Phantomas that more than one had departed the Louvre permanently. Neither kine nor Kindred had been spared in this massacre.

As if in answer to Phantomas' unasked question, a gruesome figure stepped from behind the Marly Horses. Tall and lean, he wore a rotted shroud of funeral cloth held together by strips of moldering bandage. His face was that of a long-dead corpse, with chalk-white skin streaked with red lines. Cold dark eyes stared directly at Phantomas. Slowly, the monster smiled.

"The meddling record keeper," said the Red Death. He stretched out a skeletal arm. Phantomas could feel the heat thirty feet away. "Your termination will be a fitting conclusion to the celebration."

Hundreds of years hiding beneath the streets of Paris had taught Phantomas an important lesson. When threatened, flee. Immediately. Don't search for alternative solutions, don't negotiate, don't look back. Run as fast as possible until you reach safety. It was a basic survival technique that worked in the past. It served him tonight.

Phantomas ran. He burst through the doors of the Cour Marley, raced down the halls leading to the glass pyramid, and sprinted out into the night air without turning his head once to see if he was followed. Short and misshapen, he ran astonishingly fast. And he didn't stop until he attained the relative security of the underground maze of tunnels that comprised his domain.

When he finally rested, hundreds of feet beneath the earth, there was no sign of the Red Death. He had escaped for the moment. But Phantomas felt certain he had not seen the last of the monster.

It had named him the record keeper. Somehow it knew of his great project. And the Red Death obviously disapproved.

CHAPTER 7

St. Louis—March 11, 1994

Locking his office, McCann rode the elevator to the street. At the city-run underground parking complex, he waited ten minutes for his car. It cost extra to have your automobile brought to the entrance by one of the lot's security guards, but it was well worth the price. Despite security cameras and motorcycle patrols, muggings, rapes, and murders were common occurrences in these parking garages. Rumors had it that the security patrols were the ones responsible for many of the crimes. No one knew for sure, as dead men told no tales.

McCann didn't mind spending the extra money if it avoided unnecessary confrontation. The city was a dangerous place. Urban America was increasingly becoming a jungle in which only the strongest and smartest survived. More people died these days from gunshot wounds than from any disease. The government claimed that crime was under control. But nobody believed the politicians. The truth was on the streets.

Survival depended more on recognizing the perils that haunted daily life and adjusting to them than on superior firepower. A fact of life in the nightmarish world of modern society was that someone else always possessed enormously superior weaponry.

The detective drove west, heading for the suburbs. As he rode, he mentally scanned his surroundings. He detected no evidence of being followed. Which, after the events of the past night, he found barely reassuring.

McCann lived in a small brick home in a new development a few blocks off Highway 80. Located on a wide lot at the end of a quiet street, it was surrounded by a wrought-iron security fence, isolating the building from the rest of the block. Which was exactly what the detective desired. He wanted to be left alone. In these troubled times, no one considered his security measures the least bit unusual.

He had bought the house for cash less than a year before, when he first decided to settle in the St. Louis area. He knew none of his neighbors and had no interest in meeting them. He worked at night and slept during the day. The few times he had seen anyone he had raised a hand in greeting, but said nothing. McCann considered his home a safe place to rest and relax. His office served as his base of operations. He socialized in neither of them.

Parking his car in the indoor garage, the detective laid a hand on the wall before entering the house proper. Certain arcane rituals from the dawn of civilization imbued a home with the personality of its owner. A master magician, and McCann was among the greatest ever to walk the Earth, could immediately sense any disturbance in their dwelling. There was none. McCann was safe. At least for the moment, neither the Red Death nor the mysterious Ms. Young had discovered his hideaway.

Twenty minutes later, shoes off, drink in hand, McCann let the tension of the evening drain out of his body. He sat in a padded armchair, the soft strains of an expensive stereo whispering hints of Billie Holiday in the background. The front room contained the chair, a sofa, the stereo, and a small coffee table. There was no television. A thick plush carpet covered the floor. The detective believed in simple comforts. What few possessions that mattered to him, he kept in the bedroom.

McCann was a rootless individual. He wandered from location to location, never settling for long in any one place. His complex scheme required him to keep moving. At times, he wondered why he still bothered playing the game. So many of his kind no longer struggled. Some had plunged into the great unknown from which there was no return, while others had retreated from cruel reality into a dreamworld of their own creation. He was among a handful who continued fighting. In truth, the prize hardly seemed important any longer. It was the diversion that kept him amused.

The detective shook his head and finished his nightcap. He had engaged in this mental exercise a thousand times and never arrived at a satisfactory conclusion. He was like Ol' Man River, "tired of living but scared of dying." For those like himself, there were no easy answers. Just more questions.

Idly he wondered about the identities of his foes. The Red Death was Kindred and a member of The Children of Dreadful Night. The detective could not remember ever hearing of such a cult before. That meant nothing, since the Kindred possessed a bizarre fondness for nicknames. The term *Dreadful Night* spoke of a fear of the possible approaching Gehenna. During the past few years, numerous armageddon cults had sprung up among the Cainites. They believed that the third generation was preparing to rise and devour their descendants. As it did many mortals, the approaching end of the millennium frightened them.

McCann had ignored these groups, feeling that they represented the farthest fringe elements of the Kindred. Now, with the advent of the Red Death, he wasn't so sure.

The fact that the Red Death had been aware of his existence and his psychic powers also worried the detective. For the past few decades, he had maintained a low profile, preferring to forward his schemes through unsuspecting agents. He felt certain no evidence existed associating the human detective, Dire McCann, and Lameth, the Dark Messiah of the Kindred.

Shaking his head, McCann wondered if Anis was behind the attack. She was one of the few Kindred who knew many of his secrets. And, like him, she continued to plot, undaunted by the centuries.

Rachel Young puzzled him more than the Red Death. She seemed genuinely terrified by the appearance of the specter. He was convinced they were not working together. Yet he was equally positive she was the one who had killed Tyrus

Benedict and stolen the photos of Baba Yaga. And later traveled to his office and swiped the files from overseas.

Adding to the mystery was the unexplained telephone message cautioning him about the Red Death. Reality had twisted immediately after he received the warning, which hinted that an extremely potent mage was at work. McCann had no idea who that could be. More pressing, how had the stranger known about the Red Death before it attacked?

Then there had been the attempted assassination in the alley. Two hired killers had tried to murder him for no apparent explanation. Obviously, someone had paid them for the attempt. Was it the Red Death? Or Rachel Young? The whole scenario was all terribly complex and very confusing.

Remembering the attack on the street, McCann reached into his back pocket and pulled out the wallet he had retrieved from one of the dead men. Except for the money he had removed earlier, it was absolutely empty. However, that didn't mean that it couldn't reveal secrets.

The detective rested the leather billfold on the coffee table. Placing both hands on it, he let loose the full power of his mighty will. The air wavered with titanic energies. Squeezing his eyes shut, McCann concentrated on a solitary word. *Find.*

Five minutes later, the detective sank back into his chair, a slight frown creasing his forehead. The wallet came from Washington, DC. It had been purchased from a nameless department store by a government file clerk working at the Pentagon. There was no mistaking that building in the psychic residue left by the former owner.

The killer had stolen the billfold less than a week ago. He had used it to hold the money found inside. It contained no traces of his personality.

The nation's capital had long been a source of friction between the Camarilla and the Sabbat. Though the Camarilla controlled the city, both organizations had agents in the suburbs. The constantly shifting population also brought in new Kindred. Each sect controlled numerous politicians and lobbyists. However, the frequent changes in government officials thwarted their ambitions for absolute domination of the government. The city was a potential battleground between the cults. The Camarilla held it, but Sabbat forces surrounded it. Sooner or later, warfare between the two groups was bound to explode.

McCann had carefully avoided the city. He disliked being too visible anyplace where the balance of power was in flux. He worked best when in the shadows. However, this assassination attempt hinted that perhaps he had made a mistake by ignoring the metropolis.

Dawn approached and sleep called to him. Wearily, McCann shuffled off to the bedroom. Mentally he reviewed the magical safeguards protecting the house. All were in place. Nothing living or undead could breach his defenses. He could rest in peace.

With a wan smile, he rested one hand on a small, detailed sculpture resting on the end table in his bedroom. Carved from sandstone, it depicted a man's face remarkably similar to his own. Not particularly large or impressive, the statue originally came from Egypt and was over four thousand years old. It had been with McCann for a very long time.

The detective grinned, remembering Flavia's tale of Masqueraders. It was an entertaining fable. He wondered how she would react to the truth. Maybe, someday, he would tell her.

Keeping that thought, McCann switched off the lights and let sleep engulf him.

CHAPTER 8

Venice—March 12, 1994

A black shape slipped from shadow to shadow in the late-night darkness. Weaving through the narrow streets and winding lanes of the ancient city, it moved without a sound, heading ever inward, toward Saint Mark's Square at the center of the sleeping metropolis.

The form, vaguely human in shape, traveled quickly, never hesitating to stop and stare at the stunning examples of Renaissance and Byzantine architecture that had earned the city a reputation as one of the most beautiful locations in the world. Nor did it slow down on the numerous bridges it was forced to cross. Venice, situated on 120 islands and formed by 177 canals, was laced with over 400 such spans. The dark blot lanced across them with eye-blurring speed, vanishing on one side only to appear on the other an instant later.

Saint Mark's Square, at the center of the city, was the most popular location in Venice. It was bound on all sides by famous historical monuments. At its eastern end was Saint Mark's Cathedral, over a thousand years old. Nearby was the Doge's Palace, built in 814, destroyed by fire four times, and rebuilt after each blaze, more magnificent than before. The shadowy figure glided by them both. At the rear of the palace was the famous Bridge of Sighs. Once the famous arch had led to the public prisons. Now the prisoners were gone, and in their place stood a vast, black skyscraper of glass and steel.

A number of Venetians had expressed loud and vocal complaints when plans to tear down the famous historic buildings were first announced. Opponents objected bitterly to the massive rebuilding project, declaring that the ancient jail was one of the city's most prized landmarks. As usual, money spoke louder. The city zoning commission had ignored the complaints and approved the design.

Soon after, a number of the most strident critics had disappeared from Venice. Reports by the police claimed that the citizens had angrily departed the city after being scorned by the city fathers. The more cynical inhabitants of the island said nothing and made their peace with the new skyscraper.

Forty stories high, the building was surrounded with a brick wall twelve feet high. A single gate and guardpost offered the only entrance into the compound. Whispered tales described huge, red-eyed hounds that roamed the grounds at night. No one was sure what secrets the building contained. Other than a street address, the skyscraper had no name. None was needed. Among the residents of Venice the rectangular black giant was known simply as The Mausoleum.

The presence halted at the brick perimeter. It knew better than to touch the structure. Embedded throughout the barrier were small heat detectors that would record the slightest variation in temperature—warm or cold. The top of the wall was covered by thousands of inch-high, steel needles. Each was barbed with a curve designed to rip protective garments or skin to shreds. Powerful searchlights swept the inside perimeter of the compound every few minutes. Monstrous beasts roamed the grounds, things of nightmare that recognized no friend, only prey. Entrance to the Mausoleum other than through the main gate was impossible.

Pausing for a second, the shadow crept along the wall to the lone opening. Four guards watched the barren street. Tall men dressed in black uniforms without decoration, their eyes glowed with an unnatural brightness. They were ghouls. They were the elite soldiers of the fortress, their lives dedicated to keeping it safe from intruders.

Two were stationed in a raised, glass-lined booth that offered a commanding view of the empty street. They manned a complex video and computer network that provided them with instantaneous visual access to any spot on the company grounds. Their companions, standing at attention at the gate, were armed with AK-47 automatic rifles loaded with high-powered explosive bullets. Behind them, a pair of six-inch thick steel doors that could be opened only from the control booth provided a final obstacle to anyone who made it past the quartet of sentries.

Timing was everything. The blot waited and watched for the precise moment. It was extremely patient. There were hours till dawn. And it had been planning this operation for a long time.

Even ghouls blinked. Human senses could not trace such rapid eye motions with precision. But the blot was not human.

Precisely twenty-two minutes after it arrived at the gate, all four ghouls blinked at the same moment. Their eyes were closed for less than a hundredth of a second. That was all the time the shadow needed to dart past them and flow into the microscopic space between the massive doors. Molecules in width, the blot easily slipped through the crack and into the inner grounds of the compound.

Maintaining exactly the same temperature as its surroundings, the patch of darkness raced across the earth like a reverse moonbeam. The blot had neither smell nor form for the Hellhounds to detect. Creatures of limited intelligence, they only attacked things they could see or smell or hear. They ignored the flowing blackness. Many vampires could meld their forms into the earth, becoming part of the ground. The moving shadow was one of a few that, having done so, could actually shift its location.

Two giant glass doors led into the interior of The Mausoleum. On them were engraved an ancient family crest, a symbol the shadow knew well. A solitary guard, another ghoul, sat in a booth in the center of the hall, a dozen feet back from the entrance. His gaze, like those outside, never wavered. Getting past him would be more difficult. The hall where he waited was well-lit and painted bright white. A dark patch would be immediately noticeable. A new form was needed. And that would take more than a millisecond of time to accomplish.

Gathering its willpower, the shadow projected a single thought at the watchman. *Sneeze*, it commanded, *sneeze*. The guard sniffed, scowling. *Sneeze*, projected the shadow again. The ghoul sniffed a second time, then, raising a hand to his face, sneezed.

Involuntarily, the watchman's eyes snapped shut. They were closed for only a second, but that was all the time the black spot needed. Like a whirlwind, it flowed upward out of the earth, into the night air, gathering substance as it moved. Dark shape turned into white mist. Cloud-like, the intruder flowed through a microscopic crack between the top of the door and the steel frame. As with the outer barrier, no seal was tight enough to keep a vapor from penetrating. The mist was in the hall before the guard had removed his hand from his nose.

Once inside the corridor, the cloud immediately rose to the top of the hall, flattening itself against the ceiling. Surveillance cameras and security patrols guarded the floor, not the roof. White on white, it drifted swiftly past the outer checkpoint and into the main atrium of the complex. There were other guardposts throughout the building, but the shadow planned to bypass all the rest. It knew exactly how it planned to reach its objective at the top of the skyscraper.

Though it was late at night, The Mausoleum never slept. The complex was filled with workers. Dozens of people scurried between offices. None spoke, nor did any music play. The structure was silent as a tomb.

Scurrying along the ceiling, the cloud searched for the door leading to the basement. It knew the easiest way up was by going down. A quick hunt disclosed the necessary entrance. Oozing through a crack, the entity drifted into the dark hallway leading to the Mausoleum's lower level.

Finding the switch boxes for the entire complex was the next step. The building was controlled by a computer monitoring system. Bypassing the built-in safeguards was child's play, and the shadow was no child. Mentally, it attached invisible trip wires to the proper circuits. The emergency generator proved no more of a challenge. Plans set, it went looking for the way up.

Locating the service elevator shafts was easy. Several ghouls labored close by, but none of them were security personnel. Focused on their own business and nothing else, they never noticed a white mist flow through the double doors to the lift.

Maintaining loose contact with one wall of the passage, the vapor floated toward the roof. Security cameras monitored the elevators throughout the Mausoleum. But there were none in the shafts themselves. It was a dangerous mistake.

Flowing around an elevator car stopped on the twenty-second floor, the mist rose to the fortieth floor in ten minutes. Cautiously, it mentally probed the hallway beyond the service doors. No one was there. Quickly it slipped into the corridor. This part of the building was extremely well protected. A dozen deadly spells ringed the inner group of apartments. They were triggered by thought, not physical presence. One wrong move and the invader's efforts would come to a hideous end.

Effortlessly, the misty form disarmed the traps. Instead of intertwining, so that releasing one set off another, they overlapped. The interloper's powerful mind surrounded each spell and swiftly neutralized it. Not an alarm was sounded, yet in the span of a quarter-hour, the entire top floor of the main headquarters of the Giovanni Clan of vampires was rendered defenseless from outside attack.

The whir of an elevator coming from below alerted the mist that its actions in negating the spells had finally been noticed by the building's security forces. Mentally reaching out to the proper circuits, it shut off the power to the elevators. Another touch disabled the emergency generators. Using the stairs would waste valuable minutes. No longer concerned about outside interference, the mist flowed beneath the door marked *Madeleine Giovanni*.

As expected, the chamber was empty. The mist swirled and gathered substance. In seconds it was gone, leaving standing in its place an attractive young woman with dark eyes and long black hair. Pale white skin and blood-red lips offered a sharp contrast to the black leotard that was her only garment.

Walking to a nearby closet filled with women's clothes, the intruder searched carefully until she found an old-fashioned black velvet gown. Nodding, she slipped out of her leotard and pulled on the dress. It fit perfectly, hugging her slender form as if by design. Reaching into a box on a shelf above the clothes, she extracted a stunning silver necklace and draped it around her neck. It was decorated with the same family crest that marked the front entrance of the Mausoleum. A pair of short heels completed her outfit.

Smiling at herself in a full-length mirror, she strolled across the chamber to a second door. Gently she rapped on the paneling.

"Enter," growled a loud voice from the other side. The speaker did not sound pleased. "You little witch."

Grinning, the young woman opened the door and stepped through. She was in a huge corner office lined on two sides with windows. Dark-tinted glass provided a stunning view of the city. Which seemed only proper, as the occupant of the chamber considered Venice his personal property.

"Sire," murmured the young woman, her husky voice barely concealing her amusement. "As requested, I tested the headquarters security system. I found it . . . underwhelming."

"So I gathered," said the figure she addressed. A tall man with graying hair, he had the face of an aristocrat. He was impeccably dressed in a dark, three-piece suit with white shirt and an unadorned tie. His only concession to color was a blood-red rose tucked into his buttonhole. When he walked the earth in human form, hundreds of years ago, Pietro Giovanni had had a passion for beautiful flowers. Undeath had left that sentiment unchanged. As manager of the Mausoleum and one of the most powerful Kindred in Europe, he could afford to indulge his vices. Large and small.

Pietro dropped into a huge black leather chair behind

an ebony desk. Madeleine perched herself on the arm of an armchair facing him. Politely she waited for her sire to speak first.

"Of all my childer," he declared with the barest trace of a smile, "you, Madeleine, are the most accomplished saboteur. I doubt that any other member of the clan could breach our defenses. Still, considering what you accomplished, we are obviously vulnerable to outside attack. What do you recommend?"

"We rely too much on ghouls," she declared. "They are loyal but are a weak link in our defenses. The guards at the front gate must be better trained. And their equipment redesigned to complement their efforts, not duplicate them."

"The Hellhounds?" asked Pietro.

"A minor force," answered Madeleine. "Feed them less. They need to be hungrier. Replace the earth and grass surrounding the building with artificial sod. Astroturf, lined with steel. Run an electronic current between the door and its frames, much like an electronic eye. Even that can be bypassed, but only with difficulty."

"Anything else?"

"Repaint the hallway," she said, smiling slightly. "With stripes. A multitude of color will make it difficult for a shadow to pass unnoticed."

Her eyes narrowed. "The ghoul at the entrance. His mind is too weak for the task he performs. I bent his will with minimal effort. He never realized I was manipulating his thoughts. He is worthless. Kill him."

"As you wish." Pietro pressed a button on his desk. "Summon the ghoul watching the entrance of the Mausoleum to room seventeen. Disarm him when he enters. Give the fool an hour to contemplate his sin against the House Giovanni and beg for forgiveness. Then feed him to our neonates." Pietro paused, then continued. "Make sure the other ghouls assigned to guard duty are present and watch. It should inspire them to higher standards."

The Giovanni patriarch chuckled and switched off the intercom. "Next?"

"We need security cameras in the basement. And in the elevator shafts. Motion detectors, geared for the slightest disturbance, are also a must."

"Easily managed," said Pietro. "The arrangements will be made tomorrow. Anything else?"

"The spells guarding your suite are worthless. I broke through them too easily. They need to be changed."

"You doubtless have specific ideas on how to improve the casting," said Pietro. Before he could say more, the phone on his desk rang. He listened for a few seconds, then hung up.

"Before we cover that matter, would you please turn the electricity in the lower levels back on. My clerks are helpless without their computers."

"Sorry," said Madeleine and snapped her fingers. "Power has been restored to the entire complex."

"Thank you," said Pietro. "Now, explain what you want done with the spells. Anything involving the black arts has to be approved by the clan elders."

They spent the next hour talking. Finally, Pietro raised his hands in mock surrender. "Enough. You have convinced me. I will raise your points with our esteemed ancestors at the next board meeting. There will be no objections."

"Good," said Madeleine. Standing up, she walked over to the bank of windows facing Saint Mark's Cathedral. "You realize, grandfather, I went through this escapade merely to insure you are properly protected."

"Yes, my precious one," replied Pietro fondly. "You are my greatest treasure. I thank you for your concern."

The Giovanni vampires were bound by ties closer than sire and childe. All clan members were related. Madeleine had been Embraced by Pietro, establishing their relationship in undeath. She was also the daughter of his only son, Daniel, who had met the Final Death at the hands of Don Caravelli, the Kindred master of the Mafia. It was a debt that both father and daughter had sworn to repay.

Money and death were the two ruling passions of the Giovanni. Their skill at manipulating finances was matched only by their powers of necromancy. Of all the Kindred, their clan was the most heavily involved with the world beyond. No one was sure what ghastly rituals they pursued in secret vaults beneath family enclaves. Rumors spoke of an incredible plot to control not only all life but the spirits of the dead as well.

Equally mysterious was the exact extent of the Giovanni fortune. Like a gigantic financial octopus, the family business had spread tentacles throughout the world. Connections with the Catholic Church, firmly established during the Inquisition, had further enabled the clan to penetrate markets unreachable by any other banking institutions. The Giovanni controlled billions of dollars in assets. A word from the clan elders could plunge the world into a depression that would leave entire populations destitute.

Madeleine was unique in the clan in that she possessed skills unrelated to either necromancy or high finance. Fanatic in her devotion to family honor, she had devoted her entire existence to avenging the death of her father. A century of intensive training and rigid discipline had turned her into a master of industrial espionage and corporate surveillance. She was the hidden dagger of the Giovanni empire.

Though she was responsible for many of the clan's greatest triumphs, engineered through a combination of sabotage, blackmail, and assassination, Madeleine was virtually unknown outside the Mausoleum. Those mortals or Kindred she encountered during a mission never survived to tell the tale. When she hunted, death ran at her side.

Yet despite her successes, Madeleine remained unfulfilled. Three times she had tried to penetrate the secret fortress of her ultimate quarry, Don Caravelli, and three times she had failed. The Mafia chief, controlling a criminal empire that equaled the Giovanni Clan's in wealth and power, lived in the most secure hideaway in the world. Caravelli knew Madeleine waited for him the moment he left Sicily and thus refused to travel. The Don was no coward, but he was also no fool.

"I have a special mission for you," declared Pietro. He pushed a manila envelope across the desk to her. "Everything necessary for your trip is here. You are to leave for America immediately. In the city of St. Louis, I want you to locate a human named Dire McCann. Finding him should not be difficult, as the kine has ties to the local Prince."

"And when I find him?" asked Madeleine. "What do you want me to do?"

In two words, Pietro told her.

CHAPTER 9

Sicily—March 12, 1994

Don Caravelli, Capo de Capo of the Mafia, rose to his feet as his four guests were ushered into the huge banquet hall. It was a gesture of respect coming from the supreme crime lord in the world, and the quartet of visitors grinned at each other in pleasure. It had taken months to arrange this meeting, and this slight display indicated that their trip was not in vain.

"Gentlemen," said their host, a huge man well over six feet tall, his broad shoulders stretching the limits of his impeccably tailored jacket, "welcome to my home."

He waved a hand to four empty chairs at the huge table. "My chef is preparing a special meal for you tonight." Caravelli grinned, flashing white teeth in contrast to a deep tan. "I, of course, will not join you."

The four men said nothing. They all knew that Caravelli was a vampire. That mattered nothing to them. They only cared about his criminal empire. His taste in food was none of their concern. They considered themselves businessmen, dealing with the harsh realities of the world. If necessary, they would deal with the devil if it was good for business.

"I apologize for not greeting you at the airport," continued the Don, resuming his seat. Two Kindred, bigger even than the huge Mafia leader, took positions at his sides. Another pair stood guard at the door. "However, my most dangerous enemy's whereabouts are unaccounted for at present. My advisors insist I stay within this fortress until she has been found. While I am no coward, I have barely survived three previous attempts on my life by the bitch. I prefer not to offer her an opportunity for a fourth try."

"It's that crazy Giovanni dame?" asked Tony "The Tuna" Blanchard. Head of the east coast branch of the Syndicate, he had visited Don Caravelli a number of times before and was not as intimidated by the Mafia chieftain as his fellows.

It was Tony who had arranged this meeting in hopes of forging closer bonds between the US crime cartel and Caravelli's minions. "She still after your head?"

Caravelli nodded, smiling slightly at the choice of words. He beckoned to one of the men at the door. "Some wine for my guests. They must be thirsty after their long flight from America."

The guard nodded and disappeared out the door. "Forgive me for being a poor host. Please, relax. We shall discuss your proposal after dinner. For now, you are my guests."

A bottle of fine red wine brought murmurs of appreciation from the four Syndicate bosses. Don Caravelli, though he did not indulge, maintained one of the finest wine cellars in Europe. A second bottle was delivered and consumed as well.

"I'm not sure I understand your problem, Don Caravelli," said George Kross, the Midwest representative of the cartel. A big, red-faced man with beady little eyes, he spoke with a distinctive Indiana twang. "Some crazy broad is out to get you? Why don't you just ice the dame? Fuck, you're boss of bosses. You could order the death of the President of the whole damned USA if you wanted by liftin' a finger."

"Unfortunately, your commander-in-chief is much easier to reach than a high-ranking member of the Giovanni Clan," said Don Caravelli smoothly. He folded his huge hands together, resting his elbows on the table. "Besides which, Madeleine Giovanni has proven herself a quite worthy opponent for my best agents. In the past sixty years, six of my most valued assassins have tried to eliminate her. Needless to state, none of them has returned from their mission."

"A lady taking out six Mafia hit men?" said Harvey Taylor, west coast Syndicate chief. "She sounds like one tough babe."

"Can't she be bought?" asked Kross. "Everybody's got a price in this world. Everybody. Human or Kindred."

Don Caravelli nodded. "My sentiments as well. However, the Giovanni are a tightly-knit band of troublemakers. They lust for the power I control. And," the Don shrugged in mock despair, "I made the unfortunate mistake of executing her father many years ago. Madeleine neither forgives nor forgets."

"Yeah," said Taylor. "Dames are like that. Still, you Kindred got a whole set of rules of conduct and all that. Can't you convince her clan elders to make her lay off?"

"If I was dealing with any other clan than the Giovanni," replied Don Caravelli, "that solution might work. With those leeches, no compromise is possible."

Don Caravelli rose from his chair. "Let me relate to you gentlemen a bit of Kindred lore unknown to most humans. It will make the situation I face much clearer."

The Mafia lord walked over to the fireplace. He removed an iron poker from the fireplace tools. Holding the metal rod in one hand, he slapped it rhythmically into his other palm as he spoke.

"As you are well aware, we Kindred live on human blood. It provides us with all the nourishment we need. Vitæ, as we call it, is the elixir of life. However, while mortal blood is our wine, Kindred blood is our finest brandy. We call it *the darker drink.*"

Caravelli smiled, emphasizing each word with a whack of the poker. "When the opportunity arises, my friends, we Kindred are all cannibals. The Sixth Tradition of Caine forbids vampires from drinking the blood of their own kind, but it is largely ignored. The strong obey their own laws."

Slowly the Mafia chief circled the table, stopping briefly behind each Syndicate chief. None of the four appeared very comfortable with Caravelli standing behind them.

"Diablerie describes the act of one vampire draining the blood of another. The pleasure derived from such cannibalism is beyond description. More important, however, is the result when it involves a vampire of any generation who drinks the vitæ of one of a lower generation. Remember, among my race, the lower the generation, the greater the power!"

Don Caravelli's eyes seemed to glow as he spoke. "The

life fluid consumed is such a powerful drink that *it gives the attacker all of the powers of his victim!* It is as if a child suddenly becomes his father, with all of the adult's vitality. In other words, a sixth-generation vampire who practices diablerie on a member of the fifth generation would himself become a fifth-generation Kindred. And gain all of the greater power and strength of that level.

"To lower his generation again, it would then be necessary for him to drink the blood of a Methuselah, one of the fourth-generation vampires. If that was possible, he would then experience another increase in stamina and ability. To progress further than that, he would have to find and kill one of the members of the third generation, the Antediluvians."

"I get it," said Sol Cohen, the Syndicate boss of the South who had thus far kept silent. "It's like moving up the corporate ladder. Or taking steps in our organization. To rise to a level of greater wealth and control, you gotta take out the guy ahead of you in line. That's the only way to step into his job."

"Crudely but effectively put," said Don Caravelli. He returned to his seat, still holding the poker. He smiled at the four men, but his eyes were cold, icy cold. "I am a fifth-generation Brujah. Madeleine is a sixth-generation Giovanni. Clans mean nothing in diablerie. Not only does the bitch want to kill me, but she wants to suck me dry. It would transform her into a fifth-generation Giovanni, expanding her already formidable strengths."

"Man, oh man," said George Kross. "No wonder you Kindred are so paranoid. Not only are there two sects at war, thirteen distinct clans struggling for power, but every vampire on the block is looking to murder his boss, drink his blood, and then take his place."

"Essentially correct," said Don Caravelli. "Your mention of the thirteen clans is most apt. For, as you already know, thirteen third-generation vampires, the Antediluvians, are the founders of these distinct bloodlines. But some of those thirteen are not as old as the others."

"Watcha mean?" asked Sol Cohen. "You saying that some other Kindred went and did this diablerie thing on one of the top honchos?"

Caravelli laughed, a full-bodied, deep sound that echoed in the chamber. "Honchos! You Americans use such wonderful terms. I must remember that word. It has a certain ring I like."

The Mafia chieftain tossed the poker to the side. The four Syndicate bosses breathed a sigh of relief. They were all well aware of the fact that they were deep inside an impregnable fortress where Don Caravelli's word was law. Though their host had been gracious to a fault, none of the quartet felt quite at ease.

"The original third generation consisted of thirteen vampires Embraced many thousand years ago. However, not all of them survived the centuries. Even though they were masters of incredible powers, they still could be killed. Those who performed those murders were fourth-generation vampires who, once the deed was done, drank the blood of their victims and thus were transformed into third-generation Kindred. It has happened several times in our history."

The Don paused. "You must be hungry. I shall order dinner prepared." He waved a hand at one of his lieutenants. "By the time my story is finished, it will be here."

"No disrespect, Don Caravelli," said George Kross, "but my stomach's been feelin' kinda jumpy last few minutes. Combination of that wine and this cannibalism talk. Mind if I take a trip to the john?"

"Of course not," said the vampire. "Nicko, on your way to the kitchen, show Mr. Kross the facilities."

Kross wobbled out of the room, his face a pasty green. "George never could handle wine," remarked Sol Cohen with a laugh. "He's a beer man from way, way back."

"I am sure he will be fine," said Don Caravelli.

"To continue, my own bloodline, the Brujah, are actually descended from a fourth-generation vampire named Troile who killed his sire in ancient times. In truth, our clan should be named Troile instead of Brujah."

"What about Brujah's other childer?" asked Tony Blanchard. He knew a great deal more about the Kindred than his fellows. "Weren't there other fourth-generation vampires around other than Troile? What became of them?"

"Some existed," admitted the Don, a slightly annoyed look on his face. "Their sire dead, the remaining few effectively became clanless. There were rumors of them disappearing into the far east. But no one knows for sure. Nor cares."

"I bet the Giovanni weren't among those original thirteen," said Harvey Taylor. "I don't think there was anybody with a name like that around before the Middle Ages."

"The Giovanni and the Tremere Clans are comparatively young ones," stated Don Caravelli. "Their leaders, both extremely ruthless men in life, became equally ruthless Kindred in undeath. Giovanni and Tremere lowered their generation by one act of diablerie after another. Until finally, when they were fourth generation, they each hunted down an Antediluvian and drank their blood. Thus they gained the full strength of a third-generation vampire for their clan. And thus, by Kindred law, established themselves as a true bloodline."

"If these events took place in the Middle Ages," said Tony Blanchard, "that must have left a bunch of vampires who were the childer of the two murdered Antediluvians suddenly clanless. And pretty pissed off."

"The Giovanni and Tremere proved to be quite savage," said Don Caravelli, waving a hand casually. "They methodically exterminated any members of the original clans they could find. The easiest method to prevent their enemies from taking revenge was to wipe them off the face of the Earth. By the time the Camarilla ordered them to stop, only a handful of the displaced Kindred survived. Those few became outcasts, Caitiffs. Members of an extinct bloodline, they were clanless and thus unimportant."

"Which leads us to what?" asked Harvey Taylor. "I know

there's a point to this story, but I ain't sure what it is."

"The lesson is quite simple, Mr. Taylor," said Don Caravelli. "Of thirteen clans, just these three are descended from vampires who are not eight or nine millennia old. Even immortality becomes boring after six thousand years. The Brujah, the Giovanni, and the Tremere bloodlines are younger, stronger, and more dynamic than the other ten. Though our elders are not as ancient, they possess powers equal to the leaders of any other clan. We are not as weary of undeath. Far fewer of our number have retreated into an eternal torpor. Or abandoned all hope and watched the sun rise.

"The elders among these three clans know that one of our bloodlines is destined someday to rule the Kindred. Though we forge uneasy alliances, even pursue common goals, we understand without question that the other two clans are our true rivals among the Cainites. So while I wish Madeleine Giovanni would cease her endless pursuit, I know it will never happen. The Brujah, the Tremere, and the Giovanni are engaged in a secret battle to the death. It is a *Blood War*. And, in such a fight, there are no compromises."

"George's been gone for a long time," said Tony Blanchard. He chuckled. "Hope he didn't fall in."

"I am sure Mr. Kross will be joining us momentarily," said Don Caravelli. He rose to his feet. "Ah, supper has arrived."

Three huge Kindred entered the room wheeling a gigantic rolling serving table. On it were three huge silver platters covered with immense lids. Lifting them off the cart, the attendants placed a platter in front of each of the Syndicate bosses.

"Hey," said Sol Cohen. "What about George? He should be here."

Don Caravelli smiled and nodded to his men. Each lifted the lid of a platter. The horrified screams of the three gangsters rebounded off the walls of the chamber for several moments. George Kross had returned, but in pieces. The shocked look on his face, staring with open eyes from the tray in front of Tony Blanchard, indicated his death had not been a pleasant one.

"While I recited my little tale to distract your attention," said Don Caravelli, "one of my men, an expert in reading thoughts, probed your minds. It was not very difficult to ascertain that Mr. Kross had been planning his own small deception for months. He schemed to infiltrate my fortress and learn its secrets. Afterward, he had visions of selling his knowledge to the highest bidder. The fool. He thought to play me for a fool."

The Mafia capo grinned savagely. His face no longer appeared the least bit human. His bright eyes glowed blood red.

"His trip to the bathroom was the result of an overwhelming suggestion placed in his mind by my agent. I thought it best to deal with Mr. Kross outside. It would have been inhospitable to butcher him during our talk."

The Mafia chieftain gestured and the covers were replaced on the platters. "You gentlemen came to bargain in good faith. I appreciate that. Please be aware that I expect the negotiations to run smoothly. I think you will find my terms for your organization most generous." It was not necessary for the Don to threaten them any further with the mutilated body of George Kross resting in front of them on the table.

"In any case, you now know much too much about the Kindred to leave here unchanged," he declared as the table was cleared. "My second-in-command, Don Lazzari, will shortly feed you some of his blood. The transformation from human to ghoul is quite painless. It will guarantee your silence on what I have told you tonight. And ensure your loyalty to my every wish."

Don Caravelli nodded at his still-trembling guests. "Perhaps now you understand why Madeleine Giovanni and I cannot make a bargain. Neither of us," and he laughed and laughed, "is very good at forgiving."

CHAPTER 10

St. Louis—March 12, 1994
McCann dreamed. . .

A solitary oil lamp flickered as a cold breeze rustled through the dimly-lit chamber. Huge black shadows, reflections of grotesque stone gargoyles dispersed throughout the room, danced across the sandstone walls. A spiraling arm covered with pictographs ran in a tightening noose around the polished red tile floor. The drawings ended at the base of a wide, raised table constructed of bronze, stone, and silver in the direct center of the hideaway.

A circle of thirteen green wax candles surrounded the table. They burned with a thin blue flame. On the top of the platform were dozens of baked clay pots. Each of them contained a fluid or a mixture of fluids. Two figures standing side by side, their hands gripping the table, stared at the largest receptacle. Their eyes burned with fires that matched those of the candles.

The male stood well over six feet tall, with broad shoulders and narrow hips. He wore a loincloth and a pair of sandals. His shoulder-length hair was black as night. His face was lean and drawn, with flat nose, sharp chin, and thin lips. Too-white skin and mystic symbols of black soot drawn on his cheeks emphasized that he was no ordinary man. Or vampire. He was Lameth, childe of Asshur, and the greatest Kindred sorcerer ever to walk the Earth.

The woman at his side was equally impressive. Dressed in thin garments that fully displayed her ample charms, she was as tall as Lameth but with long, flowing blonde hair the color of the new moon. Full-breasted, with narrow waist and wide hips, she was considered by many to be the most beautiful woman, living or undead, in the Second City. Her wide eyes, knowing smile, and lush lips offered evidence that even death could not silence the passions within her. She was Anis, once princess of Ur, now childe of the third-generation vampire known as Brujah.

"I worked for two centuries," Lameth declared, "perfecting this elixir. Many were the times I thought I would never finish."

"Those were the nights when I intervened," murmured Anis. "Offering you the necessary courage to continue. As befits two lovers."

Lameth laughed, a mocking sound. "The part of faithful sweetheart does not suit you well, my dear Anis. You pushed me forward not from feelings of love, but of all-consuming passion. Your motivation came from the desire to live forever, freed from the beast that lurks within all Kindred."

Anis chuckled. "Why so cynical, Lameth? I don't remember you pushing me away on those nights that I taught you that even the undead can still delight in the pleasures of physical love. You were an eager student."

"As you instructed many others," replied Lameth, smiling. "Your lovers are legion, Anis. If I was not sure of your mortal origins, I would suspect Brujah had embraced a succubus as his childe. Lately I have heard unbelievable whispers linking you and Troile. Even I find it hard to understand what you would see in that rebel."

Anis's eyes narrowed, and she peered around the room as if searching for spies. "Only to you, Lameth, would I reveal the truth. For despite your accusations, I do love you. We were lovers in life and we have been lovers in undeath. The bonds between us cannot be sundered. You are the one Kindred whom I can trust."

"As I trust you with the secret of my elixir," said Lameth seriously. "If the others discover its existence, we will both suffer the Final Death. Especially when they learn that I had barely enough ingredients for two treatments. My fate is in your hands. As you said, our fates are bound together. You can trust me with any secret, no matter how forbidden."

"I need to be free," said Anis. "Free not only of the all-consuming thirst for blood that threatens my sanity but free of the shackles that bind me to the one who made me this way, my sire. I, who once was a king's daughter of the greatest city in the world, cannot bear to serve another. I must destroy my bonds. The one who commands my will must die."

"You plot Brujah's death?" whispered Lameth, astonished. "Impossible. You could never get close enough to him to perform the act. He trusts no one."

"Wrong," said Anis. "He trusts his first childe, his favorite. *Troile.*"

Lameth looked at her in amazement. "Troile worships Brujah. He treats his sire like a demigod."

"Even demigods can be destroyed," said Anis, her lips curling in a satisfied smirk. "Troile may venerate his master, but he lusts for me. And passion is stronger than faith, my love. Passion obliterates reason. Troile belongs to me."

Slowly, sensually, Anis ran her hands up beneath her breasts, cupping them in her palms. Her eyes blazed.

"Soon, very soon, my lover will attempt to kill Brujah. If he succeeds, I am free. If he fails, there are other Kindred to seduce. Many others."

"If Troile drinks Brujah's blood, he will become third generation."

"I don't care," said Anis, laughing. "Knowing Troile, he will be so overwhelmed with guilt afterward that he will flee forever the Second City. Power means nothing to such naive idealists. It doesn't matter. Third generation or not, my mark is upon him. Now and forever."

"You are insane," said Lameth. "Gloriously mad. Yet while I question the methods you employ, I understand your feelings of bondage perfectly. Asshur demands nothing from me, but I still chafe under his rule. If I could rid myself of my sire, I would."

"Find a pawn to manipulate," said Anis. "Remain in the background, out of sight, always. Let your agent take the risk and suffer the consequences if he fails. Whenever possible, Blood Bond your confederate before acting and make sure to command him to forget your role in the scheme."

"You *are* the consummate plotter," said Lameth admiringly.

Anis pressed close to him. "You are the only one who means anything to me, Lameth. As it was in life, so it is in death. Aid me in my plans. Help me undermine the third generation. Together we can rule the world."

Reaching for the container holding the elixir, Lameth filled two cups with the murky black fluid. "Drink," he commanded. "This potion will destroy the foul hunger inside us. Drink and then we will discuss the future."

McCann dreamed. . .

The man in black smiled.

"So the clans formally made peace with the Giovanni upstarts tonight?"

"Exactly as you expected," answered his companion, his swarthy features and dark clothing proclaiming him an Assamite assassin. "They accepted the inevitable. Augustus Giovanni was recognized as a third-generation Cainite who had replaced Asshur by diablerie. The Venetian's childer were proclaimed true Kindred, with their clan taking the place of the Children of Asshur."

The man in black nodded. "Even the undead tire after a hundred years of fighting. I'm only surprised it took the clan leaders this long to come to their senses. What is the essence of the agreement?"

"The Giovanni agreed to remain involved with Kindred affairs. They swore the Oath of Caine to stay neutral in all clan disputes. And they agreed to cease hunting the few surviving Children of Asshur."

"Considering that they exterminated all but a handful of the childer, not a hard bargain to take, eh?" The man in black laughed. "The Giovanni got the peace and recognition they desired for a handful of promises that cost them nothing to honor."

"They swore the Oath of Caine," said the Assamite in protest. "They would not dare violate that vow."

"I have been a member of the Kindred for more than a millennium," said the man in black solemnly. "During that time I have witnessed the breaking of a thousand oaths, a hundred vows, a million promises. We vampires are no more noble than the seed from which we come. Mankind never honored its word. Why should the Kindred?"

"Then the Giovanni lied?"

"They will maintain a clever facade," said the man in black. "As necromancers, they are concerned more with the dead than the living. Or the undead. I doubt that they will do much to upset the other clans. Theirs is a watching and waiting game. But what they eventually plan for Kindred and kine is a mystery I do not wish to think about."

"You imagine things," said the Assamite. "The Giovanni are too few in number to ever pose a threat. They waste their energy on commerce and trade. As if money will ever matter to the Kindred."

"No one at the parley expressed any interest in the identity of the vampire who foolishly Embraced Augustus Giovanni? Or why he took the risk?" asked the man in black.

"Those questions were never raised. You worried about it for naught. The dolt paid the price for his arrogance with his life and blood. He should have known better than to challenge the will of a necromancer."

"Perhaps he had no choice," said the man in black. "No choice at all."

And Lameth, who used the man in black as his voice and ears, smiled in satisfaction.

McCann woke. . .

It was dark outside. Another night had begun. It was time for him to put on his clothes and get moving. The Prince wanted to see him again at the Club. Perhaps Vargoss would have some news about the Red Death. Or of the mysterious Rachel Young, the ghoul whose actual master was a source of confusion.

Though completely awake, McCann was still troubled by his dreams. Both conversations had taken place many centuries in the past. It seemed extremely odd that he suddenly would think of them both in the same night. McCann felt uneasy, unnerved. He suspected powers beyond his understanding were manipulating his mind. It was not a pleasant thought.

That was when he noticed a small box on the nightstand by the side of his bed. His eyes widened in shock. The package had not been there when he retired. Mentally he checked the defenses protecting his home. They were all intact. None showed any signs of being disturbed. Yet the box provided tangible proof that someone had entered the dwelling when he was sleeping.

Gingerly McCann folded back the edges of the box. Inside were the letters and papers from his office. On top of them were the Tremere photos from Russia.

There was no note. Nor was one needed. Resting on the photos was a single green sequin.

CHAPTER 11

Washington, DC—March 12, 1994

Normally, a city the size of the nation's capital could support a dozen Kindred comfortably. However, over ten million tourists visited the metropolis each year. That huge influx of new blood, along with a constantly shifting population due to political hirings and firings, enabled several dozen vampires to exist easily throughout the city and surrounding suburbs.

Last night, the Red Death had lowered that number by two. This evening, Makish planned to continue that trend. Following the instructions of his grisly employer, the Assamite intended to wipe out more than a quarter of the Kindred residing in Washington. It was an ambitious plan, but Makish enjoyed challenges. The Red Death had proposed a sliding-scale bounty for each vampire slain. The greater the number killed, the larger the reward per Final Death. Tonight, Makish was feeling very greedy. And quite lethal.

The Deadlands was a popular private men's club in the Anacostia section of the city. It was located east of the Anacostia river in one of the worst neighborhoods in Washington. No one visited The Deadlands without a bodyguard. Or tried to enter without an invitation.

The owner of the establishment was an eighth-generation Toreador Clan vampire named John Thompson. He had lived in the city, under a dozen different names, for more than a century. Well connected with the most corrupt power mongers in the capital, Thompson worked hard to satisfy the most decadent wishes of his establishment's exclusive membership.

No desire was too extreme for those who frequented The Deadlands. Sex and drugs were the norm. Orgies took place every night. Sadism, torture, even ritual sacrifice could be experienced—for the right price. More than one tax increase had been passed to help pay Thompson's fee for a Congressman's outrageous request.

Makish was, in his own twisted manner, a highly moral individual. He considered Thompson a necessary but unfortunate link between the world of the living and the undead. To ensure their safety, the Kindred needed control over important people in government. That much Makish accepted. The assassin, however, found extremely distasteful the constant pandering to the basest instincts of the politicians. He felt such acts put the Camarilla on the same level as the hated Sabbat. Removing Thompson promised to be an enjoyable artistic endeavor.

The Assamite arrived at The Deadlands shortly after 1:00 A.M. Hooked to his belt was a large black bag. Inside it were the special tools he needed for this assignment. And the others to follow.

Makish was already in good spirits. Three thugs had jumped him on his walk to the club. Before attacking, they had stupidly made several insulting remarks about the color of his skin and the nature of his ancestors. It had been bad judgment on their part. The Assamite had strangled the trio with their own intestines. Makish considered the horrified look of stunned disbelief in their eyes as they choked to death adequate repayment for their affronts to his dignity.

His feelings soaring high, he surveyed the front of the club. As he expected, a half-dozen ghouls guarded the entrance. They provided the necessary muscle to keep The Deadlands safe from both unwanted guests and neighborhood operators. All of the men were built like professional football players, and each of them carried an AK-47 automatic rifle in full view. No police patrolled this section of the capital. None dared.

Makish smiled and shook his head. Like too many of the Kindred, Thompson had grown complacent. He believed himself invulnerable. Dealing with ordinary humans had dulled the edge of his wits. Ghouls were stronger and faster and deadlier than normal humans. However, they lacked imagination and realization what a truly powerful Kindred could do if provoked. They were no match for an Assamite assassin. Especially this particular Assamite assassin. A direct assault would take too much time and give Thompson a chance to escape the surroundings. But there was more than one way to enter a fortress. Any fortress.

To think was to act for Makish. Moving with sight-blurring speed, he swept into a deserted building two doors away from the club. It took him mere seconds to reach the roof. It was level with the top of the next. Effortlessly he leapt the space between the two structures. The club was less than thirty feet away. The ghouls never looked up.

Extending his perception, Makish surveyed the sloped roof of his destination. Originally a Victorian mansion, the building had been rebuilt and reinforced when it was transformed into a men's club. The Deadlands had a number of alarms and motion detectors built into the roof and gables. However, there were no real guards keeping watch. That was all the information that Makish required.

Soaring like a bat, he covered the thirty feet separating the two buildings with a single powerful leap. The sensors recorded nothing unusual. The Assamite had mentally locked them into their present setting. Makish possessed incredible powers over machinery.

Beneath the wood-and-brick facade of the roof was steel plating. The Assamite didn't care. Again he checked the top floor of the building for inhabitants. There were only two -mortals engaged in an act of passion. He doubted they would even notice his entrance.

Hardening his fingers to the consistency of diamonds, Makish plunged his hands into the roof. Like missiles, his digits dug into the thin steel and ripped through it. Effortlessly the assassin curled his fingers and pulled back, peeling the section of the roof off like a piece of cardboard. Creating an entrance was a great deal easier than fighting his way through one. Making no sound, Makish slipped into the club, black bag dangling on his hip.

He was on the fifth and top floor. Thompson was two levels down, talking business with a pair of potential customers. Running on a tight schedule, Makish had no time for subtlety. He planned leaving no survivors of his attacks. While he disliked killing innocent bystanders, these lawmakers could hardly be described as guiltless. Murdering them was probably doing their constituents a favor.

Behind him, a woman screamed. Makish whirled. He had momentarily forgotten the human couple engaged in sexual union in the rear room. A young lady, quite attractive and very naked, was standing in the center of the hallway, a horrified expression on her face, shrieking hysterically at the top of her lungs. There was no sign of her companion.

A quick scan of her thoughts revealed that the man, an elderly politician, had collapsed unexpectedly at the height of his passion. The woman, a high-priced hooker, had come searching for medical help. Instead of finding aid, she discovered Makish descending from the hole in the roof.

"My apologies," said Makish regretfully and slapped the screaming woman hard across the temple. The blow instantly shattered her skull and she collapsed to the floor in a pool of blood.

Dragging the corpse with him, Makish entered the room from which the woman had just exited. The senator lay on the bed, clutching his chest, gasping for breath. He had suffered a mild coronary. Enough to incapacitate him, but not to kill. Makish completed the job by tearing out the man's heart. Casually, he threw the woman's body across the politician's. United in life, he felt it proper that they should be united in death.

Alarms, activated by the girl's screams, were ringing throughout the house. The assassin made no effort to use his mental disciplines to shut them off. He preferred minor chaos when he worked. Confusion served him well.

His mind fixed on Thompson's location, Makish hurried to the staircase leading down. Three ghouls armed with guns were running up the stairs.

"In there, please hurry," shouted the assassin. Trembling with emotion, he pointed with a shaky finger to the door of the room he had just left. "The senator, please. He looks very ill. I think he is dying!"

The ghouls rushed passed him. And died as he tore out their throats with three rapid strokes of his hands.

Dark hands covered with blood, the assassin continued down the stairs. He hoped there would be no more interruptions. There weren't. He found Thompson still in his office, assuring his guests that there was no cause for panic.

Slipping into the chamber, Makish nodded pleasantly to the two Congressmen and smashed their heads into pulp. Thompson, a short, squat man with a huge handlebar mustache, gaped in astonishment.

"Who-who are you?" he asked.

"I bring justice," said the assassin, aware of the hidden video camera and tape machines recording his every word and action. His rather stilted dialogue had come directly from the Red Death. "For too many years your presence in this city has offended the Sabbat. Tonight that insult ends."

"No!" cried Thompson, backing up to the wall behind his chair. Though shaken by what he had just witnessed, he was still in control of his emotions. His thoughts revealed a button beneath his desk, already pressed, summoning the ghouls from out front. And the existence of an emergency escape passage hidden behind the plasterboard a few feet to the right. "We can make a deal. I swear it. We can make a deal."

Makish toyed with the idea of letting Thompson escape into the passage, extending the hunt by a few minutes. It appealed to his sense of irony. But business was business and he had numerous other killings to perform tonight. Sometimes art had to be sacrificed in the name of expediency.

Reaching into his black bag, Makish pulled out an eighteen-inch long wooden spear. Thompson shrieked in horror when he saw it. His fingers slapped for the hidden panel but never connected. Makish moved like lightning. With a thrust of his powerful hands, he slammed the stake into Thompson's heart. Eyes frozen in shock, Thompson dropped to the floor.

Contrary to popular belief, a wooden stake didn't kill a vampire. However, it did paralyze the Cainite until removed. Thompson was unharmed, merely immobilized. Which was exactly what Makish wanted.

Out of the assassin's bag of tricks came a roll of thick gray tape and a small circular device two inches in diameter. Mentally the assassin switched off all the recording devices in the office. He preferred not displaying his special toys to the eyes of either the Camarilla or the Sabbat. His fondness for Thermit was well known. Death by high explosives was Makish's favorite artistic expression.

"Open wide, please," said Makish politely, and with one hand forced the round ball into Thompson's mouth. A thin strand of wire connected the device to the stake buried in the vampire's chest. Carefully Makish wound the heavy-duty tape around his victim's mouth and upper body. Reinforced with optical fiberglass threads, the tape was nearly indestructible. It could not be torn, only unraveled. Taking it off required hours of hard work. Removing the stake, though, took much less effort.

"Your ghouls should arrive shortly," declared Makish cheerfully. "Seeing you frozen on the floor, they will immediately think to withdraw the cause of your anguish. You will not be able to tell them not to. Unfortunately, when they pull out the stake, the action will activate the trigger of the plaything in your mouth. It is a small but extremely powerful Thermit bomb. The resulting fire should burn your body to ashes in seconds. The colors will be spectacular. It will be an artistic finish to your existence."

Taking his bag, Makish stepped into the secret passage. It was a quicker, easier escape method than returning to the roof.

"Goodbye," he said to the unmoving Thompson. "Thank you for your cooperation. Enjoy your wait."

The explosion was so loud that Makish heard it two blocks from The Deadlands. He nodded in satisfaction, deciding it was an excellent beginning for the evening's endeavors.

CHAPTER 12

St. Louis—March 13, 1994

The Prince held his council of war in his office at the rear of Club Diabolique. Attending were Vargoss, Flavia, McCann, a ninth-generation Brujah named Darrow, and an eighth-generation Nosferatu known only as "Uglyface" for obvious reasons.

Darrow, who rode a Harley, favored black leather outfits, and had tattoos over much of his body, advised the Prince on matters of policy. Despite his looks, Darrow was no rebel. He had spent most of his life serving as an officer in the British Army. He had participated in many of the major campaigns of the 19th century and was the veteran of a hundred battles. He was a calm voice of reason, not afraid to contradict the Prince when Vargoss was wrong.

No one in St. Louis knew much about Uglyface's background. Nearly seven feet tall and thin as a rail, he had lived in the city longer than any other vampire. His face came from a Gahan Wilson cartoon—wide, bulging eyes, tiny button nose, wide mouth full of yellow teeth, and ears that stuck out like antennae from the sides of his head. Uglyface's grotesque features branded him an idiot. He was not. The Nosferatu vampire possessed an incredible memory for names, dates, and facts. Like many of his clan, he thrived on gathering and processing raw data into usable information. He served as the Prince's Minister of Intelligence.

"The Red Death struck three more times in America last night," said Vargoss, resting his arms on his desk. He was obviously concerned. Troubled eyes stared at the trio facing him. To the rear, on guard as always, was Flavia. She was clad no longer in white leather but in black. And for the first time in decades, she stood alone.

"According to reports I received in the past hour, he

appeared again, in Europe, while we slept. Five perished in Paris at a reception at the Louvre. Two more were lost in Marseilles during a Ventrue Clan meeting. In total, he sent thirty-five Kindred to their Final Deaths."

"Six separate appearances in twenty-four hours?" said McCann. "Our spectral friend travels awfully fast."

"Are we positive it is the same bloke?" asked Darrow, voicing the detective's own suspicion. "That bloody mockery of a face of 'is was awfully distinctive. Maybe it was meant to attract attention, aye? Any Kindred adept at sculpting flesh could rearrange his features into that grotesque mask. Instead of dealing with a single Red Death, we may be faced with several. Maybe an entire Sabbat pack made a pact with a demon."

"Following that same line of reasoning, are you convinced the Red Death was a vampire?" asked McCann. The detective was anxious to establish certain facts he already knew as truth.

"The abomination belonged to the Kindred," said Vargoss, angrily. "My will touched his when I commanded him to stop. Blood called out to blood, McCann. The Red Death was definitely one of the Damned."

"A vampire composed of living fire," said McCann. "It's incredible. Are there such disciplines?"

"None practiced among the Camarilla," said Uglyface. His high-pitched voice squeaked like a cartoon character's.

"Darrow has it right," declared Vargoss. "The Red Death is a member of the Sabbat. Those demon lovers mock the power of the flames. One of their sacred rituals, the Fire Dance, requires them to jump and dance through a blazing funeral pyre."

"Sorry," said McCann, "but I don't accept those kinds of deductions. I'm a detective, remember? Let's use a bit of logic. Leaping over a fire like Jack-Be-Nimble is a lot different than burning your footprints into the floor. I'm not discounting possible Sabbat involvement. I just wonder why they've never used this particular method of attack before.

The war between the Sabbat and Camarilla is more than five hundred years old. Why save the Red Death until this week? There has to be more to the story than we comprehend."

"McCann raises a good point," said Darrow. "These friggin' attacks make no sense. Usually the Sabbat spends years organizing a Crusade to take over a city. We all knows the procedures. First they send in the spies. Then they place traitors into the Kindred council of elders. Next comes their efforts to expose the Masquerade through carefully planned acts of murder and terrorism. And then, during the resulting chaos, they attack in overwhelming numbers, exterminating any vampires they cannot convert to their cause. There's no place for the Red Death in such plans."

"Perhaps they have finally invented a new strategy to replace their old method," said Uglyface. "Why should the Sabbat waste the time and effort of a Crusade when the Red Death can wipe out a city's elders in a night?"

"Sounds great," said McCann, "except that's not what happened. The Prince wasn't destroyed. St. Louis hasn't been overrun by Sabbat members anxious to consolidate their control. See what I mean? The Red Death killed some Kindred. Most of the dead were later-generation vampires. The attack cut the population a little. Otherwise nothing much changed."

"Bloody hell," said Darrow, grimacing. "We've totally ignored the most important question of them all. Why did the Red Death attack here in the first place? No offense, my Prince, but St. Louis ain't a major Sabbat target. Leastwise, not according to our intelligence reports. They have their eyes on bigger, more important cities. What made us so bloody special we warranted the friggin' attention of this fire monster?"

"No offense taken, Darrow," said Vargoss. "I value your honesty more than any flattery. And your point is well presented. As best I can tell from my discussions with other Camarilla elders, the initial appearance of the Red Death last night was definitely at this club. Why?"

McCann suspected he knew the answer. However, he had no intentions of stating that the Red Death had come to the club searching for him. That would raise questions he had been carefully avoiding for centuries. It was the proper moment to swing the conversation in a different direction.

"Anyone remember Tyrus Benedict?" asked the detective. "Maybe the answer to your question is tied up with his visit."

"The Tremere wizard," said Vargoss. "Of course. I almost forgot him." The Prince scowled. From his coat pocket, he removed several folded pages of fax paper. "I sent a message to Vienna late last night regarding Mr. Benedict and his mission. This reply came from Etrius himself while I rested."

McCann, a student of Tremere history and organization, immediately recognized the name of the titular head of the vampire mage's Inner Council of Seven. Etrius served as the guardian of the founder of the clan of undead wizards, the powerful sorcerer known as Tremere. The vampire himself lay dormant in torpor in a stone sarcophagus in the catacombs beneath Vienna. Strange rumors swirled about regarding the condition of Tremere's body. Rumors that Etrius refused to confirm or deny.

"The wizard, a cold, merciless bastard like all of his clan, expressed little regret at Benedict's death. However, he was extremely interested in the tale of the Red Death. And the monster's control of fire."

"No bloody surprise, that," said Darrow. Like most Kindred, he feared and distrusted the Tremere. Though they protested that they were loyal members of the Camarilla, everyone knew that the wizards worked for their own ends. And those plans they kept to themselves. "What those devils wouldn't give to wield a power like the Red Death! They'd probably burn us all off the map. And laugh at us for providing the information while they did it!"

Vargoss nodded. What small trust he had in the Tremere vanished when his closest advisor, Mosfair, turned on him a few months ago. Only McCann's intervention had saved the Prince from the ultimate betrayal. The detective had never revealed that Mosfair had actually been acting as an agent for the Sabbat, not his own clan. McCann disliked alliances between the major Kindred bloodlines. And he worked very hard to prevent them from succeeding.

"However, what I found extremely interesting was a message on the second page of the communication. Etrius stated that Benedict had been sent merely as an envoy to personally apologize for the transgressions of his brother clan member, Mosfair. He was not carrying with him any documents relating to the Nictuku or the recent events in Russia."

The Prince paused, obviously enjoying the astonished looks on his advisors' faces. Vargoss possessed a strong sense of the dramatic. "Moreover, Etrius stated that though Benedict stated the basic facts about the mystery correctly, none of the Tremere sent to Russia to investigate the Soviet problem had returned. The name The Army of Night meant nothing to him. And he knew nothing about any photos."

"What a friggin' mess," declared Darrow. "You believe that slimy wizard, my Prince? He could be lying."

"Who can fathom the duplicity of the Tremere?" said Vargoss. "I suspect, though, from the tone of this letter, Etrius was deeply disturbed by my revelations. He urgently requested I relay, word-for-word everything Benedict said about Baba Yaga."

"I'll bet," said Darrow. "Them Tremere don't like surprises."

"According to the ancient legends of my clan," said Uglyface, "the Iron Hag was the greatest sorceress in the world. She was one of the Nictuku, monsters created by Absimiliard, the first Nosferatu, in his days of madness. Her powers rivaled those of Lameth, the Dark Messiah."

"It sounds like someone tampered with Benedict's thoughts during his journey here from Vienna," said McCann hurriedly. He was anxious to shift subjects again. "No wonder the notion upsets Etrius. Messing with the mind of a wizard is no job for a lightweight."

"I asked Uglyface earlier to backtrack Benedict's trip," said Vargoss. The Prince shifted his attention to the Nosferatu. "What did you learn?"

"Following the wizard's trail proved quite difficult," said Uglyface. "He used unconventional methods of transportation. However, after much searching, I was able to verify that Benedict arrived in Washington, DC, three nights ago. Attempts to contact my usual source of information in the capital, my friend Amos, proved useless tonight. I received no replies to my queries about the Tremere's activities in the city. Or any of my other questions."

"*Three* nights ago," repeated McCann. "Yet Benedict arrived here last evening. That leaves an entire night completely unaccounted for."

"The Sabbat has a foothold in the city," said Vargoss. "They want to add the capital to their empire."

"The Camarilla controls the capital," replied Darrow. "The Tremere are a powerful force there. Peter Dorfman is Pontifex there, and he is very ambitious. For all we know, Benedict may have received new instructions from a member of his own bloodline there. There's a bitter rivalry between Dorfman and other Tremere elders. Meerlinda, leader of the US branch of the clan, plays one against the other in order to maintain absolute control of the bloodline. In turn, she and Etrius both scheme to take charge of the entire clan. It's a frigging bloody mess, and anything's possible."

"I agree," said Vargoss. "We need an agent to personally investigate the situation in Washington. That is the only way we will learn the truth."

All eyes focused on McCann. The detective laughed.

"Why do I get the impression I've been elected?"

Vargoss smiled. "You are the obvious choice, McCann. A mortal detective, you possess the necessary skills to discover the facts. And you can function during the daytime, when the Kindred are helpless."

"Yeah, and I have my mage powers to protect me," said

McCann. "Not that they would do much good if I stumble upon the Red Death. I assume you're willing to pay well for this scouting expedition?"

Vargoss laughed. "What I like about you, McCann, is that you are so pleasantly frank. After listening to constant lies and half-truths, it amuses me to hear real, honest greed." The vampire lord nodded. "You will be well compensated for your time and trouble."

Unexpectedly, Flavia leaned over and whispered into the Prince's ear. Vargoss frowned, then rose from the table.

"Excuse me. I shall return shortly."

The Prince exited the chamber, followed by his bodyguard. McCann barely had time to deal Darrow and Uglyface a second hand of gin rummy before the two returned.

"The plans have been altered slightly," announced the Prince, taking his seat. Flavia returned to her position at his right. "You are still traveling to Washington, McCann. But you are not going alone. Flavia is going to accompany you."

"What?" said the detective. "*What?*"

"Flavia argues convincingly that a lone human, even a mage, cannot stand against the concentrated attack of a Sabbat pack. Especially if the Red Death is involved. Besides which, Flavia has contacts with the important Camarilla leaders of the city. I am forced to agree. She is right. You need protection and introductions. And she is the one Kindred who is capable of providing you with both. Darrow will take her place at my side during her absence."

"I work on my own," said McCann, feeling trapped.

"Not in this case," said Vargoss, in a voice that brooked no denial. At his side, Flavia's lips twitched in the slightest of smiles. "Do not anger me, McCann. You will discover the truth about Tyrus Benedict. And Flavia will guard your back."

"As you command," said McCann, bowing to the inevitable. "It should be an interesting trip."

Flavia nodded. Sensuously she licked her upper lip with her tongue. McCann grimaced. She winked.

CHAPTER 13

Paris—March 14, 1994

Paris is a city of many mysteries. Take, for example, the electric power lines leading into the foundation of Notre Dame Cathedral. No records exist showing why the cables are there or where they lead. They are live wires, supplying electricity to a location somewhere beneath the church. Since no one complains about the lines, the powers that be in the public works department leave them strictly alone. The policy, as in most big-city administrations, is, if it isn't broken, don't fix it.

Another unexplained puzzle of Paris is the vast network of underground tunnels that honeycomb the city. Located hundreds of feet beneath the ground, these passages are not the result of any known city engineering project. Impossible to reach, no man has walked through them in public memory. Who built them, and when, is a matter of continued speculation among the city engineers. What few records exist from the 18th century indicate that the tunnels were already in place then. Official policy states that the corridors are remnants of an underground fortress built during the Roman occupation of the area. The explanation is ludicrous, but that dating of the tunnels is much closer to their actual age than anyone realizes.

Less noticed but equally mysterious is the purpose of the Vert-Galant warehouse, located at the west end of the Île de la Cité. The building is over two hundred years old. No one knows the identity of the present owner. As has been the case with every owner for the past twenty decades. The rent is paid promptly each month by a cashier's check drawn on a Swiss bank.

No one seems interested in the fact that while deliveries are made to the warehouse nearly every day, nothing is shipped out. Yet the shelves are never full. That the shipments, ranging from computer supplies to expensive art prints, are never seen again once they enter the building is equally perplexing. Where and how the items are removed are questions that the clerks managing the building are paid not to ask. Their salaries, much higher than they deserve, come from that same Swiss bank account.

Phantomas knew the truth lurking behind the mysteries. The power lines snaked down to his hidden lair deep beneath the Crypte Archeologique in the main square fronting Notre Dame. The tunnels, constructed in secret over the centuries through subterfuge and deception, provided him with access to hundreds of locations in Paris. The warehouse belonged to him and the purchases were made through the convenience of ordering merchandise by computer. The necessary capital came from his bank account in Switzerland. The funds had been raised over the centuries by the judicious use of blackmail among the rich and famous of Paris. No one, living or undead, in the vast metropolis could keep a secret from the prying eyes and ears of Phantomas.

Tonight the ancient vampire sat in front of a computer terminal in the main room of his lair and wondered if perhaps he had overestimated his own skills. For hours he had been trying to locate some reference to the Red Death. And for hours he had not found a single clue.

Phantomas was obsessed with information. A scholar during his life, he retained the same passion for knowledge after his death. Some vampires lived for blood. Phantomas lived for facts. He collected them, saved them, ordered them, and tried to weave them into a pattern. Especially facts concerning vampires.

A thousand years ago he had conceived of his great project involving the history of the Kindred. He had been working on this masterpiece of information ever since. It was his obsession, his dream. The Nosferatu elder was writing an encyclopedia of the Kindred. It contained every fact, every scrap of information he had been able to learn about the Cainites during the past millennium. The invention of computers had greatly helped his work, eliminating the tedious work of hand-writing the information into journals. Also, the powerful database he used enabled him to cross-reference millions of vampiric acts, establishing clear links between hundreds of seemingly unrelated incidents and occurrences.

The centerpiece of his project was the most complete family tree ever attempted of the Kindred race. Starting with Caine, the diagram listed many thousands of vampires who had walked the earth for thousands of years. Along with describing each Kindred's relationship to the other Cainites, the chart also featured a detailed biographical profile of the vampire. By using this genealogy and history, Phantomas hoped to discover some trace of the Red Death. But so far his quest had drawn a complete blank.

The profiles of the Kindred were drawn from a hundred different sources. Phantomas had been using computers since their invention and was perhaps the greatest hacker in the world. He could access the files from any major data bank or information file. No security code was safe from his descramble program. The secrets of the world were at his gnarled fingertips.

Most of Phantomas' data came from the mainframes used by the Camarilla and the Sabbat. Both sects maintained extensive code-word systems to protect their files from their hated enemy. Neither were aware that a third party, uninvolved in their blood war, had been stealing data from them for years.

The American CIA, the British SAS and CID branches, the French Sûreté, the Israeli Mossad, and the Russian KGB also fed Phantomas information. He was insatiable in his quest to make his encyclopedia as accurate as possible. That it was never seen by anyone else didn't matter. Phantomas worked for his own satisfaction.

Discrete taps on phone company computers throughout the world provided details of the Red Death's other attacks on Camarilla strongholds. Together with his own information on the monster's appearance in Paris, Phantomas had fed the encapsulated data into his computer. Then he had programmed the machine to search and evaluate his files for those Kindred powerful enough to wield the powers of the Red Death. He purposefully had the machine eliminate the thirteen members of the third generation of vampires. It wouldn't require a computer to tell when they had arisen from their ages-long torpor.

A comprehensive scan had turned up twenty-seven possible vampires who might be the Red Death. A second run eliminated those Kindred engaged in major blood feuds or in centuries-old sleep. To Phantomas' frustration, the procedure left two possible names, neither covered in his file of biographies—Anis, Queen of Night, and Lameth, the Dark Messiah. Both were legendary figures of the fourth generation. But among the Kindred, legends often were based on fact.

Lameth was reputed to be the greatest sorcerer ever to walk the Earth. No two tales agreed on the identity of his tutor, but all agreed that it had been one of the primeval elemental forces that had once walked the Earth. According to myth, Lameth discovered a potion that artificially induced Golconda, the mental state that allowed vampires to exist in perfect harmony with their surroundings. Whoever controlled that elixir controlled the Kindred. That was why Lameth had been dubbed "The Dark Messiah." He had vanished into the mists of history over five thousand years ago. Though rumors of his meddling in Cainite affairs continued to surface.

Anis, Queen of Night, was a contemporary of Lameth's. Myths dating back to the Second City held her responsible for the revolt in which the third generation rose up and killed their sires. She was described as the most beautiful woman who ever walked the Earth. And among the most deadly.

The legends of the Second City described Anis as consumed by ambition. She was said to possess seductive charms nearly as intense as Lilith, the lover of Adam and one of the most powerful of demons. Anis, too, had disappeared more than five millennia ago. And, like Lameth, rumors of her reappearance circulated constantly among the Kindred.

Significantly, no legend mentioned the sire of either of the two.

Frustrated and annoyed, Phantomas had abandoned the

search for his attacker's identity. Instead, he decided to focus upon the special Disciplines of the Camarilla and the Paths of Enlightenment practiced by members of the Sabbat. Again, his efforts turned up nothing remotely resembling the incendiary grip of the Red Death. Nor was there any mention of demons gifting humans or Kindred with such a power. Phantomas even checked the latest developments in chemical and biological warfare. The results were the same. Nothing.

The Nosferatu shook his head in distress. Recent reports from America, obtained by phone taps on supposedly safe lines, indicated that there might be more than one Red Death. The possibility of an entire bloodline of vampires not included in his genealogy chart depressed him. He had worked for hundreds of years on his chronology. It was inconceivable that he had missed an entire branch of the Kindred family. Yet the facts seemed to point directly at that conclusion.

Phantomas pounded his keyboard in frustration. Lameth or Anis had to be the Red Death. Or one of them had founded a bloodline, all of whose members possessed the power of the Red Death. That was the only possible solution to the mystery. Still, he was not convinced it was correct.

Nor did any of his speculations, Phantomas suddenly realized, address the equally mysterious young man who had warned him in advance of the Red Death. And who knew his name.

Without warning, the computer keyboard sprang to life. Shocked, Phantomas lifted his hands off the console. The keys continued to type, as if being hit by invisible fingers.

A single phrase appeared on the computer monitor. Staring at it, Phantomas shivered. He had no idea what the words meant. Yet he was convinced that his stray thought about the man in the Louvre had triggered this response from his computer. Voice trembling, he read the name aloud.

"The Sheddim."

PART

2

That she loved me I should not have doubted; and I might have been easily aware that, in a bosom such as hers, love would have reigned as no ordinary passion.
"Ligeia"
Edgar Allan Poe

Chapter 1

New York, NY—March 14, 1994

The most dangerous woman in the world rose each day with the sun.

She lived in the penthouse suite on top of one of the tallest skyscrapers in New York City. The building, from foundation to lightning rod, belonged to her. Few New Yorkers realized that the owner lived on the premises. Even fewer knew what she looked like or how much she was really worth. None were aware of the other, darker secrets the structure held.

The bright yellow glow of morning flowed from the huge picture windows of the penthouse bedroom across the lushly carpeted floor and climbed up the side of the huge, king-size bed in the center of the chamber. It splashed across bright red silk sheets until it crested like a wave on the nude body of the woman sprawled in deep sleep in the middle of the crimson sea. Her dark hair flared around her head in a halo, the sleeper had the face of an angel. And the body of a devil.

Her features, young and wrinkle-free, glowing pink with perfect health, were those of a twenty-five year old. Her body was taut and lean, well-muscled and deeply bronzed. Firm breasts, long, tapered legs, and flared hips proclaimed her one of those rare beauties who looked exceptional either dressed or undressed.

The sunshine caressed her face, causing the woman to smile in her sleep. Sighing softly, she rolled over, burying her head in the silk. The warm glow, intensified by the glass of the windows, painted golden streaks across her back.

Slowly she emerged from slumber, rubbing the sleep from her eyes. Chuckling softly, the young woman rolled onto her back and stretched, raising her arms high into the air. Her fingers curled and uncurled, like steel coils tightening, then releasing. She rolled her shoulders on the silk, relishing the feel of the material on her skin, letting it caress the muscles in her neck and upper back.

It feels good to be alive, thought Alicia Varney. *It feels very good to be alive.*

Slithering over the sheets like a snake, she crawled to the edge of the bed and flicked on the intercom sitting on the nightstand.

"The princess in the tower has arisen," the young woman declared. Her voice, low and sultry, was as smooth as melted honey.

"Good morning, Miss Varney," said a man at the other end of the line. "I take it you would like breakfast served?"

"Right away, Jackson," said Alicia Varney. "Send in the usual. I'm hopping into the shower. I should be out by the time the food arrives."

"Yes, Miss Varney," replied Jackson. A former Green Beret and CIA troubleshooter, Sanford Jackson performed admirably as Alicia's manservant, chauffeur, and bodyguard. During the rare periods when she was without a lover, he handled that job with reasonable competency as well.

Thinking of Jackson's hard, muscular body sent shivers of sexual excitement rippling through Alicia. She had spent the past few nights in bed alone, a rare occurrence for a woman of her voracious appetites. It was a situation she meant to remedy as soon as possible. Alicia Varney squeezed every drop of pleasure possible out of life. She did not like being denied anything for very long.

Anxiously she headed for the bathroom and the shower. A few minutes spent under hot, pulsating streams of water, along with a session with the magnificent detachable shower nozzle, would serve for the moment. But self-stimulation was no substitute for the real thing. Later today she would go on the prowl. She needed a man.

She returned fifteen minutes later to her bedroom to find Jackson setting her breakfast tray down on a small writing table facing the window. Dressed in a totally transparent dressing robe, Alicia nodded in satisfaction at the three slices of cinnamon French toast, selection of imported fruit jellies, pot of coffee, and copy of the *Wall Street Journal*.

"Any messages?" she inquired of her assistant as she took her seat. "I can't imagine the world survived the night without something happening that needed my personal attention."

"A few," he stated, standing at attention a few feet from the table. Old habits died hard. Jackson never rested easy in the presence of his commanding officer. He always stood at rigid attention in Alicia's presence. Though he couldn't help sneak sidewise glances at her firm breasts tightly pressed against the thin material of her gown. "Nothing of great importance. I assumed you would follow usual procedure, Miss, and deal with them after breakfast."

Alicia nodded, methodically cutting a slice of French toast into sixteen small squares. She dolloped three different flavored jellies onto the plate, poured herself a cup of black coffee, and opened the newspaper. Stabbing a piece of the French toast with her fork, she dipped it into the strawberry jam, her favorite, and began to eat.

She feasted slowly, savoring each bite much like a condemned convict eating his last meal. Alicia rarely hurried doing anything. Eating, drinking, sleeping, making love, she did them all at a controlled, measured pace that defined her existence. She believed in devouring her pleasures mouthful by mouthful, chewing them to a fine pulp, then swallowing. She was never in a rush. She had all the time in the world.

As usual, the *Journal* held little of interest. Alicia had much better contacts than anyone at the paper. The biggest stories, the latest headlines, were old business to her. Money talked, and she controlled billions. Varney Enterprises, which she owned, was one of the largest corporations in the world. Estimating its actual worth was impossible, but corporate yearly reported income was more than the gross national product of many small countries. And that did not include funds from the company's more profitable but quite illegal secret enterprises.

Alicia put down the paper and stared out the window.

On a clear day like today, she could see for miles and miles. Her sharp gaze traveled past the slums of Tenth Avenue and the Bowery and across the polluted green and brown waters of the Hudson river. Beyond the river were the moldering Hoboken docks and the huge toxic waste dumps that had earned the town the nickname "the cancer capital of America." At the edge of her vision, Alicia could catch sight of the crumbling coastal palisades that guarded the New Jersey swamps.

Often, looking out her window, she felt like a medieval princess sitting in her tower surrounded by a world of peasants. It was an apt comparison. The wealthy and powerful of America reigned like aristocracy over the common herd. There was no true middle class, just the rich and the poor. Having experienced both extreme poverty and extreme prosperity many times in her life, Alicia knew without question that incredible affluence was the better of the two. She reveled in her riches, her lifestyle, and, most of all, in the physical sensations of life itself. There was no way she would give up any of it. For anyone or any cause.

"Jackson," she asked, her voice pensive and curious, "can you imagine living without the sun?"

"Pardon, Miss?" Jackson was poised, bright, and articulate. He did not, however, possess an imagination. He viewed the world in terms of blacks and whites, positives and negatives. A wonderful bodyguard and right-hand man, he was less satisfactory as a conversationalist.

She paused, gathering her thoughts. "Have you ever given any thought to what it would be like enduring in a world of eternal darkness? Without hope of ever seeing sunlight again?"

"You mean being blind, Miss?" asked Jackson. He shook his head. "Can't say I have, Miss Varney. During the war, I trained wearing a blindfold, learning how to rely on my other senses if my eyes were injured. But that never happened. I've been lucky that way. Always had perfect vision."

Alicia sighed. She wondered why she bothered. With a

shake of her head, she tried one last time.

"That's not what I meant. Not at all. If you someday discovered that you had been struck with a deadly disease so that the slightest exposure to sunlight would strike you dead, wither the skin right off your body, would you be able to stand it? Would you be able to accept the fact that never again would you be able to see the sun shining?" She drew in a deep breath. "What if the same disease denied you many of the physical pleasures you take for granted? Like eating or drinking. Would the thought of such a life, if you could call it that, drive you mad? Would you adapt? Could you adapt?"

"You mean like if I was turned into one of those characters you deal with at The Devil's Playground?" said Jackson, his rock-solid features twisting in what Alicia recognized as his thoughtful expression. "Became one of those vampire things who spend all their time plotting against each other? Or haunt the streets, drinking the blood from bums who don't have a place to hide?"

"They are not prime examples of the Kindred," said Alicia. "But close enough."

"It wouldn't make a difference to me, Miss. I'm a survivor. I enjoy my food and drink," his eyes widened suggestively, "and my lovemaking. Can't say I'd be thrilled if I had to live without them. But I ain't quite ready for the great beyond, if you catch my meaning. If I had to drink some blood to stay around, I'd do it in an instant. Did worse in the war, ma'am. Lot worse once or twice. Survival ain't pretty, Miss Varney. Still, death is awfully final."

"You are a practical fellow, Mr. Jackson," said Alicia. "Death is very final. Especially for the Damned. Still, sometimes I think an eternity spent in darkness is no better. You cannot really understand. Mankind is born of the sun. Humans are truly heirs of the morning."

"Seems to me," said Jackson, "that I once heard vampires called the Children of the Night."

Alicia chuckled. "How poetic. But it's very true."

She rose to her feet, grinning as her assistant's expression froze, his thoughts as transparent as her robe. "Keep hoping, Mr. Jackson," Alicia purred as she walked to the huge closets that covered one entire wall of her bedroom. "If I don't find a candidate to satisfy my carnal desires within the next few days, I will be forced to rely on your services. I'm positive you will rise to the occasion."

"Of course, Miss Varney," said Jackson politely. "I'll try my best."

"That will be quite satisfactory, I am sure," said Alicia. She flung open the doors of the black section of the closet. "Now get that tray out of here and bring me my messages. And bring me Sumohn. It's been days since I've seen my precious pet."

Jackson blanched. His big hands clenched into fists as he scowled at Alicia. "That beast is dangerous, Miss Varney. Black panthers aren't made to be household pets. Not even for ladies like you."

"Nonsense," said Alicia, her tone of voice brooking no disagreement. "I can assure you that Sumohn is incapable of harming me. I repeat, Mr. Jackson, *incapable*. We have had this discussion before and it does not please me to repeat it again. The subject is closed."

"Yes, Miss Varney," said Jackson, stiffly. "I'll instruct that your pet be sent up from the kennel immediately."

"You're getting better, Jackson," said Alicia, with a laugh. "But you're still not perfect. I run my life the way I want. You worry about my business rivals sending assassins after me. I'll worry about Sumohn."

"Yes, ma'am," said Jackson, his tone of voice indicating he thought his employer crazy. "You're the boss."

"Exactly," said Alicia. "Now go."

When Jackson returned to the penthouse ten minutes later, Alicia met him in the front parlor, ready for work. She wore a long, black velvet skirt, a frilly white blouse, and black toreador jacket. On her head, held at a jaunty angle to her hair by a steel pin, was a black beret.

"I sent word to the kennel," said Jackson, handing Alicia a folder containing several dozen sheets of paper. "They said they would bring up your panther as soon as possible. It should only be a few minutes."

"At least they understand the wisdom of not arguing with me," said Alicia, thumbing through the documents. Halfway into the stack she stopped, frowned, and pulled out a sheet.

"The Russians refuse to let our people into the country? What the hell is happening there? It doesn't make sense. Varney Enterprises has been doing business with the Communists since 1919. Did that fool in charge, Andropov, give any reason for the abrupt change in policy? I thought we were bribing the miserable son of a bitch plenty."

"That official's gone, Miss Varney," said Jackson. "He vanished, without a trace. Like lots of the people we dealt with over the years. Yeltsin, or whoever is behind him, has been eliminating the Old Guard and installing new people in all the positions of power. They've made it absolutely clear that foreigners are no longer welcome into the country. And that includes us."

"*Fuck*," said Alicia harshly. "That move is going to cost us millions. We spent years setting up that network in the Soviet Republics. It can't crash just because some reformer has taken charge. I refuse to believe it. Russia doesn't work that way."

"Not before, it didn't," said Jackson. "But things have changed drastically in the past few months. Our agents have been reporting all sorts of disturbing rumors about Yeltsin's secret advisors. Word is that to consolidate his position, he's cut deals with some awfully ruthless characters."

"Ruthless?" repeated Alicia. "What's new about that in Russia. Those bastards are colder than ice. They'd murder their own children and sell the bodies for medical research if it paid enough."

"Nobody knows the truth," said Jackson. "There's lots of talk, but anyone who gets too close to the real answers disappears. I've studied the reports from the past twelve months. The closest thing we have to actual facts are several garbled reports of a gigantic old bitch with iron teeth and iron claws meeting late at night with the Premier."

Alicia froze, her mouth open in stunned surprise. All the color drained from her face, leaving her white as a ghost. Her eyes clouded, as if focusing on something deep within her mind. She stood unmoving, like a statue, for nearly a minute. Then her jaw snapped shut and she ground her teeth together.

"The hag," she murmured, as if dredging a name out of her subconscious. "The iron hag."

"What's that?" asked Jackson.

"Never mind," said Alicia, her cheeks flushing red. "Forget I said it. Just remembering a story from my childhood."

The purr of the elevator cut off any further discussion. Alicia's face relaxed. She turned just as a short, swarthy man entered the parlor. Accompanying him, barely controlled by the steel chain leash around its throat and jaws, was a huge black panther.

"Sumohn," said Alicia, rushing forward. "I've missed you, baby."

Alicia knelt in front of the beast, her face level with the panther's. Gently she ran her fingers along Sumohn's neck. The beast growled, a deep rumbling sound that Alicia insisted was its way of purring.

"Glad to see me too, huh?" said Alicia, scratching the monstrous panther behind the ears.

Yellow eyes stared deep into Alicia's dark blue ones. The billionairess nodded, as if in reply to an unstated question. It appeared as if the animal and human were communicating by telepathy.

"Try to get me some more information about this Russian situation," said Alicia, rising to her feet, her features flushed. "Call our people in the State Department. Let them check with the CIA. See if you can find out what's happening by this evening. The sooner the better"

"You're going somewhere now, I gather," said Jackson.

"To Prospect Heights park," said Alicia. "Sumohn's tired of being kept in a cage. She needs exercise. It's been a while since we were in Brooklyn. I'm taking her for a walk."

Jackson frowned. "Prospect Heights isn't safe. The police

have declared it off-limits to citizens. Last week they threw in the towel and stopped patrolling the grounds, even during the daytime. Squad cars won't enter, even if they spot a murder taking place. Too many gangs and psychos hide in those woods, all armed with heavy artillery and anxious for a chance of blowing away some cops.

"The mayor washed his hands of the whole situation. He called the park a national disgrace. The city council wanted the national guard called out to clean up the place. But the legislature vetoed the funds."

Jackson shrugged his shoulders. No fan of politics, he was a strict believer in justice delivered from the muzzle of an automatic. "No way Republicans are going to help a Democratic administration. Meanwhile, the park is a free-fire zone. You'll be taking your life in your hands if you go in there."

Alicia laughed. "I'll be safe. Sumohn will protect me."

As if responding to her mistress' comments, the panther growled. Despite the big cat's mouth being muzzled by steel chains, it was a terrifying sound.

"I hope she can catch slugs with her teeth," said Jackson.

"Don't worry about me," said Alicia. "You get working on that report. I'm taking the bridge into Brooklyn. I'll be back in a few hours. Can't be too late. As I mentioned, I have plans for the evening."

"The Devil's Playground?" asked Jackson.

"You bet," said Alicia. "Alert the usual spies. It's going to be a hot night."

Which was more true than she could imagine.

CHAPTER 2

Brooklyn, NY—March 14, 1994

Huge white signs with blood-red lettering were posted on every gate leading into the park, declaring the area off-limits to law-abiding citizens. The posters, left untouched more as a grim joke than sage advice, were ignored by the crowds of people who constantly entered and left the forested area. Prospect Heights served as the major supply center of illicit drugs, assault weapons, and kept women in New York City. It was also the headquarters of more than a half-dozen major gangs and two terrorist groups.

Anything illegal could be bought for a price in the dense woods. That purchasing the goods required a certain amount of risk was a fact of life. It was all part of the New York scene. Those who couldn't adapt, left. Or died.

A fifteen-foot-high steel fence surrounded the entire park. The last attempt of a previous administration to keep the cancerous growth of the park from spreading through Brooklyn and the connecting boroughs, it worked more as a barrier to keep the police out than the criminals in. At least once a month, a body was found impaled on the sharp spikes that topped the posts. Several years ago a dozen heads had decorated the pikes for days, a grim reminder of the gang warfare that raged incessantly within the gates. No one dared enter the park alone, or unarmed. Unless that person was Alicia Varney.

The billionairess walked into the park through the gate not far from the site of the giant carousel, one of the last efforts in the futile attempt to restore Prospect Heights to its original glory. Sumohn padded silently at her side, barely held in check by a thin strip of leather. The black panther growled softly with every step. A great deal different than an ordinary jungle cat, the monstrous beast possessed more than five senses. It detected hostility in the woods. And death.

"I feel it too," said Alicia softly, talking to the panther as if it possessed human intelligence. "They're out there in the park somewhere. Watching and waiting for me. I first sensed their presence when I woke up this morning. Someone wants me dead. They're hiding in the woods. I thought it best to confront them here, on their home ground, instead of chancing their disrupting my plans for the evening."

They strolled around the first bend in the road, losing sight of the towering buildings less that a block distant. Though it was early afternoon, the woods were dark and threatening. No one else was in sight. It was as if they had left one world and entered another.

Bending over, Alicia removed the collar from Sumohn's neck. The big cat snarled its approval. Without another sound, the panther vanished into the forest.

Chuckling, Alicia tucked the leather strap into her belt. She had complete faith in her pet. It would find and eliminate those who meant her harm. It was just a matter of time.

Meanwhile, Alicia meant to enjoy her jaunt. The pressures of big business had been cutting more and more into her free time. Exercise consisted of an hour workout in the gym three times a week. It had been months since she had experienced the feeling of freedom walking in the woods gave her. She intended to enjoy every instant.

Cheerfully she wandered along the brick road leading toward the center of the park. Mentally she kept a close watch on the surrounding forests. Alicia had no desire to be surprised by any unexpected visitors. Jackson had been correct when he said that Prospect Heights park was no place for a young, unarmed woman. But Alicia was a great deal older than her bodyguard imagined. And she was not nearly as unprotected as Jackson thought.

The first hint of trouble came as Sumohn's scream of rage shattered the quiet of the forest. Alicia grinned, recognizing the sound of a kill. One less enemy to worry about.

Five others, though, she realized abruptly, were

surrounding her. She sensed their presence in the woods to the north, south and west. The last two were walking down the road toward her from the east. They were all armed with pistols or shotguns. And their thoughts were filled with murder.

"I refuse to let anyone interrupt my plans," muttered Alicia, angrily. "Death is not an acceptable option at this stage of the game. Sumohn, attend me. There is killing work to be done here."

"Hey, lady?" The speaker was a short, thin man around thirty, dressed in a pair of faded blue jeans. He wore no shirt, despite the cool March weather. A tattoo of a naked woman with an arrow passing through her breasts adorned his hairless chest. Stuck in the waist of his pants was a .45 automatic. "You lost or something?"

"Yeah," said his companion, tall and wide, with a shaven head, pencil-thin eyebrows, and a perpetual leer. He also wore jeans and no shirt. A 12-gauge shotgun, carried loosely in one hand, was his weapon. "Or maybe you're looking for some action."

Alicia sighed, realizing immediately why the assassins were holding their fire. Seeing her unarmed and seemingly helpless, they planned to rape her before killing her. She shook her head in disgust. Sex and death. The two were linked by unbreakable bonds throughout history. Her history.

"Actually," declared Alicia, taking a tentative step forward, "I was looking for some big, handsome men to satisfy the hunger inside me. I need to be *fucked*. Repeatedly. Do you two think you can help me?"

"Huh?" said the short man, her reply taking him completely by surprise. His face turned beet red. It was an old trick, but one that still worked. The jerks expected her to cower in fear, beg for mercy—not talk about sex. They weren't sure how to respond.

Meanwhile, Alicia sensed the three other assassins, drawn by her vulgar declaration, emerge from the woods. They didn't want to miss out on any of the action. All of her enemies were in plain view. They had her exactly where they wanted her. So they thought. None of them realized she felt exactly the same way, but with better reason.

"You heard me," said Alicia, raising her voice so that everyone could hear her. "I'm burning up. I want it so bad my body feels like it's on fire." She ran her hands up and down her hips, pressing the material of her pants tight against the skin. She moaned passionately. "If I don't get it quick, I'll go crazy."

"Hot damn," said the big man excitedly, his hands trembling as he fumbled with the buttons of his pants. "The bitch wants to get screwed, and I'm going to nail her right now. The rest of you jokers wait in line, 'cause I'm first."

"Like hell . . . " began his companion, reaching for his belt. He never finished the sentence. A black bolt of lightning smashed into his back, sending him sprawling to the pavement. Growling savagely, Sumohn snapped her huge jaws shut on the back of the man's head. His skull exploded in a red torrent of blood and brains.

Alicia whirled to face her other assailants. The three men were all trying to raise their guns. However, they were all experiencing uncanny problems with their coordination. Their bodies jerked to and fro in a ghastly parody of dancing as they struggled desperately to aim their guns at their swiftly advancing target.

"What the hell is wrong?" screamed the nearest of the trio, a young black man still in his teens. "I can't do nothing."

"A simple matter of paralyzing the part of the brain controlling motor skills," said Alicia with a smile. She thrust a hand at the speaker's unprotected neck. Her middle three fingers pierced the flesh right below his Adam's Apple. With a flick of her wrist, Alicia tore out the boy's throat. He collapsed to the ground, his lifeblood pumping out onto the road in a crimson fountain.

"Oh my god," cried the second man, desperately trying to swing his gun around to fire at Alicia. For all of his efforts, he could not get his finger to squeeze the shotgun's trigger. "Please, no."

"You play rough, you accept the penalties," said Alicia. Merciless but not cruel, she killed him with a sharp blow to the nose, smashing cartilage into his brain. He died without another sound.

The third man collapsed in a dead faint on the pavement. Alicia, bored with the proceedings, killed him with a quick twist of her hands that broke his neck. She was much stronger than anyone suspected.

"Very neat, Miss Varney," said a voice from behind her. "But not really very smart. You let yourself get distracted by the diversions. I'm the real threat."

Alicia turned, knowing she was too late. Sumohn was still engaged in ripping the tall man to ribbons. The panther was a wonderful ally but was too easily tempted. Her true enemy, a well dressed young man holding a Kobra submachine gun pistol, was already squeezing the trigger.

The stream of slugs never materialized. Instead, the sixth man, the one who had somehow evaded her telepathic sweep of the area, dropped to the ground, a look of bewildered disappointment on his face. Protruding from between his shoulder blades was the handle of a bowie knife. The rest of the blade was buried in his chest.

"I paralyzed his fingers so he wouldn't jerk the trigger by accident," said a blond man in a white suit and white shirt, walking over to the corpse. Bending down, he jerked the knife out of the body and wiped the blood on the dead man's clothes.

"His name was Leo Taggert. He made his headquarters in the fungus on Coney Island. Leo specialized in celebrity kills. The rest of the gang was local talent he hired just a few hours ago. You didn't detect his presence because he was a ghoul with a talent for hiding his thoughts. Fortunately, he never realized I was in the vicinity. His bad luck."

"Who are you?" asked Alicia. Though the blond man looked familiar, she was positive she had never encountered him before.

"A friend," he declared, sliding the bowie knife into a

sheath beneath his jacket. "Glad I could be of service."

He turned and started walking down the road. "Better call off your pet," he said in parting. "That man's quite dead."

Distracted for an instant, Alicia glanced at Sumohn. When her gaze returned to where the stranger had been, he was gone.

Quickly she mentally scanned the area. Discounting a drug dealer and his teenage customers, there was no one within a hundred yards of her location. It was quite mysterious. Alicia hated mysteries.

"Who was that man?" she asked Sumohn as the panther padded over to her. "Did you recognize his scent?"

Reading the thoughts of an animal, even a special beast like Sumohn, was nearly impossible. The big cat's mental images were a scramble of blood and death. There was not the slightest indication that the black panther had ever noticed the stranger. Nor had the beast noticed the man during its initial attack on the assassins. It was as if he appeared out of thin air. And disappeared in similar fashion.

"And this SOB," said Alicia, kicking the dead body of Leo Taggert in frustration, "called me by my name. He was no ordinary assassin employed by my business rivals. He was a ghoul. Which ties him in with the Kindred. And the joker knew enough about me to hide his thoughts. Damn."

She drew in a deep breath. "Assuming Jackson's loyal, and considering what I pay him I think he is, this means somebody's been studying me awfully closely for a long time. Or has links with my supposed friends at The Devil's Playground. Whoever it is wants me dead. And is willing to pay good money to get the job done."

First there had been the distressing tiding about Baba Yaga. Now came this assassination attempt, coupled with the appearance of the oddly familiar young man. Alicia wondered grimly what else could go wrong.

It was a question best not asked.

CHAPTER 3

New York, NY—March 15, 1994

Alicia entered The Devil's Playground a few minutes before one A.M. Wearing an outfit made entirely of layers of white lace, with nothing underneath, she attracted the usual stares and whispers. She never used her telepathic powers inside the club for fear they would raise questions she didn't want to answer. Still, she didn't have to read minds to know that most of the men desired her and that their dates despised her. Despite her age, and Alicia was much older than she looked, she was the best looking woman present.

Normally the billionairess arrived at the rock club several hours early and spent time flirting with the males present. Often she went home with one or several, depending on her mood and her lusts. Tonight she was late, due to certain precautions she deemed necessary after the attack in the park. Mentally she grimaced. Justine Bern was a bitch under the best of circumstances. Tonight was going to be very difficult.

Alicia was at the door leading to the private section of the club when she spotted a young blond man dressed in a white suit sitting at a booth across the floor. There was no mistaking the features of the mysterious stranger from her afternoon encounter. His head was bent in deep conversation with a stunning, redheaded woman wearing a dress covered with green sequins.

As if sensing her gaze, the man looked up and around. Spotting Alicia, he grinned and waved. Not knowing what else to do, she waved back. The club was too crowded for her to make her way over to his table. Nor did she have the time. At least, not now. She hoped the mystery man would still be there when she returned.

Unlike the Camarilla, which believed in numerous Traditions, the Sabbat was loosely organized and structured.

Caine's laws regarding sires and territories were ignored. The one principle that governed the cult was that of the jungle. The strong ruled by claiming and holding their position. As was the case with Justine Bern, the archbishop of New York.

Princes ruled cities controlled by the Camarilla. Archbishops did the same for major cities under Sabbat rule. Above them were cardinals, thirteen in number, who governed the thirteen regions of the Sabbat. Equal to them in power were the prisci, a board of advisors for the cult. Topping them all was the Regent. While technically the caretaker, not the ruler of the cult, the Regent's commands were rarely disobeyed. It was the position of ultimate power in the organization.

The current Regent of the Sabbat was Melinda Galbraith, who also served as Cardinal of Mexico City. She had ruled the cult with an iron grip for more than five decades. However, Melinda had been missing for months, following a major unexplained disaster in the region. A number of archbishops and cardinals were whispering it was time to appoint a new Regent. There were numerous contenders for the position. Including Justine.

"You're late, kine," snarled Hugh Portiglio as Alicia entered the large office that functioned as headquarters for Sabbat activities in New York. Tonight was the weekly meeting of the cult's inner circle of leaders for the city. Alicia, though human, was included because of her incredible wealth and influence. And because she was Justine Bern's ghoul.

Though the cult liked to think otherwise, the Sabbat did not completely control the Big Apple. They held the city as best they could, but the Camarilla had agents everywhere. And the werewolves, the Garou, were a force that could not be ignored.

There were nearly three hundred Kindred in the greater New York metropolitan area. Many belonged to the Sabbat, others to the Camarilla, and some were Caitiffs, loyal to neither.

"Wizards and ghouls just don't mix," declared Molly

Wade, snickering. "Hugh can't stand Justine's pet pussycat. He wants to be top dog."

"Shut up, you raving lunatic," snarled Portiglio. Molly was Justine's other advisor. A Malkavian antitribu of unknown generation, she acted, like most of her clan, totally demented. No one could tell if it was an act or she was really crazy. In either case, Molly possessed an incredibly devious mind and was a master plotter. Her advice, though often difficult to comprehend, was never wrong.

"Close your mouths, both of you," said Justine. The Archbishop of New York sat with her arms folded across her chest in a huge black leather armchair. She resided in half-light, surrounded by shadows, for darkness was the source of her greatest powers.

Embraced in her middle age during the early years of the Inquisition, Justine resembled a prim and proper matron, with dark hair drawn back in a bun, drawn features, and piercing black eyes. Plainly dressed in a shapeless brown dress, she looked like an old-maid chaperon at a school dance.

Originally a seventh-generation Lasombra, Justine had lowered her generation by killing her sire shortly after being Embraced and drinking his blood. A century later, she had trapped and killed a fifth-generation Ventrue elder, again drinking her victim's blood. Currently fifth generation, Justine harbored ambitions of yet greater triumphs. She was the personification of ruthlessness.

Less than a year before, Justine had risen to the post of Archbishop of New York. Her predecessor, Violet Tremain, had vanished under unexplained circumstances. So had Shawnda Dirrot, the priscus of Manhattan. No accusations had been made, but few doubted that Bern and her followers had been responsible for the two leaders' disappearance. In the Sabbat, the strongest survived. And rose to the top.

"I'm tired of your bickering," declared Justine coldly. "Remember who's in charge here. Neither of you are indispensable. You can be replaced without difficulty."

Portiglio's jaw snapped shut. He was deathly afraid of

incurring Justine's wrath. More than once before, she had made it quite clear to the wizard that if he annoyed her too much, she wouldn't execute him. Instead, she would drive a stake through his heart, paralyzing him, then deliver his body to the elders of the clan he had betrayed. The Tremere reserved special punishments for traitors that made the Final Death the preferable alternative.

Hugh glared at Alicia, obviously blaming her for his woes. Molly was correct. Portiglio was jealous of her influence with Justine. The wizard was a fool, but he made a dangerous enemy. Sometime in the near future, she would have to deal with Hugh. An anonymous tip to the members of the Society of Leopold headquartered at St. Patrick's cathedral would work wonders. She promised herself to have Jackson make the call tomorrow.

"Why *were* you late?" asked Justine, staring with burning eyes at Alicia. "The meeting was scheduled for midnight."

"Business problems," said the billionairess, her gaze meeting the Archbishop's own without flinching. "We are experiencing unexpected difficulties in our Russian operation. I apologize for any problems I caused."

"Apology accepted," said Justine. Though the Sabbat considered humans prey, cattle to feed their blood lust, some members of the sect used ghouls as personal retainers. Justine treated Alicia more like a favorite childe than a human pawn. It was an unusual, though not unheard-of relationship. "Don't be late again. I won't be so forgiving next time."

"Trouble in Russia, that's the pitch," said Molly unexpectedly, her face twisting at odd angles. A teenager with long blonde pigtails and crooked smile, she often spoke in rhyme. "The Old Hag is rising. And she's a witch."

"The Old Hag?" said Justine, leaning forward. "What are you talking about, Molly?"

"Baba Yaga," answered Hugh instead. "There's rumors that the Iron Hag has risen from torpor."

"Rumors, Hugh?" said Justine. "Since when have we dealt in *rumors?*"

"Facts are hard to come by, Archbishop," said the wizard hurriedly. "I've been trying to confirm the reports, but so far, all I've turned up are dead ends. As soon as I learn anything, I'll tell you. That's my job. Meanwhile, everybody's been talking about this Red Death stuff. That's been stirring up lots of talk."

"The Red Death?" repeated Alicia, not sure who or what Hugh meant by the phrase. "What's the Red Death?"

The Tremere *antitribu* shook his head. He was worried enough that he answered Alicia without his usual grimace of distaste. "No one knows. Some *thing* exterminated several of our minor drug merchants in DC. It held them in its hands and burned them to ashes. According to an eyewitness, the monster used real flames, not hellfire. It called itself The Red Death and claimed it was a member of the Camarilla seeking to destroy the Sabbat."

"Red as fire, red as fire," chanted Molly. "It's a liar. It's a liar."

"I agree with Molly," said Justine. "The Camarilla may be fools but they aren't stupid. There is no . . . "

The Archbishop broke off in mid-sentence. Eyes narrowing in amazement, she pointed to a corner of the room. "What," she asked, "is that?"

A red mist was materializing a few feet above the floor. Like a genie pouring out of a bottle, the cloud grew with astonishing speed. And, as it expanded, the cloud began to take the shape of a man.

"This can't be happening," declared Hugh Portiglio shrilly. "No Kindred can use Form of Mist and Materialization together without a linked mind on which to focus. It's impossible."

"You tell our visitor that if you dare," said Molly, suddenly sounding very sane. "I'm leaving right now. That has to be the Red Death."

The figure, solidifying rapidly in the corner, appeared to be that of a long-dead corpse. Tall and gaunt, it had a chalk-white face, decaying skin, and unblinking eyes that stared at them with utter hatred. Dressed in a tattered shroud, the creature was streaked with lines of crimson across its face and chest. Its fingers and hands glowed red, as if filled with fire.

"Death," the specter murmured as it turned solid. A gust of superheated air emanated from the monster's body, instantly raising the temperature in the small chamber. "I am the Red Death, and I bring final oblivion to the Sabbat."

"Like hell you do," said Justine. Pushing back her chair, she rose to her feet. Dark shadows clustered around her, like giant, carnivorous butterflies. Clenching her fists, the Archbishop raised her arms over her head, drawing the blackness to her fingers. Thrusting her hands forward at the Red Death, as if throwing a boulder, she evoked her most powerful summoning discipline.

"I am Master of the Night," intoned Justine. "Shades from the Abyss, attend me."

The darkness around the Archbishop swirled as if stirred by a sudden wind. Three shadowy, featureless figures, each the size of a man, coalesced in front of Justine. Shades, they were composed of solidified darkness. Denizens of hell, few vampires could summon them. Fewer still could stand before their might.

"Destroy this intruder," said Justine, and waved her shadow warriors forward.

The Red Death smiled, the ancient skin surrounding its mouth crinkling like yellowed parchment. It stretched out its arms, as if daring the three shades to grab hold. The darklings did exactly that. Their touch, the chill grip of the Abyss, normally paralyzed any being it touched. Not the Red Death.

Instead, the shades sizzled. Lines of crimson fire swept through them. The blackness forming the creatures boiled like steam rising from a kettle. Justine, her strength shared with her shadowy servants, gasped in unexpected agony. With a moan of disbelief, she collapsed into her chair as the three shades clutching the Red Death disappeared.

"I am the Red Death," repeated the spectral figure and took a step forward. "None can stand before me."

Very melodramatic, thought Alicia, tentatively launching a mental probe, *and in no rush to finish the job. This sucker wants to make a point. He's looking for publicity, not action.*

Supremely confident in her own abilities, Alicia was not ready the for searing, intense bolt of mental energy that greeted her telepathic inspection. She reeled with sudden, unexpected pain. The Red Death had been lying in wait for her probe. A bolt of psychic fire flashed through Alicia's mind, sending her staggering. Automatic safeguards, the results of lifetimes of experience, broke the contact before the Death could fry her brain to cinders. She was left with the momentary impression of four incredibly ancient vampires grinning in sadistic pleasure. They thought of themselves as "The Children of Dreadful Night," Groaning in agony, Alicia dropped to her knees.

"Out of here," snapped Justine, ignoring her ghoul's sudden collapse. Justine's universe revolved around one person—herself. Scurrying across the room, she headed directly for the exit. Grabbing the knob with both hands, she wrenched at the door leading to the hallway into the nightclub. It refused to budge.

"It's locked," shrieked Molly. "We're trapped and going to die!"

The Red Death laughed, a ghastly, gruesome sound. Shuffling forward, never lifting its feet from the floor, it reached for Alicia. Moaning in pain, the billionairess rolled away, evading the monster's grip. One touch, she guessed, meant death for mortal or vampire.

"Burning death for you all," said The Red Death. Crimson sparks flew from the spectral figure's hands. Alicia could feel the heat. The Death was a walking blast furnace.

"His touch is fire," roared Portiglio, huddling behind Justine. "We're doomed!"

"Shut the fuck up, you imbecile," snarled Justine angrily. She lashed out with a hand at the door. Wood paneling shattered like matchsticks, revealing reinforced steel plates beneath. The meeting room had been designed to resist Camarilla surprise attacks. "Stop screaming and help me."

"Burn," said the Red Death. The specter's right hand swept against Justine's desk. With a whoosh of flame, the black wood exploded. In seconds, the entire office was a raging inferno. "Burn in my wonderful flames."

"Not yet," whispered Alicia, struggling to her feet and into the corner diagonal from the Death. "Not yet."

"Fire, fire," screamed Molly, "higher, higher."

"Damned lunatic," replied Justine, slamming both hands into the steel plate. The metal crumpled and collapsed into powder. The Archbishop possessed the power to age material objects with a thought. Anxiously, she shoved her way past crumpled bits of rusted steel into the hallway leading to the club. Hugh and Molly scrambled after her—leaving Alicia alone in the burning office.

She was trapped. Trapped in the rear of the room, flames crackling all around her, facing the Red Death. Desperately, Alicia screamed to her comrades for help, but the vampires were gone. She was on her own.

"You were the only one who mattered," said the Death as it edged closer and closer. "I never planned harming the others. I needed them to survive so as to spread the word of my power. You, however, were always my target. I realized long ago that Justine was your pawn, though the fool thought she was the master. I needed you out of the picture before concluding my plans for the Sabbat."

Alicia tried to concentrate, tried to block the Red Death's words from her mind. Nothing mattered other than discovering some way out of her predicament. The bellowing flames, the stifling heat made it impossible to think. Tongues of fire licked at her exposed skin. Above her head, the ceiling ignited, dropping a shower of burning fragments into her hair. Smoke filled her lungs, making it difficult to breathe. And the Red Death stepped ever nearer.

Eyes stinging from the acrid smoke, Alicia stumbled blindly backward until her shoulders touched the rear wall. There was no place left to run. Hot ash stung her cheeks, scorched her clothing. She sobbed in frustration, the tears instantly evaporating in the heat.

"Pardon me," came a voice from the open door, catching both Alicia and her tormentor by surprise. "Would you mind if I interrupt this meeting?"

It was the young blond man from the park. His suit was sparkling white, as was his shirt. He wore no tie. His eyes, Alicia noticed in a haze of bewilderment, were a sparkling blue. He seemed completely nonplused by the flames filling the chamber.

"I really must talk with Miss Varney," said the stranger, nodding to the Red Death as if discussing the weather. "You don't mind if we say adieu?"

Not waiting for an answer, the blond man stepped into the office. Casually he walked into the heart of the inferno. Astonished, Alicia watched as he marched across the room toward her, ignoring the billowing flames. Fire grabbed at him but never seemed to make contact. His skin and clothing remained untouched, unblemished by the blaze.

Swerving around a dumbfounded Red Death, the young man arrived at Alicia's side in a matter of seconds. "Ready to go?" he asked, a gentle smile on his lips. He held out a hand. "I think it will be a great deal easier to talk in the other room. It's not as hot or noisy there."

"Whatever you say," declared Alicia. She grasped his outstretched fingers. His hand was cool and smooth. "I'm all set."

"Bye for now," said the young man, waving his other hand at the unmoving Red Death.

Alicia blinked as reality shifted. Reaching out, the blond stranger pulled open the door in the rear wall. He stepped through it, tugging Alicia after him. The flames and the Red Death were gone. They were in the main room of The Devil's Playground, close to the club's front entrance. Behind them, the portal slammed shut. Glancing over her shoulder, Alicia saw only bare wall.

"How did you do that?" she demanded.

"A trick my father taught me," said the blond man with a laugh.

He pointed to the rear of the dance floor. People were

starting to scream as tendrils of flame crept out of the hallway. "Justine and her cronies left by the emergency exit in the back. We'd better run, too. The fire is starting to spread. In a few minutes this whole place will be burning. And I sense there isn't any sprinkler system."

"Who, why, what?" sputtered Alicia.

"You sound like a journalism major," said the blond man. "The Red Death has departed. He cannot maintain Body of Fire for more than a brief interval. You are safe. At least for now. But he will return. He is a relentless enemy. You must destroy him. Or be destroyed."

"This is the second time you saved me today. I don't know why. Or who you are."

He shrugged as if dismissing her words. "We'd better move." People were shoving past them into the lobby. The screams from the back of the club were getting louder. "This crowd is turning ugly. There's going to be a full-scale riot shortly."

"You still haven't answered my question," said Alicia. "What's your name?"

"Call me . . . Reuben." He grinned. "Like the sandwich."

"And the woman you were speaking with?" asked Alicia, not sure why she asked. "Was she your lover?"

Reuben laughed. "Not likely. She's my sister. Her name is Rachel."

The young man glanced down at his bare wrist. "Oops, look at the time. I have to be going. I'm late."

"Wait," said Alicia. "Please stay. You never told me why you saved me. Or how."

"Sorry, Anis," said Reuben, "but I've said too much already." He peered over her right shoulder. "Say, is that your assistant, Jackson?"

"I'm not fooled so easily twice," said Alicia, smiling. And discovered she was talking to empty air. In the space of a heartbeat, Reuben had disappeared.

That was when she realized he had called her *Anis*.

CHAPTER 4

In the mountains of Bulgaria—March 16, 1994

The house on the hilltop was huge. And though it was well after midnight, with clouds hiding the moon and stars, the house was completely without lights.

"See," whispered Le Clair, "is it not like I told you? The ancient one lives here alone. The locals are so afraid of him that they refuse to speak his name. Or drive past the building after midnight. They say the devil lives inside."

"Close enough," said Jean Paul. "Dziemianovitch is a sixth-generation Tzimisce. His cruelty is legendary in these hills."

"All Tzimisce are maniacs," declared Le Clair. "That is why most of them belong to the Sabbat. Or live in total isolation, like this monster."

"We are all damned," said Jean Paul, nodding. "But some of us are more damned than others."

"Are we going to stand out here all night?" asked Baptiste, the third member of their party. "If we plan to drink the old bastard's blood, we'd better find him first."

"Right," said Le Clair. "Enough talk. Dziemianovitch is extremely powerful. However, in the past six months, he seems to have dropped off the face of the globe. The people from the village who clean and maintain the house and grounds have not seen or heard from him since late last year. He must be in torpor. Tzimisce need a great deal of rest. We should be able to enter the house, find his body, and destroy him without much trouble."

"Trouble or not," said Baptiste, "it will be well worth the price. You two are already seventh generation. I'm still eighth."

"Not much longer," said Jean Paul. He pointed to the massive oak door that served as the entrance to the mansion. "Shall we just knock?"

"I think not," said Le Clair. "There are windows on the

rear patio. Better to enter through them than to announce our presence. Dziemianovitch is no fool. He knows the value of his vitæ. The house is probably filled with booby traps. We must be very careful in our search. Very careful."

"Reminds me of the Great War," said Baptiste. "One wrong move and poof. You're dead."

The other two vampires nodded. Though it had been nearly eighty years ago since their experiences in the First World War, the memories of those days were still crystal clear. It was where they had met, become comrades, had fought and killed. And become vampires.

Three raw young Frenchmen recruited for trench warfare against the Germans, they had grown tough and hard after two years of fighting the Boche. Circumstances threw them together. Undeath forged them into a team.

Le Clair was the schemer of the bunch, a short, thin man with a pencil mustache and eyes that flickered from place to place, never resting. His family operated a smuggling ring in Marseilles.

Baptiste was big and strong, from the farmyards of the south. More muscle than brains, he found killing stimulating and had a cruel streak that he imparted to his bayonet.

Jean Paul was the relaxed, easygoing type. Tall and handsome, he had a taste for women and the suave, debonair charm of a Parisian bon vivant. Beneath his casual air was the soul of a sadist. He believed in sharing his conquests with his two friends. Any woman who dared protest the treatment he beat into bloody submission.

Effective, deadly fighters, they killed not for the glory of France but for the love of killing. Among foes and friends alike they became known as the Unholy Three. Often, after a major offensive, they roamed the battlefield in the dark, checking the abandoned bodies for any signs of life. What they did with the few soldiers they found pretending to be slain was never discussed in public. But more than a few badly injured German soldiers had been discovered dead in the war zone from a self-inflicted gunshot blast, choosing a suicide's death over a confrontation with the Unholy Three.

Their notoriety brought them to the attention of Louis Margali, an officer in their regiment and ninth-generation Brujah. An idealistic disciple of the teachings of Karl Marx and a veteran of the Student Uprisings of the 18th century, Margali dreamed of establishing a socialist republic in France after the war. Realizing that he needed followers capable of any excess in the name of liberty, the plotter Embraced the Unholy Three during the Battle of the Marne. However, Margali, more scholar than schemer, vastly underestimated the depravity of his new childer.

He discovered his terrible mistake the night they surprised him at an abandoned farmhouse in no-man's-land. Le Clair knew a great deal more about vampires than Margali suspected, including the fact that a wooden stake through the heart paralyzed even the most powerful Kindred. Baptiste provided the muscle, Jean Paul the distraction. With horrified expression, the Brujah officer listened as Le Clair explained their plan.

"My friends and I are not interested in your plans for a socialist utopia, Monsieur Margali," said the short man, his bright eyes glowing in the lamplight. "We care nothing for the common man or the rights of the working class. The only ones who matter are ourselves."

"You treated us like slaves," growled Baptiste, his huge hands curled into massive fists. "I ain't nobody's slave. 'Specially one of the Aristocracy."

"Perhaps crudely put," said Le Clair, "but otherwise accurate. The three of us refuse to accept these Six Traditions of Caine. Living or undead, laws mean nothing to us. We are masters of our own fate."

"We're gonna drink your blood," said Baptiste with a chuckle.

Le Clair nodded. "As leader of our little group, I claimed this first opportunity. But there will be other chances for my friends. All of us are ambitious. We plan to lower our generation through diablerie, and thus raise our powers, as often as possible. Humans will provide us with blood when necessary. But we shall prey on our fellow Kindred for our strength."

He smiled at the horrified look in Margali's eyes. Le Clair took great pleasure from mentally torturing his victims. "There are three of us. We work well as a team. It will take years, decades perhaps, maybe even a century or two. But, in the end, we plan to rule as the masters of Europe. Perhaps even the world."

"Stop playing with your food," said Jean Paul. "We want to be safely away from here before the sun rises. Kill him and be done with it."

Le Clair did exactly that. Now, nearly eight decades later, he and his comrades were stalking their ninth vampire. It was a dangerous game, but the rewards justified the risk.

"Nothing stirs within," declared Jean Paul. His hearing was a hundred times more acute than any human's. "The place is deserted."

"I doubt it," said Le Clair. "Tzimisces cannot rest peacefully during the day unless surrounded by handfuls of dirt from the place of their creation. They are poor travelers. Dziemianovitch is hiding somewhere in the mansion. Finding him is the challenge."

"You two talk too much," said Baptiste. He swung a ham-like fist at the windows on the patio. Three of them shattered in an explosion of sparkling glass.

"So much for the element of surprise," remarked Le Clair with a shrug of resignation. His companion was immensely strong but incredibly dumb. Baptiste held his own in any emergency requiring brute force. Thinking was not his specialty. He relied on his two friends for intelligence. And, too often, he grew impatient for them to act.

Jean Paul unlocked the windows and pulled them up. One after another, they crawled through the opening into the mansion. It was blacker than the night outside. Heavy curtains blocked out the moonlight.

"Sense anything?" whispered Jean Paul. The heavy darkness seemed to smother his words. "I don't hear a thing."

"Muting spell on the whole place," replied Le Clair. Recognizing and neutralizing spells was a talent of his. "That's what causes the darkness and the hearing loss. It's too powerful for me to cancel. But I think I can guide us through the place. Someone's in the basement. I sense a very powerful presence. It has to be Dziemianovitch."

"Just lead me to the old buzzard," said Baptiste. Tucked in his waistband were three wooden stakes. "I'll nail him good."

"Follow me," said Le Clair, grabbing each of his companions by the wrist. "Stay alert. There are traps everywhere. I'm trying to neutralize them as we walk. But I might miss a few."

"What sort of traps?" asked Jean Paul.

"Down!" screamed Le Clair as if in answer.

Veteran soldiers, they dropped without question. Like most Brujahs, they possessed inhuman speed. An instant after they touched the floor, the air sang as hundreds of steel-tipped arrows slashed across the room. If they had remained standing, they would have been staked by a dozen or more shafts.

"I bet the curtains slide open in the morning," said Le Clair, safely lying flat. "Letting the sunshine pour in and baking anybody caught to a crisp."

"Effective," commented Jean Paul. "Is it safe to rise?"

"Give me a few seconds more," said Le Clair, his face wrinkled in concentration. "There, that should do it. No more arrows. I disabled every similar mechanism in the mansion."

The three vampires rose to their feet. It was still as black as a coal mine in the chamber. "No more linking hands," said Le Clair. "It slows us down too much. Besides, we are safe now. The stairway leading to the basement is in the hallway about a dozen meters from here."

"You are positive there are no more traps?" asked Jean Paul. For all of his good looks and bravado with women, he was at heart a coward. It was a trait that served him well. Too often vampires followed their blood lust, succumbed to the beast within. Jean Paul never rushed in where the proverbial angels feared to tread. He walked slowly, always guarding his back, and ready to retreat at the first sign of danger.

"I told you," said Le Clair, inching his path across the floor. "I found and neutralized every mechanism in the . . ."

The small man screamed as the wood beneath his feet suddenly collapsed. He dropped like a stone, knowing that a horrible fate awaited his landing. But his feet never hit the ground.

Instead, Baptiste, stronger than an ox, grabbed him by the back of the neck. Effortlessly the big man held Le Clair dangling over the pit that had appeared as if by magic in the center of the chamber.

"Smells like acid below," commented Jean Paul, the barest trace of mockery in his voice. "There must be a pool of it covering much of the lower level. I am not sure what the lasting effects of a fall into it would be. Assuming it is a strong solution, the pool would most likely melt the flesh right off our bones, perhaps damaging our skeletons as well. It would take years and years to regenerate." The Parisian hesitated for effect. "The pit appears to be another trap to me."

"Quiet, you mealy-mouthed gigolo," snapped Le Clair angrily as Baptiste swung him back to the edge of the pit. "The fiend fooled me. Evidently, when this room was prepared for the unwary, he used sorcery to age the boards from here to the door. It was not an active, but an inactive trap. That was why my work failed. There was no mechanism involved, just my own weight."

"He is an ingenious devil," said Jean Paul. He ignored Le Clair's flashes of temper. The short man calmed down as quickly as he grew angry. "It will be a great pleasure killing him. How do you propose we make our way to the door if the rest of the floor is equally insubstantial?"

"I'm not sure," said Le Clair. "Let me think."

"I know what to do," said Baptiste. "Point me in the direction of the door, little man."

"Why do you ask?" said Le Clair, sounding puzzled, as he nevertheless turned his huge companion so that he faced the exit from the chamber.

"I'm tired of shuffling," said Baptiste. "Gotta move."

Before Le Clair realized what his companion planned, the big man grabbed him around the waist, lifted him over his head, and tossed him like a shotput across the decayed boards. The short man crashed head-first into the closed door, smashing it to bits. Cursing in rage, he collapsed into the outer hall. Le Clair noted with dulled senses that at least this corridor was well lit.

A second later, a shrieking Jean Paul followed him into the hall. With the door between the rooms gone, there was nothing to slow his flight. He hit the floor on the fly and bounced twice before coming to a stop only a few meters from the stairway leading to the basement.

"Watch out!" roared Baptiste from the darkness. "I'm coming through."

Hurriedly, Le Clair rolled to the wall. An instant later, his giant companion came hurtling through the smashed entrance. Baptiste had vaulted the acid pit without effort. Vampires possessed strength many times that of ordinary humans. Baptiste possessed strength many times that of ordinary Kindred.

"Well, we made it this far," declared Le Clair, struggling to his feet. "Time to descend and confront our foe."

He turned and glared at the giant. "Baptiste, your efforts are appreciated. But, please curb your impatience. Let Jean Paul and me do the thinking. Agreed?"

Shrugging his shoulders, Baptiste nodded. "I was only trying to help."

"Can you detect any activity below?" asked Jean Paul, staggering over to Le Clair. Jean Paul disliked surprises, especially ones that sent him unexpectedly flying over a pit of acid. "We've made enough noise to wake Dziemianovitch from the Final Death, much less torpor. In the future, I suspect we will be remembered not as the Unholy Three but as the Stooges Three."

"I sense a presence there," said Le Clair. "The same as before. He remains unmoving." Le Clair grimaced. "He knows we are here. And he finds our antics . . . amusing."

"Should we continue?" asked Jean Paul nervously. "If

Dziemianovitch is aware of our intentions, are we not doomed?"

"Oddly enough," said Le Clair, frowning, "I sense no hostility in his thoughts. He merely waits."

"Maybe he's tired of undeath," said Baptiste. The big man jerked open the door leading to the cellar. "We can't turn back. I want his blood."

Le Clair looked at Jean Paul and shrugged. "What the hell? We can only die."

"Once was enough for me," said Jean Paul.

"There's steps leading down," said Baptiste, ignoring his comrades' remarks. "And there's a light shining at the bottom of the stairs. I'm going."

"Onward, brave soldiers of France," said Le Clair grimly. He scuttled after the giant. "Liberty, equality, fraternity."

"Don't forget stupidity," added Jean Paul as he hurried after the others. "Slow down, you two. It's probably another trap. Where better to spring one than on steps?"

The warning was appropriate. Halfway down the staircase, the entire structure collapsed, much like the floor above the acid pit. Instead of a pool of acid, dozens of wood spikes a meter high were embedded in the basement floor, waiting to impale their victims.

Brujah speed, coupled with lightning reflexes, saved them. When the staircase crumbled, they leapt forward instinctively. They landed a few meters beyond the circle of stakes. And found themselves teetering on the edge of another acid bath.

"Diabolical bastard," grunted Le Clair as he edged around the deadly pool. The small man pointed to an open doorway. "But not as brilliant as he thinks. His coffin lies in the next room."

"Too easy," said Jean Paul as they peered through the entrance into the crypt. A single, dim light lit the room. In its center stood a massive stone sarcophagus. "It is too easy."

"Are you undone, Jean Paul?" asked Baptiste. "We have defeated darkness, arrows, acid, and stakes. Our reward, my reward, awaits." The giant tapped the three wood staffs beneath his belt. "I thirst for the old buzzard's blood."

Baptiste lumbered forward. He was just about to pass through the doorway when Jean Paul shouted, "No!" and pushed him to the side. "It's another trap."

"Trap?" questioned Baptiste. "The passage is clear."

"I sense nothing amiss," said Le Clair. "The floor is sound. And there are no mechanisms in operation."

"The best snares are the simplest," said Jean Paul. "Shall I demonstrate? Give me one of your stakes, Baptiste."

The big man handed over a wooden rod. Holding it by the end, much like a sword, Jean Paul slashed in an overhand stroke at the open doorway. The wood blade seemed to hesitate for the barest of instants in his hand, then continued on its downward path. However, it was no longer one piece of wood but three. Jean Paul held a stump in his hand, as the other two sections clattered to the floor.

"Magic," said Baptiste, making the word into a curse.

"Wires," replied Jean Paul. "Very thin, very tautly strung wires anchored to the doorposts. It is the probably the same type of material used in space satellites. It is made from incredibly dense, razor-sharp steel. Anyone rushing through the doorway would behead themselves."

"Sliced into pieces like a summer sausage," said Le Clair. "A gruesome end. How did you guess?"

"Why leave the door open?" asked Jean Paul. "After the traps we faced, it seemed extremely unlikely that Dziemianovitch would not have another trick up his sleeve. The entrance was too innocent, too obvious. That's when I focused my vision and spotted the wires crossing it."

"How do we pass them?" asked Baptiste, impatiently.

"The walls, of course," said Le Clair. "I am sure the wires are securely anchored to the doorposts. Those are probably booby-trapped. Ripping them out would be near impossible. The easiest method of defeating a trick is to discard the rules. We will not use the doorway. Instead, we will make our own."

Baptiste proved equal to the task. His immense fists smashed a large hole through the brick and mortar a meter past the door. Cautiously, Le Clair waved a hand through the opening before risking his body. By now, he was feeling quite paranoid about Dziemianovitch's preparations. A pack of hellhounds hiding in the shadows wouldn't have surprised him.

There were no more traps. But there was one more surprise.

Together, the trio of killers approached the stone sarcophagus. Baptiste trembled with excitement. "I'll drink his blood and lower my generation," he declared, his head bobbing like some giant Tinkertoy. "I'll drink his blood and become lots stronger. Lots stronger."

Le Clair nodded, unable to imagine his companion any more physically powerful. Baptiste already possessed the strength of an elephant. Instead, Le Clair hoped that perhaps the elder's vitæ would increase Baptiste's intelligence. It definitely could not lower it any.

Cautiously, the trio peered into the huge coffin. It was empty, and judging from the thin layer of dust on the bottom, had been empty for months.

"Impossible," declared Le Clair. "I sensed his presence here. I swear it." He paused, concentrated. *"He is still here. Somewhere in the room."*

Growling in frustration, Baptiste poked the coffin with a stake. "Not invisible. Maybe it's a trick box. He could be underneath it."

"Or hidden somewhere else in the room entirely," said Jean Paul.

"Or," said another voice, one colder than ice, "you mistook the thoughts of another Kindred for those of your prey."

"Shit," said Le Clair. He stepped away from the sarcophagus. He retreated to the wall, his friends at his side. "Who are you?"

A horrifying figure shuffled out of the shadows. A creature of blacks and whites, crimson stains kissed his face and chest. Tall and thin, the stranger wore a single garment consisting of a tattered old shroud. His face was that of a long-dead corpse, with decayed flesh, paper-thin lips, and hollow cheeks. "I am known as the Red Death. I have been waiting for you."

"Waiting?" said Baptiste, his huge fingers curling and uncurling into fists. "Why? What do you want with us?"

The Red Death chuckled, an unnatural sound that made Le Clair shiver. "I wanted to see if you could avoid the traps in the mansion. And, if you did, to make you an offer."

"Where's Dziemianovitch?" asked Jean Paul.

"The Final Death claimed him a few months ago," said the Red Death. "I'm afraid you were doomed to disappointment whether I waited or not." The monster's face twisted in a grotesque mockery of a smile. "His blood did not go to waste."

"Why should we listen to you?" asked Baptiste. The giant took a step forward. "Why shouldn't we just drink your vitæ instead?"

"Good question," said the Red Death. His body started to glow. Thin traces of smoke rose from his bony fingers. Sparks flew from his chest, his arms, his legs. His eyes glowed red. "Would you like to learn the answer?"

"No thanks," said Le Clair quickly. He could feel the heat coming from the Red Death's body. It was unnatural. He knew instinctively that a touch of the fiend's hand meant death. "What was that offer you mentioned?"

"I thought you might see reason," said the Red Death. "Besides, the venture holds a certain appeal to those of your persuasion. I want a certain Kindred killed. He annoys me but I don't have the time or patience to track him down. Instead, I want you three to do it. He is fifth generation but harmless. You can have his potent blood as your reward."

"Hey, that don't sound so bad," said Baptiste. "A Methuselah's blood. I like that."

"Besides which, he lives in Paris," said the Red Death. "It will be a homecoming of sorts for the three of you. His name is Phantomas. He is a Nosferatu and lives in catacombs of his own making beneath the streets of the city."

"We get to keep his possessions?" asked the always practical Le Clair.

"Of course," said the Red Death. "My only interest is that he is destroyed. Phantomas has lived beneath the city for two thousand years. I suspect he has numerous trinkets you would find quite valuable. Claim as many of them as you wish as part of your reward. I am a generous employer."

"With such terms, I see no way that we can refuse," said Le Clair. "We have a deal."

Cautiously, he stated the obvious. "I assume that we really didn't have a choice in the matter."

"Not," said the Red Death, "if you ever expected to leave this chamber."

CHAPTER 5

New York, NY—March 15, 1994

Alicia found Jackson at their usual rendezvous point a block away from The Devil's Playground. Fire engine sirens shrieked in the night as he opened her car door.

"All of our agents were in position tonight?" she asked as she slipped into the rear seat of the limo.

"Of course," replied Jackson, sliding behind the wheel. "Home?"

"Yes," she answered, "but just for a quick stop. I need to change clothes and perform a small errand. Then we will be going out again. There is a person I want to see about the situation I endured this evening. While we are at home, check with our spies. Also, have someone review the video tapes from the hidden monitors. I need to know everything possible about a creature that calls himself the Red Death. And a young man and woman named Reuben and Rachel."

"Anything you say," declared Jackson as he steered the car through late-night traffic. "I'll start checking as soon as we reach the penthouse."

The Devil's Playground was just one of the many buildings in Manhattan that Alicia secretly owned. Through subtle but intense mental manipulation, she had persuaded Justine to set Sabbat headquarters up in the club. The Archbishop, for all of her power, had no idea that her every movement was being monitored by secret video cameras built into the structure's walls.

"Justine, Molly, and Hugh left in a rush tonight," said Alicia, stretching out on the soft, white seat of the gigantic limo. "Your team manage the situation without any trouble?"

"No problem," said Jackson. "It's amazing what money can buy. I have the entire club surrounded by operatives. There's more than a dozen inside the premises as well, including several people on the staff. Overtone's equipped with a subvocal transmitter. Whenever the unusual occurs, the word goes out immediately. All three of your inhuman friends were picked up as soon as they departed. You'll have their destinations in the morning."

"Fine," said Alicia, "just fine."

She needed Justine. At least, she required the Archbishop's position for the moment. But Alicia also liked knowing where the Kindred rested during the daytime. It gave her an extra measure of power over them if the situation at The Devil's Playground ever soured. Or if Justine discovered the real truth about their relationship.

Wheels within wheels within wheels, thought Alicia as she closed her eyes and let the smooth hum of the car wheels lull her senses. *The game never ends. It just grows older and more complex.*

Fifteen minutes later, Jackson steered the limo into the Varney Building's garage. A special express elevator took them from the underground level to the penthouse in seconds. Entering the apartment, Alicia shed layers of lace as she walked. By the time she reached her closet, she was completely nude.

"Anything more on the Russian situation?" she asked Jackson as she pulled out the correct attire. Anonymity was required for her next trip. A full-length black bodysuit, long dark gloves, and a hooded jacket worked perfectly. Though before doing any more traveling, she needed to make a stop elsewhere first.

"Nothing conclusive," answered Jackson from the parlor. "I've been pressing our representatives, but, for a change, they are as much in the dark as us. Whatever is taking place in the Soviet republics is a mystery. It's as if someone has put a cork on all the news exiting the country."

Alicia grimaced in annoyance. And worry. Legends called the Iron Hag the most powerful sorceress ever to walk the earth. If she had indeed risen from torpor, anything was possible. Alicia shuddered. If the Nictuku were awakening, the Antedeluvians might be stirring as well. That thought was the stuff of nightmares.

"I'll return shortly," she told Jackson. She pressed a

section of the wall in the rear of her closet. Noiselessly, it slid to the side, revealing a compact elevator big enough for a solitary passenger. It descended to a level far beneath the bottom floor of the Varney building. A place where no other human being had ever walked. A crypt.

Fifteen minutes later, Alicia reappeared. Her cheeks glowed with an almost inhuman vitality. Her eyes sparkled. All of her fears, her doubts had vanished. She brimmed with self-assurance. With a laugh of savage amusement, she pressed the panel to close the entrance to the hidden elevator.

"The Red Death and the Queen of Night," she murmured to the walls. "We shall see who is the stronger."

"Did you say something, Miss?" asked Jackson from the other room.

"Just thinking aloud," said Alicia, raising her hood and drawing it around her head. She strolled into the parlor. "What do you think? Is the executioner's face well hidden?"

Jackson, putting down the telephone receiver, stared at her in bewilderment. "Say that again, Miss?"

"You don't listen to Bob Dylan, Mr. Jackson," she said with a smile.

"No, ma'am, can't say I do. I prefer classical music. Mozart and Bach are my favorites."

"Amadeus," said Alicia, her eyes clouding for an instant. Then, shaking her head as if to clear the cobwebs of memory, she walked over to the huge picture window overlooking the city.

"What did you learn?" she asked, staring into the night.

"Nothing particularly useful," said Jackson. "Your three friends split up shortly after leaving the club and returned to their usual hideaways. The fire department put out the blaze. It was confined to the rear of The Devil's Playground. Three people were trampled in the stampede to get out. That's about it."

"My friend with the blond hair and white suit?" asked Alicia. "The man I described to you. He said his name was Reuben."

"One of our agents on the police force questioned the chief bouncer for the bar. Implied that he was searching for this Reuben character in regards to the fire. The stooge came up blank." Jackson raised a hand, anticipating Alicia's next question. "Nor did he remember the woman in the green dress."

"Our cameras?" asked Alicia, expecting the worst.

"Amazingly, your mysterious acquaintance avoided being taped. I thought the machines were angled so as to completely cover the floor of the club. But I must be mistaken. He wasn't in any of the videos."

"Don't be so quick to fault the equipment," said Alicia, her eyes rising to the heavens. She stared at the full moon as if searching for an answer. "Reuben is a mage. The greatest I have ever encountered. He twists reality to suit his purposes."

"A mage?" said Jackson. "You mean a magician? Like those guys in Las Vegas with the tigers?"

"Not a showman or a trickster, Mr. Jackson," said Alicia. "A person who alters the universe with his mind."

"Whatever you say, Miss," replied Jackson dubiously. A hard-headed materialist, if the ex-soldier couldn't touch it, he didn't believe in it.

"These are strange times, Jackson," said Alicia. "Too strange for my tastes."

She turned from the window and started for the door. "There's only a few hours of darkness left. No time to waste. There's an old woman I want to visit in the Bowery. Now."

"The Bowery," repeated Jackson. "Another fine neighborhood. A step above Prospect Heights Park because there's no fence around it. Same gangs, same problems, though."

"You have your gun?" asked Alicia as she pushed the button for the garage.

"Of course," said Jackson. "I always carry it."

"If anyone bothers us, use it. Shoot to kill. No second chances tonight."

"Yes, Miss," said Jackson. "Whatever you say."

The drive ended in front of a dilapidated old brownstone in the shadows of the elevated subway line. Five young men, dressed in black leather, heads shaven, sat on the steps leading into the building. They stared at Alicia and Jackson with undisguised hostility.

"Whatcha want, lady?" asked the biggest of the quintet, his gravelly voice dripping menace. Pale gray eyes flickered from Alicia's limo to Jackson, then back to her. He was obviously trying to decide if she was worth a struggle.

"Yeah, whatcho want?" echoed another member of the gang. He opened a palm and revealed a switchblade knife. With a sigh of air, the six-inch blade slid into view. Looking straight at Jackson, the teenager sneered. "You too, motherfucker."

The former Green Beret smiled. His gaze met Alicia's and she dipped her head in answer to his unspoken question. Normally, Alicia tried to avoid violence. She didn't like attracting attention. But after dealing with frustration all evening, she had reached her limit.

"What's wrong, moth. . . " the same punk started to ask when Jackson acted. For a big man, he moved incredibly fast. Years of jungle warfare had filed his nerves to a razor's edge. Two steps forward brought him level with the teenager. One hand caught the boy by an ear and wrenched his head back. The punk's jaw dropped in shock. As if in reply, Jackson pulled a massive .357 Magnum Police Special from beneath his coat and slammed it between the gang member's teeth. The boy shrieked in pain as red blood spurted onto the stairs.

Alicia, never satisfied with merely watching, stood inches away from the leader of the group. One hand was buried in the soft flesh of his neck, her long, painted fingernails embedded in white skin. "Don't say or do anything stupid," she remarked calmly to the young man, who stood paralyzed with fear. "Squeezing my fingers shut will rip out your carotid artery. It's a very painful way to die. Don't give me an excuse."

"Anybody feel like a hero?" asked Jackson, wrenching

his prisoner about by the ear so that he was directly in line with the other gang members. Jackson's hand on the gun sticking in the punk's face remained steady. The boy's eyes were glazed in shock. "I can blow you away firing *through* this sucker's skull. Might be sort of messy. Your call."

"Hey," gasped the punk in Alicia's grasp. "We don't want no fuckin' trouble. We were just talking."

"Well," said Alicia, tightening her fingers just enough to start blood oozing, "learn to keep your *fuckin'* mouth shut. Understand?"

"Yeah, yeah," said the young man anxiously. There was death in Alicia's eyes. "I understand good."

"That's nice," said Alicia. "Now, you be a nice boy and tell us where Madame Zorza resides. Then maybe I'll let you and your buddies loose."

"The old witch?" asked another member of the gang, frozen during the entire encounter. "She lives on the third floor. Fuckin' weird bitch."

"Isn't she," said Alicia, nodding. With a shove, she sent her captive stumbling down the stairs. Seemingly by magic, she held a compact automatic in one hand. She waved it at the others. "You can release our foul-mouthed young friend, too, Mr. Jackson. Enjoy the rest of the evening, children. If I see you nearby when we leave, I will assume you are planning something nasty. And Mr. Jackson and I will respond in kind."

Dragging their wounded with them, the quintet disappeared into the night. "They'll be back," said Jackson. "With plenty of reinforcements. All armed with heavy-duty firepower and ready for war. Kids don't take threats seriously these days."

"Pity," said Alicia, holstering her gun. "Children should not be seen or heard. Their presence complicates life a bit. I'll be inside a little while. Madame Zorza speaks in riddles usually. It takes a remarkable amount of patience to comprehend what she means."

"We've come to this slum," said Jackson, "to visit a gypsy fortune teller?"

"*I've* come to these slums to visit a fortune teller," said Alicia. "You stay here. I need to speak to Madame Zorza alone. In the meantime, use the car phone. Summon aid. If these punks want trouble, give it to them. Scorched earth policy. No mercy. Use whatever manpower you need."

"You'll be okay in this rat hole with a crazy woman?" asked Jackson.

"Madame Zorza and I are old friends," said Alicia, wrenching open the door to the tenement. "We go back years and years."

Climbing the rickety steps that led to the third floor, Alicia reflected that years was not quite the proper term. She had known Madame Zorza for centuries.

The gypsy fortune teller was a Kindred mystic, a member of the Gangrel Clan. Of unknown generation, she had lived in New York City for nearly two hundred years. Before that, Alicia, in other guises, had known her in Europe during the time of the plague. A seeress with unexplained powers, Madame Zorza predicted the future with unwavering accuracy. She spoke, however, in vague, secretive riddles. And like all fortune tellers, she always demanded a price.

Only one apartment remained on the third floor. The other two were gutted ruins. Carefully, Alicia drew the black hood around her face so that only her eyes showed. Madame Zorza refused to speak to anyone if she saw their face. Alicia refused to speculate why.

She knocked. Three times, in a pattern she had been taught five hundred years before.

"Enter, Queen of Night," came a voice from inside. "The door is unlocked. I have been expecting you."

Zorza spoke English with a harsh, guttural accent. It was often difficult to understand what she was saying. Alicia shook her head in dismay. She had decided only a few hours ago to visit the fortune teller. How had the witch known she was coming?

Alicia pushed open the door and stepped into the apartment. The parlor was in near total darkness. A lone candle, nestled in a polished skull, burned on a round table at which there were two chairs. On one of them sat Madame Zorza. She was a tiny, thin woman with haggard, wrinkled features.

A black cloth decorated with mystic symbols stitched in silver thread covered the table. Alicia remembered seeing the same cloth on her first visit to Madame Zorza seven hundred years ago. Like the fortune teller, it never changed.

"Sit," said the vampire, gesturing to the other chair. Her aura burned bright. Madame Zorza was small in body but great in spirit. "I know why you are here."

"Of course," said Alicia. "You always do. What is the price to be paid?"

The fortune teller remained silent. Instead, she waved a hand over the candle in the skull, making strange symbols in the air. The flame quivered, as if exposed to a sudden draft. The fire appeared to dance to the intricate pattern woven by her ancient fingers. "Tonight there is no charge. I will tell you what you wish to know for free."

"Free?" said Alicia, immediately suspicious. "Why?"

The fortune teller smiled but said nothing. Alicia sighed in frustration. Madame Zorza's mind was a closed book. Reading her thoughts was impossible. Whatever secrets the ancient vampire held in her mind she kept well hidden.

A gun cracked outside. Then another. The sullen throb of a submachine gun filled the air. Alicia stirred uncomfortably. Jackson could take care of himself. Still, sooner or later, major gun battles like this drew police attention. She did not have much time to waste with Madame Zorza.

As if reading Alicia's thoughts, the fortune teller began to speak. The candle's flame swayed with each word.

"Thirteen, three, and one," Madame Zorza murmured. "The numbers always matter. Many are not what they seem. The numbers always matter. The answer is in the past. The answer is in the future. The children play the game. The rules are in no order. The numbers always matter. The ratman knows the answer. But he has not been asked the question. And most of all, the numbers always matter."

Alicia stared at Madame Zorza. "That's it? That's it! I'm supposed to make sense from that gibberish?"

The fortune teller nodded. A faint smile crossed her lips. Legends tied the Gangrel Clan with the Lupines, the werewolves. Many of the bloodline had wolfen features. Not Madame Zorza. Her face resembled that of a mythical beast—the sphinx.

"Go," she said. "You have what you came for. Use the knowledge well. The future of the Kindred depends on your actions."

"*The future of the Kindred?*" repeated Alicia with a harsh laugh. "Since when has the Queen of Night ever worried about what happens to the Children of Caine?"

"We are all dancers in a Masquerade of Blood," said Madame Zorza. "Your disguise cannot hide your interest, Anis."

"Damn," said Alicia, rising. "That name again. Second time tonight I've been called that. I must be losing my touch. Soon I'll be getting letters addressed to Anis. Maybe even junk mail."

Madame Zorza did not respond. Alicia hadn't expected that she would. With a nod of respect, Alicia left the apartment and headed back down the stairs outside. It had been a long evening. She needed rest. And a chance to ponder the meaning of the fortune teller's words.

CHAPTER 6

New York, NY—March 15, 1994

Walter Holmes looked astonishingly ordinary. He stood a shade under six feet tall, weighed 180 pounds, had a plain but unremarkable face, with cool, slightly hazy eyes that never seemed entirely focused, and a constantly bemused look of quiet desperation. His hair was brown and his skin unnaturally white. Unlike many of his kinsmen, he dressed conservatively in brown or black slacks and light-colored dress shirt. He spoke softly, with a slight accent that sounded vaguely Scottish or Welsh.

To the Kindred of New York, Walter was a late-generation vampire of no particular note. He was a regular at the Perdition Club, a hideaway frequented by anarchs, the rebellious, younger vampires of the city. Walter stayed in the background, avoiding trouble, sipping his glass of blood at a dark table, watching the world pass by. Unlike most of the Kindred who spent their nights at Perdition, he never bragged of his killings or deceptions. As far as anyone could tell, he had no ghouls nor any childer. The few vampires who spoke to him with any regularity assumed he was Caitiff, a loner without clan or prestige. Walter never said or did anything to change that impression. No one knew much about him, nor did they care. Vampires possessed little curiosity about their perceived inferiors. And even less compassion. In the darkly-hued world of the Undead, Walter Holmes was nearly colorless.

Walter's only claim to uniqueness was his overwhelming obsession with playing cards. He was never without a deck. When alone, he dealt himself hand after hand of solitaire. Studying each card intently, he played with a passion that bordered on mania. Other vampires joked that Holmes thrived not on blood but printer's ink. When he could persuade others to join him, Walter indulged in his greatest infatuation—poker. He played five card draw, seven card stud, dead man's call, blind man's bluff, and a hundred other variations. He played for dollars, for markers, for drinks. The amount didn't matter. He lost as often as he won. The results weren't important. Walter gambled for the sheer pleasure of gambling. It made undeath bearable. Or so he told anyone willing to answer.

Paranoid to an extreme, suspicious to a fault, the Kindred of Perdition never once questioned Walter's identity or motives. He was much too obvious, too weak, to be a concern. None of them realized that oftentimes, instead of hiding, the best disguise was staying in plain sight.

Walter Holmes was a much better gambler than any of the anarchs at Perdition realized. He had had plenty of practice over the centuries. Those few who knew his true name and history understood his obsession. The terribly ordinary-appearing vampire was actually two thousand years old. Once he had been a Roman centurion. Now he was the Inconnu Monitor of New York.

Before there was the Sabbat, before the Camarilla was formed, there was the Inconnu. It was the oldest and most mysterious sect of Kindred in existence. Few outside of the order knew its history. Or who belonged. Or the unstated goals of the organization. But there were stories. Many, many stories.

Legend had it that only fourth- and fifth-generation vampires belonged to the Inconnu. Other tales said that the group was founded by Vlad Tepes, perhaps the most famous vampire of all time, during the Middle Ages. A third report claimed that Saulot, the mythic third-generation Kindred who had first achieved Golconda, was the original leader of the sect. And that Tremere, who had practiced diablerie on Saulot a thousand years ago to raise his bloodline to cult status, had also been trying to destroy the Inconnu through the same action.

The purpose of the sect, some said, was for the pupils of Saulot to follow their master into oblivion by achieving Golconda. The purpose, argued others, was to obliterate their blood enemies, the Tremere. Or perhaps the Sabbat. Or even the Camarilla. Or maybe all of them. Or none.

A popular tale said that the leaders of the Inconnu lived in a castle that transcended the barriers of space and time. This collection of vampire elders known as "The Twelve" consisted of the most powerful group of Cainites belonging to any sect on Earth. Whatever their wishes, they could not be denied. Another story described the feud between the Inconnu and the Tremere as an offshoot of the Jyhad. According to this scenario, the Inconnu were the guardians of the status quo, seeking to destroy the one cult whose members might someday challenge their control of mankind.

Unconfirmed reports said the Inconnu secretly moved among the Kindred, manipulating their descendants as pawns in an ancient games of intrigue. Just as common were the stories that said that the Inconnu had one rule—never interfere in the affairs of the Undead.

Watch and wait. Conspire and plot. There was a glimmer of truth in the stories—and lies in them as well. Exactly as the Inconnu desired. Most of the stories originated with them. And were spread for a purpose only they understood.

Tonight Walter Holmes played solitaire and watched. His soft eyes scanned the club, seemingly without interest. No one realized how much he saw. Or how well he heard. Walter missed very little. It was his job to wait and listen. And report what he learned to the leaders of his sect.

Carefully, he shuffled the cards and dealt. His fingers moved smoothly, handling the deck like an old friend. Walter could do miracles with the cards when he wanted. Each one had a certain distinct feel. To someone with his raised senses, he could tell what each card was by touch. Sorting them in a specific order, dealing from the top, bottom, and even middle of the deck, was easy with practice. Walter was very patient. And very persistent. He practiced constantly.

"Mind if I sit in for a hand or two, dealer man?" asked a familiar voice. A teenage girl with long blonde pigtails and crooked smile slid into the chair directly across from

Holmes. "I feel lucky tonight."

"Always glad to engage in a game of chance," answer Walter, smiling faintly. He pulled a thick handful of chips from his pants pocket and split them up into two stacks. One went across the table and he kept the other. "The usual stakes?"

"Of course," said Molly Wade. "Whoever has the most chips at the end of an hour pays for drinks." She licked her lips. "I hear the blood is fresh tonight. They caught a couple of thugs trying to break into the back room the other morning. Ghouls sliced and diced and drained them dry."

She grinned. "Like Marion Crawford said, *For the Blood is the Life*."

Holmes nodded, shuffling the cards with extra care. His fingers moved faster than seemed possible. "Great title. Terrible story."

"I met Crawford in Italy about eighty years ago," said Molly. "Told him how much I liked 'The Dead Smile.' He remarked how I seemed rather precocious to be reading such stuff." She grinned. "If he only knew."

"You are older than you look, Molly," said Holmes and dealt the first hand. The game was seven card stud. "Ace showing," he declared softly. "Your bet."

"One chip for Molly," she chanted. "Two for luck."

"I'll chance that bet," replied Walter. He matched her chips with his own, then turned over another card. "Ace and jack. You're still high."

To anyone watching, it was an ordinary game of cards. With only two players, both evidently familiar with the other's style of play, it moved swiftly from hand to hand. The cards ran good and bad for both participants. The level of chips in front of them varied, but after nearly an hour, neither of the pair was appreciably ahead.

The story told by the cards was another matter entirely.

There are fifty-two distinct cards in a poker deck. Twenty-six letters make up the alphabet. Twenty-six multiplied by two gives fifty-two. A brilliant cryptographer could easily assign a letter to two cards of the same number and color, and thus spell messages in code by dealing several hands of poker. It was a unique method of carrying on a conversation and of learning important information in the midst of a crowd.

Why are you here tonight? Holmes asked through the course of several hands. *We were not scheduled to meet until later in the week.*

Molly replied in short word bursts as the deal passed between them. *Major troubles I thought you should know about immediately. A mysterious Kindred calling himself The Red Death attacked Justine a few hours ago. He claimed to be part of the Camarilla. Used fire.*

Walter Holmes' eyes narrowed slightly, an indication to those few who knew him well of intense surprise. *The Red Death? I never heard that name before. Did you recognize him? Was anyone destroyed?*

Molly shook her head. "Cards are running against me." She took the deck from Holmes' fingers. "Let me do a quick run on the table for a change of luck."

The Malkavian girl shuffled the cards and quickly spun them out on the table in a backwards pyramid. Her deft fingers never hesitated. Card followed card, forming an intricate pattern that only she and Walter Holmes understood. Six times she dealt, studied the markers for an instant, then swept them up in her hands and dealt again.

I concentrated on reading his bloodline, signaled Molly. *Without success. It was impossible to determine his clan or generation. His control of flames was flawless. A deadly trick. Justine, Hugh, and I escaped without harm. Alicia was left behind. Justine was upset later that we forgot her pet. I don't know if she survived.*

"Nicely done," said Holmes. He retrieved the cards, mixed them casually, then dealt out a new hand. "Five card draw. Jacks or better to open. Trips to win."

Alicia escaped, he messaged. *She was spotted elsewhere by my agents tonight.*

Killing her is not easily done, he continued. *She has a powerful protector.*

Justine, was Molly's message when the deal returned to her. *The bitch is Justine's ghoul. She has been for a hundred years or more.*

Perhaps, came Holmes' answer. *Have you ever actually seen Alicia drinking any of Justine's blood? Or wonder why the Archbishop treats her so well?*

No, replied Molly. *Some questions cannot be asked. Even by one supposedly as mad as me. Justine would have my head. Are you implying that Alicia is more than an ordinary retainer?*

There is a dark cloud hovering behind that woman, Holmes spelled out in the cards. *Be careful around her. If you appear to threaten her schemes, she will crush you like a bug. She has ambitious plans. And possesses the power to carry them out.*

Molly appeared amused by the warning. With a sly smile, she dealt out a new message. *You worry too much about the shadows, my friend Walter. You act almost as if this Alicia was the Queen of Night.*

"I think she is," said Walter Holmes aloud, his voice trembling just the slightest. "I think she is."

CHAPTER 7

New York, NY—March 15

Alicia's mood was as bleak as the afternoon sky. Dark, gray clouds hung over the city, pounding the metropolis with a steady downpour. The world outside her windows was cold and grim, ashen as a shroud. The incessant patter of the raindrops on the penthouse roof made deep thought impossible. There was no escape from the gloom and despair of the weather. Alicia lived for the sunshine.

Restless, she prowled back and forth, wearing a groove in the thick plush carpet of the parlor. Playing in the background on her stereo was "Siegfried's Funeral Music" from *Götterdämmerung*. The somber, melancholy music, with its slowly rising crescendo, perfectly fit her thoughts. The twilight of the Gods was approaching. And she seemed powerless to stop it.

As the music rose to its final climax, with its clash of cymbals and roar of horns, then dropped to the grim, subdued conclusion, Alicia's face twisted with impotent rage. She refused to let circumstances become her master.

Returning to her apartment nearly at dawn, she had slept in all morning, rising only a short time before. There had been a message on her machine from Justine, directing her to come to an anarch nightspot known as Perdition located on Manhattan's south side at midnight. The Archbishop sounded worried.

Alicia didn't blame Justine. She was equally worried. In her entire existence, she had never encountered a being like the Red Death before. She had never even suspected that it was possible for a member of the Kindred to control fire as easily as the monster managed. If it had not been for Reuben, Alicia had no doubts she would have been burned to ashes at the club.

Thinking of Reuben made her wince. Physically, the

young man was quite striking. However, at the present time, the last thing Alicia wondered about was whether he found her equally attractive. The mysterious stranger was an enigma. He possessed unexplainable, undreamed-of, powers. And he knew much too much about the Kindred—and Anis.

"Are you interested in looking at the mail, Ms. Varney?" asked Jackson, breaking her train of concentration. "No messages of any importance. All of our ongoing inquiries and investigations are still unanswered."

"How wonderful," said Alicia sarcastically. She walked over to her assistant and took the letters from his hands. "The universe is coming to an end. But our spies can't seem to discover what is going wrong."

"They're trying," said Jackson. He grinned. "They don't want to face your temper."

She laughed in spite of her foul mood. "Better me than Justine Bern. If they failed in a mission for her, she wouldn't be so pleasant. Or so forgiving. She doesn't tolerate excuses. Death is the least of her punishments."

"Hard to keep employees with that sort of policy," said Jackson, grimly. He knew, having seen Justine in action on videotape, how vicious the Archbishop could be.

"Remember that the Sabbat think of humans as cattle," said Alicia. "The kine supply them with blood and sometimes render minor services. Mortals are otherwise worthless. That's why Sabbat members routinely kill anyone suffering from AIDS they meet. To them it's not murder, merely cleansing the blood pool of harmful diseases."

Alicia glanced quickly at the mail. The first two pieces were from her lawyers, regarding business matters that needed immediate attention. She quickly scanned the contents of each missive, then walked to the phone and dialed the legal department. It only took a few minutes to clear up both problems.

That finished, she opened the rest of the letters. Nothing appeared important until she ripped apart the bottom envelope. It came from her clipping service and contained two newspaper articles. They were from an Australian newspaper and were dated from last week, a day apart. As Alicia read the two clippings, she felt the chill of the grave creeping through her veins.

The first piece described a riot that had taken place the night before in the city of Darwin in the Northern Territory. Hundreds of Aborigines had raged through the streets for hours in what was described as the worst incident of native unrest in the history of the territory. Eighteen people had been killed—three shopkeepers and fifteen Aborigines. The police had first used water cannons and rubber bullets, but when they proved ineffective, had opened fire on the crowd with live ammunition.

The mayor and town councilmen, in a rare display of unity, praised the handling of the affair by the lawmen. Moreover, the officials made it quite clear that any further activities by the natives would be treated as "civil war." They further stated that they would then not be responsible for the actions that followed. Alicia knew something of the bitter history of Australia. *Genocide* was the first word that came to mind.

Tucked away in the bottom of the article was the reason for the violence. Earlier that evening, the first government trucks had arrived in the native shanty town. They had come to begin the task of returning the Aborigines to their home at the foot of the Macdonnell Ranges. Evidently, it had been the news of this forced relocation plan that sent the natives out into the streets. They did not want to return to the Tanami desert. Though no colonial in Darwin was sure why.

The second newspaper clipping was from the next day. It was a short, terse report describing a frightening slaughter that had taken place, the same evening as the riot, on a cattle ranch thirty miles outside the city. Police had gone to the location at the request of the rancher's brother, who had been trying unsuccessfully to raise his relative on the phone the entire day. The bodies of the man, his wife, and their three children had been discovered lying in the grass outside the main building, with their heads missing. There was no sign of a struggle, though the ground around them was soaked with their blood.

Though the victim's wounds were not delineated in great detail, it was clear from the article that their heads had not been found. And that from the gnawed, mangled condition of their necks, it appeared as if their heads had been chewed off by the teeth of some colossal beast.

Adding to the horror was the mention that a check of the barn and fields revealed that every farm animal on the ranch -from cattle to chickens to the family dog—had also been killed in the same manner. Something unimaginable had passed through the area and sliced off and taken the heads of every single living mammal. It was all very puzzling.

"Are you all right, Miss Varney?" asked Jackson. He sounded concerned. "Bad news?"

Alicia nodded. "The worst, Jackson. The very worst."

"Anything I can do?"

"I doubt that anyone can do much," replied Alicia. She paused, as if the words brought back an old memory. "Perhaps there is one. An old friend, a very old friend. I haven't seen him for many years. He always seems to have a solution for every mystery."

"Maybe you should give him a call," suggested her assistant. "Very old friends don't mind being bothered."

Alicia smiled. "He's different than me, Mr. Jackson. A rolling stone, he never stays long in any location. I have no idea where he is or how to find him. This mess is my problem, and somehow I have to deal with it."

With a sigh, she passed the two newspaper articles to her assistant. He scanned them without comment. Working for Alicia, he was no longer surprised by anything she showed him

"Do we have anyone in Australia?" asked Alicia. "Specifically, the North Territory?"

Jackson shook his head. "Not that I recall. Our business interests are handled by companies jointly held with the Asian Conglomerates. They supply the cheap labor and resources. We're responsible for the technology."

"What about our less *publicized* operations?" asked Alicia.

"No luck," said Jackson. "The Triads control the Australia underworld with a steel fist. Nobody can break their grip. Even the Mafia steers clear of the Triads."

"I want one of our top men in Darwin within the week," said Alicia. "Smart, tough, and quick on his feet. Find me someone and get him into the country quickly. I want first-hand reports on the situation there. Meanwhile, instruct the clipping service to search the Australian newspapers for follow-ups to these stories. In particular, alert them to the name Nuckalavee."

"Spell it for me," said Jackson. "Why don't I like the sound of that word?"

"The Skinless One," said Alicia quietly. "It's a creature in Australian Aboriginal mythology. One of the hideous demons of darkness, according to legend, it sleeps beneath the Macdonnell Ranges until the end of the world. That's when it's scheduled to emerge to devour all the wisdom left on Earth."

"Devour the wisdom?" repeated Jackson.

Alicia tapped the side of her head. "Up here. That's the home of a man's intelligence. In his head. Take away a man's brain, and you take away his wisdom."

She sighed. "There are hundreds of different Aboriginal dialects, Jackson. However, there is one word common to them all. *Nuckalavee*. It baffles the few professors who bother studying the natives' languages. They just can't seem to be able to translate the term into English. But I know the significance of the word. It means Devourer of Skulls."

CHAPTER 8

Vienna, Austria—March 16, 1994

Etrius dreamed. . .

He was waiting impatiently in an ancient stone chamber, deep in the bowels of the fortress known as Malagris. Located in the heart of the Transylvanian Alps, the keep served as one of seven chantry houses for the magi of the House Tremere. Its master was his hated rival, Goratrix.

Tonight, seven of the most powerful mages in the world stood there, anticipating the arrival of their leader. They had been summoned from throughout Europe to this location by the master of their order, the wizard Tremere. In his messages, he had specified this particular night and this specific location. He had not indicated why, and no one dared questioned his commands. They were among the most powerful mages alive. Tremere quite possible was the most powerful.

Of them, only Goratrix seemed strangely at peace. The sardonic smile on his lips proclaimed that he knew more about the night's events than he was telling. The Experimenter, as he was known by the other members of the Council, was, in the opinion of Etrius, a hotheaded, impulsive fool. He posed a terrible danger to the entire Order with his secret delving into immortality and eternal youth. That Tremere had demanded that his most important disciples travel to Malagris disturbed Etrius greatly.

Someday, when Tremere died or was killed, Etrius planned to rule the Order. Goratrix had made it quite clear that he had the same plan. Only the sharp discipline of Tremere had prevented open warfare between them. Though each had more than once tried by subtle means to slay his rival. Etrius considered himself the voice of reason on the Council. He had obeyed his master for hundreds of years. It was only logical that he be selected to succeed Tremere. He was the obvious choice.

With a crash of steel on stone, the door of the chamber swung open. Tremere, tall and aristocratic, features dark and sardonic, strode into the room. Etrius frowned. Following his master, a few steps behind, was the enigmatic Count St. Germain. The nobleman was a longtime confidant and friend of Tremere, but Etrius didn't trust him. St. Germain was a bit too mysterious, a touch too cold-blooded, for Etrius's taste. He always remained in the shadows. Everyone knew that the Count was an extremely powerful mage. It was whispered that he was also a vampire. No one was sure exactly what bond existed between him and Tremere. First Goratrix, now St. Germain. To Etrius, it was an ominous, dangerous combination.

"You are all here," said Tremere, his powerful voice oddly subdued. "Good. We can begin the ritual immediately."

"Ritual?" asked Meerlinda. The only woman in the Council, rumors named her Tremere's longtime mistress. She said nothing to dispel the tales. They didn't matter. Meerlinda was a member of the circle because of her skills using magic. Not her abilities in bed. "What ritual?"

"Goratrix has discovered the secret of immortality," said Tremere. His gaze swept across his disciples. "Tonight we shall drink the elixir of eternal life. This evening will live in our memories for millennia to follow."

"Where does this miraculous drink come from?" asked Etrius, compelled to speak. "There have been certain stories circulating recently. Tales of Goratrix dealing with . . . the Children of Caine."

Goratrix smiled at Etrius, his sickly-sweet smile indicating his triumph. "The tales are true. A year ago, two of my most trusted assistants were Embraced in the mountains by an ancient member of the Cainite race. I slew the fiend instantly, of course, but the damage had been done. Knowing that the Kindred were immortal, I decided to take full advantage of the unique opportunity presented to me. For the last year, I closely studied my hapless servant's condition. I conducted numerous experiments on them, until I finally understood the secret of their vampire blood.

Working with that vitæ, I concocted my elixir of immortality."

"You've made a potion containing the blood of the Damned," said Etrius anxiously. "The results could be disastrous. Dare we take the risk? There are worse fates than death."

Goratrix laughed, a harsh, annoying sound. "Name one, coward." He waved one hand in the air. "Etrius the Bold, my friends. Only the Conscience of the Tremere would worry about the possible consequences of eternal life."

"I am no coward," said Etrius, striving to control his temper. Now was the time for cold reason, not hot passion. "But I know that the Children of Caine are not happy with their lot. They are cursed for eternity. And you are proposing that we join their lot."

"Enough debate," said Tremere, his tone brooking no dissension. "Etrius, your point is well taken. However, you ignore the fact that the Kindred are linked directly to Adam's son through the act of the Embrace. By drinking the elixir made from their blood, we are avoiding that bond. We shall enjoy all the benefits of immortality without any of the penalties."

"It sounds like a splendid opportunity," said Abetorius, another of the Council. "I, for one, am willing to take the risk."

"Agreed," said Meerlinda. "Etrius, you worry too much. Remember, we are Tremere wizards. We fear nothing."

"There's truth," exclaimed Xavier de Cincao. "Why, then, is *he* here?"

There was no need to indicate who de Cincao meant. None of the Council trusted the Count St. Germain. There were too many unanswered questions about his identity— and his goals. And they all felt he wielded too much influence with Tremere.

"I asked the Count to attend me tonight," said Tremere, a nasty ring to his voice. "He knows a great deal about the Kindred and has advised me on them for decades. We need his assistance. Does anyone object?"

No one did. Tremere was master of the Order by force of his will. His word was law.

St. Germain, still half in shadow, bowed from the waist. "I am here merely to observe and assist," he declared. "The interests of my dear friend, Tremere, are mine as well. As are those of his disciples."

Etrius doubted that, but he recognized that expressing his doubts would be worthless. Glancing around, he saw that his companions obviously felt the same way. Tremere was in no mood to be crossed.

"We have talked too much," said Tremere. "Goratrix, where is this miraculous drink you have prepared?"

"Follow me," said Goratrix, pressing a brick in the chamber wall. With a rumble of gears, an entire section of the room shifted, revealing a stone stairway leading down. "Immortality waits below."

They descended into the heart of the mountain. Goratrix's laboratory was located nearly a hundred feet below his castle. It was brightly lit with lamps that glowed without flame. Resting on the experimenter's table in the center of the room was a huge bowl and nearly a dozen beakers of unknown essences. To the side were eight empty silver goblets.

"All is ready for the final incantations," declared Goratrix. "The mixture requires specific spells chanted with each addition."

"The blood?" asked St. Germain, the barest hint of curiosity in his voice. "Where is it?"

Goratrix laughed. "The formula specifies fresh blood, Count." He pulled a lever on the far wall. As before, a section of the chamber shifted, revealing a small room. Chained to the bricks were what appeared to be two haggard young men.

"My sources of vampire vitæ," said Goratrix cheerfully. He walked close to one of the prisoners. Sharply, he slapped the man across the face.

Dully, the captive looked up at his tormentor. Seeing it was Goratrix, the man snarled. Goratrix laughed again, the sound grating on Etrius' nerves.

"My spells, and a lack of human blood, keep them weak. I have kept them here in this chamber for nearly a year. It won't be the same without their presence."

"They served their Order in good fashion," said Tremere. "Now let them die in the same manner. Let us begin."

It had taken hours of spellcasting and incantations to ready the potion. In dreams, it was the matter of an instant.

The two vampires were dead. Their blood, along with the rest of the magical ingredients, were properly mixed and prepared. St. Germain, acting without being asked, had carefully filled the eight goblets and passed them out to Tremere and his disciples.

"Stand ready if necessary," said the chief mage.

"Your wish is my command," said St. Germain.

"Drink," commanded Tremere and raised the cup to his lips. It had been agreed, as a small matter of trust, that they would all imbibe the liquid at the same instant. "Drink."

Goblet at his lips, Etrius found his gaze on St. Germain. There was a sly look of satisfaction on the Count's face that Etrius found unsettling. With a flash of intuition, Etrius suddenly realized that the Count's back had been turned to them as he prepared the drinks. He could have easily added something to the mixture. It was too late. Liquid fire burned Etrius' throat. He swallowed.

And screamed and screamed and screamed. As did his companions. Etrius' insides were ablaze. Senses overwhelmed with pain, he dropped to the floor, unconscious. The last thing he remembered seeing was the face of St. Germain. The smiling, pale white face of the Count St. Germain.

When he returned to his senses, he knew that Goratrix, Tremere, and the others had been wrong. Ingesting the blood of the Children of Caine had indeed made them immortal. It had also turned them into vampires. And numbered them among the Damned.

Etrius woke. . . .

Shakily, he rose from his coffin. It had been decades since

he had last dreamed of that foul night when Goratrix's brew had destroyed their souls. This time, however, the memories were clearer, sharper than they had been in the past. He had long forgotten his suspicions about St. Germain. Now he wondered if he had forgotten or if the memories had been deliberately suppressed. By the will of another.

Etrius frowned. There were odd holes in his memory, ones that he never before realized existed. St. Germain was without question a member of the Kindred. For centuries he had served as one of Tremere's closest advisors. Yet Etrius could not remember when the Count had been Embraced. Or by whom. Or when. After his dream tonight, Etrius was no longer sure that the mysterious mage was actually a member of the Tremere Clan. And yet none of the Council had once raised a question about him or his heritage.

Was it possible that the Count had already been one of the Cainites that fateful night in Transylvania? Etrius was beginning to wonder—and worry. His memories, so clear on most details from long ago, were hazy on St. Germain's appearance that evening—and on many of his actions during the ceremony.

The notion frightened him. It seemed quite possible that St. Germain was in part responsible for the very existence of the Clan Tremere. What advice had he given his "dear friend" Tremere? What help had he provided Goratrix in developing his secret formula, the formula that had changed them from mortals to Kindred? And, most worrisome of all, what had he added to the potion before giving it to each of them to drink?

The frown on Etrius' face deepened. He had a terrible feeling that he had been manipulated for centuries. That the entire Council had been likewise exploited. It seemed quite possible that Tremere, now in torpor, a member of the third generation by diablerie, had acted on the secret instructions of another. That the entire Clan Tremere had been the unknowing pawn of the Count St. Germain, a vampire of unknown origins and unknown powers. It was not a pleasing thought.

Then he was struck by another realization. Somehow, after all this time, he had suddenly become aware of that subtle twisting of his memory and will. St. Germain had successfully stayed in shadow for centuries. Now, unexpectedly, a dream had revealed his plotting. Etrius did not believe in coincidence. No Kindred did. Especially not of this magnitude. Was the dream another lie, another attempt to twist his thinking? Or was it a warning? If so, of what? And equally troublesome, from whom?

CHAPTER 9

St. Louis—March 16, 1994

Her shoes beating a sharp tattoo on the sidewalk, an attractive young woman with dark eyes and long, black hair approached the Club Diabolique. Curious eyes turned as she approached. The stranger wore a short black velvet dress, dark hose, and stiletto heels. The outfit hugged her slender body as if painted on. Her pale white skin glistened in the bright moonlight. Her lips were blood red. Around her neck she wore a silver necklace decorated with an ancient, ornate cross. Though she resembled the Goths, she was not one of them. She was what they strove to be.

Brutus, the doorman, massive and unyielding, watched with curious gaze as she walked past the several dozen people impatiently waiting for admission to the club. The stranger ignored the crowd and walked directly up to him. Her voice was soft but unyielding. There was steel in her tone.

"I am Madeleine Giovanni, of the Clan Giovanni," she stated just loud enough for him to hear. "I am a visitor in this city. As per the Six Traditions of Caine, I have come to pay my respects to the Prince of St. Louis."

The giant smiled, a slow, easy grin that stretched from ear to ear. "Pleased to meetcha, Miss Madeleine. My master, Prince Vargoss, appreciates dose who honor the ancient laws. You'll find him in the private meeting room on da second floor of da club."

"Thank you," said Madeleine, with a smile of her own. Unlike many Kindred, she treated humans and ghouls no differently than those of her own race. Madeleine held no prejudices against any group. Instead, she reserved her hatred for specific individuals.

"Hey," a man called angrily from the crowd, "how come the babe doesn't have to wait in line like the rest of us?"

Brutus' smile vanished. He scowled. His expression cut off any other protests.

"'Cause she's better," he answered, as Madeleine entered the club. "Understand? Anybody else wanna wait here all night?"

Able to see perfectly in total darkness, Madeleine had no problems navigating through the dimly-lit club. Carefully picking her path through the crowd, she soon found the stairway leading to the second floor. Climbing to the upper landing, she discovered her entry blocked by a big, powerfully-built man in black leather trousers and a black leather vest. His chest, white as chalk, was covered with tattoos and there were naval insignias on both his arms. He looked at Madeleine with undisguised curiosity.

"Darrow, of the Clan Brujah," he said in a deep bass voice. "I have the pleasure of addressing . . . ?"

"Madeleine Giovanni," she answered. Her last name proclaimed her clan. "I've come to pay my respects to the Prince."

"He will be delighted, I'm sure," said Darrow. He bowed gallantly, though Madeleine noted with amusement that his gaze never left hers. Darrow understood the difference between respect and stupidity. He was a gentleman, but not a fool. "The Prince holds the Giovanni in high regard."

That Madeleine doubted. The Ventrue, like most members of the Camarilla, feared and mistrusted her clan. Nor did she blame them much. They had good reasons for their worries.

Darrow pushed open the door to the inner chamber. A huge room, it was nearly deserted. A few Kindred and ghouls sat clustered around a small group of tables, nursing drinks and listening to the plaintive wail of a jazz trombonist. Split off from the main group, his back to the far wall, was a distinguished-looking Cainite, dressed in a black tuxedo with red cummerbund. He was engaged in deep conversation with an extremely tall, extremely thin, and incredibly ugly Nosferatu. There was no need for Darrow to tell her which vampire was the Prince.

A dozen heads turned instantly as she entered the room. Blazing eyes stared at her with undisguised hostility and suspicion. Madeleine, perceptions trained to spot the slightest irregularities, noted that much of the furniture in the chamber was new. As was a section of the floor. Something had happened here within the past few days that had left the Kindred wary of strangers. She wondered what. And if it tied in with her mission.

Alexander Vargoss was standing, waiting for her, when she reached his table.

"Prince Vargoss," she said softly, "I am Madeleine Giovanni of the Clan Giovanni. I am sixth-generation Kindred and the childe of Pietro Giovanni."

Madeleine, taught always to be polite to her elders, refrained from saying anything else. She waited for her host to formally welcome her. The tradition of Domain varied from location to location, but a common thread binding the ceremonies was respect. The Prince of a city welcomed his visitor and asked whatever questions of the stranger he felt necessary before extending the hospitality of his realm.

"I bid you welcome, Madeleine Giovanni," said the Prince, with the slightest nod of recognition. Like most early-generation Ventrue, the vampire treated the traditions of Caine very seriously. "I am Alexander Vargoss, Prince of St. Louis. The hospitality of my city is extended to you. I know your sire. It is a pleasure to receive his childe."

Madeleine was not surprised that Vargoss knew her grandfather. Many centuries old, the Prince had left Europe two hundred years ago. He still maintained close contacts with many vampires on the Continent. Vargoss, though he chose to reign as Prince of a comparatively small city, was a force among the inner circle of the Ventrue.

Born in an earlier age, she smiled her most winning smile and curtsied for Vargoss. She was rewarded, as was often the case with older members of the Children of Caine, with a brief smile of his own. There were certain traits death could not alter. Old manners were never forgotten.

"I thank you for the welcome, Prince Vargoss. I am traveling on a mission for my clan elders. Passing through your city, I felt it only proper that I pay my respects."

"How commendable," said Vargoss, resuming his seat. He waved at a chair for Madeleine. "In these changing times, few Kindred respect the old traditions. Please sit down and join me for a drink. I am curious about your trip."

"Strictly business," said Madeleine casually. "The Giovanni Clan has invested huge sums of money in the coal industry of southern Illinois. I have been sent on a fact-finding tour to make certain that our funds are not being misspent by unscrupulous underlings."

"I find it hard to believe kine or Kindred would be stupid enough to try and cheat the Giovanni," piped in the Nosferatu at Vargoss's side. "Hell hath no fury worse than that of a banker scorned."

Madeleine laughed. "Well put," she declared. "I have to remember that line for my sire. He appreciates a good turn on words, no matter whom the subject."

"You will be staying in St. Louis long?" asked Vargoss nonchalantly.

"A day or two at the most," said Madeleine. "My schedule has me traveling throughout much of the country. The Giovanni have many business interests in the United States. I am investigating most of them. I regret that tonight will probably be my only evening in your city."

Vargoss looked relieved that she was not staying for any length of time. He was no fool. Madeleine was obviously lying about her trip. The Giovanni were much too careful to leave any operation to chance. They kept an extremely close watch on their investments. Whatever the reason for her appearance in St. Louis, Madeleine was not there to study the company books.

"A glass of blood, perhaps?" he asked. "It is always fresh at The Club Diabolique. Curious mortals anxious to learn what takes place in this private area provide us with a constant supply. Besides, we were forced to eliminate several curious kine hired the other evening to do some necessary repairs to the chamber. They made the mistake of looking in the wrong place at the wrong time."

"Life is wasted on the living," added the Nosferatu, twisting his face in grisly fashion. It took Madeleine a few seconds to realize that he was grinning. With a wave of a hand, Vargoss ordered drinks for them all.

The blood arrived promptly. Scented and spiced with exotic seasonings, it smelled delicious. Though Madeleine rarely indulged in public, she decided to make an exception in this case. Especially since she did not want to insult her host.

Vargoss raised his glass. "To Undeath." It was a familiar vampire toast. "To eternal night." Then the Prince added an unexpected third line. "To the destruction of the Red Death."

The vitæ tasted as good as she had expected. Her body sang with the familiar surge of pleasure brought on by the blood.

"The Red Death?" she repeated, unable to keep the curiosity from her voice. "Who is the Red Death?"

"You have not heard?" asked Vargoss suspiciously. "I thought the Giovanni were aware of the latest news before it occurred."

Madeleine grinned. "A reputation that, perhaps, is slightly exaggerated, Prince Vargoss. Besides, I have been traveling and out of communication with my brood."

In short, clipped sentences, Vargoss described the attack two nights ago by the Red Death. Twice, in passing, the Prince mentioned Dire McCann, the mortal mage who served as his advisor. Madeleine couldn't help but wonder if her current assignment was in some mysterious fashion related to the appearance of this bizarre phantom. Her grandfather was often too secretive for her liking.

"This human detective?" she asked cautiously, ready to retreat at the slightest sign of reticence, "do you actually think he can discover the truth about the Red Death?"

"I have learned from experience that McCann possesses a unique talent for unraveling the most complex mysteries," said Vargoss. There was an unspoken challenge in his voice. "Kine or Kindred, I believe in using the best tools available.

In this case, McCann, though mortal, is the right one for the job."

"I meant no disrespect," said Madeleine hurriedly.

"He won't fail," said Vargoss. Madeleine found the Prince's overwhelming confidence in the detective slightly bewildering. It was almost as if Vargoss had been brainwashed. "Besides, he has Flavia at his side. My Dark Angel is determined to confront the Red Death in a return engagement. She has sworn to destroy him."

"They sound like a dangerous combination," said Madeleine. "I wish them good hunting. Where in this vast country did you say the clues pointed?"

"Washington, DC," answered Vargoss.

Inwardly, Madeleine grimaced. Remaining at least outwardly faithful to their covenant with the rest of the Kindred, her clan stayed clear of areas involving conflict between the Camarilla and the Sabbat. Though they wielded a great deal of behind-the-scenes influence with the government, none of the Giovanni maintained quarters in the capital. As usual, she was entirely on her own.

She had to get to Washington as soon as possible and find Dire McCann. And she could only hope that she reached him before the Red Death did.

CHAPTER 10

St. Louis—March 16, 1994

Madeleine Giovanni departed less than an hour later. Darrow nodded his goodbye as she walked past. "Good hunting," he said impulsively.

The dark-haired woman smiled, her eyes flashing, but said nothing. Darrow watched as she made her way down the stairs and wove a path through the crowd to the exit. Madeleine walked with a lithe grace he found fascinating. Now that he had met her in person, Darrow had no doubts that she was as deadly as all the stories he had heard indicated. Dealing with her was going to be the greatest challenge of his career.

A silent, telepathic message broke his train of thought. Prince Vargoss wanted to see him immediately. Instantly, Darrow banished all thoughts of Madeleine Giovanni from his mind. Vargoss was more trusting than most Kindred elders. But his recent betrayal by Mosfair had made the Prince jumpy. The slightest indication of cross-loyalties by another member of his inner circle would mean the Final Death. Darrow, who served two masters, was walking a very fine line. He couldn't afford to make even the most trivial mistake.

Vargoss waited at his usual table, Uglyface still in attendance. His intense gaze bored into Darrow's face like a drill. "Well?" asked the Prince as Darrow sat down next to them. "What do you think?"

"Not my type of woman," said Darrow, grinning. "She struck me as the type of bitch who likes to be in charge of anything she does. Anything, if you gets me meaning. Friggin' well power hungry, they is."

The Prince nodded in agreement. Raising a hand, he signaled for another round of drinks. "I, too, was struck by the power of her personality. All of the Giovanni are related. When I commented on the striking similarity of her features to those of her sire's, she admitted that Pietro was also her grandfather."

"Pietro Giovanni," declared Uglyface, his high-pitched voice even shriller than usual, "the master of the Mausoleum. Even among the Giovanni he possesses a reputation for ruthlessness."

"Blood runs to blood," said Darrow. "Always was true. Always will be. That's a dangerous lady, Miss Madeleine Giovanni. She ain't travelin' around the country on an accounting trip."

"My thoughts exactly," said Vargoss. He swallowed his goblet of blood in one gulp. His cheeks flushed crimson. "The Giovanni rely on ghouls to do their bookkeeping. Pietro's childe is visiting our city on other business. Since she saw fit to stop here, I believe it is in our best interests to learn the purpose behind that mission."

"I will check my sources of information," said Uglyface. "The Giovanni think they can keep secrets from the Nosferatu. But their efforts only serve to increase our desire to learn their plans."

Darrow laughed. "Best the buggers did everything in the open. Then nobody would ever take notice."

The Prince scowled, his eyes narrowing. "Your words might not be so farfetched, Darrow. Madeleine Giovanni was quite open in asking me about the Red Death. And she also inquired about McCann's mission to the capital to locate the monster."

"You think the bitch is hunting for the bugger, too?" asked Darrow. He made no secret of the fact that he trusted the Giovanni no more than the Tremere. Though Darrow trusted no one very much. "That would be typical of those Necromancers. Send their agent right to us for ask for important information."

"Negate our suspicions by being direct?" replied Vargoss. "How clever. And, as you say, how like the Giovanni."

Vargoss' dark eyes flashed. "See if you can discover Madeleine Giovanni's next destination," he said to Darrow. "I suspect she is heading to Washington, DC."

"And if she is?" asked Darrow. "What then?"

"We will do nothing," said Vargoss, shrugging his shoulders, "other than warning Flavia that company is coming. There is nothing else we can do. We dare not openly accuse the Giovanni of meddling without real proof. Our suspicions are not enough."

"The Dark Angel will handle Madeleine Giovanni if necessary," said Uglyface. "Flavia knows how to take care of herself."

"That she does, mate," said Darrow, rising to his feet. "I'm off, now. Not many hours of darkness left. Gotta run if you wants some results, Prince."

Vargoss nodded his dismissal as Darrow hurried for the door. The Brujah advisor had meant what he said to the Prince, but there was more to the words than Vargoss realized. Darrow had plans of his own regarding Madeleine Giovanni, and he knew exactly how to put them into motion.

CHAPTER 11

New York—March 16, 1994

Alicia found Perdition depressing. Which was not really surprising, because she found most modern Kindred traditions and society equally tiresome. A plotter who thought not in terms of years or decades but centuries, she considered the constant posturing and bragging by the supposedly decadent anarchs little more than the babbling of tiresome children. Anis, Queen of Night, was an authority on decadence and depravity. She came from a time when such pursuits were done with style and grace. These recent additions to the Children of Caine had no idea of the true meaning of the words. Alicia licked her lips. Someday they would learn. Those few who survived the Final Death would understand why many thousands of years ago her sire had dubbed her Queen of Night.

A punk rock band of five Kindred with the less-than-clever name The Fingers of Death was roaring through a set of much too loud songs as Alicia entered the club. It was fifteen minutes before midnight. After one late arrival that week, she was determined to be early to this meeting.

The club was half empty. Scanning the crowd, she recognized few faces. Though anarchs usually sided with the Sabbat in philosophy, most of them professed loyalty to neither the Sabbat nor the Camarilla. They were the Young Turks of the Kindred, the rebellious youth of the Children of Caine. To Alicia, they were the savages lurking at the fringes of the fire, the enemies of all civilization. Part of her loved them. Part of her despised them.

She wore basic black tonight—a pair of black trousers, a ruffled black blouse, black leather boots, and black gloves. Her hair was swept back and tied with a black ribbon. She wore no makeup other than deep black eyeliner and blood-red lipstick. More than one vampire glanced at her with inquiring eye—then hurriedly looked away. Most recognized her immediately as Justine's ghoul, and the Archbishop was universally feared. And there was something in Alicia's eyes that troubled the Undead. She was too . . . aware.

Bored and unimpressed by the music, she sat down at a small table at the rear of the club. Justine and her two advisors were nowhere to be seen. Alicia let her gaze roam across the room. She smirked, suppressing the desire to laugh out loud. Most of all, anarchs amused her with their bloated egos and their inflated notions of their own importance.

These later-generation Kindred were all fools. Their emotions and desires were so easy to read, so easy to manipulate. Toying with their thoughts was a trivial exercise in mind control. They never guessed that often their most basic desires were not their own but those of another, more powerful mind. Stupid puppets, they pranced to her every desire. They existed only to satisfy her wishes. Even if it was the suicidal command to attack her mentor, Justine Bern, when she entered the club.

Alicia sighed and abandoned the idea. It was a tempting surprise but not a practical one. She still needed Justine. The Archbishop was her latest pawn in her ongoing attempt to gain total control over the Sabbat. She doubted that her plans would succeed, but at present, it was her only available option. Justine was safe for the immediate future. Or until Alicia came up with a better scheme.

A flicker of motion at a nearby table caught Alicia's attention. A very ordinary-looking male vampire, a colorless, drab member of the Kindred, was playing solitaire. He dealt out the cards with astonishing elegance. Alicia watched his hands, marveling at the dealer's skill. She had watched men play cards for centuries and had never seen anyone handle cards with such dexterity.

Rising to her feet, she sauntered over to the vampire's table. "You're incredibly talented," she declared. "Is it physical skill or magical ability?"

"A tremendous amount of practice," declared the player, his gaze fixed on his cards. He was completely engrossed in the game. "I've had plenty of time to learn my trade. The one thing Kindred never lack is time."

"A philosopher and a card player both," said Alicia, grinning. "A novelty among the Undead. Do you mind if I sit and watch?"

"No, of course not," he replied. His gaze rose for an instant and met hers. The barest trace of a smile crossed his lips. "My name is Walter Holmes. You, of course, are Alicia Varney."

"My fame precedes me," said Alicia, dropping into the chair across from the card player. "I am flattered."

"No need to be," said Holmes, his concentration once again focused on the cards in front of him. "You are notorious, not famous. I think your sponsor, Archbishop Justine Bern, is a dangerous megalomaniac, capable of any atrocity in pursuit of her goals. She gives vampires a bad name."

Alicia chuckled. "You are quite perceptive. And astonishingly honest. However, such words hold a certain risk. If I report them to my mistress, she would rip your heart out with her hands. Then make you eat it."

"You won't tell," said Holmes, calmly, his eyes never leaving the cards. "I'm not worried."

"You *are* a gambler," said Alicia.

Holmes intrigued her. Curiously, she probed his thoughts. Cards filled the vampire's mind, along with the usual surface concerns about blood, boredom, and identity. There was nothing to indicate that the dealer was anything more than he seemed to be—a late-generation Kindred with extraordinary physical skills. Yet, instinctively, Alicia felt certain that Holmes was not what he appeared. The vampire possessed far too much confidence for the mental picture she was receiving. Somehow, he was keeping his real thoughts from her. She just wasn't sure how. Or what method she could use to break through that barrier.

"Tell your fortune?" Holmes asked unexpectedly, breaking her concentration.

"What?" She looked at the cards, then back at the gambler. "I thought you needed a tarot deck to forecast the future."

"Nonsense," said Walter Holmes, gathering the playing cards together. He shuffled them with blinding speed. "That's an ugly rumor spread by the Gangrel and Ravnos Clans to maintain a monopoly on the prediction market. Anyone with the slightest bit of skill can spin the web. Regular cards work as good as a tarot deck. Connecting the strands properly is the real skill."

"Go ahead," said Alicia. "What does tomorrow hold for me?"

The cards flew from Holmes' fingers as if alive. Seven stacks of seven cards formed, in a circle, with the three remaining rectangles in the center. "The wheel of destiny," he announced solemnly. "In the circle are the secrets of the past, the mysteries of the future. And, like all circles, it has neither a beginning nor an end."

Holmes passed his hands three times over the cards. Then, proceeding from the group nearest to him and working counterclockwise, he proceeded to turn over the top card in each stack, placing it in a second ring surrounding the first.

"The cards speak of conflict," he declared, surveying the numbers. No pictures showed. "You are scheduled to encounter dangerous situations that cannot be avoided. They must be face and conquered. Or you will die."

He turned over the second card in each stack. Two queens, both black, appeared, along with the two red aces. "The Queen of Night meets the Red Death," pronounced the mystic. "I see conflict. I see . . . " he paused then in one smooth motion, gathered all of the cards together, " . . . someone looking for you."

Alicia turned. Justine, with Hugh Portiglio and Molly Wade trailing close behind, was walking across the dance floor, heading for the private meeting rooms in the rear of the club. Anarchs scuttled like frightened bugs from her path. The Archbishop's expression was grim.

"A fascinating experience," said Alicia to Holmes. "I wish we could have finished."

"Another time, perhaps," said Holmes.

"Perhaps," said Alicia and hurried over to Justine. She could feel Walter Holmes' gaze following her. But when she glanced back over her shoulder, he was once again concentrating on a game of solitaire. Mentally promising herself to investigate Holmes' background, Alicia switched the focus of her attention to Justine and her cronies.

Molly Wade grinned merrily and winked as Alicia fell in beside her. "The ghoul didn't die," she recited, "and that's no lie."

"Too bad," muttered Hugh Portiglio, scowling. "I entertained hopes she had been cooked."

"I'm glad to see you too, Hugh, my love," said Alicia. "Thanks for your invaluable help the other night."

"My pleasure," replied Portiglio, with a sneer. "You can always count on me for the same whenever danger threatens."

"Shut up," said Justine. The anger in her voice silenced them immediately. "I am in no mood tonight for quarreling. Annoy me at your peril."

No one said another word. None of them dared.

CHAPTER 12

In the Mountains of Bulgaria—March 17, 1994

Le Clair stared into the depths of the fire. The flames burned with an intensity only slightly less than those of the Red Death. Staring at the blaze, the little Frenchman shivered at the thought.

"Cold?" inquired Jean Paul politely. In his arms he held the corpse of the innkeeper's daughter. Gently he stroked her long golden hair. She had been among the first to die when they had slaughtered the inhabitants of the tavern a few hours ago. Jean Paul had hit her with more force than he had planned. She had perished without a sound. Fortunately, after decades of undeath, he was not particular whether his women were alive or dead. In either case, all he did was fondle their hair. And ruefully shake his head, remembering the times when sex actually meant something to him.

"I am always cold," replied Le Clair sorrowfully. He shook his head, staring at the bodies littering the floor. "Since the day I lost my soul, my insides have been locked in a sheet of ice."

"Not me," rumbled Baptiste. Clutched in each of his huge hands was the limp body of a man. Neither of them was dead, though both were barely alive. Baptiste had been noisily sucking their blood for the past thirty minutes, switching from one victim to the other as the mood struck him. His appetite for vitæ was enormous. Given the opportunity, he could drain dry a city. "I'm nice and warm. Blood keeps me hot."

Le Clair stared at Jean Paul and shrugged. At times, it was difficult to believe that Baptiste had been born French. There was no poetry in his soul. The giant had the personality of a German. Or, even worse, that of an English shopkeeper.

"Finish off the pair of them," said Le Clair. "We can't

remain in this dive all night. When the sun rises, I want to be in the forest hours from here. Someone from the village is sure to investigate. When they discover a dozen corpses drained of blood, it will raise the hue and cry. Better that we are not in the neighborhood when the peasants find their torches."

"You are thinking about the Red Death?" asked Jean Paul, changing the subject abruptly. With a grunt of dismissal, he pushed the girl's lifeless body to the floor. The chamber was littered with bodies. After spending the daylight hours sleeping in the basement of Dziemianovitch's mansion, the Unholy Three had emerged with an incredible hunger. It had taken them nearly two hours before they found an isolated tavern filled with weary travelers in the mountains. They had slaughtered the inhabitants like cattle, feasting on the fresh blood with gusto. Evading traps always made them hungry.

"The Red Death," repeated Le Clair. "But of course. After these many years together, my friend, I believe we have formed a telepathic bond. Yes, my mind was on the fiend. And our bargain with him."

"A deal is a deal," said Baptiste, letting the two bodies in his hands drop to the floor. They were empty of blood and devoid of life. To his simple mind, there were no shades of gray, only black and white. "We promised. We don't have no choice."

"Not true, mon ami," said Jean Paul. "Now that we are free of his clutches, the choice is ours. We can obey the monster's commands. Or not. The decision rests with us, not him."

"My feelings exactly," said Le Clair, somberly. He stirred the wood with a metal shaft. Sparks flew up the chimney. "After so many years of independence, I do not relish once again obeying the orders of a commanding officer. One tour of duty was enough for my liking."

"I, too, value my freedom," said Jean Paul. "But the taste of hot blood is quite sweet on my tongue. The Red Death strikes me as an unforgiving foe." Jean Paul threw a stray stick into the fireplace. It vanished in the inferno. "Undeath is highly preferable to the fires of oblivion."

Baptiste, his face solemn, nodded. He made the sign of the cross on his chest. He was a vampire with religion. "We are the Damned. Once we perish, hell awaits us. And there the fires are not quenched. We are destined to suffer eternally."

Le Clair scowled. A hard-headed materialist, he disliked being reminded of his supernatural origins. An avid reader of science fiction, he preferred thinking that the Kindred were actually a race of mutants. It was an absurd theory, but he cherished the notion, constantly looking for shreds of evidence to prove himself correct.

"Forget that supernatural crap," he declared. "It's typical church propaganda."

"Does it matter?" asked Jean Paul, knowing his friend's quirk. "Who cares what happens after the Final Death? Our main concern is avoiding that fate at any cost."

"I agree," said Le Clair. "I do not trust this Red Death fellow. But I see no other choice than to follow his instructions. At least until the opportunity arises to turn on him."

"Killing him would yield some powerful blood, I bet," said Baptiste. "He has to be fifth or maybe even fourth generation."

"Most certainly," said Jean Paul. "Methuselahs are defined by their arrogance. I think his actions place the Red Death squarely in their ranks. Draining him of vitæ will be a pleasure."

"Then we are agreed?" asked Le Clair. "First, to Paris, where we find and destroy this Nosferatu elder. The Methuselah called Phantomas. Then, when he is gone, we turn on our erstwhile employer, the Red Death?"

"It sounds like the only logical course of action to me," said Jean Paul. Reaching out, he grabbed a burning faggot from the fireplace. "I think setting this place ablaze would conceal our activities tonight. It should burn quickly, destroying the bodies beyond recognition."

"The sacred Masquerade," said Le Clair, with a laugh. "Considering our multiple crimes against the Kindred, I don't know why you continue insisting that we hide our presence from humanity."

"Caine's Traditions mean nothing to me, either," admitted Jean Paul. His handsome features twisted into a devilish grin. "However, we cannot take chances. As you stated before, revealing our presence to these mountain peasants might result in a great deal of unpleasantness. These Bulgarians have traditions of their own, dating back many centuries, for dealing with the restless dead."

"Bah, human scum," said Le Clair. "Would they cause us any more trouble than the dozen we murdered tonight? I think not."

"Then consider the Camarilla Justicars," said Jean Paul. "We have managed to avoid their attention thus far. Which I feel is to our distinct advantage. Those bloodhounds are relentless in their pursuit of those who shatter the Masquerade. We do not need them on our trail."

The Justicars were the enforcement arm of the Camarilla. Deadly Kindred avengers, they upheld Caine's Traditions, especially the Masquerade, with fanatical devotion. Possessing great powers, they acted entirely independently of the Camarilla hierarchy. They served as both judges and executioners. Their word was law. And, once unleashed, they could not be recalled.

"Light your fires," said Le Clair. "I stand corrected. I forgot those devils. And their infernal Blood Hunts."

"Don't forget," said Jean Paul. "Not even for a moment. Those of us who feed on our brethren must never underestimate the Justicars. They are extremely efficient. And extremely patient."

Even Baptiste, usually eager to proclaim his courage in the face of any adversity, remained silent.

The tavern burned satisfactorily. They watched the blaze race through the structure until the roof collapsed with a roar. "That should wipe out all traces of our visit," declared Jean Paul. He nodded to Le Clair. "Scattering the wine bottles among the bodies was an excellent idea. Obviously, the poor fools drank themselves into a stupor and never realized their peril until it was too late."

"An incredible tale," said Le Clair. "But humans are such fools. Manipulating their thoughts is hardly a challenge. They believe the most incredible fabrications without question."

"Don't we all?" asked Jean Paul, always the philosopher.

CHAPTER 13

New York—March 18, 1994

"Don't think about sleep tonight," declared Alicia three hours later, as Jackson drove them back to the skyscraper. "I doubt if there will be much rest for either of us before dawn."

"Ms. Bern was not in a good mood, I take it," said her assistant dryly.

"That's putting it mildly," replied Alicia. Inwardly, she was seething. Though she maintained some minor control over Justine's mind, she was careful when they were in Manhattan not to tamper to much with the Archbishop's thoughts. Justine associated with too many other powerful vampires in New York for one of them not to notice the telltale signs of mental manipulation. Alicia could sway Justine by strong arguments into making the proper decisions, or focus on one point instead of another. However, she never planted ideas in the Archbishop's mind during their stays in the city. It was much too risky. Unfortunately, that decision sometimes led to minor disasters.

"We are going to Washington, DC," announced Alicia. "Our nation's capital, a city long coveted by every faction of Kindred society. It has been held by the Camarilla since the early 19th century. However, the Sabbat has been working diligently for years to undermine that rule. And there is talk of the Inconnu focusing their efforts there as well. Justine has decided the time is ripe to rip the city from the grip of her enemies."

"I gather this trip is going to occur in our near future," said Jackson, steering their auto into the underground parking lot at the base of the Varney Building.

"We leave tomorrow morning," said Alicia, "acting as the advance crew for my Kindred friends. We need to make sure everything is prepared for Justine and her cronies when they arrive in the city late tomorrow evening."

They rode the elevator up to the penthouse in silence. Alicia was annoyed at herself for not guessing Justine's reaction to the Red Death's attack. Jackson was already planning what they needed to do for their trip.

"I assume you want Ms. Bern and her two advisors safely ensconced in a location we own?" asked Jackson as Alicia headed for the bar to make herself a stiff drink.

"Of course," she replied. "The usual. With video cameras to record their every action. And twenty-four-hour spy crews to keep track of their every trip."

"The works," said Jackson. "As DC is only hours away, I can pull a bunch of our regulars out of this city and send them to the new location. Most of them have participated in surveillance work for the government, so they know the capital quite well."

"Let's go for an old warehouse," said Alicia, gulping down her scotch and soda and then immediately fixing another. "Hugh finds such locations appealing. He has the mind of a peasant."

"Perhaps in the less reputable area of town," said Jackson, thinking aloud. "I believe we own several that fit the bill. Installing the electronic gear should only take a few hours. Anything else?"

"Hugh is getting to be a pest," said Alicia, remembering a thought from the night before. "I've let him survive this long because I worked on the assumption better the devil you know than the one you don't. But he has become a major nuisance. Tolerating him is not worth the effort. I think the time has come for him to meet an unfortunate end. You know what to do."

"A few words to the Society of Leopold headquarters should do the trick," said Jackson. "Their new bureau chief, Victor Lindsey, is quite ambitious. The prospect of executing a vampire of Portiglio's stature will insure a full-fledged assault on your enemy's hideaway. I think you'll find the results satisfactory."

"Excellent," said Alicia, sipping her second drink. While

she possessed extraordinary control over her body, she could not directly affect its chemical processes. A few more drinks would have her flat on her back. And she didn't have the time to waste being drunk. Or recovering from a hangover.

"Another thing," she said, her thoughts dancing from one subject to another. "There's a Kindred at Perdition I want to know more about. His name, and I don't think he was lying, is Walter Holmes. He plays cards. See what else you can find out about him."

"I'll put out the usual inquiries," said Jackson. "How long do you expect to be in DC? Should I set up a field headquarters for our operations? Or just have information sent to our bureau chief there as needed?"

"I'm not sure," admitted Alicia. "Justine has declared a secret blood war against the Camarilla in the city. Depending on the success of the attack, the battle could last for days. Or weeks. Or months."

"A blood war?" said Jackson. "Why does that phrase sound ominous to me?"

Alicia laughed without humor and finished her drink. "Justine has sent secret messages to all Sabbat packs on the East Coast informing them that the Red Death is working for the Camarilla. She refuses to acknowledge any facts to the contrary. Since the first reports dealing with the specter came from DC, Justine has seized upon that information to announce that the city serves as the monster's stronghold. Using that statement as her rallying point, she has called upon the sect members to wipe out all traces of the Camarilla in the metropolis before the Red Death can attack again. Destroy the Camarilla in Washington and you destroy the Red Death. Or so she declares."

Alicia shook her head in annoyance. She had been outmaneuvered by her puppet. Justine had acted, and there was nothing Alicia could do other than to follow along.

"As one of the leaders of the Sabbat," Alicia continued, "Justine has full authority to call for a blood war. The Archbishop, as we already know, is extremely ambitious. She understands that controlling both New York City and

Washington, DC, would make her the most powerful leader of the cult in America. Which is exactly what she desires. This situation with the Red Death offers her the excuse to attack the capital she has been searching for ever since she rose to power in Manhattan.

"The word has gone out to every Sabbat cell within hundreds of miles of the capital. Some bands will refuse to participate, but many exist for just such a summons. Tomorrow evening, hundreds of late-generation Sabbat vampires will invade Washington. Their mission is to seek out and destroy any Kindred not belonging to the sect. Starting twenty-four hours from now, the streets of the city are going to run black with Cainite blood."

"The situation sounds pretty grim," said Jackson. "How is the Camarilla going to react?"

"I don't know," admitted Alicia. "We are not dealing with the usual circumstances involving a battle between the two sects. Normally, the Sabbat leaders plan these campaign with great care, working for many months to insure that they run smoothly. Initially, they send bands of spies and saboteurs into the city disguised as members of Camarilla Clans. Working slowly and cautiously, these fifth columnists establish themselves in the Kindred community, working hard so that they rise to positions of power among the unsuspecting ranks of the enemy. Thus they learn all of the secrets necessary to guarantee the success of a sneak attack. Nothing is left to chance. When the strike finally takes place, these spies turn on their former comrades, destroying them without mercy.

"The attack is fueled by hundreds of late-generation Kindred acting as shock troops, overwhelming the most powerful vampires in the city. It always takes place as a complete surprise, so as to maximize the chances for success. Using the information supplied by the spies, the Sabbat soldiers try to break the Camarilla stranglehold on the police and government of the city. If that is accomplished, the siege is a success. Wiping out individual pockets of resistance is easy.

"Sometimes the strategy works, sometimes it doesn't. Much depends on the strength of the vampire elders in the metropolis, and how fast they react to the unexpected assault.

"In this case, however, Justine has forfeited any advantages gained by fifth-column work by calling for an immediate surprise attack. She hopes to catch her enemies unprepared and unawares. It is a bold, cunning stroke. And it just might work. However, considering the size and scope of the assault, the dangers are many.

"There are Camarilla spies scattered through the Sabbat. They will be desperately trying to inform the Camarilla elders in Washington of the coming attack. Stopping them will not be easy. That is why Justine called for an immediate attack. Less chance of traitors betraying the mission if it takes place immediately.

"Though I know very little about him, Marcus Vitel, the Prince of Washington, is reputed to be an extremely powerful member of the Kindred. Breaking his grip on the city isn't going to be easy. The Ventrue and the Tremere Clans are both powers in Washington. They will not surrender the metropolis without a fight. Justine is hoping that sheer force of numbers and the relative quickness of the attack will overwhelm Vitel and his minions."

Alicia frowned. "According to Hugh, the capital recently has become a hotbed of intrigue and dissension. The Camarilla is not the unshakable rock there it once was. Justine is evidently hoping that internal bickering among the city elders will hamper their efforts to marshal enough forces to combat the Sabbat invasion. Bound by the strictures of the Masquerade and the Traditions of Caine, the Camarilla often experiences difficulty reacting to immediate challenges."

"That's a big if," said Jackson.

"You bet," said Alicia. "That's why such an assault is called a blood *war*. If Prince Vitel survives the initial onslaught and calls for assistance from other Camarilla princes on the East Coast, this mess could erupt into a full-scale conflict between the sects involving tens of thousands of vampires. We could find ourselves in the midst of mass carnage."

Jackson shrugged. "I am starting to feel I am being underpaid. After this episode is over, I'd like to renegotiate my contract."

Alicia smiled. "No argument from me, Mr. Jackson. You are a rare treasure. You are worth your weight in gold."

"Don't give me ideas," said Jackson, grinning. "In the meantime, I think I'll order our agents to acquire several of those special flamethrowers developed by the Secret Service. They could prove to be very useful. And there's some NASA stuff in Washington that I think you'll find intriguing."

"I want security in this building doubled while we are gone," said Alicia. "I'm sealing the underground vault, but there are some very determined Kindred out there."

"Whatever you want," declared Jackson. He hesitated, then continued. "This upcoming battle between the Sabbat and Camarilla? I understand what you say about Justine Bern's ambitions and all that. Still, she needed an excuse to act. Now she has one. Am I being paranoid, or does it appear that the Red Death is directly responsible for the conflict?"

"No need to feel paranoid," said Alicia. "I'm convinced of the same thing. No real agent working for our enemies would ever announce that fact to an Archbishop of the Sabbat. Especially in such dramatic fashion. The Red Death is counting on Justine's ambitions. He's exploiting her lust for power for his own ends. I'd be very surprised if we didn't discover that he is also behind many of the problems experienced by the Camarilla recently in Washington.

"The Kindred often let their lust for power overwhelm their good sense. They act passionately, not rationally. For all of their great powers, the Undead are easily duped. This war is being orchestrated by The Red Death. My only question is why? What does he stand to gain from it?"

"Power?" said Jackson.

"No doubt," said Alicia. "But over what? And how?

That's what I don't understand." Her features hardened into a look of fearful intensity. "But I definitely intend to find out."

PART

5

Even with the utterly lost, to whom life and death are equally jests, there are matters of which no jest can be made.
"The Masque of the Red Death"
Edgar Allan Poe

Chapter 1

Washington, DC—March 20, 1994

There was a whisper of sound in the room. McCann, sitting on the couch watching the TV set, reacted instantly. He dropped to the floor and ripped the Ingram submachine gun from his shoulder holster. Eyes narrowed, he surveyed the dark chamber. Nothing moved in the harsh glow of the light from the television.

"Nervous, McCann?" asked a voice with the slightest sarcastic edge. "You seem rather edgy."

"Hell, yes," said the detective, rising to his feet and returning the gun to its sheath. Grimacing, he switched on the lamp on the table. Night had fallen in DC and he had not bothered switching on any of the lights. "I feel like I'm skating on the edge of a razor. Don't do that again."

Flavia chuckled. She rested easily against the door to the hotel room. The Assamite assassin was dressed conservatively, in a plain dark dress, flats, and dark gloves. A trace of blush kissed her pale white cheeks and her colorless lips were touched with pink lipstick. She was working very hard at blending in with the local populace.

To McCann's surprise, Flavia had proven to be quite adept at disappearing in crowds. Though he should have known better. Assamites killed with style. But they knew the importance of going unnoticed when necessary. They could kill with stealth as well as with panache.

"You read the newspapers?" she asked. The assassin held up the late edition of the *Post*. *Huge* boldface letters screamed out their protest. *Gang Warfare invades the streets. Dozens killed during past twenty-four hours! Police Helpless! Mayor calls for state of Emergency. Asks for help from the governors of Virginia and Maryland.*

"I missed the paper," said McCann. He nodded at the silent television. "But I was just catching up on the details of the story on the local news station. There's fires and looting all through the District of Columbia. It's going to take more than the National Guard to stop this insanity. The White House is talking about bringing in regular troops."

The detective shook his head in disgust. "It seems as if we arrived in the capital just as this whole situation broke." His voice grew heavy with sarcasm. "What an odd coincidence that these riots started the same day we arrived in the city."

"My thoughts exactly," said Flavia.

"What did you learn?" asked McCann. "Any word on Benedict's actions during the time he was here?"

Flavia shook her head. "Not a clue. Same as what you told me. Information has dried up. Every trail leads nowhere."

"Were you able to find Thompson?" asked McCann. Vargoss had given him that name as their contact in the city.

"He's gone," said Flavia. "Permanently gone. Details weren't clear but word is that he got fried in spectacular fashion. His club ain't there, either. It's a smoking ruin, destroyed in that riot last night."

"Burned to death?" said McCann. "You think the Red Death was somehow involved?"

"I don't really know," said Flavia. "Like I told you, I can't dig up much information. There just aren't very many members of the Camarilla willing to show their faces in public at the moment. Peter Dorfman, the Tremere Pontifex, is in hiding. The Octagon House, which normally serves as the wizard's chantry, stands empty.

"Prince Vitel can't be found," continued the assassin. "Rumors are circulating that he has been destroyed, though I find that hard to believe. I suspect he is gathering his brood, waiting for the proper moment to strike back at those who dare invade his territory."

"What a mess," said McCann, shaking his head in disgust. "What a goddamn mess. My telepathic powers are useless with this many Kindred in the city. Their minds create a psychic jungle I can't penetrate. Finding any traces of The Red Death in that tangle has proven to be impossible."

"A gnarled, twisted Nosferatu named Amos I encountered in the subway system," said Flavia, "mentioned stories of someone using Thermit bombs."

McCann frowned. "Thermit? Since when have the Children of Caine been messing with high explosives?"

"Most professionals prefer the old-fashioned methods," said Flavia. "Knives and swords are the weapons of choice."

Effortlessly, she drew her two short swords from sheaths somehow concealed in the folds of her dress. The twin blades gleamed in the moonlight pouring through the window of the room. "Cold steel is so satisfying," she said, almost purring with pleasure. "The finishing stroke, slicing your enemy's head from her body, there is nothing like it."

"It sounds delightful," muttered McCann sarcastically. "We were discussing Thermit?"

"There is a rogue Assamite who delights in flaunting the rules of proper clan behavior," said Flavia. "In the last few years, unconfirmed stories have described him using Thermit bombs in bizarre death traps."

"You're not sure if these rumors are true?" asked McCann.

"There are never any survivors to verify the tales," said Flavia. "Makish is quite thorough."

"Makish," repeated McCann. "He's good?"

"The very best," said Flavia. "And he works for the highest bidder. If he is in the . . . "

The Assamite never had a chance to finish her sentence. With a whomp of exploding wood and metal, the door of the hotel room exploded inward. Hissing like snakes, nearly a dozen figures dressed in black leather tried to squeeze through the entrance of the chamber. McCann got a jumbled impression of chains and switchblades and scythes. "Kill the buggers!" shouted a voice from the crowd. "Sabbat forever!"

Damn, thought McCann, pulling his machine gun pistol from the holster for the second time in less than five minutes, *they even have their own cheers. This is insane!*

The leader of the pack, a huge vampire with shaven head, wild eyes, and daggers tattooed on his cheeks, lunged forward. He held a machete in each hand but never got a chance to use them. Calmly, McCann pressed and held the trigger of the Ingram. A dull roar filled the room as thirty high-powered shells slammed into the Cainite from near point-blank range. It was as if a giant hand lifted the vampire by the neck and threw him back into his comrades. Arms and legs thrashing, they collapsed in a heap in the smashed door frame.

Flavia's short swords decapitated three of the pack before the rest could scramble into the hallway. Laughing wildly, the Assamite stepped forward, ready to follow. She stopped abruptly as McCann grabbed her by the shoulder.

"Don't act crazy," he declared, pulling her away from the opening. "There could be a hundred more coming up the stairs right now. Someone you talked to squealed. You were followed here. We gotta get out of this place before they overwhelm us by sheer force of numbers."

"Sabbat scum," said Flavia loudly, waving her knives menacingly at those peering through the doorway. The faces vanished.

"Quickly," she murmured. "Out the window. Much as I want to stay and fight, you're absolutely correct. I can't destroy every anarch in the city. Escape is the answer."

McCann followed the Assamite to the far side of the apartment. A huge picture window dominated the wall. Thick clouds hid the moon and stars. Except for the dim glow of street lamps, it was pitch-black outside. They were six stories above the ground. There was no convenient pool beneath them like many spy novels. Nor was there any fire escape. "Can you fly?" asked Flavia.

McCann was not sure from her tone of voice if she was serious or not. In either case, the answer was the same. "No. Nor can I turn into a bat."

"Neither can I," said Flavia. "Which leaves us with one choice. We climb down."

There was noise in the hallway. "They're gathering up their courage for a second assault," said the Assamite. "We'd better get moving."

Savagely, Flavia kicked out at the protective glass of the picture window. Supposedly unbreakable, it shattered into a million pieces. She turned and beckoned to McCann. "Climb onto my back. Quickly."

The detective stared at her. "You plan to make your way down the sheer wall of this building—in total darkness—with me hanging on for dear life?"

"You have a better idea?" asked Flavia. "It's that or face the Sabbat pack. And you know what they do to humans or mages who work for the Camarilla. It takes several long weeks to die."

"I'm convinced," said McCann. He pulled himself onto her back, one hand snaked beneath her right arm and across her chest. He wrapped his legs around her waist. The detective felt like a human backpack.

In his left hand, he retained a tight grip on his reloaded machine gun pistol. Under normal circumstances, he knew the weapon wouldn't do much good against their enemies. But, if necessary, he could change that. War called for desperate measures. As did personal survival.

Even burdened with McCann's two hundred pounds plus, Flavia moved with the grace of a stalking cheetah. Fingers of immeasurable strength reached outside the opening and sunk into the stone facade of the hotel.

"Here we go," said Flavia. "Don't lose your grip. Humans don't bounce off concrete well. Even Masqueraders, I suspect, would not survive the fall unscathed."

She swung out of the room and onto a decorative ledge a few inches wide that circled the building. Her fingers, instead of searching for holds in the stone, made their own, sinking into the building material as if it was soft clay. Slowly, carefully, the Assamite inched her way along the ledge, retaining her grip with one hand while she reached with her other for the next spot. It was an incredible feat of balancing, considering she was carrying McCann on her back.

Howls of rage and frustration boiled from the apartment they had just vacated. "Can you steady yourself so we won't fall no matter what the shock?" asked McCann.

"I believe so," said Flavia. "There's another window up ahead. If I balance one foot on that ledge and keep my hands in the stone, we should be firmly anchored. Why do you ask?"

"I packed some special cartridges for my pistol," lied the detective. He raised the gun and pointed it in the general direction of the window from which they had just exited. "When those pack members stick their heads out the opening looking for us, I plan to cause them major damage."

"Go ahead," said Flavia. "I'm set."

"Where are those motherfu . . . " screamed a black woman, leaning out onto the ledge. Like her fellow anarchs, she was dressed in black leather, her jacket adorned with studs and chains. McCann didn't give her a chance to finish her question.

He squeezed the trigger of his pistol three times. At that range, the bullets couldn't miss. At the exact instant the bullets slammed into the vampire's exposed body, McCann reached out with the full force of his will and mouthed a word that could not be said aloud. The resulting explosion lit up the night sky and caused the entire building to tremble.

"What was in those bullets?" asked Flavia as she watched the headless body of the anarch tumble to the pavement below. Already, she was moving again, sliding along the wall, heading for the center of the building where ornate decorations on the wall would make descending easier.

"Special loads for riot police," said McCann smoothly. There were such bullets, but not of the magnitude just demonstrated. "They're made for stopping armored vehicles. I thought a few rounds might generate some excitement."

"Let's hope these pests did not leave a rear guard waiting for us on the ground," said Flavia as she carefully started descending. "Blood Bound by their sires, these anarchs have no control over their actions. The Sabbat treats them as cannon fodder. The sect elders are willing to sacrifice dozens, even hundreds of neonates, to bring down a Camarilla elder."

"Now that they know you exist . . . " began McCann.

"The horde will not rest until I am dead," completed Flavia. "Or I kill them all."

"Sounds like the odds are pretty much even," said McCann. "Just in case we get separated, though, let's plan on meeting tomorrow at midnight at the Lincoln Memorial. If the city is still up in arms and one of us can't make it, then we'll try again the night after."

"Good idea," said Flavia. They were about twenty feet from the ground. "I can hear the whelps approaching below. Hold on tight. I'm going to jump. Be prepared to run once we reach the pavement."

The detective didn't argue. Flavia had been sent by Prince Vargoss to provide him with protection. There was no reason to be noble. Strange things were taking place in Washington-events directly related to the Red Death. McCann meant to know what the monster was planning. And he did not intend on letting a horde of Sabbat anarchs stopping him from learning the truth.

They hit the ground with a thud that shook McCann's teeth and set his ears ringing. Releasing his grip on the Assamite, the detective staggered to the wall, reestablishing his equilibrium. Flavia seemed to experience no such problem. She had her short swords out and appeared ready for action. It wasn't long in coming.

Screaming obscenities, five anarchs came charging out of the bushes surrounding the hotel. Two carried knives, two others were armed with metal clubs, and one, astonishingly, wielded a pitchfork.

"Leave them to me," said Flavia, with a quick glance at McCann. "Get going before any others show up."

"I'm history," said the detective. "See you later. Don't make any mistakes and get killed."

Flavia laughed, her swords spinning in her hands. "Against scum like these? Not likely, McCann." Her eyes glowed with anticipation. "Beware Makish, detective. He is extremely dangerous. And Amos whispered to me that the assassin is working for The Red Death."

Then there was no more time for talk, as Flavia charged into battle. McCann, all six senses alert, sprinted in the other direction, heading for the hotel parking lot.

Having taken the red-eye flight to DC several nights ago, the detective was driving a rented, late-model Executive Land Cruiser. It had cost a bundle to obtain, but the money came from Vargoss' near-unlimited funds. Powered by a turbocharged V-8 engine and covered with an outer shield of bulletproof fiberglass netting, the Cruiser offered a small measure of safety traveling Washington's deadly streets.

A reception party waited for him by the Cruiser. Two young women, or so they appeared at first glance. Tall and slender, one blonde, one brunette, they sat perched on the hood of the car. Dressed not in black leather but silky white butterfly lace dresses, they looked like they were in their mid- or late twenties. McCann was not fooled. Their bloodless faces, too-bright eyes, and hungry stares made it clear they were members of the Undead. As did the butcher knives in their hands.

"Get the hell out of my way," said McCann, raising his pistol. "I'm tired of this crap. These bullets will blow your heads apart like ripe tomatoes."

"He talks so dirty," said the blonde, sliding to the ground. "It really turns me on. A tough guy. I bet his blood tastes really sweet."

"Yeah," said her companion, joining the blonde on the ground. She pointed her butcher knife at McCann's chest. "Wonder if he's gonna say when he realizes his gun won't work no more. What's he gonna do when he discovers we got the power?"

McCann cursed and squeezed the trigger. Nothing happened. The brunette laughed.

"What now, big man?" She licked her lips, revealing a mouthful of gleaming white teeth. "Did you know that drinking blood is better than sex? At least it is for us."

With a whoop, the two Kindred rushed forward. McCann, disgusted with his own stupidity, dropped the Ingram and stood his ground. He let his awareness expand, taking in the entire hotel grounds. There were nearly forty anarch vampires roaming the area, but, except for his two foes, none were aware of his presence in the parking lot.

Satisfied that he was unobserved, the detective let long-dormant reflexes take over. Two butcher knives flashed up, then down. They caught McCann in the shoulder and chest. And exploded into a flurry of metal fragments as they hit a body solid as stone.

"Never, never underestimate your opponent," chided the detective, grasping each Cainite under the neck with an unbreakable, vise-like grip. The women were too stunned to struggle. Effortlessly, he raised them into the air. "This world of ours is filled with too many surprises not to be extremely cautious."

McCann squeezed. The vampires gasped in pain as he crushed their bones beneath his fingers. Nodding with satisfaction, he dropped the pair to the earth. Kindred could be killed by diablerie, sunlight, burning, or decapitation. As if by magic, a long, thin steel wire appeared in the detective's hands. Its edge was razor-sharp.

McCann knew exactly what to do. Over the centuries, he had had plenty of practice.

CHAPTER 2

Washington, DC—March 20, 1994

"He's here," whispered Alicia, her eyes widening in surprise.

"Did you say something, Miss?" asked Jackson from the front seat of Alicia's limo. "Sorry. I wasn't paying attention. Driving through this neighborhood on an evening like tonight takes my full concentration."

"Nothing to concern yourself with," said Alicia. "I was merely thinking aloud. Stay alert. The closer we get to Justine's headquarters, the more likely we are to run into anarch packs. At present, I'd like to avoid them if we can. The Archbishop's lost control of the situation. No Kindred is safe. Or human."

"We'll make it through," said Jackson, not the slightest doubt in his voice. "This car is constructed like a tank. Nothing can stop it. And the warehouse is only six blocks away."

"I hope you're correct," said Alicia, leaning back against the cushions. "According to the last reports, the riots have spread throughout the city. It's no longer just the Kindred causing damage. There's fire and looting everywhere. The whole metropolis has gone berserk."

"You were right," said Jackson, sounding grim. "It's a war. A blood war."

Alicia said nothing. She was still slightly in shock. Some words could not be said aloud. Even the thought of them sent disturbing ripples through the umbra. Such a phrase had been uttered a few moment ago. Among the Kindred, only two extremely ancient, extremely powerful figures knew its correct pronunciation and its use. Anis, Queen of Night was one. And Lameth, called by many the Dark Messiah, the lover of Anis, was the other. Tonight, for the first time in more than a hundred years, they were present, in mind if not in body, in the same city.

Like the Inconnu, there were many whispered tales but few facts available about the mysterious duo. Many Kindred spoke of how Anis and Lameth unquestionably still walked the Earth, but yet none admitted having met either. Dozens of stories circulated about their involvement in the Jyhad, the eternal war waged for control of the Cainite race, but no actual proof of their involvement could be found. There were legends, but no one could separate myths from reality.

According to the storytellers, the pair had attained Golconda, the state of absolute mastery over the beast within, by the use of a potion developed by Lameth in the Second City. The drink had given them immortality free of blood lust, but it had not brought them peace. For the elixir did not dull ambition. And both Anis and Lameth had been consumed with the desire to rule the world.

They had been lovers. That too was part of the legend. Working together, using their powers in concert, they had constituted perhaps the most dangerous Kindred duo ever to walk the Earth.

Anis was the schemer, the plotter, the seducer. The daughter of the king of a vast prehistoric megalopolis, she was in life and then in undeath the most beautiful woman of the primordial world. Her beauty rivaled that of Lilith, first wife of Adam, mother of demonkind.

Lameth was the master of magic. Before his Embrace, he was the greatest sorcerer of the lost island empire of Atlantis. None knew his true age or history, but it was rumored he had entered into unmentionable bargains with the Lords of Hell in exchange for his knowledge. None of his contemporaries expressed the least surprise when he became a member of the Undead. It was, they whispered, a desperate attempt to escape the unending punishment that awaited him beyond the grave. That he had succeeded in his scheme could be measured in the fact that while his jealous rivals were gone and forgotten with Atlantis, six thousand years later Lameth still roamed the Earth.

Queen of Night and Dark Messiah, they were among the earliest members of the fourth generation. Methuselahs dating from before recorded history, they were gifted with incredible powers and vast and terrible disciplines. Ambitious in life, they were no less rapacious in Undeath. Not even their sires, the demigods known as the Antediluvians, were immune from the duo's treachery and duplicity. Tales passed down from the days of the Second City claimed that it was Anis' schemes that brought about the death of Brujah. And that the secret struggle for Lameth's formula had led to the destruction of the Second City.

Anis and Lameth—their names were linked forever in the mythology of the Kindred. Theirs was a love that transcended death. However, such powerful beings, no matter how deep the ties that bound them, could not coexist in harmony. Each dreamt of absolute control of kine and Kindred. Neither was willing to share their empire with the other. Lovers became rivals and, over the centuries, rivals became enemies. And then, like so many others of the fourth generation, with the fall of the Second City, they vanished into the dark sea of history.

Alicia wondered what Lameth looked like. She had no doubts that she would recognize him the instant she saw him. There was no hiding his distinctive life force, even if it was buried deep within mortal flesh and blood. She knew all of his tricks, just as he knew hers. Alicia smiled. She had needed a new lover for days. Lameth knew her moods, her desires, better than anyone else in the world. A truce, she suspected, would be as much to his liking as hers. It had been too long since their last encounter.

"Trouble up ahead," warned Jackson unexpectedly, breaking into Alicia's thoughts. "Looks like there's barricades set up in the street."

Alicia peered over her driver's shoulder into the darkness. A line of smashed furniture, oil drums, and barbed wire stretched from one curb to another. Several indistinct figures armed with torches prowled behind the makeshift barrier. Mentally, she tried to scan the area ahead, but with no luck. Too many Kindred in the city made her telepathic powers worthless.

"Smash through it," said Alicia. "We can't waste the time backtracking."

"It might be a trap," said Jackson. "There could be metal spikes planted in the pavement right beyond the barrier. It's a sucker trick from years back. We'll be moving too fast to stop."

"Chance it," said Alicia impatiently. She had to reach Justine. This carnage had to be brought under control. The surprise attack had caught the city unawares. Yet the elders of the capital were nowhere to be found. Somehow they had received advance warning of the Sabbat invasion. There was a traitor in the ranks of the Sabbat, but finding him was impossible at the moment. Nor did it matter. Alicia suspected that all the Kindred present in the city were actors in a drama orchestrated by The Red Death. And that some monstrous finale waited for them in the wings.

"You're the boss," said Jackson and pushed the accelerator to the floor. "Hold on."

The big car shuddered and leapt forward. Motor roaring, the limo hurtled like a meteor down the street straight at the barricade. It struck the piles of furniture like a hammer, smashing the wood to splinters. The auto seemed to hesitate for a moment, then with a growl of mechanical fury, was through the obstructions. Wheels screamed as they fought for traction. The muscles in Jackson's arms bulged as he fought to keep the steering wheel straight. Then, glancing ahead, he cursed in frustration. Caught in the glare of the headlights, less than twenty feet away, were a row of steel X's—tire shredders—that could not be avoided. His suspicions had been correct. They had been lured into a trap.

Instinctively, Alicia acted. Drawing upon the core of molten energy burning deep within her brain, she exerted the full force of her will. The discipline, known only to the original childer of Brujah, was called Temporis. Outside the car, time froze.

"What the . . . " began Jackson, his eyes bulging at the motionless surroundings.

Ignoring her assistant, Alicia focused on the metal spikes ahead. Temporis required an incredible amount of mental energy. Inhabiting a human body, her mind could only maintain the unnatural state for a few heartbeats before the time field collapsed. It offered a brief respite from impending disaster. Hands clenched into fists, she reached out and transformed the steel X's into chalk. Then, with a gasp of relief, she released her hold on the time stream. As if lifting a finger from the corner of a rubber band stretched across the room, the universe returned to normal.

" . . . hell?" finished Jackson, spinning the steering wheel wildly as the limo crashed onto and over the tire shredders. And then continued speeding down the thoroughfare, leaving behind a stunned gang of street outlaws.

"The . . . the . . . " stuttered the big man, as he gradually slowed the automobile to a manageable pace. "The spikes . . . in the street . . . the metal . . . ?"

"They must have used cheap material," said Alicia, physically exhausted by her effort. "Don't question. Drive."

Sighing, she reached for the bottle of brandy kept in the limo's bar. Mentally, she noted the location of the ambush. Sooner or later she would return to this area and find those who had manned the barricade. Alicia believed that despite slogans to the contrary, revenge served as the best revenge.

"Next time," she told Jackson angrily, "remind me not to be in such a hurry to get killed."

Annoyed by her own stupidity, Alicia gulped down the liquor. A second glass quickly followed the first. By using Temporis, she had revealed her presence to any other Methuselah in the city. Now Lameth knew she was here. And, more worrisome, so did the Red Death.

They arrived at Justine's headquarters, a huge abandoned warehouse not far from the center of town, without further incident. Jackson parked the limo in the rear of the building, at one of the loading docks. He turned to Alicia for instructions.

"Wait for me here," she commanded, a harsh edge to her voice. The events of the past few days were finally making themselves felt. Alicia hated being manipulated. Thus far, she had been merely reacting to the Red Death's actions. It was time for her to take the offensive. "Anyone approaches the car you don't recognize, use the flamethrowers. Burn the bastards to ashes. They want trouble, we'll give them trouble."

"I thought you came here to defuse the situation." asked Jackson, his composure regained. "Wasn't it your idea to stop the killing?"

"No more senseless murders," said Alicia, opening the door of the limo. She grinned without humor. There was no reason to be subtle. "Anybody bothers me, it's not senseless. It's personal."

Normally, Alicia shielded that part of her that was Anis. Not now. As she walked through the warehouse, her body blazed with unnatural energy. Her anger and frustration made her dangerous.

Nearly twenty Kindred, heavily armed, were scattered throughout the building. Known as the Blood Guard, they were Justine's shock troops. All of them were battle-scarred veterans of a dozen campaigns against the Camarilla. Tough, vicious fighters, totally consumed with the desire to take control, they were followers of the Path of Power and the Inner Voice. Each of them was ambitious, anxious to rise in the world of the Undead. They obeyed the Archbishop not out of a sense of responsibility to the sect but because they felt their best chance of advancement came from allying themselves with her. Their ultimate loyalty was to themselves.

Usually this inner circle of vampire warriors treated Alicia with the same respect accorded a stray dog or cat. Oftentimes they mocked her, taunted her in her role as Justine's ghoul. To them, humans were cattle and deserved no more respect than livestock. Not tonight. There was something undefinable in Alicia's gaze that sent the Blood Guard scurrying for cover.

"Look who's here," said Hugh Portiglio, his voice dripping sarcasm as Alicia entered the small office in the front of the building where Justine was holding court. "The princess of the kine has finally arrived."

"Shut the hell up," said Alicia, letting a glimmer of her wrath touch the Tremere antitribu. Hugh's jaw dropped. A frightened look on his face, he hurriedly stepped back to the wall.

Molly Wade peered at Alicia curiously, but the Malkavian antitribu said nothing. She smiled and nodded as if mentally answering a question never stated.

"The riots in the street have to be gotten under control," said Alicia directly to Justine. "The kine are growing suspicious of the mysterious violence rocking the city. If things get much worse, the Masquerade could be threatened."

"Who cares?" said Hugh Portiglio, regaining a small amount of courage. Though he carefully avoided staring directly at Alicia as he spoke. "That's always been our method of attack. Keep the Camarilla off balance as they try to maintain the Masquerade while we seize control of the local seats of power."

"We're not managing to take over a *fuckin'* thing, you moron," said Alicia harshly. "*That's the problem*. Our neonates are tearing the city to shreds. But they haven't wiped out any of the major Camarilla power brokers.

"So far, we've succeeded in killing a few unimportant cogs in Vitel's brood, but no one of any real importance. We gambled on our enemies being taken by surprise and being overwhelmed by our forces. That didn't happen. The Prince and his advisors fled our attack. Somehow, they learned of our plans in advance. The elders escaped, leaving their human puppets to fight in their place. This blood war has turned into a battle between kine and Kindred. And that's a conflict we can't win."

"Nonsense," said Hugh, an expression of disdain crossing his features. "The humans are fools."

"No worse than some Kindred," said Alicia, making it

quite clear who she meant.

"Alicia is right," said Justine, breaking her silence. The Archbishop grimaced. "We came here to seize control of the city from Prince Marcus Vitel and the Camarilla. The Red Death provided a perfect alibi for our actions. But, despite the slaughter, we have destroyed neither enemy."

Justine paused. "If the Prince returns and drives our forces from the city, the loss of Sabbat prestige will be blamed on me." She glared at Portiglio. "And my advisors."

"The other Archbishops supported your actions," said Molly, sounding quite sane. "They agreed to this venture. All of them feared the Red Death."

"They *fear* him," said Justine, an edge to her voice. "But they *hate* me. More than a few of the Inner Council would secretly rejoice in my failure. My rivals would take intense pleasure in accusing me of endangering the survival of the Sabbat for my own personal gain. The punishment for such action, of course, is the Final Death."

"The anarchs must focus on the hunt, not on random acts of violence," said Alicia, concentrating her will on the Archbishop. "With them under control, the riots will subside. All of our efforts need to be concentrated on finding the Prince and his allies."

"Vitel must be destroyed," said Justine. "That much is clear. Unless he is found, we have lost."

The Archbishop gestured to Molly. "Tell the Blood Guard to spread throughout the city. I want the chaos to end. Immediately. Those who do not obey my wishes are to be destroyed. Without exception."

"I protest," said Hugh Portiglio vehemently. "Stopping the destruction is a stupid mistake. If the riots continue, Vitel will have to surface—or watch his city burn to the ground. Ceasing the attack will give him a chance to regroup and reorganize. Control of this city is within our grasp. We cannot waste such an opportunity."

"Your objection is duly noted, Hugh," said Justine. "Now shut up, and don't open your mouth again. If you dare disagree with me one more time, I will hand you over to the Blood Guard. I think they would enjoy teaching you some of their more interesting rituals."

Alicia stifled a smile. She felt quite satisfied with herself. Sometimes, pointing Justine in the proper direction took just a few words. The Archbishop always responded to logic. Especially when it concerned her survival.

For more than six thousand years, a handful of members of the fourth generation had been engaged in a struggle for control of the world. They called it the Jyhad. But though they controlled forces beyond belief, few Methuselahs cared to risk their survival in actual combat.

Instead, they conducted their secret war through pawns. Using their awesome willpower, the Methuselahs had deceived the unsuspecting Kindred of later generations into fighting their battles. The Jyhad was a complex, multiplayer chess game with the world as the prize.

Anis, in one guise or another, had been participating in the contest for millennia. She had over fifty centuries of experience manipulating the pieces on the game field. Strangely enough, that she also might be a puppet of yet even more powerful schemers never once crossed her mind.

CHAPTER 3

Washington, DC—March 20, 1994

"Excuse me," said Makish politely, "but do you know the correct time?"

"What?" growled the heavyset man, spinning around in surprise. He had been rummaging through a pile of boxes stacked at the side of an empty tenement and had obviously not heard the Assamite approach. Gaze fixing on Makish, he grinned, revealing a mouthful of yellowing teeth. "Who the hell cares? You're dead meat, you little Jap bastard."

"My apologies," said Makish, sounding properly contrite. Seemingly without effort, he drove the oaken stake he had held concealed behind his back into the anarch's chest. With a grunt of shock, the astonished vampire collapsed to the ground. Makish shrugged his shoulders. "However, I am not Japanese. Nor am I dead meat."

Out of his coat pocket came one of his prized thermite bombs and a tube of super glue. Nodding cheerfully to his paralyzed victim, the Assamite bent over and carefully poured several drops of the solution on the bridge of the his nose. Carefully, Makish placed the explosive between the anarch's eyes. Letting it bond for a few seconds, he tested the adhesion with his fingers. The bomb was held rigidly in place.

"I think your death will be quite artistic," said the diminutive assassin. "I have set the timer for one minute. When the device explodes, it will effectively burn your skull to ashes, beheading you. Please feel free to contemplate the mysteries of the great beyond while you wait."

Makish rose to a standing position. "I will be close at hand, making sure that no one interferes with your meditations. Do not worry. This neighborhood appears uninhabited."

The Assamite paused, then smiled. "The answer to my question about the correct time, in case you were wondering, was that it is later than you think. Goodbye. Thank you for your contribution to my art."

The explosion sixty seconds later proved to be quite satisfying. Makish enjoyed terminating anarchs. Their brutal, nihilistic approach to existence offended his delicate sense of true beauty. He considered them to be the barbarian hordes of the Kindred. In his own unique manner, Makish considered himself a solitary voice defending positive values in a cultural wilderness. Those vampires who could not appreciate art deserved to die. And he felt it was his duty to release them from the burden of immortality.

"That gentleman makes sixteen vanquished in the past three nights," he declared to the silent buildings that surrounded him. After working the Anacostia neighborhood for the past two nights, he had returned to Washington's east side this evening. The riot gripping the city made for wonderful cover and Makish firmly believed in taking advantage of the moment.

He wasn't sure if the violence was related to the Red Death's schemes or not, nor did he care. Higher motives meant nothing to the assassin. Money and art were the guiding lights in his unlife.

"You handled him with ease," said a familiar voice behind Makish. "It is always a pleasure watching a craftsman at work."

The Assamite grimaced in annoyance but wiped the expression off his face before turning. He disliked intensely the fact that the Red Death could take him so effortlessly by surprise. The talent, coupled with the specter's killing touch, did not promote a strong feeling of trust between employer and employee.

Makish was under no illusions about dealing with fanatics. Too often they decided to change the terms of a contract once the required service had been performed. Usually, convincing the plotters that they had made a terrible mistake was not very difficult. Makish could be extremely persuasive. Bargaining with the Red Death, however, could prove to be a problem. It was a dilemma whose complexity Makish had pondered for many hours already. But he had yet to arrive at a satisfactory solution.

"The number of potential victims in the city has increased enormously in the past few days," said the assassin, his voice bland and polite as ever. "It is a wonderful opportunity. I can pick and choose my targets."

"I thought you would be pleased," said the Red Death. His waxen lips curled in what Makish assumed was intended to be a comradely smile. "Amazing, is it not, what a few threats and pyrotechnic displays can accomplish?"

"Your plan proceeds as expected?" asked Makish.

"It continues to progress in a most satisfactory manner," answered the Red Death. He beckoned Makish to follow him. "Come. Let us walk. My body burns with unnatural energy. I find it very uncomfortable standing too long in any one place. My feet melt the pavement."

"Whatever you wish," murmured Makish, mentally filing that information in his memory. "Please lead. I will follow close behind, as is the duty of a loyal servant."

"How polite," said the Red Death sarcastically. But Makish noticed that the specter didn't argue. Like most low-generation Kindred, it had an ego as wide as the ocean. To Makish, cautious to the extreme, it was another character flaw to be exploited when necessary.

"You have been destroying members of both the Camarilla and the Sabbat?" asked the Red Death as they walked down the empty streets. Far distant, a fire illuminated the night sky. The faint wail of sirens echoed through the darkness.

"Exactly as you instructed," said Makish. "Eight of each, to be precise. I alternated my murders between the two sects. It was the easiest method of obeying orders and keeping track of my kills."

"Hopefully, not all of these executions involve Thermit bombs," said the Red Death. "The presence of the explosive might indicate to an inquisitive mind that a lone killer is behind the attacks."

Makish shook his head. "I use my toys a few times and

very selectively. Not often enough to raise any suspicions. They leave hardly any evidence. Besides which, I vary the method of killing from victim to victim. It offers me the chance to sharpen my various techniques of extermination. A dedicated craftsman likes to stay in practice."

"Dire McCann has arrived in the city," said the Red Death, switching subjects. "The detective searches for me at the bequest of the Prince of St. Louis. He is accompanied by the remaining Dark Angel of the Kindred. She is here as his bodyguard."

"Ah," said Makish. "How very, very interesting. I heard many stories about those talented twins. They were Embraced and became members of the clan long after my departure. Their style sounded fascinating. I regretted learning one had died before I could observe them in action."

"The remaining bitch, Flavia, has sworn to kill me," said the Red Death, small sparks of rage flying from his fingertips. "She blames me for her sister's demise."

"Were you responsible?" asked Makish.

"She made the mistake of attacking me," said the specter. "I had no choice but to defend myself."

"Of course," said Makish. "However, knowing Assamite conditioning and tradition, I am quite certain your nemesis does not consider your reasoning an acceptable excuse. Can this Dark Angel actually harm you?"

"I am invulnerable while using Body of Fire," said the Red Death. "But maintaining the discipline is extremely difficult. It drains me of energy quickly. Fifteen minutes is my limit in this unnatural state."

"Interesting," said Makish, his tone neutral. Inwardly, he rejoiced.

"The knowledge is useless to a pile of ashes," said the Red Death ominously. "Remember that."

Makish grimaced and shook his head. "Do you truly believe I would betray my patron?" he asked, his expression solemn. "Never. I am an honorable Kindred. When I make a bargain, I stick to it. You have paid me for my services.

With me, deals are sacred."

The assassin did not consider it prudent to add that a broken promise voided any such agreements. He was as honest as necessary with the Red Death. But no more than that.

"Alicia Varney has also entered the capital," said the Red Death. "She came with Justine Bern and her brood."

"The honorable Archbishop of New York," said Makish. "A female of great talent and small patience. I gather she is the Sabbat leader responsible for the blood war taking place in the city."

"I counted on Justine's greed acting as a powerful incentive," said the Red Death with a ghastly chuckle. "She was searching for an excuse to attack the capital. I offered her the necessary motive. She leapt at the chance."

The specter turned and faced Makish. "I will be departing in a moment. Justine is relatively unimportant. Sabbat Archbishops need not concern you. Concentrate on Alicia Varney. She is the one we are after. My plan has many purposes. But killing her is extremely important."

"Another human?" said Makish. "Like this Dire McCann, am I to understand she is much more dangerous than she appears?"

"She is deadly as a rattlesnake," said the Red Death. "Do not underestimate either her or the detective. Fortunately, neither of them grasps the full extent of my scheme. And due to the vast number of Kindred in the city, they are unable to use their psychic powers to discover my secrets."

The gruesome figure wavered, shimmering like a shadow exposed to the light. "I must leave. My binding spell is slipping. One last bit of advice before I withdraw. My efforts have been thwarted in several instances by another pair of mortals. I know nothing, absolutely nothing, about them other than their names—Reuben and Rachel. Beware of their interference. Their powers are beyond my comprehension."

"I am cautious by nature," said Makish. The Red Death was barely more than a mist, drifting apart before the assassin's gaze. "However, I appreciate the warning. I will stay alert."

"In two nights," whispered the Red Death as it vanished into the darkness. "The trap is complete. You know what to do. Prepare yourself. McCann and Varney will discover the truth about the Red Death."

Makish remained silent long after the specter had disappeared. He did not trust the Red Death. Which was not unusual, because he did not trust anyone. That was how he had survived hundreds of years as an assassin. And intended to survive many hundreds of years more. With or without the approval of the Red Death.

CHAPTER 4

Lexington, KY—March 20, 1994

"It's a fuckin' big rig," whispered Junior.

"MG Enterprises?" said Sam. "What's MG stand for?"

"Mucho Grand," said Pablo, laughing. Pablo considered himself the comedian of their gang. At sixteen, he was two years older than Junior and Sam. He thought he knew everything. "Damned truck gotta be loaded with lots of high-priced goods. It's sittin' heavy on the blacktop. With that much weight, there's gotta be lots of goodies inside. Stuff just call for us to take it home."

"Well, we sure ain't findin' out standing around here shooting the breeze," said Junior. "You brought the cutters?"

"Right here," said Sam, pulling a pair of heavy-duty bolt cutters, the kind you needed both hands to use, from beneath his overcoat. "This'll cut through any fuckin' lock."

"Well, what the hell we waitin' for," said Junior. Standing just over five feet tall, baby faced, with limpid blue eyes and a shrill child's voice, he was the leader of their group. Junior had the brains and ambition of a man twice his age. "We ain't got all fuckin' night. Old man Adams checks this section of the lot a couple of hours from now. Let's move."

Carefully, the teenager pulled up the loose section of the fence circling Adams' Long Haul Parking and Storage. Bright red and black signs posted along the entire length of the barrier warned of deadly electrical voltage. Junior and his cronies knew better. Old Man Adams was too cheap to spend the money electrifying the fence. Affixing phony warning signs was a lot cheaper.

The lot was located in the worst section of Lexington, not far from the access road leading to US Highway 64. It served as a safe haven for long-distance truckers who needed a break from long hours spent hauling merchandise cross-country. A dozen bars, three cheap motels, and a notorious whorehouse, all within walking distance, made the depot a favorite among drivers.

Under normal circumstances, the lot also would have been a favorite target for hijackers and truck poachers. The pickings were sweet and security minimal. However, Old Man Adams had the right connections. Word was out on the street that making trouble on his tract was bad news. Gangs, big and small, avoided the Adams property like it was a graveyard. Junior and his two buddies were the only thieves brave enough to risk stealing from the trucks. With the brashness of youth, they were confident that they were beyond such mundane concepts as crime and punishment.

The truck, massive, sleek, boldly painted in silver, black and red, stood alone at the farthest end of the lot. The three boys scurried along the blacktop, a trio of human beetles circling their prey. Moving swiftly, they reached their destination in seconds. As per Junior's instructions, they regrouped between the rig's huge back tires.

It was the perfect night for a break-in. Thick clouds hid the moon and stars. A solitary lamppost cast a dim glow across the empty cab. The rest of the huge vehicle lay shrouded in blackness. The three youngsters crouching by the truck's rear door were invisible from more than a few feet distant.

"Pablo uses the cutters," said Junior. "Sam, you drop your coat over the lock to muffle the sound. Once we snap the fuckin' chain, pull it out quick. I'll slip in first, do a quick survey with my flashlight. Once I find the stuff worth takin', I'll signal with a knock. Coupla' minutes after that, I'll start handin' the goods out the door. Stack it like we planned underneath the wheels. Once we got enough, out we go."

"Hot fuckin' damn," whispered Pablo. "I love this part. Makes me feel like a kid at a birthday party. Never know what presents are waitin' inside."

"Yeah, yeah," said Sam, the most pragmatic of the three. "We've heard it before, birthday boy. You wanna take those damned choppers and snap that lock? I'm gettin' fuckin' cold listening to you gabbing."

The first surprise came when they discovered that there was no chain or lock holding the big doors of the rig closed. The second surprise was that the massive steel doors swung inward, not out. It was as if they were designed for leaving, not entering, the cargo space. The third, and most intense, shock came when silently, noiselessly, the two big doors started opening without anyone touching them. And that there was a light inside in rig.

"What the fuckin' hell is goin' on?" whispered Sam.

"I'm not stayin' to find out," said Pablo. "I'm gone."

That was when the trio discovered they no longer controlled the actions of their bodies. Despite curses and threats, which quickly changed to whimpers and tears, they could not move an inch. They could only wait and watch.

In the space between the doors, a solitary figure appeared. Expecting a monster, the boys found themselves staring at a beautiful young woman. Dressed in a tight-fitting black shift, she seemed amused at their predicament.

"More children," she declared softly, speaking with an odd accent. "Adults in this country do not understand how to raise their young properly. There is a terrible lack of guidance. How sad."

Smiling at them, the woman snapped her fingers. "Come inside," she commanded. And, like automatons without a will of their own, they shuffled meekly into the truck. Behind them the steel doors slammed shut.

Junior blinked in amazement. The inside of the trailer was decorated like an office. There was a desk, several chairs, and a row of filing cabinets. Screen glowing, a computer rested on the desktop. Against one wall was a huge, complex-looking telephone system. There was even a fax machine. All of the furniture was fastened to the floor, so as not to shift while the truck was in motion.

Past the office equipment was a large closet filled with women's clothes. With a few exceptions, all of the outfits were black. An open case revealed gleaming silver jewelry.

Beyond the apparel, at the front of the cargo container, closest to the cab, was a large, black coffin. The handles and decoration were in silver, as was the satin lining. The lid was open, but there was no body inside. Junior had seen enough horror movies to know that the occupant of that box stood before him.

"Three young outlaws," said the young woman. Slender and not too tall, she had black hair and piercing dark eyes. Her skin was snow white and her lips, blood red. "Three children pretending to be adults."

Her gaze fixed on Sam. She grimaced. "What is your name? And why are you not home, pursuing your schoolwork?"

Sam's tongue was loosened. "I-I-I'm Sam Carroll. My mom threw me out of the house six months ago. Her boyfriend hated me. He made her do it. Mean son of a bitch—I was lucky he didn't tell mom to strangle me. She was dumb enough to do it.

"I didn't have any place to go. No way I was selling my body to some perverts just to keep eating. Instead I hooked up with Junior and Pablo.

"We live together in the burned-out motel around the corner. They're my family. I ain't seen the inside of a school for a year. They don't want kids like me."

Junior wanted to tell Sam to shut up, not to reveal any of their secrets, their hideaways. But he couldn't. He was unable to speak.

"What about you?" asked the lady in black, looking at Pablo. "Tell me your name and why you steal."

"I'm Pablo Luis Alvardo Cortina," said Pablo. "My mother and father died in the big riots two years ago when the Klan burned down the barrio. The fire killed everybody in my family except me. I had six brothers and sisters. They all died. A terrible accident, the fuckin' cops said afterwards. What a god-damned fuckin' lie. Two of the blueboys belonged to the KKK. Even without their sheets I recognized them. They knew it, too.

"They came searching for me in the wreckage, the dumb shits. That was their big mistake. I was waiting for them. Junior helped me fix the traps. First one, a fat slug named

McGraw, tumbled into a pit we dug. Impaled himself on a nice, sharp steel spike. He screamed like a stuck pig for an hour before he finally bled to death.

"His partner, a holy-roller loony, Sergeant Grayson, panicked and tried to hid in a big steel garbage container. I couldn't have planned it any better. We fastened down the lid so he couldn't escape. Then we pumped gasoline into it until it was half-full. Junior gave me the match." Pablo laughed. "Whoosh!"

Pablo drew in a deep breath. "Ain't no place for guys like me. If the blueboys get me, it's curtains. I'll have an accident, just like my family. The street's where I live. And stealin's the only way to eat."

With a shake of her head, the dark woman turned to Junior. "You are the ringleader of this wild bunch, I gather. Well, Junior, since your two companions both have told me their sad stories, why don't you reveal to me something about yourself as well."

Junior didn't want to talk. He swore to himself he wouldn't talk. But when their captor told him to speak, he spoke.

"Everybody called me Junior," he began. "That's because nobody knew my real name. They found me on the front steps of the hospital. My mother, whoever the hell she was, left me there. No note, no nothing. Not even a fuckin' diaper. At least she abandoned me in the front of the building. Who the hell knows what would have happened if she dropped me off in the back.

"I got raised in an orphanage with lots of other kids. Got sent to a bunch of foster homes, but I never lasted. Those people weren't lookin' for children. They wanted little slaves. Or were sicko perverts. I ran away from every home they placed me into. But they always caught me and brought me back to the orphanage.

"I escaped the damned place when I was eleven, three years ago. Climbed out a hole in the roof and never looked back. I've been on the run since then. Don't got no real name, no family, no money. Pablo and Sam are my only friends.

"The world's screwed me since I was born. So I decided when I got free to screw it back. Been doing it ever since. Until you caught us tonight. What the fuckin' hell do I care. Nobody lives forever."

"How true," said the dark lady. She snapped her fingers. "You can move again. That's not an invitation to try anything stupid, like jumping me. Sit. Relax. Unfortunately, I cannot offer you any refreshment. There is no food here."

Pablo and Sam sank to the floor. They looked scared of the dark lady. Not Junior. He hadn't been afraid of anybody in a long, long time.

"You're a vampire," he said. "You drink blood."

"Good," said the woman. "You're better educated than I expected."

She smiled, revealing perfect white teeth. But no fangs. Junior thought for sure she would have fangs. "Sorry," said the dark lady. "No fangs."

"You read my mind!" said Junior.

"I can detect surface thoughts," said the vampire. "Many of my kind possess that talent. Don't complain. It enabled me to detect that three children were assaulting my vehicle instead of a band of outlaws. If you had been a few years older, you would not be my guests at the moment."

"What would we be?" asked Sam, nervously.

"My dinner," said the dark lady, chuckling. Even Junior shivered when she said it. The dark lady wasn't joking.

"My name is Madeleine Giovanni," she continued. "I am a vampire, a member of the Undead. There are thousands of us living among humanity. We call our race the Kindred. And mankind are the kine."

"Whatcho want with us?" asked Pablo. "Late-night snacks?"

Madeleine Giovanni laughed. "Actually, I need you for a much more mundane service. The last few nights I have been involved in a running battle with a band of rogue vampires. They made travel difficult. Finally, earlier tonight, I tracked them to their lair and destroyed them.

"However, these events led me to believe that my cover

has been compromised. I am on an important mission in this country for my clan elders. Someone, perhaps a member of my own bloodline, is a traitor. I can no longer trust my regular contacts. But my assignment requires allies who can serve me during the daylight hours. *Human* allies."

"You want us," said Junior, his eyes bulging with shock, "to work for you? That's nuts. We're kids."

"Children make the best spies," replied Madeleine Giovanni. "Adults rarely pay them any attention. Youngsters are seen but ignored. Besides, as I stated, you can move about in the sunshine, a privilege I am denied. I think you would serve me quite well."

"Sounds fuckin' dangerous," said Sam. "If you got enemies, working for you could be suicidal."

"The risks are great," said the dark lady. "But so is the reward. I will pay you extremely well for your assistance."

"How well?" asked Junior.

"A million dollars for each of you," said Madeleine Giovanni, smiling. "In cash."

"Lady," said Junior. "You got yourself three spies."

CHAPTER 5

Sicily—March 21, 1994

Nicko Lazzari, assistant to Don Caravelli, Capo de Capo of the Mafia, read the fax for a second time. Then he laughed. A deep, booming laugh that filled his office, startling the giant standing in the doorway.

"A funny message, Don Lazzari?" asked Luigi, who had just delivered the transmission. "It makes you happy."

"Very happy," said Nicko, grinning. "It is good news from America. Excellent news from across the ocean. I am sure Don Caravelli will be pleased. Surprised and pleased."

Nicko's eyes narrowed in thought. An opportunist, he believed in taking advantage of every opportunity to make himself popular with the Mafia security brigade. "In fact, I suspect the boss will be so happy that he will order a blood feast to celebrate the news. Those soldiers sent by the Italian government to annoy us are still in the dungeons, are they not?"

"They are, Don Lazzari," said Luigi. A huge figure, seven feet tall, weighing close to four hundred pounds, he was slow-witted but deadly in a fight. A tenth-generation Brujah, he served the Mafia well, doing whatever was required of him without question. "I checked on them the other day."

"I suspect that tonight they will meet their just reward," said Nicko. "Prepare the large meeting room for a carnival. With the approval of Don Caravelli, we shall hang the interlopers by their heels and bleed them dry."

Luigi nodded, a broad smile creasing his Neanderthal features. "Fresh blood is the best blood."

"Now leave me," commanded Nicko. "Make things ready, but do nothing to the prisoners until I obtain Don Caravelli's approval."

"I understand," said Luigi, backing out the door of Nicko's chambers. "The Don is Capo de Capo. His word is

240

law." The giant hesitated. "I hope he finds the message as funny as you do."

"I am sure he will," said Nicko.

Alone again, Don Lazzari studied the fax. It was written in a complex code used by Mafia spies to report important information to the organizational headquarters in Sicily. Knowing that untapped phone lines were impossible, cryptographers working for the crime cartel had devised a nearly unbreakable secret language for communication. The code was based on a randomly generated number sequence derived daily from the temperatures of twenty-seven cities throughout the world. As a member of the inner circle of the Mafia and an eighth-generation Brujah, Don Lazzari could decode the message mentally. Scanning the document, he nodded in satisfaction. The information was straightforward and to the point. The news could not be much better.

He found Don Caravelli in his study at the center of the fortress. The Capo de Capo, studying an ancient scroll on his desk, looked up as Nicko entered the chamber. The Don smiled, but there was no warmth in the expression. Of all the Kindred he had encountered over the centuries, Nicko considered the Mafia chieftain as possessing the least amount of humanity. There was no pity, no cheer, no soul left inside the boss of bosses. Don Caravelli, though he still resembled a man, was no longer mortal. He was Undead in mind and spirit.

"You seem excited, Nicko," said the Don, his deep voice calm and smooth as always. He rolled up the document and dropped it into a drawer in his desk. "What makes you smile?"

"Another fax arrived from America," said Nicko. "It came directly from St. Louis, where our midwest representative resides in deep cover working for the Prince of the city."

"I remember," said Don Caravelli, his white teeth flashing in contrast to his deep tan. "He reported earlier in the week about the appearance of this mysterious being known as the Red Death. The monster who is stirring up trouble everywhere."

"Our agent's name is Darrow," added Nicko. "He is smart, suave, and very ambitious. He dreams of vastly expanding and controlling our North American operations."

"Good," said Don Caravelli. "I like ambition. Our organization is based on greed and zeal and selfishness. If this Darrow wants the position badly enough, he will seize it, strangling those who oppose his wishes."

The Capo paused. "What did he send now? More news of this grisly apparition?"

"No," said Nicko, savoring the moment. He still possessed enough measure of humanity to enjoy catching his usually imperturbable boss off guard. "The Prince of St. Louis had a different sort of visitor the other night. Darrow double-checked her identity before passing along the information to us. Madeleine Giovanni came to pay her respects."

"What!" bellowed Don Caravelli. Like a rocket, he exploded out of his armchair and around the desk. In three long strides, he made it to Nicko's side and grabbed the fax out of Don Lazzari's fingers. Swiftly, the Capo's gaze scanned the paper.

"The bitch is in the United States," he said, smiling. "How nice. For a change, I believe the Giovanni elders have overreached themselves. Dear, sweet Madeleine is on her own in a hostile environment without any backup. Despite their great wealth, the clan has no real strength in the Americas."

"Nor do we," reminded Don Lazzari. "The Sabbat anarchs control most of the East and West Coasts. The Camarilla holds the rest of the country in its grip. Our agents are few and work mostly in secret. Darrow sent several Caitiffs after Madeleine, but he doubted they would do much more than slow her down."

"Wise words, Nicko," said Don Caravelli. "However, the Giovanni are a close-knit, unapproachable bunch of necromancers. They are universally despised by ordinary

Kindred. That is not the case with the Mafia. While we are widely feared, we are also widely respected. We shall exploit that difference in perception to our advantage."

"How so?" asked Nicko. He thought of himself as a master schemer. But he was an amateur compared to Don Caravelli. The Capo de Capo was a master of intrigue.

"You gave me the idea with your mention of Darrow's ambition. We shall give him a chance to make his dreams come true. Or anyone else of equal ambition. I want you to fly to Washington, DC, immediately to take charge of this operation. Take whatever and whomever you need. The full force of the Mafia stands behind you.

"Upon your arrival in the American capital, I want you to immediately announce a blood bounty on Madeleine Giovanni. By then, she should be somewhere in that city. Spread the word secretly, to avoid any possible interference from those fools who oppose us in the Camarilla and the Sabbat. The Cainite who kills the bitch will be made Capo of America. And I promise him the opportunity to lower his generation one level."

"The Camarilla Justicar of North America is not going to like the notion of you calling a Blood Hunt for personal vengeance," said Nicko. "According to the Camarilla interpretation of the Six Traditions of Caine, only the Prince of a city possess such authority."

"I place that problem in your able hands," said Don Caravelli, smiling. "If the question arises, solve it. Justicars have great powers. But so does the Mafia."

"As you command," said Nicko, bowing his head slightly. He knew better than to argue with Don Caravelli. "I thought, perhaps, the good news would be cause to celebrate in the fortress. Might I suggest a blood feast . . . "

"An excellent idea," said the Capo de Capo. "Those soldiers captured on our property?"

"My thoughts exactly," said Nicko. "I gave the necessary commands. All needed was your approval."

"Go and attend to the details," said Don Caravelli, with a wave of a hand. "Enjoy yourself, Nicko. But do not delay too long. I want you on a plane to America before the night is over."

"I exist only to serve my Prince," said Nicko.

"I know," said Don Caravelli, his dark eyes burning. "Otherwise, one of your ambition would long have met the Final Death. Before you leave, Nicko, a few more thoughts for you to consider."

Don Lazzari's muscles tightened. The boss of bosses had a habit of saving his worst news for the last possible instant. "My lord?"

"This human, Dire McCann, for whom Madeleine Giovanni is searching. I have no idea why she wants to find him. Perhaps he did some wrong to her clan. Or owes them money. I don't care. Kill him anyway. Leave no loose ends."

"It shall be done," said Nicko. "Anything else?"

"This mission is an important one, Nicko," said Don Caravelli. "Madeleine Giovanni has been a thorn in my side for too many years. Of all my lieutenants, you are the most ambitious. Here is your chance to prove your worth. Your reward for putting an end to her existence will be substantial."

Inwardly, Nicko exalted. Then the joy turned to dust as the Capo de Capo's voice grew colder than ice. "Fail me and you need not return. Either Madeleine Giovanni meets the Final Death. Or you do."

CHAPTER 6

Paris, France—March 21, 1994

Cautiously, Phantomas crept through the silent hallways of Notre Dame. For the past few nights, ever since his frightening encounter with the Red Death, he had avoided the art museum. Actually, he had been so worried by the spectral killer that he had remained hidden in the twisted catacombs far beneath the city that he called home. This trip tonight was his first venture outside the tunnels. And it had him very nervous.

This late, the cathedral was deserted except for a few priests on solitary errands and the usual police necessary to guard public monuments from thieves. The huge church contained objects of art worth millions. More than one band of thieves had tried to ransack the treasures in the central nave. None had succeeded.

Police and priests, they all ignored Phantomas. Using his Mask of a Thousand Faces discipline, he appeared to each of them as a familiar, unthreatening figure. They all saw a person with full rights to be there no matter what the hour. The only possible danger in using the masquerade came when he encountered several men at the same time. Since it directly affected each person whom he met, three guards spotting him at the same time would see three very different people. Such a confrontation invariably led to complications.

Phantomas tried very hard to avoid such confrontations, but even he could not redirect destiny. Once, unexpectedly, a hundred years ago, while examining Nicolas Coustou's "Pieta," he had been stumbled across by three priests and three nuns en route to a secret revelry definitely not sanctioned by the church. Their astonishing visions, due partly to Phantomas' power and partly to the incredible amounts of wine they had already imbibed, caused such an uproar that it had brought guards running from throughout the cathedral. The Nosferatu had been lucky to escape before being discovered. The offending sextet had been severely punished, their revelations dismissed as the products of alcohol and debauchery. Even after a century, the memory of one particular buxom nun throwing herself at him, screaming "Lord Satan, Lord Satan," still made Phantomas smile.

Tonight he stayed in the shadows. Making not a sound, he crept past the South Rose Window, beyond the entrance to the sacristy, and finally arrived at the hall to the treasury. It was here that the religious treasures of the cathedral were stored, including numerous ancient manuscripts and reliquaries. Phantomas had spent decades poring over the fragile documents, searching for obscure references to the Kindred for his encyclopedia. The vampire was perhaps the greatest authority in the world on the secrets of Notre Dame.

Usually, several guards and priests were stationed in the outbuilding. Not at the moment. Using the full force of his powerful will just before entering the church, Phantomas had sent them a vague summons to the Crypte at the front of the west entrance to the cathedral. He did not have much time before they returned. But if what he suspected was true, time was the least of his worries.

He located the manuscript in seconds. It was in the same exact location where it had been during his last examination of its contents, sixty years earlier. No one had touched it during the intervening decades. He was not surprised.

Few scholars were interested in the Cabalistic concept that God created worlds previous to this one. It was a subject that annoyed religious fanatics and disturbed nonbelievers. Few mages were aware of the idea, though it helped explain several of the most vexing mysteries regarding their view of the cosmos. Phantomas didn't care. He felt no responsibility to explain the wonders of the universe to mankind. Or the Kindred. Neither group understood the truth about the shifting nature of reality. But the Red Death knew. And was using his knowledge for evil.

Phantomas quickly read through the few short paragraphs

that interested him. He memorized the relevant sections. Now, at least, he knew the source of the Red Death's Body of Fire discipline. Though the knowledge provided him absolutely no idea how to combat it.

The Nosferatu shrugged his misshapen shoulders. The best way to avoid the Red Death's fury was to remain hidden. Which was exactly what Phantomas planned to do. After this trip, he was going to stay in his nice safe tunnels for years and years. Though he still could not guess why the specter wanted him dead. He had not been able to discover a thing indicating the monster's lineage in his encyclopedia. Nor had he ever seen him before the other night in the Louvre.

Or had he? Recalling his visit to the fabulous museum the evening of Villon's party set Phantomas' mind spinning. The Red Death's garments and demeanor distracted attention from his face. The monster's features, grim and foreboding, were distinct. And, the more Phantomas considered them, vaguely familiar.

With a groan, the Nosferatu knew that he had to return to the Louvre. The answer to the Red Death's identity waited for him somewhere in the majestic halls of the converted palace. It was a trip fraught with danger. If the mysterious killer appeared a second time, Phantomas was not so sure he could escape as easily. The Red Death had killed a sizable number of Kindred in his attacks during the past week. He could be fooled once, Phantomas suspected. But not twice.

Muttering angrily to himself, the ancient Cainite slipped out of the treasury. He was resigned to his fate. Most vampires worshiped blood, the vitæ that served them as both food and drink. A few glorified death, claiming that their greatest pleasure came from the act of murder. Several bragged that sex kept them immortal. But only Phantomas craved knowledge. It was the drug that kept him eternal. Without information, he was nothing.

He entered the Louvre with nothing to guide him but his subconscious. Somewhere in the greatest art collection in the world he had seen a face, and the features of that grim visage had matched those of the Red Death. Fortunately, he could retrace his journey of a few nights past without effort. He had walked these steps a thousand times.

His senses alert for the least disturbance, Phantomas flitted from gallery to gallery. He felt like the infamous criminal returning to the scene of the crime. In a reversal of roles, however, he was the victim backtracking the locale of his escape, searching for a clue to the identity of his attacker. It was not a role Phantomas relished, but one he accepted. By now, he realized that the Red Death wanted him exterminated. And that the only way to save his life was bring about the specter's demise.

Knowledge, Phantomas understood, was the key. His encyclopedia project frightened the Red Death because it contained important information about the earliest members of the Cainite race. Buried deep in that storehouse of information was a clue, or clues, to the Red Death's identity. And, equally likely, to his weaknesses.

That was why the spectral figure wanted Phantomas destroyed. The Red Death was neither invulnerable nor unstoppable. The past held the key to the crimson specter's future. If the Nosferatu vampire could find the data before it was too late.

For all his concentration, he nearly missed the object of his search. In his usual manner, he stopped in the Egyptian hall for a moment to stare at the veiled statue of Nefertiti. Her perfection called out to him across the centuries. She was as beautiful as he was ugly. Phantomas shrugged. The Queen was also a vampire, one of the Children of Set. She was eternally fair and eternally evil. There was no justice in the world.

Turning, his gaze swept across the crypt of Osiris, with its depiction of the deities of the First Kingdom. They remained unchanged as the day of their carving, thousands of years ago. They had been old long before he was born, two thousand years ago.

Suddenly, his eyes stopped moving. His attention

fastened intently on one of Egypt's ancient Gods. Phantomas blinked in astonishment. Sometimes the extent of his memory even amazed him. There, surrounded by a coterie of seven identical hawk-headed servitors, was a squat, powerful figure possessing the gruesome features of the Red Death.

Phantomas had hoped to discover somewhere the identity of his mysterious foe. He had not expected to find them on a carving thousands of years old. Quaking with a mixture of fear and excitement, he studied the plaque in front of the tomb which listed the identities of the Gods. The brutish entity was Seker, one of the most ancient of the Egyptian Lords of the Underworld. He was associated with the darkness and death of the tomb, and he reposed in the night.

He was, without doubt, concluded Phantomas, a member of the Kindred. According to the brief paragraph describing the deity, the inhabitants of the ancient city of Memphis had worshiped Seker over five thousand years ago. Seker had to be a Methuselah, a vampire of the fourth generation.

Phantomas grimaced in frustration. According to his records, the only two Cainites powerful enough to be the Red Death were Lameth and Anis. Now he had discovered a third candidate. He was positive there was no Seker in his encyclopedia of the Damned. Which meant the spectral figure belonged to an unknown and unsuspected bloodline. It was very confusing.

After a few seconds, Phantomas shrugged. More work was what it meant. Seker existed, and thus possessed a sire. A determined search would reveal his antecedents and his history. No one, not even the greatest of the Kindred, existed in an information vacuum. Somewhere there existed data about the Red Death. And he, Phantomas, would find it.

That thought firmly in place, Phantomas spun on his heels and headed for the exit. It was then that serendipity struck. Eyes focused straight ahead, he found himself staring at a carving depicting the face of Khufu, the fabled ruler of the First Kingdom and builder of the largest pyramid known to man. For the second time that evening, Phantomas realized he recognized those features. Except for the slightest variations, the face of Khufu was identical to that of the handsome young man who had warned him about the Red Death a few nights ago.

CHAPTER 7

Vienna, Austria—March 21, 1994

Etrius sorted through the six sheets of paper he held in his hands, rereading the contents of each letter carefully. The words had not changed in the past five minutes. The replies to the questions he had raised the day before remained the same as they had been for hours. None of them pleased him.

Snarling in rage, he squeezed his fingers together, crumpling the white sheets into a thick wad of paper. Normally, he saved his correspondence, especially letters concerning major issues of policy. They served as powerful information in the bitter fights that often broke out at meetings of the Inner Council. Etrius knew the value of the printed word. Once an opinion was put on paper, it could not be easily abandoned. More than once he had used such documents to sway the council to his point of view.

Features contorted in anger, he tossed the wad of paper into the fireplace. He had no reason to save these responses. The six other councilors had all been of the same mind. None of them remembered St. Germain attending the events at Malagris Keep centuries ago. Nor did they recall the mysterious figure helping prepare the drink that turned them all into vampires. Though none of them came out and said it, several implied that Etrius was experiencing delusions. Or worse.

Etrius was no coward. Tonight, however, he feared, not only for his own continued existence, but for the fate of the entire Tremere bloodline. He knew already that his own unlife was in deadly danger. Somehow he had learned the darkest secret of his order. A secret that he was not supposed to know.

For nearly a thousand years, an incredibly powerful Kindred who went by the name St. Germain had manipulated the wizards of the Order of the House of

Tremere. He had intrigued with Tremere to convert them from mages to vampires. And, while assisting in that abominable ritual, he had gained a measure of control over the Council through a mixture of black magic and Blood Bonding.

More frightening to Etrius was the fact that the diabolical Count had managed effortlessly to conceal his efforts from his victims. The other council members were entirely ignorant of St. Germain and his work. To the rest of them, the Count was a name vaguely remembered as being a sixth- or seventh-generation vampire of the clan, one long missing and presumed destroyed. Only Etrius recalled St. Germain's many visits to Vienna, his numerous consultations with Tremere, his attendance at dozens of Inner Council meetings. And Etrius felt quite certain that the memory of those events had been locked inside in his deepest memories and forgotten until less than a week ago.

Last night he had spent hours carefully checking the record books of Clan Tremere. Etrius himself had written those diaries over the centuries and until now would have sworn that they were the absolute, complete truth. To his horror, he had learned how wrong he was. There was no mention of St. Germain in any of the journals. Not a word existed in print about the mysterious count. It was as if he had never existed.

St. Germain was a shadow. He was an unseen apparition, a specter, a ghostly schemer, always in the background, who haunted the Tremere. He possessed incredible powers, but what they were, Etrius could only guess.

One fact was terribly clear. Many times over the centuries Etrius had experienced a vague, unsettling feeling that his mind was not entirely his own. It felt as if someone else was staring out at the world through his eyes. He had always assumed that that being was Tremere, keeping watch over his clan even while in torpor. Now Etrius was not so certain. He worried that the unseen overseer might have been St. Germain.

Distraught, Etrius rose from his chair and stood before

the fireplace. He could expect no help from his fellow council members. Even in the best of situations they were not a cooperative group. Most of them hated him, just as he hated them. The Council of the Tremere consisted of some of the most ruthless, powerful vampires in the world. There never could be peace between them. They all wanted the same thing—mastery of the clan and ultimate power over both kine and Kindred. None of them trusted the others. They lived in an unsteady truce because Tremere, their absolute master, dictated that it remain so. Otherwise the bloodbath would have started centuries ago.

Etrius' left hand rose to his neck. Circling his neck was a black cord from which dangled a steel key. For all his other fears, Etrius felt confident that St. Germain had never been able to remove the key from his neck. The cord was protected by the most powerful binding spells in the world. It could only be used by Etrius, and never when he was under the mental control of another. It opened the locked door that led to the underground chamber containing Tremere's coffin.

In the past century, Tremere had spent more and more time in torpor. Their founder had rarely risen to direct the business of the clan. The last time he had left his coffin had been only for a few short hours to lead the discussion focusing on the events in Russia. Nothing definite had been decided at that time, but Tremere had not emerged from his sleep to offer any new ideas.

Etrius had been hoping that somehow the revelations of St. Germain's duplicity would summon Tremere from his rest. But when the minutes, then the hours, then the nights slipped by, Etrius had come to accept the fact that the clan founder was not going to help. In his fight with St. Germain, Etrius was entirely in charge.

With a grunt of annoyance, Etrius walked to the door of his study. As in life, so it was in death. If you wanted something done right, you had to do it yourself. No matter how busy you were with other projects. A pass of the hand made the entrance become one with the wall. Until he willed it, no one could enter—or leave—the room.

A muttered spell cleared the chamber of any outsider's spy probes or binding commands. No one, human mage or vampire wizard, could penetrate the protective web that circled the study. Even St. Germain's unknown powers could not bypass the basic laws of magic.

Satisfied with his precautions, Etrius walked over to the fireplace. A huge construction of red brick, it dated back to the original building of the mansion. Only a few wizards other than those of the Inner Circle knew its secret.

Etrius twisted three fingers in a mystic sign and the fire died. Resting a hand on the massive wall of brick, he spoke a word aloud. It was a word of great power. Etrius stepped back as the fireplace slid to the side, revealing a massive oak door. Only one key in the world opened the lock in that door. The key that hung around Etrius' neck.

Nervously, Etrius slipped the cord over his head. Holding the key in his left hand, he inserted it into the lock. A twist and the bolt clicked. The door swung open smoothly, revealing a dark tunnel leading downward. Etrius grimaced. It was two hundred and thirty seven steps to the vault. He knew. He had walked up and down these steps several thousand times.

He descended into the blackness. Tremere headquarters was centered over a huge network of underground caverns beneath Vienna. No one was sure who had built the catacombs but they definitely were not natural. And they had been here before the coming of the Kindred.

Tremere had become a member of the third generation by committing diablerie on Saulot while the Antediluvian was in torpor. Concerned that he someday might suffer the same fate, he spent years designing a special resting place for his body. The only known entrance to the tomb was through the door behind the fireplace. Etrius, though, suspected that there were other exits, known only to Tremere. And beyond the sarcophagus was a pitch-black tunnel none had ever dared enter, leading farther downward.

A hundred different spells protected the passage through

which Etrius descended. Torches that burned eternally lined the walls, for no electrical devices worked inside the passageway. Nor could any vampire materialize in the space. Or use some sort of Earth magic to pass through its walls. Tremere had foreseen every possible method of attack. Or, at least, so he thought.

The gigantic stone coffin rested in the center of a small cavern some twenty feet long by fifteen feet wide. The stone roof stretched thirty feet into the stone. At one end of the cave was the stairway from above. At the other, just beyond the front of the coffin, was the entrance to the passageway leading farther downward. Nothing had ever emerged from that dark hall, but at times, Etrius swore that he had heard voices whispering in the depths far below.

Cautiously, Etrius approached the sarcophagus. He rarely came here, other than when mentally summoned by Tremere. At times, reality and fantasy mixed and Etrius had difficulty remembering what was truth and what was nightmare. He had vague recollections of seeing a third eye open once in Tremere's skull. A more frightening memory— or dream, for he wasn't sure which—was of once opening the lid of the coffin and finding a giant, mucus-covered white worm within.

With a shudder, Etrius pushed open the tomb's lid and stared inside. A brief, somewhat relieved smile crossed the mage's lips. Tremere peacefully rested within the velvet-lined box. His features were those of a dynamic, powerful man—the same as they had been for more than a thousand years. His face appeared untroubled, at rest.

Nodding in relief, Etrius quickly closed the lid. Seeing Tremere safe and unharmed gave him a boost of confidence. His dream, Etrius knew, had been not only a revelation but a warning. St. Germain still existed and plotted. His continued presence was a danger to Clan Tremere. He had to be destroyed. And Etrius was the only one who could do it.

He spent the entire hike up the steps deciding his next move. It was less a matter of what to do than whom to use.

The choice, the more he thought about it, was not difficult to make. Etrius trusted very few Kindred, primarily those of his own brood. Of them, the most relentless, the most ruthless, the most determined, was Peter Spizzo.

Though Blood Bound to Etrius and thus unable to harm him, Spizzo made no secret of his desire to someday become a member of the Inner Council of Seven. Etrius knew Spizzo would do anything for a chance to become a councilor. Once the fireplace was back in place and the flame again burning, Etrius summoned the mage to his chamber.

"I want you to find a renegade Kindred," said Etrius, deciding the direct approach would work the best. There was no reason to lie to Spizzo. He just would not tell his childe more than he needed to know. "Do it and the reward will be great."

"How great?" asked Spizzo. A short, stocky man with jet-black hair, wide shoulders, and swarthy features, he burned with restless energy.

"Seek out and destroy the one I name," said Etrius, "and a seat on the Inner Council will be yours."

"There are no vacant positions in the Council of Seven," said Spizzo softly.

"Not yet," answered Etrius. "But that situation could change overnight."

His voice sank low. "Hundreds of years ago, one of Tremere's original disciples, Abetorius, was sent to the Middle East to spread the influence of our clan into Asia. He failed, badly. Ashamed of his defeat, he remained in Constantinople, where he reigns as the most unimportant member of the Council. No one would complain if he was suddenly replaced by a more forceful Cainite. Someone, for example, *like you.*"

"Tell me the name of the Kindred you want destroyed." said Spizzo.

"The Count St. Germain," said Etrius.

"St. Germain," repeated Spizzo slowly, letting the syllables roll off his lips. There was an odd glow in his eyes. "An interesting name." He looked at Etrius and nodded. "It shall be done. *No matter what it takes*, it shall be done."

CHAPTER 8

Washington, DC—March 21, 1994

It was midnight at the Lincoln Memorial. McCann waited in the shadows clustered around the rear of the huge statue. He was the only visitor on the grounds. With the riots continuing and much of Washington still burning, there were no tourists. Besides which, the police detail assigned to the Memorial had been pulled to help keep the peace. Despite being located in one of the safer regions of DC, only the bravest—or dumbest—people visited the monument at night even when the guards were present. Gang graffiti boldly painted on the walls and floor of the structure trumpeted the reason. There were even gang markings on the marble statue of Lincoln.

McCann sighed and shook his head in disgust. Anarchs, human or otherwise, had no respect for the past. Or, for that matter, the present or the future. They cared only for the moment and themselves.

The detective grimaced. The statue deserved better. Lincoln had been one of the greatest men in American history. He had accomplished a great deal during his few years in office, so much so that the Kindred secretly controlling the country finally ordered him killed. They dared not let him live during the Reconstruction. Otherwise he might have healed the hatred the Undead wanted to reign unchecked. And what the Kindred wanted, they usually got.

Lincoln had freed the slaves over a hundred years ago. Yet, many blacks in the United States still lived in abject poverty, denied their basic civil rights by local governments dominated by the KKK and right-wing extremists. The rich got richer and the poor continued to get poorer. The military-industrial complex thrived while common citizens went hungry and homeless. It was not the government of the people, for the people, by the people that Lincoln had envisioned, but a government by a few for a few.

It was a situation that appealed to both the Camarilla and the Sabbat. Massive federal intervention was needed to rebuild the country. But with a Congress controlled by wealthy special interest groups, poor people had no voice in national affairs.

Anxiously, the detective glanced at his watch. It was five minutes past the hour. He was starting to worry about Flavia. He found it inconceivable that the anarchs the night before could have pulled her down. If she was missing, something else had happened. And to McCann, that something else had to be an assassin named Makish. Or a Methuselah named Anis.

He had been stunned the night before when, as he drove out of the parking lot, the fabric of time rippled for an instant. McCann immediately recognized Temporis, the secret discipline of the True Brujah. Conceivably, it could have been another Kindred elder. But the detective felt certain it was Anis. She, too, was involved in some manner in The Red Death's plot.

The faintest whisper of air put McCann's fears about Flavia to rest. A gleam of white leather, seen for an instant, assured him he was not mistaken. When a hand tapped him on the shoulder and a woman's sultry voice whispered "I'm here," in his ear, McCann was prepared.

"You're late," he said, keeping his voice steady. He saw no reason to express his earlier concerns. Flavia and her obsession with Masqueraders was already a problem. Any indication that he had been worried would merely make her twice as insufferable.

"My deepest apologies," said the blonde, appearing seemingly out of thin air in front of the detective. Tonight she was dressed in her white leather jumpsuit. With a blood war raging through the city, worrying about disguises seemed foolish. "A gang of street punks thought I might need assistance with my clothing. They offered to remove it. I declined their invitation but they refused to take me seriously. It took me a few minutes to convince them that I meant what I said."

"How many died?" asked McCann.

"Five," said Flavia. She smiled. "I rearranged their bodies so that they appeared to have killed one another in an argument. That's why I was late. Murder is quick. Positioning corpses takes a few minutes."

"Judging from the radio and TV reports, no one will notice," said McCann. "The last figures I heard were nearly five hundred dead. And several thousand wounded."

"Needless to say," added Flavia, "those numbers don't include Kindred casualties, since our bodies usually disintegrate upon death. I have no way of estimating how many anarchs have suffered the Final Death the past few nights. But it must have been hundreds."

"Things seem to have quieted down tonight," said McCann.

"Justine has drawn in her followers," said Flavia. "Take that for what it's worth. Once unleashed, the Sabbat anarchs aren't very good at obeying orders. A small number refuse to stop rioting. The Archbishop's personal Blood Guard is dealing with them."

"What an unholy muddle," said McCann. "And we still have absolutely no idea how the Red Death is involved with the situation. Or where he is hiding."

Lameth, whispered a voice in McCann's mind, as if in reply to his questions. *The Red Death speaks. Are you willing to listen?*

Startled, the detective looked at Flavia. She stood a few feet away, waiting for instructions. Her bored expression made it clear that she had not heard a word.

"Check out the grounds," said McCann. "I have the oddest feeling we are not alone."

"Whatever you say," declared Flavia. "I'll be back in a few minutes. Don't wander off."

"I'm not moving," said McCann.

Mentally, he focused his thoughts into a reply. *I can hear you just fine. What do you want?*

I wish to make you an offer, was the near instantaneous reply. *Don't bother having your Assamite look for me. I am nowhere near you. Like many of our generation, I can broadcast my thoughts on a narrow beam aimed at a particular individual. Besides, locating you is not difficult. Your mind burns with a fire as fierce as my own.*

You assume too much about me, broadcast McCann, *but I see no reason to correct your mistakes. I repeat. What do you want?*

A peace parlay, declared the Red Death. *I wish to discuss an alliance between us. Attacking you was a mistake, I realize now. We both strive for the same goals. Together we might succeed. Working separately, we are doomed to failure.*

McCann grinned. Like so many of the Kindred, the Red Death was too arrogant for his own good. He thought everyone else the fool. A trap was a trap no matter what the excuse. The detective was anxious to confront the spectral figure face to face for a second time. But he didn't want to appear too eager.

I work on my own, he declared. *Why should I trust you?*

I pledge I will not harm you, flashed the Red Death. *I swear it by my sire's honor.*

It was a powerful oath, but McCann was not impressed. He had made and violated such sacred promises many times. *Give me one reason why should I meet you. One.*

Though prepared for deviousness, the detective was caught by surprise by the Red Death's reply.

The Nictuku are rising, telepathed the specter. *Remember, I was the one, using Benedict as a messenger, who sent those photos of the Iron Hag to Vargoss. I knew you would see them. The monsters cannot be defeated alone. Only our combined powers can destroy the horrors.*

Out of the corner of an eye McCann spotted Flavia returning. He preferred that she not learn of this mental conversation. Hurriedly, he sent his answer.

You raise a valid point. Where to meet? And when?

The Washington Navy Yard, returned the Red Death.

Tomorrow at midnight. Come alone. Or do not come at all.

Agreed, thought McCann and broke off contact.

It was a ruse. The detective was positive that The Red Death had no real interest in working with anyone. There was a reason behind the confrontation and it wasn't cooperation. McCann didn't care. Traps often had a nasty habit of backfiring on those who set them. Especially when Lameth, the Dark Messiah, was involved.

"Find anyone?" he asked Flavia.

"Not a soul," said the Assamite. "You look happy. Why the big smile?"

"I think I came up with an idea how to find the Red Death," said McCann. "It's a long shot, but one that might work. Unfortunately, it's going to take some legwork in the daylight hours. Meet me here, same time, same place, tomorrow night. By then I should have the answer."

Flavia's eyes narrowed as she stared at McCann. The Assamite, he guessed, was trying to read his mind. That was impossible. He kept even his surface thoughts shielded. "I don't care for this idea, McCann," she finally declared, her voice cold. "I dislike being played for a fool."

"The Red Death," the detective repeated. "I can locate him. Tomorrow night. Give me twenty-four hours."

Unexpectedly, Flavia smiled. It was one of the few times McCann had ever seen the assassin smile, and the sight of it caught him by surprise. "You are a schemer, Dire McCann," she stated, with a low chuckle. "It's one of the many reasons I believe you are more than you pretend. Much more.

"You play with words. I will not bandy terms or definitions with you. Proceed as you wish. I will be waiting here tomorrow as you request. Show up. I do not like to be deceived. No matter who does the tricking."

Then Flavia was gone, with the same soft whisper of sound as she had arrived. McCann shook his head. He would have almost favored Flavia accompanying him on his meeting with the Red Death. She would have provided a strong backup against treachery. However, the specter had specified that he come alone. The condition bothered McCann not at all. He preferred keeping some aspects of his identity hidden even from his closest allies. For while the detective knew he was walking into a trap, he was not without a few surprises of his own.

CHAPTER 9

Washington, DC—March 21, 1994

"I wish," said Alicia Varney to Sanford Jackson as the clock in her suite tolled midnight, "that I had brought Sumohn with me."

"Transporting a black panther several hundred miles by limousine might have proven difficult," replied her aide. "I doubt if your cat would have stayed hidden in the trunk."

Alicia shrugged. "I know. But my psychic powers are useless with so many vampires in the area. The black panther, with her special hunting skills, would find The Red Death a lot quicker than Justine and her anarch army."

"They're not an army," corrected Jackson, bristling slightly. "Soldiers have discipline and obey orders. These vampires are mindless rabble. They are worthless cannon fodder."

"Not entirely worthless," said Alicia. "The Sabbat anarchs have plunged the city into a state of total chaos. The police and fire departments are helpless. The National Guard can't stop the looting. The rule of law has collapsed. Those few members of the Camarilla who are still active are desperately scrambling to maintain the Masquerade. Justine has no such worries. If she somehow finds Marcus Vitel in the next few days and destroys him, the city will be hers. Washington, DC, seat of power of the US government, will be controlled by the Sabbat."

Alicia smiled. Justine's success here would establish the Archbishop as the leading contender for Regent of the Sabbat. Though things had not proceeded exactly as originally planned, they had not gone as badly as Alicia had feared. Only the mystery of The Red Death remained to be solved.

"Won't the Camarilla strike back?" asked Jackson. Though he knew more about the Kindred than most humans, his knowledge came directly from Alicia. And she was careful not to tell him too much.

"Not if Vitel is eliminated," said Alicia. "It's the old problem of descending to the level of your enemy to defeat them. Destroying the Sabbat leadership in the city would require a full-scale attack like the one we witnessed these past few days. However, a second such effort, coming shortly after the these riots, would threaten the Masquerade. The Camarilla won't risk that possibility. Bound by their traditions, the sect is unable to use the only technique that might bring them victory."

"I'm not so convinced about that," said Jackson. "Justine has tried using an army of Undead fanatics to overrun those in positions of power. It hasn't worked because the targets were warned in advance. That's the problem with the direct approach. A team of trained assassins could have accomplished the same goal a lot easier. And they would have done it faster and with a lot less commotion."

Alicia frowned. Her aide made a good point. In fact, it made her wonder if such a scheme wasn't being used already. A number of Camarilla Kindred had died the Final Death during the past two days. As had numerous members of the Sabbat. There were odd rumors about the death of John Thompson. As well as whispers among the Blood Guard of a mysterious assassin named Makish. Nor had anyone discovered who had warned Prince Vitel of the blood war.

"Why," she asked aloud, "would anyone kill leaders of the Camarilla and the Sabbat and forsake any credit for the murders? What possible motive would an assassin have for exterminating members of each sect and blaming the other?"

Jackson snorted in amusement. "You didn't pay much attention to your military's involvement with the Vietnam War, did you, Miss Alicia? Whenever the boys at the Pentagon wanted an increase in spending, they faked a new crisis overseas. Pressed the right button and Congress and the President jumped through hoops. Killed a few bigwigs in Saigon and Hanoi and the money flowed like water. Stirred the pot a little, got both sides steamed, and the war continued bigger than before. Escalation needed provocation. Winning the conflict wasn't what the military wanted. Their power came from making war, not making peace."

Alicia stared at her aide in bewilderment. "You mean our Generals deliberately fabricated disasters to further their own careers? They murdered our allies and blamed the other side?"

"Sure," said Jackson. "The more dangerous the enemy appeared, the faster the top brass rose in rank."

"And you're suggesting that the Red Death might be doing something similar here?" said Alicia. "That by secretly helping both sides in the battle he's actually intensifying the conflict between the Camarilla and the Sabbat?"

"It makes sense to me," said Jackson.

"But why?" asked Alicia. "What does he stand to gain if the conflict between the sects continues to grow?"

Anis, whispered a frigid voice deep within her mind. *The Red Death speaks. Are you willing to listen to what I have to say?*

Alicia didn't believe in coincidences. Somehow the specter had been mentally eavesdropping on her conversation. Evidently it didn't like the possibilities being discussed. She promised herself to return to the puzzle later. Now she needed to concentrate on the Red Death.

Her expression must have alerted Jackson to the fact that something odd was taking place. He stiffened to attention, awaiting her commands. With a faint smile, Alicia sent her thoughts hurtling across the mental pathway opened by the Red Death.

I am always willing to listen to reason, she declared. *You attacked me without provocation. I did nothing to you.*

That was a serious mistake on my part, came the near-instantaneous reply. *I vastly underestimated your powers. And those of your mysterious friend. Fortunately, I learn from my errors. Your strength and determination are legendary. I realize now that I should never have attacked you. I wish instead to make you an offer that I think you will find most attractive.*

Alicia saw no reason to correct the Red Death on his

assumption about Reuben. She believed in taking advantage of any misconception her enemies might have about her. And, despite the specter's words of moderation, Alicia had no doubts that The Red Death was her enemy.

Make your offer, she broadcast. *I am always willing to listen to reason.*

A peace parlay, declared the Red Death. *I wish to discuss an alliance between us. We both strive for the same goals. Together we might succeed. Working separately, we are doomed to failure.*

Alicia sighed. Six thousand years of intrigue had taught her never to trust anyone, especially another member of the fourth generation. No Methuselah ever lacked the confidence that it wasn't powerful enough to handle any problem it faced. Their egos were all-consuming. The Red Death, despite his claims to the contrary, was no different than the rest. She knew he was lying. He was an arrogant fool, incapable of realizing the transparency of his actions. Over the centuries, Alicia had encountered his type many times. They never learned that trying to seduce a seductress was impossible. But, they kept on trying.

I have my own agenda, she declared pompously. *Why should I waste my time with you?*

Though expecting some sort of convoluted logic, Alicia was caught totally by surprise by the Red Death's reply.

The Nictuku are rising, telepathed the specter. *The situation in Russia is continually getting worse. The Iron Hag has taken over the country. And monstrous events are about to unfold in Australia. The entire Kindred race is threatened.*

Alicia shivered. The Red Death was no fool. She almost believed he wanted her cooperation. Still, she was not impressed enough with his answer to walk into a trap without first protesting further. He would have been suspicious if she hadn't.

How do I know you are not merely using the circumstances to lure me to my doom? she asked.

I pledge I will not harm you, replied the Red Death. *I swear it by my sire's honor.*

It was a powerful oath. The specter sounded like he was deadly serious. But Alicia was not that credulous. Oaths were words, nothing more. They were made to be broken.

Where do you want to meet? she asked. *And when?*

The Washington Navy Yard, returned the Red Death. *Tomorrow at midnight. Come alone. Or do not come at all.*

Tomorrow at midnight, thought Alicia. *Agreed. I will be there.*

Contact ceased. Alicia laughed harshly. "This time, you arrogant bastard, I'll be prepared."

"What was that about?" asked Jackson, looking flustered. "One second we're talking. The next, you're not moving, with a strange expression on your face."

"A direct telepathic link between me and the Red Death," said Alicia. "He wants to meet me tomorrow evening. And make friends."

She saw no reason to mention the Nictuku. Jackson knew more than most humans. But there were some secrets of the Kindred that were not meant for mortal minds.

"You're not planning to confront this monster?" asked Jackson. "It's a trap."

"So I expect," said Alicia. "I'd be disappointed if it wasn't. The Red Death wants a second chance at killing me. So he's politely asked if I would stick my head into a noose. We're to rendezvous at the Navy Yard at midnight. Alone. I, of course, agreed to his terms."

Jackson frowned. "Alone? That might be a problem. The Navy Yard is awfully big. Especially if you want the usual support crew. It's going to require a lot of manpower."

"I leave the details in your capable hands," said Alicia. She smiled her nastiest smile. "Remember the machinery I mentioned we could borrow from the government. Make sure it's ready. I don't care what money you need to spend. I want the arrangements made and everything ready and waiting. The Red Death thinks he's very clever. It's time he learns that I can be clever too."

CHAPTER 10

Washington, DC—March 21, 1994

The handsome young couple sat in a rear both at Geppi's restaurant, nibbling on thick-crust pizza and drinking Coca-Cola. None of the staff remembered exactly when they had entered. Or who had taken their order. But since they seemed to be having a good time, no one worried. Somehow their presence in the restaurant seemed perfectly natural.

The man appeared to be around twenty-five years old. He was slender, with wavy blond hair and bright blue eyes. His skin, slightly bronze, glowed with good health. He wore an open-neck white shirt and white slacks. Even his shoes and socks were white.

His companion was dressed in dark blue slacks and a glittering blue sequined tunic top. Her eyes matched the color of her clothes, while her hair was a brilliant shade of red. She wore a hint of makeup. The looseness of her clothing could not conceal the lush lines of her figure. While the man was merely handsome, she was stunning.

A careful observer might have noticed a faint facial resemblance between the two. Anyone asking would have learned that they were brother and sister. But no one in the restaurant gave them a second look. That was the way they wished it. And their wishes always came true.

"They've both accepted the so-called truce," the young man declared. His voice was mellow, incredibly smooth and relaxing. Though it was not his real name, he called himself Reuben. "Tomorrow evening, at midnight, our Masqueraders are both scheduled to meet the Red Death at the Washington Navy Yard."

"I know," said his sister, who called herself Rachel. Her voice was deep and sultry, sexy without being threatening. "I followed the two telepathic conversations as well. There should be fireworks. I'm astonished that neither Anis nor Lameth has guessed the truth. They don't realize the full scope of the Red Death's bizarre identity."

"Not yet," said Reuben. "McCann almost stumbled upon it at the nightclub, but then the thought eluded him. Alicia never had any reason to be suspicious. In Washington the telepathic babble due to the invasion effectively shields his secret from their mental probes. I suspect you're correct in your assessment of the situation. They're both walking into a deadly trap, thinking that they are entirely safe."

Rachel shook her head. "You misunderstand what I mean. These aren't naive young anarchs we're discussing here. Between the two of them, shared and alone, they have participated in more than ten thousand years of duplicity, betrayal, and treachery. They understand full well that the Red Death is plotting their destruction. They suspect he somehow plans to circumvent his oath. They don't care. All they want is a chance to strike back at the monster. Neither of them suffers from stupidity, just incredible vanity."

Reuben nodded. "That's why pointing them in the right direction has been so difficult. The two of them are almost incapable of believing they are ever wrong."

"They sound just like you," said Rachel, sipping delicately from her Coke. In the background, the jukebox in the corner started playing "You're So Vain" by Carly Simon. No one in the restaurant seemed to notice that the machine had begun working without anyone depositing coins.

The redhead smiled at the mixture of annoyance and dismay displayed on her brother's face. "Actually, though we have yet to meet in person, I find this Dire McCann quite fascinating. I hope he survives this encounter."

"I feel the same about Alicia," said Reuben, brightening. "She is, unquestionably, the most dangerous woman in the world. Miss Varney is both beautiful and brilliant." He smiled back at his sister. "And I think she likes me."

The brother and sister stared at each other for a moment, then burst out laughing. No one else in the restaurant noticed the couple's behavior. No one never did.

"We think much too much alike," he declared, still chuckling. The jukebox slipped into "Shut Up and Kiss Me" by Mary Chapin Carpenter.

"The peril of being twins," she replied. "Do you believe McCann or Varney have any idea who we really are? Or why we have acted on their behalf?"

"Not yet," said Reuben. "Lameth, however, communicates with McCann through dreams. Sooner or later the Methuselah is going to realize why your features are so familiar. That's when things will get interesting."

"Phantomas already suspects," said Alicia, changing the subject. "He saw the carving of Khufu in the Louvre."

"I forgot all about that picture," said Reuben, shaking his head in annoyance. "I wish I hadn't. That Nosferatu is awfully smart. And that encyclopedia he's working on gives him an unfair advantage."

"The Red Death wants him dead," said Rachel. "The specter made a bargain with those three oafs to destroy Phantomas. The Nosferatu is in terrible danger."

"Don't underestimate our ugly little friend," said Reuben. "He hasn't lived for two millennia running away from trouble. Phantomas avoids confrontation, but he is no coward. Remember, he traveled with Caesar's legions. He destroyed Urgahalt. I suspect the Unholy Three, as they like to think of themselves, are going to be very surprised by their intended victim. He won't die easily."

"I like your trick with his computer," said Rachel. She attacked another slice of pizza as she spoke. "You have a flair for the dramatic."

"It caught his attention," said Reuben. "Plus it gave me a chance to play with the machinery a bit. Phantomas needed a tiny shove in the right direction. The message supplied the push. Since then, he filled in the blanks nicely."

Rachel took another sip of her Coke. "He has the information. Lameth and Anis have the power. If they connect, do you think the three of them can defeat the Masquerade of the Red Death?"

Reuben shrugged his shoulders. "I'm not sure. Seker has

planned this coup for centuries. His bloodline has always been extremely powerful. Cooperating with The Sheddim makes him and his followers nearly omnipotent. I truly don't know whether the Red Death *can* be stopped."

"*We* could thwart his plans," said Rachel.

"*Perhaps*," said Reuben. "I'm not as convinced as you. Reality can only be twisted so far. And Father has made it quite clear that our involvement with the Jyhad must be minimal. At present, we can merely watch and wait."

Rachel pouted. "I hate waiting."

"Tell me about it," said Reuben. "The price of immortality is learning how to endure infinite boredom. I'm convinced that despite numerous Methuselah statements about it being their destiny to guide the Kindred, those still engaged in the Jyhad are participating primarily to keep from going crazy."

The jukebox switched from country back to rock. The patrons never said a word as Queen's "Who Wants to Live Forever?" blared from the speakers.

"Maybe," replied Rachel. "However, as we've argued in the past, I'm not entirely convinced that you're right about that. I hope you're wrong, for our sakes." She sighed. "The only one who knows for sure is Father."

"Correction," said Reuben, solemnly. "There is another."

"We'd better leave," said Rachel. "The conversation is turning too serious. I've had enough pizza. And it's getting late."

"Later than they think," said Reuben.

He waved over a nearby waitress and handed her a fifty-dollar bill. "We have to get moving," he said pleasantly. "Can you handle our bill? We had a thick-crust cheese pizza and a pitcher of Coke."

The young woman blinked, looking slightly bemused. "I'm not exactly sure whose table this is," she declared. "No problem, though, if you're in a hurry. Wait a 'sec and I'll bring your change."

When the waitress returned, the couple was gone. The manager, worried about the size of the tip, questioned the rest of the staff about the pair. No one could remember the two exiting. Or, for that matter, the duo entering or being served. Actually, nobody could recall much about them at all.

CHAPTER 11

Washington, DC—March 22, 1994

It was near midnight at the Lincoln Memorial. Clouds covered the moon and stars. It was cold, icy cold for March in Washington. A lone figure stood by the side of the huge statue of Abraham Lincoln. It was a blonde woman dressed entirely in white leather. Her gaze darted back and forth, scanning the shadows. She was anxiously waiting for someone. But no one approached.

The black shape, deeper than the darkness, traveled like a blur across the earth outside the building. Reaching the marble stairs, it flashed up the white steps and into the hollow recess between the pillars. It moved silently, hardly making a sound. Yet it generated enough noise that the face of the woman in white leather snapped around, searching for the culprit. Eyes blazing, she dropped into a fighting position, arms held out before her, bent at the elbows.

"Who are you?" she asked. "What do you want?"

A dozen feet from the woman in white, the shadow solidified, turning into a young woman with long, dark hair, dressed only in a black leotard. She nodded, as if confirming her suspicions.

"I am Madeleine Giovanni of the Clan Giovanni. I gather you are the Assamite once known as Sarah James, now called Flavia, the Dark Angel?"

Flavia nodded but didn't lower her hands. Madeleine would have been surprised if she had. Assamites weren't notorious for their trusting nature.

"You know my identity, Giovanni," said the woman in white. "And your reputation is known throughout my clan. Though we work for different masters and different causes, I believe we acknowledge the same rites of conduct."

"Honor above all else," said Madeleine, solemnly. "Debts of blood must be repaid in kind."

Flavia smiled. However, she still remained on guard.

"What does a notorious Giovanni saboteur want with me? Especially in a city where the Sabbat anarchs battle Camarilla elders."

"I visited with your prince, Alexander Vargoss, earlier this week," said Madeleine. "He told me you were in Washington, accompanying a human named Dire McCann. The two of you were hunting a spectral figure who called himself the Red Death."

"Correct," said Flavia. She was no longer smiling. "Why does that concern you?"

"I need to find McCann," said Madeleine. Lying to Flavia would serve no useful purpose. When necessary, it paid to be direct. "My sire sent me to locate him. As he is human, I cannot use my special talents to trace him in a city this big. However, I am mistress of a discipline that enables me to sense the presence of powerful Kindred in the immediate surroundings. Even the company of hundreds of other vampires in the locale does not dampen my ability. It is a skill that has served me well during a Blood Hunt. When I arrived in the capital, I cast my psychic net and detected two powerful Assamites in the area. I came here first. From Vargoss' description, I recognized you immediately."

"You detected me and *another?*" asked Flavia. "That had to be Makish. The rumors were true."

"The rogue assassin?" said Madeleine. "I had no idea he was in the city. Is he working for the Camarilla or the Sabbat?"

"I'm not sure," said Flavia. "A number of members from each sect have disappeared lately. Most of the deaths have been attributed to the blood war being waged by the Sabbat. But too many have died or disappeared without anyone claiming credit for the kills. It seems suspicious to me."

Madeleine nodded. She, like Flavia, knew that most young neonate vampires couldn't resist bragging about their exploits. Slaying an elder Cainite was major news. For Kindred to vanish without anyone blustering about how they accomplished the task was very odd. The dark lady could think of only one possible explanation.

"Makish never boasts about his murders," said Madeleine. "He considers himself an artist. As such, he lets his endeavors speak for themselves. Still, why would he kill Kindred on both sides of the conflict? Surely one group or the other must be paying his wages. The rogue does not come cheap. And he definitely doesn't work for free."

"It is a mystery," said Flavia. "One that I do not like."

The Assamite hesitated, then continued. "McCann is not here. I expect him any minute, though."

"I will wait," said Madeleine.

The two vampires, dark and light, stood silent, unmoving. Patient. Unobtrusively, each studied the other, pondering skills, weaknesses. It was part of their nature, their training. Though completely dissimilar in background and appearance, they were closer than sisters in spirit.

It was Flavia who broke the quiet. "What do you know of The Red Death?" she asked apprehensively.

"Nothing more than your prince told me," said Madeleine. "I heard the story of his attack and the death of your sister. Vargoss seemed positive that the specter was a Sabbat elder."

"You were not convinced?" said Flavia, tilting her head slightly and smiling.

"I believe in facts, not supposition," said Madeleine. "From your tone, I suspect you feel the same."

"McCann thinks The Red Death works for himself and no other. In the short time I have known the detective, he has rarely been wrong."

"Vargoss said McCann was a mage?"

"Euthanatos tradition," replied Flavia. Madeleine, trained for centuries to detect the slightest hesitation or doubt in a voice, Kindred or kine, noted that the Assamite paused for an instant. There was something Flavia was not revealing about McCann's identity. It was not important. At least not right now. "He is the most interesting mortal I have ever known. And by far the most dangerous."

Again Madeleine detected an odd note in Flavia's remark. As if challenging her to disagree. There was something odd, very odd, about this Dire McCann. She wondered if that was the reason behind her mission. By now, she was anxious to finally encounter this unusual human. For several reasons.

"You are definitely meeting the detective here tonight?"

"At midnight," said Flavia, sounding the slightest bit concerned. "Usually, he is very prompt."

The woman in white frowned. "You said you sensed Makish? Where? When? There were rumors he was allied with The Red Death. And last night McCann mentioned something about finding a clue to the specter's hideaway."

"Would he dare investigate without you?" asked Madeleine.

"McCann would dare anything," said Flavia.

Madeleine's eyes narrowed, her fingers curled into fists. She stood motionless, mentally scanning the city with her tremendous will.

"I have him again," she whispered. "South of here. To the east." Madeleine grimaced, as if in pain. "He is not alone. The assassin is in the company of several others. They are waiting for someone. I can sense that. They are all waiting."

"Several?" From Flavia's lips, the words sounded like a curse. "More than one other?"

Madeleine's lips pressed together into thin lines. "I am distressed to admit that I cannot fathom how many others are there, or their clan identity. There is something strange about their minds. They seem tied together, perhaps by telepathy. Nor do they exhibit any of the distinguishing characteristics of the thirteen clans. Yet I sense that they are extremely powerful Kindred. They pulse with raw, elemental energy."

"*The Red Death*," said Flavia, a note of desperation in her voice. "We discussed the possibility before leaving St. Louis, but never gave it much thought. There are *several* monsters, not one."

"You think McCann is walking into their trap?"

"I'm sure of it," said Flavia. "But they'll soon discover that he is no easy target."

"South and east," repeated Madeleine. "South and east."

Her body wavered, grew indistinct. What was form became shadow. A patch of darkness bulleted down the marble steps and into the night.

With a snarl of fury, Flavia followed.

CHAPTER 12

Washington, DC—March 22, 1994

"Quarter to twelve," said Jackson, checking out the last of the electronic equipment in the van. "Still time to change your mind. You sure you want to go through with this insanity?"

Alicia grinned. She was dressed in slacks, a mid-weight winter jacket, and a plain black hat. The clothes worked wonders, hiding her body armor and communications gear. "Tonight is what being alive is all about, my dear Jackson. I wouldn't miss this confrontation for the world."

Her aide shook his head in astonishment. "How do you know this monster will even show up? This whole scheme could just be a elaborate death trap."

"The Red Death will come," said Alicia confidently. She understood the monster's motive. It was the same as hers. "He wants to eliminate me. And he's convinced the only way to insure my death is to personally supervise the execution."

"That sounds like a very good reason to stay away," said Jackson. "Remember the power this guy controls. He can fry you to a crisp in seconds. Living is about living. Not dying."

"That's all a matter of perspective," said Alicia. Her eyes grew wide, almost hypnotic in intensity. "Did you ever own a favorite suit, Mr. Jackson? A suit that was so comfortable that when you were wearing it, you hardly noticed it was on? The perfect fit, the perfect style, everything about it was just right. When you have clothing like that, you hate to give it up. You never want to let it go. But sooner or later you realize that it's only a suit. Nothing more. And there's always more suits."

"Whatever you say, Miss Varney," replied Jackson, looking bewildered. "But we're not talking clothes here. You get killed out there, it won't matter what you're wearing."

With a smile, Alicia leaned over and kissed her aide on the cheek. "It depends entirely on your point of view, Mr. Jackson."

Then, without a backward glance, she was out the rear door of the van and onto the street leading to the entrance to the Navy Yard.

"You hear me okay, Miss?" came Jackson's voice, twenty seconds later, over the intercom she wore in her hair.

"Perfectly," subvocalized Alicia. The microphone attached to her coat picked up and amplified her replies and relayed them to the control van. "Am I starring on TV yet?"

"Yes, ma'am," replied Jackson. "Got you on two different monitors. The whole Navy Yard is covered by our cameras. Unless you enter one of the buildings, you'll remain on-screen."

"Good," said Alicia. Supremely confident, she marched forward onto the grounds of the old Navy Yard. Originally the home of a major naval gun factory during the 19th century, the Yard had served primarily as a tourist attraction for the past four decades. At this time of night, it was deserted.

"There's a replica of the original gun factory at the edge of the river," said Jackson in her ear. "Along with a Navy museum and a Marine museum. Somehow I doubt that this Red Death character wants to do any sightseeing. Keep to the right. That's the Parade Grounds. Nice and open there. It's the perfect spot for a meeting."

Alicia nodded. They had gone over this information several times when making their plans. And installing their equipment.

"The pods are in place?"

"Yes, Miss," said Jackson. "I'm getting readouts from all three. Watch for a storage depot on the edge of the march area. One of the units is inside."

Unlimited funds had their advantages. Three escape pods built by NASA for the space program then never used, had been transported to the Navy Yard earlier that day. The construction crews, following orders, had left them in strategic locations throughout the Yard. It had cost millions in bribes getting the units moved and installed, but Alicia had money to burn. Each designed to protect their occupant from the destructive power of an atomic explosion, the pods served as Alicia's last line of defense against The Red Death.

"Any signs of movement?" she asked as she cut across the brown earth, heading for the parade grounds. "What time is it?"

"Seven minutes to zero hour, Miss," said Jackson. "Not a sign of life anywhere. All stations are ready and anxious."

"Well, the Red Death said midnight," replied Alicia, "so I guess patience is the password."

"Uh, uh," said Jackson, sounding surprised. "A car's just pulled up to the front entrance. Man's getting out. Big, powerful-looking guy. He's heading into the Yard. No resemblance at all to your buddy, The Red Death. Any ideas? Should we blast him?"

"Hold your fire," said Alicia. She shook her head, then smiled, realizing who it had to be. She should have guessed. "He'll locate me in a minute. It's fine. I know him."

"You do?" said Jackson. "Who the hell is he?"

"An old acquaintance," said Alicia. "I told you about him in New York. Remember? He's my oldest, closest friend."

He was big. Alicia guessed two-fifty and six foot six. A massive man, with wide shoulders and deep chest, he wore a thin topcoat through it was below freezing. The weather never bothered him, in life or in undeath.

She grinned when he drew close enough that she could see his face. Though his features were different, they were the same. There were certain characteristics that never varied, no matter what body they inhabited. Alicia wondered if she was equally as obvious in her choices. The stranger was clean-shaven, with thick, dark hair, bushy eyebrows, and dark, penetrating eyes. He held his head in a certain manner that had not changed through countless centuries.

"Lameth," she declared. "You're not The Red Death, I hope?"

The big man sighed. That habit, too, had not wavered over the millennia. He always sounded world-weary. The weight of the world rested on Lameth's broad shoulders. "One personality is more than enough for me," he declared solemnly. For all of his dramatic gestures, the big man possessed a cynic's humor.

"You're looking well," said Alicia. "Very healthy. Alive and kicking."

"Anis, you are radiant as ever," he replied. "Alicia Varney, the billionairess, right? I've seen you interviewed on TV news several times. And there was that appearance on the David Letterman show. I didn't realize it was you when I was watching, of course. I'm Dire McCann these days."

"The detective," said Alicia, nodding. "I remember now. You uncovered Mosfair." She shook her head. "You cost me a good agent. My fault, I suppose. I should have guessed anything involving Lameth's elixir had to be a trap."

McCann chuckled. "Your memory slipped. If you recall, there was just enough of the potion for two. You and me. That was all that ever existed. Several of the scarcer ingredients came from animals that are long extinct. Fables of the elixir being rediscovered, I'm afraid, are exactly that. Fables."

"Still manipulating the Giovanni?" Alicia asked.

"Money makes the world go round," said McCann. "I don't have to ask if you're still involved with the Sabbat. The evidence is spread out through the city."

Alicia couldn't suppress a grin. "It did get slightly out of hand."

"Slightly," said McCann dryly.

"Why are you here?" asked Alicia.

"The same reason as you, I suspect," said McCann. "The Red Death invited me to a parlay. He swore an oath on his sire's honor that he would not attack. He asked for no such promise in return. So I decided to come. And see what he had to say."

"Likewise," said Alicia, smiling. The detective winked,

confirming her suspicions. Left unsaid was the real reason he had traveled to the rendezvous. It was the same as hers. Neither of them intended The Red Death to survive this parlay. "Same promise, too. Any idea who he is?"

"Not a clue," replied McCann. He glanced down at his watch. "Minute till twelve. I expect he will be exactly on time. He strikes me as the type who's never late."

"Obsessive-compulsive personality," said Alicia, chuckling. "I know what you mean."

Reaching out, she patted McCann on an arm. "Good to see you again, my sweet. I've missed you."

"And me, you," he replied. "Paris was fun. But it was a hundred and nine years ago."

"If the situation becomes messy here tonight," she said softly, "let's meet there again. Its a rendezvous that only we remember."

McCann nodded in agreement. "Too many strange characters seem to know much too much about me." There was an odd look on his face. "Kindred and kine."

Alicia licked her lips. "A young man with blond hair? Who said his name was Reuben?"

"No," answered McCann. "A redhead named Rachel. Her powers to reshape reality were frightening."

"That sounds like my friend Reuben," said Alicia. "We have to talk."

"Not now," said McCann. He pointed to a spot a few yards past Alicia. "I believe our host is arriving. "It's midnight."

The red mist rose like a ghost from the dark earth of the parade ground. Indistinct at first, it gradually solidified into the frightening figure of The Red Death.

Alicia's pulse quickened. Until this moment, despite what she had said to Jackson, she had not been sure that the Red Death would show up. The entire truce could have been a trick, aimed at luring her and McCann into some outlandish trap. But, her basic instincts had proven correct. The Red Death was here.

"He won't be leaving using the same trick," murmured

McCann at her side. "If I focus my will, I can stop him from dematerializing. However, the trick takes a great deal of effort. "I wasn't sure how I was going to finish the job. Why don't you handle that? We always worked well as a team."

"That sounds like a wonderful proposition," replied Alicia. "He deserves to die, the arrogant fool. Imagine, thinking he could defeat both of us at the same time. What nerve!"

McCann nodded. "The Red Death will pay the price for his stupidity."

"He's arrived," subvocalized Alicia, wanting to make sure nothing was amiss with her troops.

"I see him," replied Jackson from the control center. "I've alerted our agents. They're ready."

"I wonder what treachery he has planned," said McCann softly. The detective actually looked cheerful.

"Nothing pleasant, I'm sure," replied Alicia. She also found herself smiling. "But then again, neither do we."

CHAPTER 13

Washington, DC—March 22, 1994

"Greetings, Lameth and Anis," said the Red Death. Its voice was the wind rolling across a cemetery. It was filled with the chill of the grave. "I appreciate your heeding my call. Tonight the future of the Kindred lies in our hands. We must join together or perish."

McCann inhaled a deep breath. He had expected nothing less, but hearing it still made him sigh. Despite being Undead and thousands of years old, most Methuselahs were not evil monsters beyond redemption. Those who had lost all traces of humanity had either accepted the Beast and descended into the madness which led to the Final Death or drifted into an eternal torpor where their minds only tangentially touched reality. The majority of fourth-generation vampires engaged in the Jyhad were motivated by complex, powerful desires that went far beyond ruling the world. Both he and Anis had their own, distinct visions about the future of the Cainite race as well as about humanity. Evidently the Red Death had another.

"I'm listening," said Alicia, at his side. "But let me warn you. I've heard that line before. Many, many times over the ages. Others have predicted a terrible end for the Kindred. It's never happened. So convince me differently."

"It's been more than six thousand years since the destruction of the Second City," said McCann. "The Jyhad has raged that long. What makes this particular year different than those that have passed?"

"You know the answer, Lameth," said the Red Death. There was a note of sincerity in the monster's voice that the detective found amusing. The Red Death believed in what it was saying. It truly thought it was working for the good of the Kindred, not just itself. Though McCann had long since discovered that altruism and self-interest had a habit of merging together after a millennium. *"The Nictuku are rising."*

"Bad news travels fast these days," said Alicia. "I assume we all know that Baba Yaga has awakened in Russia. And Nuckalavee is haunting the deserts of Australia once again."

McCann shrugged. "So what? It's depressing stuff, but we've had bad news in the past. According to my sources, Gorgo rose from torpor in South America a year or more ago. Since then nobody's heard a word about the bitch."

The detective half-turned to Alicia. "Remember her? The One Who Screams in Darkness was the title given her by the inhabitants of the Second City. Even Absimiliard, her sire, found her repulsive. That's how she ended up in those caverns in Peru."

He turned back to the Red Death. "Who cares about the Nictuku? I see no reason to abandon plans forged over the centuries just because a few monsters have resurfaced."

"The entire Kindred population of Buenos Aires has disappeared," said the Red Death.

"Interesting if true," said McCann. "But the monsters have existed in torpor for millennia. Now a few of them have awakened. I'm concerned. But I'm not *that* worried."

"I, as well, had schemed for thousands of years," said the Red Death. "However, unlike most Methuselahs, I maintained a low profile. None of the Kindred knew of my bloodline or my plans. I watched and waited and planned for the day when all was in readiness for my emergence as leader of the Cainite race. Carefully, I closely spied upon my possible rivals. In particular, the two of you, since you were the only other vampires who had any chance of success." The monster paused. "The emergence of the Nictuku, the brood of Absimiliard, forced me to drastically revise my schedule."

The monster's gaze burned with fanatical intensity. "Gehenna approaches," said the Red Death. "I know it. *I feel it.*"

The monster's voice wavered for an instant, almost as if puzzled by what it was saying. Then, his voice regaining confidence, the Red Death continued. "We are nearing Armageddon's final call. The facts speak for themselves. The rising of the Nictuku means that the third generation are stirring. The Antediluvians will awaken from their torpor. And they will be hungry for blood. Our blood. We must defend ourselves. The Kindred must stand united or perish."

"Not good enough," said Alicia. "I dealt with the third generation in the Second City and survived." She laughed. "Actually, I managed quite well. The Thirteen control amazing powers. But they are not invincible."

"Together . . . " began the Red Death.

"Allies?" said McCann, grinning. "After trying to destroy me, and, I assume, Anis, you now propose cooperation? The three of us against the entire third generation? With you as leader, I assume."

"You object?" asked the Red Death. "I am by far the most powerful. Body of Fire makes me omnipotent."

"Perhaps," said Alicia, with a nasty laugh. "Perhaps."

"Besides," said McCann, "we know nothing about you. Why should we obey the orders of a mysterious Kindred of unknown origin?"

"Good point," said Alicia. "From what you said, you evidently know quite a bit about the two of us. Yet we know nothing about your sire or your brood. You mention your bloodline, but neither of us is aware of any such clan. Who is the Red Death? What are these plans you mentioned? And why have you been pitting the Camarilla against the Sabbat?"

The Red Death shook its head. McCann grimaced. The monster was starting to glow. The air around it shimmered as heat burst from the vampire's body. Mentally, the detective readied his own defenses. He had a feeling that the time for talking was just about over.

"Let us cut out the rest of the small talk," said the Red Death. "I offered an alliance, but I knew neither of you would accept. You are both too self-centered to realize the value of collaboration. It took no effort on my part. And served as a necessary distraction until I was ready to act. The time has come for an end to this charade. Consider the invitation withdrawn."

The specter laughed, spots of blood forming on its cheeks

and forehead. "You two are the only Methuselahs I fear. You are the only others who had a chance of winning the eternal war. But no longer. The Jyhad concludes tonight."

The Red Death seemed to expand, take on size. It was growing hotter by the second. "You came here to destroy me. However, the situation is much different than you suspect. My attacks in St. Louis and New York, along with this blood war, were all designed to serve dual purposes. As you stated, they accelerated the conflict between the Camarilla and the Sabbat. At the same time, they drew the two of you into my net. Here, in the center of the maelstrom. The conflict in the city worked as a wonderful distraction. Surrounded by hundreds of Kindred engaged in violent conflict, you never sensed my secret. And now it is too late."

McCann scowled. He didn't like what he was hearing. Glancing at Alicia, he noted her expression mirrored his. She had no more idea than he what the monster meant.

The Red Death held out its hands. They burned with unnatural fire. "My flames will totally consume the human body you each use as a marionette. It will take you months, perhaps years, to successfully reestablish a new identity—and regain a small measure of your influence among the Kindred. Long before then I will be master of the Cainite race!"

"So much for the oath on the honor of your sire" said Alicia, with a sneer.

"I swore it to you," said the Red Death, chuckling. "*But not to her.*"

"And I swore it *to her* and not to you," declared an identical voice a few feet *behind* them.

"Hell," said McCann, whirling around to confront a second creature, an exact duplicate of the vampire in front of him. "There are two of them."

"I swore it to *either*," came the voice of a third, from McCann's right.

"I made no such promise," came a voice from the detective's left.

"Four of the bastards," said McCann. Now he understood

the purpose of the specter's proposed alliance. The talk had served to distract their attention while the other monsters surrounded him and Alicia. The detective recalled his conversation with Vargoss and Darrow in St. Louis less than a week ago. "That's the secret of the Red Death. No wonder they seemed to be everywhere at once. They *were* everywhere!"

"*We are the Red Death,*" said the monsters.

Waves of incredible heat poured from their emaciated figures. They advanced a step. Then another. Stopping, they raised their arms like cannons. The air crackled as bolts of crimson fire streaked like red whips at the two humans. "We are the Red Death," the monsters chanted. "We are your doom."

"Not likely," said McCann. Hands clenched together into a massive fist, he exerted the full force of his will. Out of nowhere, a blue bubble ten feet in diameter appeared around him and Alicia. Tongues of fire touched the glowing sphere and were repelled. "This time, at least, I was prepared for your tricks."

The detective made no attempt to read the thoughts of his attackers. He knew everything he wanted to about them. After listening to the first Red Death's tirade, the meaning of their chosen name, The Children of Dreadful Night, was quite clear. The entire bloodline fought what they perceived as Armageddon approaching—by seeking absolute mastery of the Kindred.

With hundreds of Kindred in the city, the presence of the quartet of powerful Cainites had gone completely unnoticed by McCann. They were four among many. The Red Death had not lied. The entire blood war had served as a shield for the vampires' plot. McCann had come to crush the Red Death. Instead, he found the roles reversed and his survival in doubt.

The attack continued with increasing ferocity. The flames bursting against the blue circle grew more and more intense. McCann guessed that, as with most disciplines, the four monsters could only maintain Body of Fire for a certain length of time. If they did not break through his defenses by then, their fire power would disappear. And they would be helpless.

The odds, however, favored the Red Death. The leader of the group was of the fourth generation. His three doppelgängers were slightly less powerful. McCann guessed they were fifth-generation vampires. Together, they controlled incredible energies. It took all of McCann's strength to maintain the psychic shield. He had no excess power left to return their attack. And slowly they were smashing down his defenses.

The detective looked anxiously at Alicia. "Remember our earlier conversation?" he asked. "Forget about waiting until later. Now's the time to pull that trick out of your hat. Unless you have another solution in mind."

"You know me too well, Lameth," replied Alicia, her eyes glittering with excitement. McCann had to smile. Anis thrived on danger. The greater the peril, the greater the thrill. "I planned a small treat for our friend. That he brought company along doesn't matter."

Alicia moved her lips without making a sound. She nodded slightly, as if answering an unheard voice. Then, distinctly, McCann heard her say, "attack."

Engines roared. From a dozen locations around the marching grounds, small, oddly-shaped vehicles came lumbering out of the darkness. Five feet long, three feet high, riding on four huge balloon tires, they resembled rolling gas tanks with a large spray nozzle on the front. McCann noted with interest that painted in bright red on the white bodies of the devices were the letters N-A-S-A.

"Army surplus?" he shouted, trying to make himself heard over the growl of the machinery.

"On loan," replied Alicia. "I have friends in the right places. These babies are constructed to work on other planets. They're built to withstand incredible extremes of hot and cold. Computer-controlled from off-site by my agents, they're virtually indestructible. And wait till you see what they're carrying inside their tanks."

The NASA vehicles surrounded the four Red Deaths. Their concentration directed on maintaining Body of Fire, the quartet were unable to shift any of their attention to the machines. Carefully, the robots raised their nozzles in direct line with the vampires' torsos. A second later, a thin stream of white liquid spewed forth, hitting the monsters in the chest.

The chemical disappeared in a cloud of steam. The Red Deaths howled in agony. The fire from their fingers vanished, as the four vampires writhed in uncontrollable pain. "Liquid nitrogen," explained Alicia, smugly. "Pressurized in the tanks at a temperature only a few degrees above absolute zero. Body of Fire or not, I thought extreme cold might dampen the enthusiasm of our hot friend. It was an expensive trick to arrange, but well worth the price."

"Fools!" screamed the original Red Death, the one who had done all of the talking. "You think to thwart me so easily?"

The monster's form quivered, grew insubstantial. It was dissolving into mist. As were its three duplicates. McCann, exhausted from deflecting the four attacks, was unable to stop them.

"I hoped to destroy you myself," declared the Red Death. "But I realized defeating you might not be so easy. So I made *other plans.*

"My triumph is complete," came a final whisper as the monster departed. "Now is the time of the true red death."

The spectral figures were gone. McCann cursed. In a flash of understanding, he mentally scanned the marching field—above and below the surface of the earth.

"That damned Makish," he gasped, turning to Alicia. "There's enough thermite bombs planted beneath us to blow the whole complex to kingdom come!"

A black shadow slammed into McCann, lifting him off his feet, hurtling him through the air like a toy balloon. He sensed time distort for an instant. And then the world exploded into an inferno of chemical fire.

Afterword

Gasping for breath, a man's head emerged from the frigid waters of the Anacostia River. Behind him, the Washington Navy Yard burned in huge crimson flames that lit up the entire night sky. It was a scene right out of Dante's *Inferno*. Hell on Earth, it was unquestionably the red death.

Hardly causing a ripple, a woman's head broke the surface a foot away from the man. Her long, black hair was pasted against snow-white features, and her dark eyes reflected the fury of the blaze.

"You are Dire McCann," she asked her companion.

"That's me," answered the detective.

"I am Madeleine Giovanni, of the Clan Giovanni," said the woman. "My sire sent me to America to find you."

"You found me," said McCann, treading water. "Now what?"

"My instructions were simple," said Madeleine. "Pietro Giovanni commanded me to *protect you*."

"Good start," said Dire McCann.

At length I would be avenged. . .
"The Cask of Amontillado"
Edgar Allan Poe

About the Author

Robert Weinberg is perhaps the only World Fantasy Award winning writer ever to serve as the grand marshal of a rodeo parade. He is the author of eight novels, five nonfiction books, and numerous short stories. His work has been translated into French, German, Spanish, Italian, Japanese, Russian, and most recently, Bulgarian. A noted collector of horror and fantasy fiction, he has edited nearly a hundred anthologies and short story collections of such material. At present, he is serving as Vice-President of the Horror Writers Association, teaching creative writing at Columbia College in Chicago, and finishing work on the second novel in his "Vampire: The Masquerade of the Red Death" trilogy, *Unholy Allies*.

BUY THESE TITLES AT A BOOKSTORE NEAREST YOU, OR USE THIS CONVENIENT ORDER FORM FOR MAIL ORDER SERVICE.

White Wolf Publishing
Suite 100
780 Park North Boulevard
Clarkston, Georgia 30021

Please send me the books I have checked above.
I am enclosing $_____.
(please add $4.00 to cover postage and handling).
Send check or money order (no cash or C.O.D.s)
or charge by Mastercard, VISA, and Discover
(with a minimum purchase of $15.00).
Prices and numbers are subject to change without notice.

Card # _____

Exp. Date _____

Signature _____

Name _____

Address _____

City _____

State _____ Zip Code _____

For faster service when ordering by credit card,
call 1800-454-WOLF.
Allow a minimum of 3-4 weeks for delivery. This
offer is subject to change without notice.

HAWKMOON

THE ETERNAL CHAMPION VOL 3

WRITTEN BY MICHAEL MOORCOCK

The time is the distant future...

The animal-masked warriors of the Dark Empire of Granbretan threaten to conquer the Earth. Alone against this mighty force stands the tiny province of Kamarg, where dwell Count Brass and the Last Duke of Köln, Dorian Hawkmoon. At first a duped pawn of the Dark Empire, Hawkmoon quickly becomes Granbretan's most potent enemy. To have any hope of defeating the Dark Empire, Hawkmoon must call upon arcane sciences and ancient artifacts — including the fabled Runestaff.

This third volume in the Eternal Champion series presents four of Michael Moorcock's novels: The Jewel in the Skull, The Mad God's Amulet, The Sword of the Dawn, and The Runestaff. These novels chronicle the fate of another aspect of the Eternal Champion — Hawkmoon, Duke of Köln. This omnibus collection features revised text and a new introduction by the author.

ISBN   1-56504-178-X
Retail Price: $19.99 US
                 $27.99 CAN

AVAILABLE IN APRIL 1995

Midnight Blue

The Sonja Blue Collection

Written by Nancy A. Collins

Enter the nightmare world of Sonja Blue: an independent, strong, and beautiful woman who also happens to be a murderous vampire — and vampire slayer.

To avenge herself on the monster who turned her, against her will, into one of the undead, Sonja Blue hunts the vampires who prey on unsuspecting humans. She haunts the shadows of the world's greatest cities, continually searching for her prey. Sonja's greatest enemy, however, is the Other — the demon that has shared her mind since her resurrection twenty years ago.

Follow Sonja Blue as she descends into a hell on earth — a world where reality can be swept aside at any moment to reveal a shadowy domain of monsters and miracles.

Midnight Blue collects, for the first time anywhere, the award-winning Sonja Blue Collection: Sunglasses After Dark, In the Blood, and Paint It Black.

ISBN   1-56504-900-4
Retail Price: $14.99 US
                    $20.99 CAN

Available from White Wolf in April 1995